Noëmi's Promise

K McCity

Dedicated to my beautiful children whom I love with all my heart and soul.

ACKNOWLEDGMENTS

With grateful thanks to my incredibly
talented cover artist, Emma City
@emmacityart

And special thanks to my editor for their help
and encouragement.

CONTENTS

PART ONE – REASONS

Ainsi que la vertu, le crime a ses degrés

Phèdre, Jean Racine

PROLOGUE

7 October 2019, Grey Street, Newcastle.

'You'll not get away with it.'

Alura Honeyfield

"Noëmi, Noëmi…" He moaned.

Disturbed, Alura Honeyfield rolled over. Eyes already adjusted to the dark, mind racing, body tense. At her side in their bed, her husband Digby turned, exhaled loudly and seemed to settle.

"Noëmi, Noëmi…" Alura's husband whispered again.

Sitting up, she stared down at him. His mouth was half open, dribble leaked from one side, he was nothing like the woken version of the huge persona that was the Reverend Digby Honeyfield.

'Just the basic raw materials of a so-called man.'

Flinging herself back down, she sank into the mattress they had shared these past nine years. She clenched her fists. Her jaw locked.

'He's starting again!'

The next morning, unrested, they prepared for their day; quick showers, much huffing, mutual irritation.

"Ready for your first day of prosecution poker!" His eyes were glacial.

"Not really, I didn't sleep." She sat down at her smart, dove grey dressing table.

"What kept you awake?"

"The usual." Her mascara was sticky.

"Or rather the unusual. Never forget, Bertha." Passing behind, he jabbed her on the shoulder as he spoke.

"Shut up! Stop calling me that!" Alura glared at him via the mirror. His image was distorted like her emotions; inverted front to back.

"And now given your promotion, just ironic! You're good at what you do!" His voice was flat.

Ignoring his comment, she finished her make-up, tossed her head, then shook her shoulders. He disappeared downstairs to start the coffee machine. She stuck to him like Echo following Narcissus.

"When will you be back from London?" she asked, sounding like she hoped the answer would be never. "Wednesday evening. We've got that mission conference to set up. Pitching to some big charities, they're always ready to splash cash on marketing so it's looking good. Ah and we're in the money! Got that education contract with St Wolbodo's. The head teacher has just emailed me, it looks like I impressed everyone with my pitch last Friday!"

'He really thinks he's the chosen one.'

Thirty-nine years old, ambitious and intimidating, Digby stood tall before the full length hall mirror. A Ralph Lauren suede jacket in a deep rust, a Thomas Pink crisp, white shirt and indigo denim jeans by Hugo Boss. He was someone worth a second glance.

"It's a matter of class." He said, unsmiling as he slicked his thick, dark blonde hair. Next he moved to their immaculate, pewter grey kitchen and poured an espresso coffee into a glossy, black demitasse.

"Are you travelling first class again?" She stood open-mouthed.

"Calm down, this new school contract will cover the cost!" He popped his dog collar in his laptop bag and brushed past her, adding, "You're such an old nag. Really nasty."

His soft French lilt emphasised the insult in his pronunciation of *nasty*.

Mustering every ounce of self-control she resisted all temptation to erupt. *'You've got the trump card, remember.'*

And so the couple began their day. Silence replaced incessant sniping as they left their duplex in Grey Street, central Newcastle and went down to their cars in the basement. Snuggled next to each other were matching Mercedes; one night black, one polar white. Today they chose his. She yanked the door open and huffed as she thumped down onto the driver's seat. Without a word she rearranged the mirror and put her sunglasses on. Her husband was barely in the car when she screeched off. Digby swayed as he put his phone into the car audio system and did up his seat belt. She swerved round corners until early morning stop start traffic jerked them to a halt. Neither spoke. Just before 7:30am, Alura pulled into the station drop off zone. Commuters scurrying like beetles towards the Monday morning light, jolted her momentarily out of her miserable thoughts.

"Here you are, get out!"

Digby opened the door of his night black Mercedes-AMG C43 convertible. Stopping for a minute she looked straight ahead and adjusted the Bluetooth settings for the car audio.

"I'm sure you won't miss me." She muttered.

"Can you get all those prayer partnerships followed up?"

As he spoke, she glanced at him; His blue eyes were far away. *'Is he dreaming of her? He never notices me. I could be dead for all he cares.'* Digby climbed out and opened the boot to get his suitcase and laptop bag. A car behind beeped its horn.

"Who's Noëmi?" Alura could wait no longer.

"What?" Hand on bag handle he stopped.

"Who's Noëmi?" Head over shoulder, her eyes drilled into him.

He scoffed, "I have no idea who or what you're talking about!"

"Noëmi."

"No enemy? I'm sure you've got a few with your track record!" he laughed, hyena-like in her face.

"Don't give me that, we've been here five minutes and you're at it again!"

"You're imagining things. In any case, what are you going to do about it? What are you going to do about anything?"

"You'll not get away with it!"

"Maybe I already have!"

He slammed the door shut. Watching him march off to catch his train she cursed her husband. Shaking, she sat in her seat and breathed deeply to avoid involuntary tears falling from her eyes. *'You'll not get away with it.'*

7 October 2019, Newcastle Royal Victoria Infirmary (RVI).

Marcus

Emergency doctor Marcus McKenzie was a tall, fit and eye catching man. Dark eyes, soft afro hair and good teeth. His extremely attractive exterior hid an, at times, overly serious character. Each day the RVI emergency department, in Newcastle, offered up its usual gamut of cases; falls, pains and strains. Yet there were also the more unusual complaints, courtesy of the more experimental individuals. Today Dr Marcus McKenzie was dealing with a patient whose DIY piercing had become infected. Marcus reassured the patient as he signed off the notes;

"Complete the course of antibiotics and absolutely no activity in the area until it's healed. Then in time if you want to get the piercing done, go to a specialist."

The patient nodded sheepishly and left as quickly as they could. Once again Marcus never knew what to expect as he sat at the urgent care centre staff base to review his list. Looking at the notes for his next patient he suppressed a sigh,

'Will these roads ever be safe?' He put his shoulders back as thoughts of Noëmi being lifted, broken, bloody and unconscious from the tarmac, filled his mind. *'Focus on the good outcome.'* The post accident counselling had served him well. He went back to his patient details.

'Forced off bike. Query fractured left clavicle?'

He knew his patient had already been to X-ray, so he turned to the patient records system to see if the images were ready. Having gathered all the information, he went straight to the first emergency bay. Pulling back the sky blue curtain, his patient was slouched in a chair, arm in a sling, t-shirt ripped. He was attempting to use his phone with his right hand.

"Hello, I'm Marcus, your doctor for today, can you just confirm your name, date of birth and first line of your address, please."

"Oliver Legatt, 13 March 1987, Flat 2b, 199 Old Durham Road."

"Yep, you're my patient! So, what happened?"

"Got cut up cycling to the station. A muppet in a flashy, black Mercedes turned left without indicating so I gave them the finger and fell off my bike. My fault I guess but I'm in high vis with lights everywhere. How did they not see me? And how do they not know how to use their sodding indicators?" Oliver grimaced and put his good hand to his shoulder. "I need to text my manager. Otherwise, work will be on my case." He continued trying to use his phone, "I'm left-handed!"

"Sorry to hear this. My wife cycles a lot, so these drivers really wind me up! Where do you work? We can call them for you."

"Oh mate, that'd be amazing! Yeah, it's the Radisson in Durham, security office. Cheers."

"You cycle a lot then?" Marcus took Oliver's blood pressure on his good arm.

"Yeah, I do marathons, triathlons, iron man challenges, anything, can't sit still! Won't be doing all that for a while, eh?" Oliver laughed but grimaced again.

"True but good for you, I'm planning my first marathon so any tips would be most welcome."

"Just build it up day by day and taper for the week up to the event so you're fresh! Sleep twelve hours the night before!" Oliver tried to sit up, exhaled deeply and slumped back to his original position.

"Thank you, that's good to hear! Not too sure about the sleep! With three month old twins, I can't get more than four hours undisturbed!" He moved to complete Oliver's notes.

"No way, I've got a four month old boy, Rudi, best thing that ever happened to me but bloody knackering...bloody brilliant too!" Finally Oliver grinned.

"Totally agree, I've got a girl and a boy! Now let's look at these images together, you can see here you've fractured your collarbone, which is causing pain as the humerus here is also dislocated anteriorly."

"Ooh that's not funny!"

"Indeed! We need to give you gas and air and get that back into place. For the fracture you just need to keep the sling and take it easy."

"No cast then?"

"No, it's in its correct position, just fractured here. It'll heal perfectly well and our clinic will keep an eye on you. But no cycling for a good six weeks I'm afraid. You'll be signed off work for a bit then they should allocate you to different duties, front of house or so on. Make sure you see occupational health. So let's get these grazes sorted out. Trauma nurse Penelope here will see to that."

Marcus turned to his colleague, Penelope Rivera who had just entered the cubicle. "Pen this is Oliver, fitness fanatic and devoted dad! He'll be swearing as much as you do when he gets that reduction, lots of gas and air required I think!"

Oliver grinned but writhed with pain as he tried to give Marcus a wave with his injured arm.

"Cheers mate! Good luck with the twins, see you at soft play, swimming and McDonald's parties, all that hardcore stuff we never dreamed we'd be doing!" Oliver called after Marcus who left the bay and disappeared behind the sky blue curtain.

"He's a great bloke!" Both said about the other.

CHAPTER 1 - PERSON OF INTEREST

Friday, 4 October 2019…three days before. St Wolbodo's School, Durham.

Digby

Educational consultancy bid over and now taking tea in the staffroom at St Wolbodo's school, Digby was not listening to whoever was talking to him. Glancing over the shoulder of his conversation bore, through the picture window, he spotted the dark haired 'Miss McAllister' rushing across the car park. *'Definitely a person of interest! Why's she limping?'* His eye trailed her to a Fiat Tipo Station Wagon in Passione red. The door was flung open and there appeared to be someone else inside, passing things to her. Returning his attention to the room, Digby eventually became aware that his interlocutor had moved away.

Noëmi

Flinging herself into their new red family car, she gasped, "Oh my God, my breasts are going to explode!"

Pre-empting the situation Marcus handed over a grizzling, three month old. She fed the twins in turn. Everyone sighed with relief.

"Thank you for helping with this!" Noëmi strained across to give

11

her husband a kiss. Marcus had his day off and was keen to help his wife with the logistics for this extraordinary meeting.

"How was it?"

"Big sigh! They're outsourcing a whole chunk of the school's pastoral responsibilities to a consultancy. I'm triggered as this will include Attila's duties and my school charity role during my mat leave. Unbelievable!"

Attila Varga was the vicar, from the local church in Durham, who provided spiritual support for the school.

Noëmi continued, "A new youth church pitched for the work. The guy seems pretty passionate but what a waste of money! Something about a drive to appeal to the younger generation! What rubbish!"

"Ah well you'll be back soon enough to sort it out! Time now to forget work and just enjoy motherhood!" Marcus said.

As a teacher of maths at St Wolbodo's school in Durham, Noëmi was proud of her efforts to fundraise for the End Noma Campaign. This charity was close to her heart.

"One more meeting to handover to the successful consultancy and then that's it, I swear!"

He grinned at her.

"What?"

"The estate agent has literally just called me! Our offer has been accepted! There's no chain so we'll be in before Christmas!"

She screamed with excitement. Finally, a small, terraced house, slightly further up the road from their flat in Jesmond would be theirs.

Saturday, 5 October 2019, Jesmond, Newcastle.

Marcus

Until then Marcus and Noëmi's one bedroom flat was bursting; babies were everywhere. Space, quiet and time were forgotten concepts for the couple. The day after the school meeting, Marcus was returning from work, when the smell of Sudocrem and tanning foam filled his nostrils. Suddenly he remembered. *'Yumi's hen do. Oh here we go!'*

Marcus' best friend, Guy Castle, was preparing to marry Noëmi's best friend, Yumi Watanabe.

Creeping further into the flat, he noted a suspicious semblance of organisation; kitchen tidy, babies sleeping and evidence of dinner having been prepared. Resplendent in a short, black, sequined dress, she limped into the hallway. Noëmi was looking good; her long, lustrous hair swung around her shoulders and her 'top hourglass' figure was trim and shapely. Putting his rucksack down he smiled at her.

"You've caught the non-existent Newcastle sun!"

Never having had a hen do of her own, his wife had evidently decided this event belonged also to her.

"You look good too!" She checked her reflection.

"You don't look good…you look absolutely gorgeous!" He reached his hand out to her. Taking him with it, she hugged him, not letting go after the usual five seconds.

"Do you have any idea for how long I've been absolutely mad about you?" He said.

She giggled, "About the same amount of time I've been crazy for you?"

He ran his hands softly over her body.

"That's the 2016 New Year's Eve dress, isn't it?"

"Yep, I've not worn it since that night." She pulled at the fabric around her hips to adjust the fit.

"Let's hope it doesn't bring bad luck!" He tried to joke, blocking out memories of that evening.

"Urgh! No, it won't! I've already had an emotional overload with my dad this morning so no more! Everything's ready. Chilli is in the oven and I made my guacamole. B and E will wake in an hour or so. Bruno's more clingy than usual, you know how he is. Lots of breastmilk in the fridge."

"Perfect night in! Bring it on!"

Holding onto her stick, she checked herself in the mirror again and smoothed out her dress.

"First night out, eh?" He moved behind her, gently held her shoulders and looked at her in the reflection. Her silver heart necklace gave refracted glints. Her dress sparkled as iridescent, blue goldstone. Her hair rippled over his hands as she adjusted herself. Reminders of brushing it when she was in the coma sprang involuntarily into his head. He shut his eyes.

"Actually, maybe I should…" She hesitated.

He knew that she too had been struggling with dark thoughts. He would have loved for her to stay. That way he could keep her safe like putting her into a little box.

"No! You're going! Have fun!" He took her shoulders and turned them to the door. Next, he grabbed her faux fur, animal print coat and held it open for her.

"Time for the leopard to change its spots and have a break from nappies! Go out and have fun!"

"Actually, it's cheetah print and leopards don't have spots, they have markings like rosettes, cheetahs have spots, if you look…"

"Go out!" He thrust her mustard handbag and the National Trust walking stick, she had borrowed from his grandmother, into her hands.

"Watch out for big game hunters!"

"Ha, I literally have a stick to hold them off with!" She brandished it with a glint.

"You'll need to fight them with big swords!" his eyes shone.

The muffled sound of Yumi giggling filled their ears. Marcus rolled his eyes and Noëmi grinned. She limped to the door and as she opened it Yumi fell inside. Holding a bottle of fizz with disposable cups and bedecked in a short silk dress, covered in cheap, plastic decorations, Yumi looked nothing like her usual sophisticated self.

"Wow, you're nightclub perfection Yumi!" Marcus said.

"Offensive to fun loving women everywhere! At least I know how to enjoy myself Marcus!" She poked him on the chest and glanced down at her hot pink 'condemned woman' sash.

"This was the classy one! Bri's got all sorts of different accessories in the limo, Marcus, anatomical shapes! They're huge! Come and see!"

Bri Francis, one of Noëmi's colleagues at St Wolbodo's, was also part of the group. She had been introduced to fellow maths teacher, Yumi, when the latter moved to Durham, eighteen months earlier. Yumi handed a beaker of bubbly and a neon pink cowboy hat to Noëmi.

"I'll tell A & E to look out for you all!" Marcus called out as the women's excitement filled the hallway.

"Off you go! Where's Guy by the way?"

"He's coming over to keep you company!" She was giggling again. "He's bringing a new friend!"

And they were gone in a flash of pink polyester. A white stretch was doing the rounds to pick up eight of Newcastle's finest for a night of clubbing and dancing. Marcus thought of Yumi's comment and felt cold. A message pinged through from Yumi's fiancé Guy.

'Let me know when they're asleep and I'll be over with my buddy!'

'Yesss! Both sleeping! Food's ready!'

'Who's he bringing? God have I been replaced by this new person of interest? I already don't like this dude.' Marcus felt jumpy. Within the hour Guy had arrived with a bouncing working cocker spaniel called Rolo.

"It's because she's brown and caramel coloured like the sweet." Guy and the loyal hound did not take their eyes off each other.

"Yeah, I did work that out!" Marcus bent to stroke the docile dog. "Is she yours?" Rolo's big supplicating eyes now fixed on him.

"No, she's a police dog, but she's getting on, so she's got a special role in our unit. She does a bit of work and she's allowed in my police office for our well being. As her attachment figure, I'm authorised to take her home too. She'll come and go, so you need to get used to her." Rolo quickly sniffed out the whole house.

"No cocaine here then!" Guy laughed, "She's a tracking dog. Rolo has a sense of smell tens of thousands of times greater than ours! She's smart. I'm absolutely smitten. That much easier than a baby!" Guy grabbed a beer from the fridge. Marcus declined as he was on twin infant alert. Guy continued. "She's friendly with everyone but she loves me the most." Rolo sat, beseeching at his feet.

"Naturally!" Marcus agreed.

"Plus she can sniff out scheming people, she's pretty amazing! Tbh, I think Yumi's even a bit jealous!"

"Jealous! God that's silly!" Marcus felt himself burn up.

With a face full of child-like wonder, Guy stroked and cuddled his faithful new canine friend.

Yumi

Yumi and Guy were Noëmi and Marcus' closest friends. Yumi's hen do was the exact opposite of what everyone would have expected for her. No stylish Stockholm city break, sipping cocktails in Gamla Stan, no it was a Newcastle big night out. Privy to the plans, Yumi's face resembled that of a cat in water. However, she soon realised there was no way that Noëmi could travel to Ibiza, owing to breastfeeding and fracture recuperation. More than anything she wanted her best friend at her side so the 'Toon' was on.

Noëmi

Saturday night streets were buzzing. Car horns, shouts and laughter. Everyone wanted to relax. Cries of excitement as friends grouped up. Music pulsated out of pubs and bars. The scrape of heels announced Yumi's troupe arriving at the first club. Noëmi was hyped.

"Digital! Eight years ago! I couldn't get in that summer because I was eight days too young!"

Responsibilities were fading away with every thump of the beat; Noëmi began to feel seventeen again. Leaning on the bar, she ordered lots of prosecco for the group. The neon backlights glowed from pink to lilac to turquoise to yellow. Spilling into the lounge area, their legs took over a black vinyl sofa and matching low chairs. With laughter and shrieks they discussed the drinks menu with a young barman who grimaced knowingly at their size related banter. Noëmi explained to Yumi what had happened when she was too young to get into the club.

"Yumi, I finished with Marcus that night, just before my eighteenth birthday. It killed me, I've always wondered what would've happened if I'd not done that…" she felt so cold.

"We probably wouldn't be sitting here and you'd have some boring, simpering, unfun best friend and oh my God I may never have met Guy! Thank God you dumped Marcus!" Yumi's desperate hand clutched her arm.

"Owww your fingers are digging in. Six years of utter pain and misery in exchange for you and Guy, so worth it!"

The now neon tangerine lights bathed Noëmi.

"I'd say so! You should wear dayglo orange, it's quite your colour!"

Digby

Also out enjoying the Newcastle nightlife was Digby Honeyfield and a visiting friend, Jacques. They sauntered into the club, Digital. Digby surveyed the scene with some disdain and turned to his companion who spoke first.

"These women are cheaply dressed."

Digby agreed. "Yeah, but there'll be a couple that'll keep us entertained. Turn on zee charm and zee accent et voilà!"

"I don't want any of that next morning hassle." Jacques shrugged his shoulders as he surveyed the clientele. A woman with long, dark hair, sitting alone, caught his eye and he gave his friend a pat on the back and left the bar. Digby followed.

"Celle-là m'intéresse!'

Sauntering to the young brunette's side he stood next to her seat and spoke in a low voice to Digby.

"Elle est belle, elle a de beaux yeux! Elle a de la classe!"

The woman turned and replied, "En fait il y a des anglais qui comprennent le français!"

She was upfront.

Lip curling, Digby composed himself as he watched Jacques' face pale with shock. Digby moved forward and gave a smile.

"Not dancing?"

Digby asked in a thick French accent. The brunette jumped up and back. Jacques grimaced as a pair of strappy, block heeled sandals crushed his toes.

"Oh, oh re-bonjour, I mean bonsoir! Hello again! Thank you for coming in for the meeting yesterday! We loved your pitch!"

Digby touched her shoulder, "Merci! But now relax! This is leisure time, let's leave work behind!"

Jacques scowled at his friend and excused himself.

Grabbing his wine and his glass, Digby sat down with Noëmi. He poured himself a glass of pinot noir. "So, not dancing?"

"Ah non! I got injured in the summer, so I have to sit it out!"

"Playing sport?"

"A car accident but I'm fine!" Her voice was determined. She sipped her wine.

Digby was intrigued. "What's your first name? During the

19

presentations yesterday, they only introduced you as Miss McAllister, which is a bit formal! Made me feel like a naughty schoolboy!"

Without sparing him a glance, she replied, "Rumpelstiltskin." Her glass was finished.

Digby burst out laughing. He could see she was trying to suppress a grin.

"I know zat story!" He filled her glass without her noticing.

"You're the first person who does, most people just look puzzled!"

Her eyes were bright.

"You know me, I'm Digby, but really what's your name? I'm not trying to bother you, just new 'ere in zis town and checking things out, avant que…sorry, I've just moved up here! I can just about understand zee Newcastle lilt. An accent is forever it seems!"

Noëmi

Relaxing, she grabbed her drink. They continued in French.

"Yes, my mother never got rid of hers, she was Italian!" Noëmi could tell he was impressed. *'I love feeling this smart.'*

"She gave you grace, beauty and style!"

Digby, with his sandy hair and lightly freckled face, was now sitting next to her. She drank some more.

"Sorry I just can't help my friendliness, enchanté!"

Silence. *'Should I tell him my name? He seems pretty safe.'*

"My wife would love someone to show her around zee Toon and of course, Durham. She knows no one."

"Lovely to meet you, I'm Noëmi." She relaxed, *'Totally safe, he has a wife!'*

Refilling his glass, he smiled.

"Enchanté!" He took her hand and gave it a kiss.

"Where were you living before?"

"Londres, Teddington really. What 'appened to your leg?" He put his left foot on his right knee.

"I told you I was knocked over by a car. What's the word for 'coma' in French?"

Digby's mouth was gaping, "It's the same!"

"I was in a coma for three weeks, but I'm really doing well now!" She played with her now empty glass.

"Mon Dieu!" Digby sidled closer and in a move worthy of a Vegas magician, reached for the bottle of wine behind him and filled her glass once more.

She tasted the wine, "Mmm, that's lovely. Merci!" She sank into the abyss of what could have been. Pulling herself up, she resurfaced. Warm and woozy she joked,

"Luckily for everyone, I survived! Still here to nag my husband!"

They burst out laughing. Yumi glanced over. Digby spoke quietly, she felt his hot breath on her ear as he leant in. She sidled away from him.

"I bet you're beautiful even when you're nagging!"

The wine was intoxicating and she failed to notice his arm around the back of her chair.

"I hope we will be working together soon on zee charity thing!"

"Indeed! I believe the head teacher will make a decision by Monday morning! What a happy coincidence to bump into you here!" She said.

"Or could it be destiny? Whatever the difference may be! I hope to work with you, Noëmi!"

She smiled.

Joe Le Taxi by Vanessa Paradis suddenly began playing, the two sang along. Swaying together. Digby's arm was brushing hers. Soon it was round her shoulders but Noëmi was oblivious; hazy with wine. Digby was moving in closer. Distracted, Noëmi was chuffed, *'All my hard work has paid off, I spent hours learning these lyrics as a teenager. Mum would play this song. 1987 it came out. I remember Mum telling me that summer was her and Dad's first trip to Italy. As students, they drove from Edinburgh through France and this was the song of that summer! This is so clever! I look just so clever!'* Digby crooned the lyrics into her ear, his lips breathed into her hair. Suddenly she noticed Yumi was staring open mouthed, she shook herself out of his arms. The image of the taxi she had ordered the night of the accident, instantly filled her head. Her mouth was dry.

"I'm here tonight for my friend's hen do lovely to meet you." She stood up and stumbled. Steading herself she began to move away, he caught her arm. He held her hand and gazed into her eyes.

"I know it's a bit forward, but I'd really like to see you for a coffee sometime, get to know you. We could spend some time together…I can't help feeling we've met for a reason."

His other hand was now on her upper arm, his fingers played with the ends of her hair. His eyes were pleading, puppy-like.

"Coffee? No, no, sorry, no coffee!" Flustered, she could see Yumi in the corner of her eye. Yumi's eyes burnt into her.

"Oh I understand. A cocktail zen!"

Noëmi gave a yelp. "No you don't understand!" Her heart was beating.

"Noëmi, I like you. I really like you. I'd love to see you again. Just the two of us! Sorry this is out of my control. Ah c'est vrai, sometimes attraction cannot be ignored."

"Même pas en rêve! I'm not looking for anything."

"I just can't bear the thought of living without you!"

"Listen, let me paint you a picture with words; not interested, never going to be, happily married…" She stiffened her body and set seriousness on her face.

"Really I don't care about that! Nothing is insurmountable! I must see you…"

"No, just leave me alone! Fuck off!" She hissed at him.

Digby jumped back with shock. Yumi, now behind them, gave a loud cry as Digby stood on her toes. Without apologising he walked off. Noëmi was pale.

"Proper actual flirting? That's horrible! It's a really bad look, Noëmi!" Yumi scowled, nose in the air.

"No! I wasn't flirting!"

"You make me sick! That wasn't a bit of fun, look at him! That man's into you!" Digby kept glancing their way.

"No, stop! Don't say that!"

"You play all sweet and innocent, don't you!"

"No!"

"Did you flirt like that with Guy when you and Marcus were apart? Was he a person of interest? The back-up plan? Or was it, *oh which one shall I choose?*" Yumi spat her words out.

"There's never been that kind of vibe! Guy's one of my dearest friends!"

Yumi turned away; her silky hair following.

Feeling decidedly sober, Noëmi checked the time on her phone.

'Everything's good, aliens are sleeping ;) Have fun!'

She bit her lip. Regret flooded over her.

'In Digital! I love you so much xxx'

Noëmi spotted Yumi at the bar and marched up to her.

"Yumi, don't talk like that. Guy and I were both single when we met and nothing. He meets you and within seconds you two are superglued together. Stronger than an ionic bond."

Reluctantly Yumi gave into her smile.

"It's an iconic bond!"

Then she leant across and then whispered something to her friend with a cat like smirk,

"Yumi! Stop with all the details! I'm pretty sure Guy doesn't want me to know that!"

Digby

Taking her stick, he saw her limp away. Whatever her injuries he was interested. Her figure was tight, she had dark glossy hair that swung round her soft shoulders and her eyes were bright. She seemed classy; someone he could easily spend time with when his wife was busy. Sidling back to the bar he found Jacques and ordered a gin and tonic.

"Pas de chance?"

"Non, zat one is not a cheater!"

"Evidently but it's just a question of persistence n'est-ce pas?"

CHAPTER 2 - ST WOLBODO'S

Thursday, 10 October 2019.

Noëmi

Walking into the school foyer she felt a rush of nausea. Students pushed past her, obviously oblivious to her new status as a proud mother of two people for whom she would instantly die. She settled on a low, leather look chair, outside the head teacher's office. The smell of cotton fresh cologne and the glint of an Omega Seamaster watch heralded Frank Sprague's arrival at her side. Her good friend was now Deputy Head at St Woldbodo's.

"Frank, hello! How are you mio caro? I've been up half the night breastfeeding."

A beaming Frank straightened out his jacket cuffs and smoothed his tie.

She carried on, "And of course you look immaculate, in control...Frank, I'm so underprepared, I can barely form a sentence let alone lead a handover meeting."

"Relax, it's only the new head teacher, Cathal Shelmerdine. You know he's a bit of an arse. Plus that new funky preacher the school's wasting money on. Flashy McFlashface, he's pushed Attila Varga out of his role and apparently he's taking charge of the End Noma Campaign?"

"Urgh, Digby Honeyfield!"

"Yes! That's him! Arse number two."

"I feel terrible for Attila."

On cue the door swung open and Digby appeared, smirking. Noëmi took a sharp breath. He ushered her in. She moved quickly to avoid a loose hand at hip height. Standing to greet her was the new head teacher, Cathal Shelmerdine. Forty years old, brown suit, puffy faced with thick auburn hair which he had combed flat against his head. He shook hands vigorously. His clothes gave off a musty scent. The office was familiar; it was dominated by the huge dark oak desk with two massive screens that dwarfed the beady eyed head teacher. A large picture window to the side, gave an excellent view of the jostling and shrieking of students lining up for the canteen. Like busy ants, pupils arranged themselves. *'How often our previous Head, Maurice Mundy, must have ignored the chaos of queuing kids.'* Given the disruptive behaviour of an unchallenged minority, lunchtime had been reduced to forty minutes, which was not nearly enough time for everyone to be fed. She remembered the number of times tearful younger students would arrive hungry to afternoon lessons, having been shoved out of the lunch line.

"Noëmi, how wonderful to see you!"

She sat down, obediently, in front of the pair.

"Reverend Honeyfield this is Noëmi McAllister,"

The reverend gave crocodilian teeth. "We know each other!"

Regret gnawed inside her like a parasite. She continued.

"Yes but I'm now going to be known by my new married name, Mrs McKenzie."

"Congratulations, for so many things Noëmi McKenzie; the wedding, the twins and most of all for surviving!" Mr Shelmerdine thought himself quite the wit.

"Twins?" Digby spoke for the first time.

She felt sick for too many reasons.

"Yes! They're, what, three and a half months old…" The head teacher read from his notes. "And your maternity leave comes to an end at Easter?"

"No mid-July 2020 actually."

"I was hoping you'd return sooner than that!" He simpered. "You do realise there's a vacancy for Head of Sixth Form coming up as the current incumbent is leaving at Easter?"

Noëmi felt overwhelmed *'Head of Sixth Form. I've got a real chance!'*

"Now Digby here, sorry Reverend Honeyfield, needs to find out all about your noma fundraising!"

"Yez Noëmi, it sounds completely fascinating!" He put a foot on one knee, just as he had done in Digital and leaned towards her. She cleared her throat and her mind,

"It's been two years now since we've been sending a doctor from the Newcastle RVI hospital out to Nigeria during the summer holidays. As you know I also went the first year. Now we've got a nurse practitioner place too."

"Excellent stuff! Just so you know, your fellow maths teacher, Bri Francis, has very kindly offered to help too! I wonder if you and one of your doctors could come along to the school prize giving, which is…er sometime in November, to represent the charity?" Cathal looked up from his notes.

"Absolutely!"

Digby slowly smiled, "Perfect, I can manage all the tax affairs through my consultancy. Save the bursar the bother!"

Noëmi felt her pulse quicken. "The terms of reference do say that the school governing body should administer all charity accounts, so they would need to approve this change."

Digby and Cathal turned to each other. They were synchronised.

"That's us! So that's passed!" Bursts of infantile laughter followed. The men sobered up. Cathal's walkie talkie buzzed into life on the desk and the end of lunch bell sounded. A small blackbird sitting on the window ledge outside flew off. Digby gallantly held the door open. Walking out together, she decided to come clean.

"Thank you. By the way I just wanted to apologise for how I spoke to you when I met you the other week." Small students dodged past them.

Digby smirked and stage whispered, "We nearly got caught out!" He teased by glancing furtively over his shoulder. She was unsure if she noticed a wink. They walked down the corridor, side by side, like chess players unsure of their next move.

"Right Digby, there's nothing to uncover!"

Digby stopped melodramatically and put his hand to his head.

"You and me, we were out in zee Toon together!"

"We actually call it the Town, and no, not together!"

Reverend Honeyfield swung round "But of course! Our little secret!" This time he definitely winked.

"Stop twisting things! Everyone will get the wrong idea!" She said in a hush.

With a curl to his lip he said, "Oh come on don't be a bore! Let's 'ave coffee!"

She rolled her eyes and followed into the staff room. Today she chose the faded mint green itchy woollen seat, as there were new stains on the others. Perched on the arm of the pastel chair next to the hot water urn she watched Digby at work.

"Of course in Paris we 'ave proper coffee! And in Italy?"

"Assolutamente!"

He smiled and brought her coffee to her. They settled to talk.

"I apologise for my persistence! I'm such a romantic!"

"Of course! Silly me that must mean you can do as you please!"

Digby grinned, "Alright, alright! Don't worry I have the message that you're 'appily married! Quel dommage!"

"I'm sorry, I was a bit drunk that evening. But you're married! And a vicar!" She did not hide her confusion.

"Yes, yes but like all unreliable men, I 'ave a wife who doesn't understand me!"

"Oh for goodness' sake! Maybe you could try not flirting with other women!"

"C'est vrai but you know, I lost my true love. She died…"

"I'm so sorry to hear that!" Noëmi stuttered. Digby gazed out at the playing fields.

"Never mind, it's been a while, she died of a heart condition, undiagnosed…my own heart was broken."

"My God! That's awful…now you've found love again?"

"I must go, would you like a lift back to Newcastle? Just the two of us!" Again, she was sure to see his eye twitch.

"No thank you, my car is here too!"

And Digby was gone. As she pondered on his openness, her phone pinged, it was Yumi sharing the hen party photos. After a brief scroll, she took a deep breath and turned her phone to silent.

CHAPTER 3 - LAURA

10 October 2019, Guy and Yumi's flat, Jesmond, Newcastle.

Guy

A text pinged through. Sighing as he read, he replied then flopped onto his pillow. Yumi stirred but did not wake. He put his phone down. A couple more pings but he ignored them. Yumi rolled over, yawned and snuggled into him,

"Breaking your own rule about phones in bed! Who's that? Your secret girlfriend?"

"Yeah, sorry I thought it might be to do with our flights! Yumi, it was Laura."

Yumi groaned. She knew all about Guy's relationship with Laura.

Friday, 2 February 2018...eighteen months before. London.

Guy Castle and Yumi Watanabe's relationship took off, the first weekend he had visited her in London. Since they had met, on New Year's Eve 2017, they could only communicate over the internet as they lived three hundred miles apart. Yet they had spoken every day. Although they were desperate to see each other, their visit had been long delayed on account of Yumi leading a school trip to Japan that January. Finally the first weekend arrived that they could spend together; 2 February 2018.

Clapham in south London, was not unfamiliar to Guy as his eldest sister lived in Balham, just nearby. Arriving in a flurry of nerves, he parked his car and texted Yumi who shot out of her front door with a parking permit for the weekend. Slender and elegant with glossy, long dark hair; Yumi was a stunningly beautiful woman. Guy leapt from his car and they fell into a long kiss. Yumi lived alone in the first floor maisonette with high Victorian ceilings and original iron fireplaces. A large bow window gave out to a wide street lined with London Plane trees. The sash window was thereby shaded with sage green leaves that gently fluttered in the wind. Yumi had decorated the flat with whites and neutrals; keeping the design simple and modern. Many Japanese touches such as the low, heated Kotatsu table and the foldable screen decorated with peacocks and cherry blossoms made Guy feel warm inside. Everything about Yumi was gorgeous. She showed him to the single guest bedroom. He smiled to himself. They avoided each other's eyes and then she suddenly said,

"Don't get a negative vibe. It's because I'm serious about you. I have rules."

He understood. He broke the awkwardness.

"There's a logic there somewhere and what would be happening if you weren't serious about me…would I…?"

"No, you wouldn't have even made it through the front door!"

"So I'm doing well then!" He grinned, put his case carefully on the chest of drawers and popped his rucksack on the bed.

"I like things to be special." She passed him a pile of fresh white fluffy towels.

"And on that note, we need to go straight to my sister's and you can meet my family!"

"This is the weirdest first date ever!"

Having freshened up they were straight back in the car driving to Balham. By chance his parents were visiting before a ski trip to France and his sister Poppy had arranged dinner. His other sister Beth also lived in south London but was away with friends. Before long Yumi, Guy and his family were sitting together in his eldest sister's stylish kitchen having supper.

"When did you meet my baby brother?" Guy's sister, Poppy, asked as she served out portions of homemade moussaka. She was six months pregnant and evidently taking this in her stride. The Castle family were aptly named; strong, stoical and resilient.

"New Year's Eve! At a restaurant party in Durham! I live in Clapham but Guy and I, we've got mutual friends up in Newcastle."

"Oh long distance!"

"Yes but I've got to know all about him: gym, his DIY, Cluedo, Newcastle, mates, pub, a love of Japanese culture…and family obviously! This is our first date!"

"In a nutshell! You're a brave woman!"

Guy could feel everyone sizing them up. His father smiled chummily although his mother was more reserved. The meal progressed with chit chat about jobs, holiday plans and future family events; Poppy's baby and Beth's upcoming wedding. Poppy wanted to show her mother the plans for the baby's nursery, so Guy accompanied them upstairs. Yumi stayed at the table chatting with the others about the cost of wedding canapés.

Surveying the future baby's small buttercup yellow room, Guy's mother suddenly started, "Guy! Guess who we saw back in the village the other day, Laura!" His mother's voice was loud with wine.

"Right!" Guy's voice was strained.

"She was visiting her parents, she's got some problems with Tom you know! Your father thinks he's not right for her."

His mother's face was expecting a reaction which was denied. Poppy rolled her eyes in sympathy with her brother,

"Mum just because you and dad were college sweethearts, doesn't mean to say Guy has to be one too! They broke up years ago!"

Ignoring the comment their mother continued.

"You and Laura were such the perfect couple! Maybe you should give her a call? See how she is?"

Guy turned to his mother and snapped back, "That's of no relevance to me."

Guy and Laura had met on day one of Durham University when they were both lodged in the same college, Trevelyan. Having quipped that he should be in the college named after him, Castle, Guy was already showing himself to be the bright eyed joker of the freshers. His muscular frame and boyish good looks made him popular with everyone. Guy had thick dark brown hair and sparkling hazel eyes. Laura was equally self assured and attractive with wavy dark blonde hair and bright blue eyes. She was sporty and fun and they were instantly a match. They began their relationship, the first serious one for them both and were together throughout the whole of their three years at Durham. The day they left they broke up following a simmering row they had been having for most of the third year about Guy's plans to travel. Guy went to Japan. Laura went to London and began studying to become an accountant. That was that. Laura soon was in love again with a fellow graduate trainee named Tom. Life had moved on for them both.

"But you were ideal for each other."

Guy turned to his mother. He was exasperated, "I don't need to hear this stuff! Yumi's the one. I know that!"

"Ridiculous! You hardly know each other! You've not even spent any time together!" His mother examined the heavy chintz curtains that were decorated with lambs, baby rabbits and chicks.

"That's unfair! We've spoken for hours every night, even when she was in Japan! I know enough about myself to know when I've met the right person! And tell Beth that Yumi will be coming to her wedding as my partner!"

"Honestly Guy, you have no idea how successful Laura is! She's the kind of girlfriend you need; a high achiever! She earns a six figure salary!"

"Mum, stop! Don't make me tell you exactly why Laura and I were unsuited!" Guy marched out of the room, only to find Yumi on the stairs.

"I'm looking for the loo!" She said quietly, eyes like one of the rabbit kittens from the nursery curtains. Guy stepped from one foot to the other and then opened the bathroom door. Without a word Yumi went in and Guy went downstairs.

Presently Guy and Yumi drove home. During the journey he noticed she was pensive.

"Maybe I might've overheard your conversation." Finally, she confessed.

"And the best bit was?" He drew up to her front door.

"Can't quite remember… perhaps it was *the one* bit or was it *the right person* bit?"

Smiling, he turned to kiss her.

"Yumi, it may be early days but I know how I feel about you and all my hopes for our relationship."

"I feel the same. Big hopes!"

"And I bet you're really desperate to know exactly why I wasn't suited to my ex!"

"It would help!" They sat in the car. The night was still.

"None of this is quite the romantic plan I had for the evening. Okay Laura and I were together for three years. First love. We got on, well suited, similar backgrounds, our parents live near each other and all that. Everything was great but soon the cracks appeared. She didn't want me to go travelling, she didn't want me to join the police, I'd earn more in the City but it was when she didn't like me seeing my friends that things really got tricky!"

"That won't be a problem for us!" Yumi's eyes were bright in the darkness.

"I know! But there were other more serious things, I'll tell you sometime, we don't need to worry about all that now!" Yumi did not persist and he was glad, a memory of Laura scrolling on her phone as they were making love jumped into his head. Her lack of tenderness and her functional attitude to sex was not something she cared to change even after many a discussion. Laura liked the outward show of a long term relationship without the same enthusiasm behind closed doors. Her plans for the future involved more discussion of curtains and carpets than it did their growth together. She became bad tempered and ill mannered. Eventually the emotional gap between them could not be bridged by shared memories. Exiting the car, Guy and Yumi returned to her flat where they enjoyed a nightcap and made plans for the next day. Finally, he went to shower as she locked up.

Yumi

Waiting for the bathroom Yumi was pacing her room. Her head was full of the evening and her heart full of Guy. She popped her head into the hallway as she heard the bathroom door open. In the half-light, she moved to see Guy strolling, towel around his waist, towards his room. He threw her a big smile as he saw her standing in her bedroom doorway.

"Missing me!"

She tried not to grin. She could not resist, "Question or statement? Guy, I've decided I might be lonely all alone in this big bed." Yumi gestured to her room.

He burst out laughing. "Yes! What happened to the rules?"

"Koketsu ni irazunba koji wo ezu…if you don't enter the tiger's cave you won't catch its cub."

"Mamoritai. I want to protect you." He took her in his arms. And that weekend they both enjoyed the intense physical pleasure of their emotional connection.

10 October 2019, Jesmond, Newcastle.

"What does she even want?"

Guy showed her his phone.

'Hi Guy. How's things? Would love to hear from you. Laura xxx'

'I'm good, hope you and Tom are too. Busy being Guy of the north upholding the law! Plus, I'm getting married soon! Send your parents my best wishes. Guy.'

'Tom and I broke up. It was a massive mistake. Been

thinking about you xxx'

'I'm sorry for you both. I hope you find happiness again soon.'

'You made me happy. Can we meet up? I miss you xxx'

'Laura, you need to stop these comments. Good luck with everything.'

'I really miss you xxx'

Yumi read the messages and wrinkled her nose.

"Up to you, but it's probably best to ignore these!"

"Otherwise you'll be sending her a reply!"

Yumi mumbled something in Japanese. Then added, "Just what we need right before our wedding, your university sweetheart trying to rekindle things!"

He hugged her tightly, "Our love is all that matters!"

* * *

And the following day Guy and Yumi made for Tokyo to go through the legal process of getting married. This was the official registration of their marriage according to the Japanese Civil Code. They would also spend time with Yumi's family. The couple had decided to postpone their actual wedding vows and celebrations for two reasons. The first, so that Noëmi and Marcus could make the journey to Japan, once their children were six months old and the second, so that they could affirm their marriage in the snow in Hokkaido. It worked out serendipitously for them as they chose 31 December 2019 which would mark exactly two years since they met. However the legal marriage would come into effect immediately so they would be a couple with two wedding anniversaries.

This massive effort was repaid with the first trip coinciding with the Rugby World Cup and the pair getting tickets for a number of England matches. Yumi was also smug with delight at getting tickets for Scotland vs Japan. With Japan shirts already being sold out before the tournament began, Guy borrowed Marcus' 2015 shirt in order to support his new team. Everything went well apart from typhoon Hagibis interrupting their plans. On Sunday 13th October Yumi sent Noëmi a text.

'Japan 28 - Scotland 21 - I'm wearing my Japan shirt with pride!'

'Ngl - same!'

And Noëmi attached a photo of herself in her well loved shirt.

* * *

With half term over, Yumi needed to be back to work. The anticlimax of returning to Newcastle coincided with a renewed attack by Laura.

Guy

'Mum says you're married now! Wow, so grown up! If u want any help with tax stuff as a married man (*0*) do reach out! You can save a fortune putting assets into different names / setting up a company #taxevasionislegal Lol xxx'

'Thanks. Hope all good with you!'

'Sorted out your shit then! Let's meet up for a drink soon! Lol xxx'

Guy sent a thumbs up emoji to finish the conversation.

Yumi looked over his shoulder.

"Stop looking at that phone!"

Guy was pragmatic, "I won't be going for that drink by the way!" He turned off his mobile.

"That tax scheming offer is a trap!"

"Dramatic!"

Yumi turned onto her side and he cuddled up to her. She felt warm and good.

"Lol…" Yumi said all of a sudden.

"You okay?"

"Laugh out loud or lots of love?" She held his gaze.

Guy sighed. "I dunno but either way I don't care. All I care about is you! Mrs Castle!"

"How come she always texts when we're in bed?"

"Mimi, that's a coincidence!"

"You're such a rubbish detective! Ask my advice when you want to know the female mind!"

"Now I'm scared!"

Giggling they snuggled under the duvet.

CHAPTER 4 - PRIZES

14 November 2019, St Wolbodo's School, Durham.

Noëmi

St Wolbodo's annual prize giving ceremony was about to start. Former students of the illustrious school swarmed around Noëmi and her double buggy. All citizenship lessons that had ever been given to put anyone off having a 'life ruining' baby were completely negated by her uber adorable four month old twins. Noëmi's well publicised survival had also awarded her a kind of celebrity heroine status in the local community. To top it all off her young emergency doctor husband was 'well fit'. Eventually students excitedly took their places for the evening awards which had been clipped to a fast paced forty-five minutes, as the teachers' authority was now as fragile as a spiderweb. The odd shout and teenage shriek were the only tricky moments for the head teacher and MC for the evening, Cathal Shelmerdine. After each interruption he would respond with a pause and a look. In contrast everyone listened respectfully to the noma presentation given by Marcus. Most students escaped the school faster than they had ever moved in PE, apart from a number who lingered to talk to Noëmi.

"I love you, Miss, you're the best teacher ever. You and Mr Sprague." The girls were saying. "You were alright, Miss, Mr Sprague's decent too." The boys would say. Eventually, just the so called grown ups were left to enjoy a short drinks reception. Bruno was getting grizzly so Noëmi went to the school office to feed him in privacy. Having settled as he latched on, she heard the door open and gave a start.

"Sorry I just need a minute!" Noëmi cried out.

"Only me!" a gentle voice called. "Don't worry, I just want to say hello! I've brought you a drink before that lot in there guzzle it all away. You know how measly school budgets are!" Hearing a fellow female voice, Noëmi felt safe. As she cupped her son's head to her breast, a willowy, flame haired woman of about thirty-two entered her field of view. She was wearing black, wide legged trousers and a cream, silky shirt, her ruby red hair was cut smartly to her shoulders. She felt herself go pink with overheating and embarrassment as breast milk began to squirt as Bruno looked round, aware of an intruder. Flapping, she mopped herself with a muslin.

"Alura Honeyfield!" her new companion announced with gusto.

"Lovely to meet you Alura, I'm Noëmi, I've met your husband a couple of times already," she said pointedly.

"Digby's such a charmer, don't believe a word he says!"

'You're spot on there! Mrs Honeyfield.'

Her gold bracelets jangled as she threw herself into the chair next to Noëmi. Alura put two glasses of something resembling prosecco on the office desk and began to swivel as she spoke. Alura was fresh faced with a clear skin, plum like lips and Armitage Shanks white teeth.

"What do you teach?"

43

"Maths! Everyone's favourite subject!" Noëmi moved herself slightly round.

"Well done you! I studied law, down in London, that's how I met the reverend! We had a flat share in Fulham. Friends for a while before we finally got our act together!"

Noëmi relaxed, "I know what you mean, my husband and I were a bit like that!"

Alura crossed her legs and leant forward.

"Does that hurt? We won't be having children since I was ill. I've always wondered how it is to feed a baby."

Noëmi felt awkward and awful for the woman at her side. Being a mother was the best thing that had ever happened to her.

"No it doesn't hurt and I'm sorry to hear that. Parenting definitely has its ups and downs!" She could not think what else to say and went bright red.

"Anyhow, we feel that God has a plan for us. Plus Digby and I don't need anyone else. So no matter." Alura sipped her drink. The door clattered open and the women looked around.

"Diggers, you can't come in! I'm just with Noëmi! She's feeding her baby!"

Burning up, Noëmi saw Digby stare his wife out. His narrow eyes were snakelike. Finally, without a word, he left. Uncomfortable, Noëmi focussed on her baby who was now sated.

"Anyway God's called us here to the North East and I would never have time to deal with a baby. Although Digby's an infant, come to think about it!"

Alura gave a sigh, finished her drink, smiled and walked out. She flicked the light switch off. It was pitch black, Noëmi gave a yelp. Moments later the fluorescent light flickered back on.

"Sorry, I'm so sorry, I hit that switch by mistake!" Alura called out in a soft voice. The door slammed behind her.

Holding Bruno close, Noëmi sighed as she got herself together, turned the light off and left the office. *'Digby Honeyfield, the holiest of creeps.'*

15 November 2019, Eldon Square, Newcastle.

Noëmi

Eldon Square shopping centre. The tank-like double buggy was on its way to John Lewis. Moving quickly Noëmi needed to find somewhere to breastfeed before meeting Yumi. She had fifteen minutes. Finally, she found a secluded bench just away from the fast food area and positioned herself behind a large but rather limp looking fern. Grateful mouth latched on; grateful hands patted her skin. Her baby sighed with relief, she felt him relax as he fed. Gently she caressed his soft curls. "I love you." she kissed his head, "and I love you!" she gazed at Emmanuelle who was wriggling and giving the odd whinge.

"Noëmi!"

'What the hell?'

A perfect white, padded, fur collared Moncler coat appeared before her.

'That coat should be in St Moritz not the Eldon Square food court!'

She raised her eyes, Alura was looming over her, taller than she had remembered.

"Hello! Are you shopping?" Noëmi asked without thinking.

"No! Just plotting mass murder!"

"Sorry, stupid question!" She felt herself burn up. Alura gave her the warmest smile and rubbed her arm affectionately.

"I'm in between meetings. I'm a lawyer working on an international people smuggling case. And you?"

"I need to get a few bits…" she thought to herself, *'nipple shields, breast milk collection cups…'* Noëmi put her son down and strapped him back in. Picking up Emmanuelle she wondered how long she had. Yumi would be waiting. Next baby feeding, her phone began to buzz. In this deserted side of the food hall, she fumbled to get to her bag which was hanging behind the buggy.

"Let me help!" Alura dived into Noëmi's handbag. Assuming her new acquaintance would be passing her the mobile, she wiped the breast milk from her hand.

"Noëmi's phone!" Alura answered the call.

Noëmi gave a cry. *'The absolute cheek!'*

"One of her friends… she's just breastfeeding! Yes, mmm, aha, hold on! Yes, that's fine, we'll be along in a moment! Bye Yumi!" Alura returned the mobile to Noëmi's tired looking mustard handbag. Simmering, Noëmi avoided looking at Alura. Feeding finished, she tried to manoeuvre the baby buggy.

"John Lewis cafe. Let's go!" Alura cried.

Silent she followed Alura. Negotiating the various benches and plant holders, Noëmi refused to talk. Alura live streamed,

"Digby and I don't need anyone else. We're good just the two of us, I'm his baby. Of course even if Digby had wanted a baby, he would never have wanted me to breastfeed. He sees my body really as his own!"

They carried on through the shopping centre. Hearing the monologue, Noëmi was not listening until Alura opened up about her marriage as they moved along.

"It's enough to have each other eh?" Noëmi offered occasional platitudes.

Alura stopped dead. Suddenly she seemed small.

"The problem is that I'm not enough for him. I used to be but not anymore. He's a sex addict!"

"What?" Noëmi was aghast. The women stood as shoppers breezed by. McDonald's doorways were perfect for confession it would seem.

"It's one woman after another!"

"He's a vicar!"

"You're so naïve! It's the perfect cover!"

"My God! I thought he was a flirt but…"

"Noëmi, the flirting turns into affairs. The first liaison, he said, was 'impossible to resist' indeed, 'unstoppable, given the attraction'. I mean what does that even mean? Then there was a second and a third. They're only the long term ones. There have been countless one night stands, little flings. He doesn't even bother hiding the condoms anymore." Alura sighed deeply. Noëmi bit her lip and saw Alura forlorn; a little bit lost, like a lone swan.

"That's awful."

"Noëmi. You just can't trust men."

"But he loves you?"

"I'd give anything to capture what we had…the time he loved

me. Now I fear we're too broken."

"It's just not right! Why do you stay with him? You should out him! Reveal to everyone what he is! He can't be allowed to get away with it!"

"So now it's my fault? Like everything else." Alura dropped her head and stared at her feet.

"No...I..."

"He literally drives me crazy Noëmi, but you're right, I won't stay silent! I will out him!"

"That's the spirit! Show the world what he is!" She pushed hard on the double buggy as they set off again.

"You know, we're just the worst of friends and the best of enemies!" Alura seemed faraway.

Noëmi wondered what she meant. Arriving at John Lewis coffee shop, Noëmi raised her eyebrows at Yumi.

"Noëmi, thanks for the chat, see you soon!" Alura gave her an air kiss and was gone.

"Who's that?" Yumi hugged her friend. The shiny, white coat strode into the distance.

"Alura Honeyfield, wife of that preacher I told you about."

"The one you were flirting with?"

Yumi grabbed the double buggy and disappeared to find a table. Rolling her eyes and with a huff, Noëmi followed. Coffees sorted, Yumi played with the babies.

"They're just gorgeous, look at those grins!" Yumi snorted with laughter. "That preacher, why's he at your school?"

"He's working as a consultant; pastoral outreach. Expensive! What's worse is that he shoved the previous vicar out of the role, and he was working for nothing!" She checked the brake was on the double buggy as the babies drifted off to sleep, full and content. "Forget about all that! Tell me about wedding number one Mrs Castle!"

"It was beyond beautiful. I'll share the wedding album we've put together for the official ceremony, don't worry! No hen photos!" Yumi teased.

"I'm ignoring that comment but I think you should've included the one of you upended trying to eat a kebab at 4am after Digital!"

"Ha! Me too! You know I kept some photos back. The ones of you and him! The real prize!" Yumi was pointed.

"What the? Honestly, so a woman can't talk to a man anymore? What century are we in again?"

Yumi got her phone out and proceeded to scroll through the singalong from that evening. Each photo looked worse than the one before. Eye contact, smiles, cuddles. At one point Digby's arm was wrapped tightly around her as she gazed back at him. Noëmi felt her skin go cold.

"Just delete those okay!"

"They're not mine are they! They're Bri's, you'll have to ask her. She's posted them but not tagged anyone… luckily!"

"They give the wrong impression!"

"The camera never lies!"

"Just shut up Yumi!" Noëmi grabbed her bag and tried to push the double buggy, forgetting the brake was on. Baby blankets slipped down with the force.

Yumi rolled her eyes, "Someone can't take a joke."

"It's not funny!" Noëmi hissed as she turned to tuck up her babies like a pen protecting her cygnets.

CHAPTER 5 - UNEXPECTED

2 December 2019, Jesmond, Newcastle.

Noëmi

Noëmi had no time to think further on the Honeyfields as she and Marcus had just completed their first house purchase. In an unexpected turn, they were the only couple in history whose move had gone smoothly and ahead of time. Marcus was on his way back from Guy's stag do in Prague. Therefore, to avoid babysitting issues, the school charity committee had decided to meet at the new McKenzie house to discuss the End Noma Campaign handover. Having settled the babies, she scurried around scooping up infant paraphernalia in an attempt to make the house momentarily more grown up. Shoving numerous teethers and primary coloured, plastic distractions into a toy box, Noëmi ran to the kitchen to prepare the drinks and arancini.

A quiet knock at the door.

"Digby! I thought the head teacher was coming, not you!"

Debt collectors would have been made more welcome.

"Pleased to see you too!"

Digby entered wearing a midnight blue cotton shirt and a light wash jean. His presence and expensive cologne filled the room. Noëmi rushed to organise the antipasti to avoid the reverend coming anywhere near her, although he still managed a wink. Eventually the pair sat awkwardly under a naked light bulb in the undecorated living room.

"Your husband's out of town! Cathal texted me to say he's not coming, Bri's late, so just the two of us!" He was smirking as he raised his eyebrows.

"Bri should be here any minute!" She rolled her eyes, moved a box of toys with her foot, and set about connecting her laptop to the smart TV. She could feel her skin creep. Doorbell. She charged from the front room.

"Bri, thank God!" Her voice gave her thoughts away.

"So sorry I'm late! Noëmi I could murder a glass of wine…"

Noëmi felt her body relax Bri Francis was also a maths teacher at St Wolbodo's and a loyal friend to Noëmi. She was in her late twenties, gregarious, dark eyed, tall, slim with thick dark hair which she wore in a messy bun. As she saw the preacher, Bri's words stumbled out,

"Oh! Hope I'm not interrupting!"

Noëmi gave her friend a withering look as she went to fetch drinks.

Bri laughed, "We all met out on the Toon! Remember that eh?"

Reverend Honeyfield wrinkled his nose, "Of course!"

Noëmi was rushing back in with the snacks and she passed them around.

"Arancini, they're Italian, these are ham but I've made vegetarian ones too!"

Bri and Digby helped themselves. In-between mouthfuls, Digby commented,

"Delicious! Your Italian mother not only gave you beauty but taught you well!"

"Oh lay off it you two! Didn't we see enough of you flirting and teasing each other at Yumi's hen do?" Bri was pointed.

Noëmi pursed her lips. "Bri you're imagining things!"

"Err no I don't think so! Did you get the pictures, Noëmi?"

Noëmi sent her friend the darkest of glares. Digby was smirking as his ego was rubbed. He gave Bri a wink. Bri's arancini spilled out as she bit into it. Playfully Bri licked her lips and gave Digby a grin, their eyes locked, both sparkled. Noëmi felt the full force of their moment.

Their energy evidently animated Digby and he took the floor to outline his vision for the school charity outreach. *'Here we go, the Digby Honeyfield show.'*

Noëmi focussed on connecting her laptop to the TV but was distracted by which input to use.

"This is terrible!" Digby said as he saw the slides.

"Yeah, I think what's especially difficult is that many of the victims of noma are the age of the school students."

Digby shook his head, "No! We need more shock factor to up the donations!"

Noëmi continued. "No! We need to balance raising awareness with not traumatising students."

Her slides had been carefully prepared with the devastation of noma conveyed by graphics.

"Each patient has to give consent for their story to be told…"

"Shock tactics! For me this approach works every time!" Digby spoke over her.

"With respect, we need to ensure that the patients are treated as people!"

He glared at her. Noëmi had the correct medical safeguarding approach. Frostily, the meeting continued with decisions regarding the school charity arrangements. All evening the only thing Noëmi saw was the energy between her colleagues. No doubt bold and warmed by wine, Bri played off Digby. Noëmi was panicking, *'I need to warn her he's a married, cheating sex addict, I feel dreadful for Alura.'* The evening drew to a close.

"Thanks N, got to dash, I need to get to the train station, asap! Just sorting an Uber…"

Digby insisted, "No Bri, don't worry I can take you, it's on my way!"

"No!" Noëmi screeched like a banshee.

"Eh? That's unexpected! Are you alright?" Bri giggled as she grabbed her duffle coat.

"Come with me!" Digby crooned in a heavier French accent than usual. The pair disappeared into the darkness. As the door clicked shut, the ten O'clock grizzles began upstairs.

* * *

Bri

The night black Mercedes was purring its way to Newcastle central station. Snug in her bucket seat, hearing only the muffled sounds of the city she was hyper aware.

"What's that perfume Bri?" Digby drove with one hand on the wheel.

"A new spa has opened in the city and they were gifting products as part of a promotion." She thought about her inane conversation, *'Am I feeling nervous?'*

Digby slowly added, "It smells wonderful...like you Bri."

Bri smiled. The car pulled up at the drop off bay outside Newcastle station. Digby jumped out to open the passenger door.

"I'll get your bag, hold on."

"Thanks so much!" Bri exited the car. Digby touched her arm.

"Thank *you* so much, Bri, for...making me feel...well, amazing!" Hedylogos, Greek god of flattery, had nothing on this man. She blushed and he clearly noticed. Giving a smile, he slithered back into the black leather driver's seat. He adjusted the mirror and watched her leave. As he plugged his phone into the car system, Bri was returning. He pressed the button to open the window,

"Everything alright?"

"Yeah, sure..." she was searching her bag. She looked over at him.

"Bri?"

"Sorry I can't find my purse. Could you lend me ten quid until tomorrow to get home?" She was still frantically fishing around.

"Where do you live?" He asked. Shining above them, Venus was paled by the glint of his eyes in the night.

"Yeah, Durham...I just love being on the school doorstep!"

"Then I shall drive you to your door!" Digby was decided.

Soon, the car was speeding over the Tyne bridge to pick up the A1(M). Digby arrived outside Bri's flat, turned off the engine and was at the passenger door in a millisecond. He opened it wide and Bri exited feeling something between intrigue and excitement. Digby walked her to the front door of her building.

"Cheers, very good of you Digby, to be honest I wasn't expecting that!"

Digby kept her gaze. Bri was silent. He moved his head towards hers gently and then suddenly pulled away.

"I'm so sorry, you're just... I must go, please forgive me... you're just...just so beautiful."

Digby locked on like a Nile crocodile. His hands cupped her face. Before she knew it they were kissing. Stumbling into her hallway Digby was feverish,

"I've never felt like this before Bri, I never realised how much I could feel..."

Bri put her hands onto his shoulders,

"No, Digby, this is not what I want. Aren't you married? We need to press pause. I don't do affairs. For me having a bit of a flirt is just a bit of fun!"

Fumbling for her hall light she put it on. The royal blue carpet on the stairs leading up to her top floor maisonette had worn threadbare. Bits of mail were scattered around them. She straightened her navy duffle coat which Digby had already unbuttoned.

"My wife and I are no longer together, we're divorcing, we live separate lives just putting on a united front for our consultancy, but you're right...this is wrong, how much I feel for you is wrong. Forgive me. I must go."

And into the darkness Reverend Digby Honeyfield slid. Bri stood, hand on the dark oak stair bannister, her lips tingling. *'God how strange! This is too weird!'*

Her fingers touched her lips where he had kissed her.

CHAPTER 6 - JOTI

3 December 2019, New College, Oxford.

Tianna

Marcus' younger sister, Tianna McKenzie, was now two months into studying at Oxford and like her eldest brother she had chosen New College. With huge brown eyes, perfect skin and soft black ringlets that framed her pretty face, she was a true beauty. Her equally good looking boyfriend, Joel Rivera, was settled at the nearby Oxford Brookes university. As the son of Penelope Rivera, Marcus McKenzie's colleague in the trauma department, Joel was studying to become a paramedic. A fitness fanatic, he was self-assured, funny and most importantly kind, a quality which Tianna valued above anything. Having met the year before in their mutual hometown of Newcastle, Joel and Tianna were enjoying student freedom far away from her family's strict rules. Together they explored the city, made friends at their respective universities and immersed themselves in the joys of student life. As others around them broke up or formed new relationships, Joel and Tianna were like a small ship, safe in the maelstrom.

Tianna's college room was adorned with the de rigueur fairy lights, pin boards covered with smiling pictures of loved ones and her collection of pretty tea cups. Relaxing on her bed atop a pile of heart plushies and sloth cushions, was Joel in his Oxford Brookes football strip. He pulled out one of the pillows which had a badly taken picture of them, in garish colours, printed on its cover. She flopped down next to him in her Oxford hoodie and faded jeans. Together they lay, sipping from their water bottles, Joel positioned their happy faces behind his head.

"That pillowcase is mad!"

"Yeah, my mate across the corridor got it made for me! The one who calls us JoTi. You know she's just broken up with her boyfriend from school. She said, they're too young to be serious, that they need to try other things, see other people." Tianna turned onto her front and fiddled with the drawstring of his sport's jacket, "she said no one can last in a long term relationship if they meet as teenagers. She's already slept with someone else and she says she's just enjoying herself; not interested in a relationship! Do you think we've met too young?"

She lay her head on his shoulder.

"That's so negative and it depends what you want. It worked out for your brother."

"No, but they split up before uni didn't they?" Sitting up, she stared at him. "That too young thing was Noëmi's point!"

"Was it? I think she said she had low self-esteem that's why she ended it. He was broken, messed up. Whatever, they both regretted it! Not everyone wants to stack up relationships and hook-ups. Maybe it's alright for us to have all this time together, plus the future! We're sharing everything!" Joel's face was earnest.

Tianna could not resist a grin. "I do love that!"

"Yeah, when we're fifty we can be like, remember when we got off our faces at Fever!" He turned onto his front.

"We wouldn't remember that though would we!"

She lay back down next to him. She saw him throw his head back with laughter. Everything about him was warm and genuine. They were quiet for a moment.

Suddenly she said, "We're not quite sharing everything. I think we're ready." She held his gaze.

"No problem with that! What's jarring is our upbringings." He rolled onto his side. She put her head back down on the pile of cushions, so she was facing him and cuddled up close.

"You mean my family and all the rules. Look at my brothers, they just do what they want! Why shouldn't I? I'm sure mum just turns a blind eye because they're boys! When they got with their girlfriends it was pretty clear it was more than having tea and biscuits!"

Joel burst out laughing. "Or maybe it's not!"

"Eh? Anyway you know what I'm saying and this is our decision. I want our relationship to be everything it can be; complete."

Joel

"Ti, things just keep getting better between us." He saw a McKenzie group photo sitting on her shelf; her family were a solid church going unit of Jamaican origin, "but this decision has to be up to you. I don't want anything to ruin what we've got. There's no rush. When the time's right for us…and that's totally your call." He kissed her forehead. "I've got my personal tutor meeting now, then football training. Don't forget there's a gathering at Malik's tonight!" Joel pulled himself up, shoved his trainers on and set on his way.

CHAPTER 7 - THE MORNING AFTER

3 December 2019, the day after the noma meeting, Jesmond, Newcastle.

Noëmi

"Dad, can babies get colic at 9am?"

Stereo screaming surrounded her. Two babies kicked out on playmats, seemingly in competition for the most volume.

"Sorry I didn't catch that?"

"Why do they cry so much?"

"It's just them getting used to the outside world, just keep cuddling and breastfeeding! I'll pop over in my lunch hour to see how you all are!" her father yelled down the phone.

Relieved, she glanced at the time. *'Three hours. Ah the doorbell?'* She dashed to it.

"Alura? Hello!" Her visitor kept walking until she was in the lounge. Her heart began to race.

"God how do you put up with that racket!" Alura sat in the same chair Digby had occupied the night before. Ignoring her comment, Noëmi took baby Emmanuelle into her arms.

"I'd hold the other one for you but this blouse is silk and…anyway he won't want me…no one does…" Alura dropped her head.

"Give me a sec, I'll pop the kettle on, are you alright?" Noëmi rubbed her baby's velvety back. Within seconds Emmanuelle was sleeping.

Putting her in the travel cot, she began soothing Bruno, who wriggled and kicked.

"Shall I do the tea?" Alura was out in a flash. Noëmi felt hot and cold as she heard doors and drawers being opened.

"Just popping to the loo!"

Still calming a wrestling baby, Noëmi realised Alura was already up the stairs. After the longest time Bruno was finally settled. Muslins and soothers tumbling to the floor, she dashed out of the lounge to check where Alura was. Footsteps coming down the stairs answered her.

"Lovely up there isn't it! That photo of you and your husband is just scrummy! I didn't know you kept a diary!"

Lip quivering, body burning Noëmi snapped, "You can't go into other people's bedrooms!"

"Sorry, I was just looking for the loo! Now let me get that tea sorted. Tell me about this fascination you have for what three words (What3words.com)?"

Shaking with anger she finally replied.

"If you've got a special place you can look up the three words for it. You can use these words to pinpoint an exact location."

"How funny, let's have a go!"

Alura messed about on her phone for a few moments and grinned. "Icon, Coins, Zoom!"

"I need to get on, my husband will be home soon!"

"Yes! Where is the wonderful Dr McKenzie?"

Biting her lip she followed Alura, wondering how she could get her to leave.

"He's on his way back from a stag do, so home very soon!"

"Quite a late night for you then with that meeting and then all alone after that?" Alura helped herself to mugs and opened the fridge.

"No, everyone was gone by ten." Noëmi rearranged her feeding bra. Suddenly her unwelcome visitor burst into tears. Kettle whistling, Alura sobbing, Noëmi was confused.

"Digby came back well past midnight, about one in the morning."

Noëmi thought of Digby leaving with Bri. *'No, there's no way Bri would be so easily persuaded.'*

"Come on, sit down, you need to think of yourself." Noëmi thought what pointless advice this was.

Alura wiped her eyes. "Those women! I'm pretty sure he's got a new one on the go!" Her sobs became sighs.

"No, this is too much, you need to stand up to him!" She rushed to put the tea bags in the cups.

Alura gave a long gasp, "And after my illness…it's just too much!"

Noëmi brought the cups to the table. Alura bowed her head.

"Cancer, it was a terrible time but it actually brought us closer…"

Noëmi felt her heart race; her head filled with memories of her mother's illness. Her throat was suddenly dry. *'What an absolutely terrible way to treat someone.'* Leaning across the table, she took Alura's hand.

"Are you still getting treatment?"

"No, I'm cured! But it was traumatic."

"That's amazing that you're cancer free! Where were you having treatment?"
"At the Marsden."

"Oh which site?"

Without answering, Alura's eyes flickered, "It's in the past now, I don't want to talk about it."

Noëmi wanted to remind her that she actually brought the subject up but decided this was not helpful. "Thank God you're better."

Ignoring her comment, Alura's eyes turned to her mobile. It pinged. Noëmi saw her brow furrow as she read the screen. Quickly gathering her soft, caramel leather handbag, Alura stood up.

"Time for me to go, I'll be keeping an eye on him, just you wait, he won't get away with this! I'll see myself out."

The door slammed, the stained glass panel shook, Alura was gone. Both babies began to scream.

3 December 2019, Blake's Coffee shop, Newcastle.

Tariq Azzara

Blake's coffee shop on Grey Street was a cosy beacon in the Tuesday morning drabness of Newcastle city centre. With two more days to heave through until Friday, Tariq was on an early break. Drumming his fingers, he checked his watch then stared at his almost orange cup of tea. *'I'm cutting it really fine here, my meeting with Guy is in an hour.'* Tariq's mentor was DS Guy Castle and he was helping him become a fine policeman. An alert pinged through from his bank about his overdraft status. *'Why's everything so expensive? All we want is a place of our own.'*

"Tariq Azzara?"

"Yes, Alura Burford?" Tariq stood up and offered a handshake. She clutched his hand with both hands. After a few seconds he slipped it out and indicated for her to take a seat.

"Do you want something to drink?"

"Loads of wine, but I guess 11am is a bit early! I'm fine for now thanks." Alura pulled off her Barbour jacket and smoothed out her mint green, silk blouse; she was formally elegant.

Tariq felt his neck itch.

"If I dumped my horrible, cheating husband and got with you I could be Alura Azzara, makes me sound like a superhero!"

Evidently Alura was an imaginative individual. His neck was itchier, he did not appreciate her crossing his boundary. *'The hidden cost of moonlighting.'* He reasoned.

"Ms Burford, I think you wanted to discuss how my private surveillance services could help you?" Tariq drew out a folder he had prepared.

"Yes! Tell me about yourself!" She put her elbows on the table and leaned forward.

"Tariq Azzara, trainee detective in my second year of police work. I'll be honest, you would be my first client but I *am* excellent at my job. Discreet surveillance is not something that would compromise my position as a police officer, as long as it's restricted to public spaces."

"Sure but can you look someone up on that police database for me? Find out juicy secrets?"

Tariq scoffed, "No! I'd lose my job."

"So you won't be looking me up?"

"No questions asked but I do need to run a criminal record check on you and I can't do anything against the law. Tracking someone's movements in a public space is what this is about." Tariq sipped his tea and reached for the sugar.

"That's fine, let me fill you in." She sat back and Tariq took out a brand new, oxblood leather notebook and a Bic biro borrowed from the office.

Alura took a breath and began. "I'm married to Reverend Digby Honeyfield. My name, Alura, means God-like advisor, very apt don't you think? Burford's my maiden name. My horrible husband and I have moved up from the south and settled in Newcastle to set up one of our churches in the area. We already own a few buy to let flats in the area and we have a number of businesses helping charities but the church is our main outreach. Digby's ordained; he studied philosophy and theology in Paris at the Grande École, ENS, that's the École Normale Supérieure. With that he felt his calling. We met in London when he was setting up the London Church of Glory. I was one of his first converts! He's so utterly charming."

Tariq glanced up, *'I have no idea what that French place is, but it sounds fancy.'*

Alura was far away.

"I was under his spell completely. He's older than me by eight years. I'd just graduated, I was shy, confused and immature. There was nothing I wouldn't do for him. We started sleeping together, my first proper lover; he taught me everything. I'm good at what I do Tariq,"

She was staring at him, squirming he wondered where this monologue was going. Sighing to himself, *'I'm selling my soul'*. She continued.

"I knew it was wrong, him being a church leader, us not married and so on. Soon, I sensed he was getting bored of me, he started spending time with other girls and I panicked, freaked out. I called him and told him I wanted to die and that I'd taken hundreds of pills. I don't remember anything else apart from waking up in St George's accident and emergency department. He rushed to see me, there were TV cameras and everything there! Digby, maybe caught up in the drama, proposed at my bedside. Romantic you might think?"

Tariq could not imagine anything less. Without looking up, he nodded at her to continue.

"The wedding was six weeks later and a bit small. Just thirty of us. Not quite what I'd imagined but Mum went all out. Digby was reticent, but our honeymoon was good. Lots of sex! We came up to Northumbria. That's why the place means a lot to me. We travelled extensively around Newcastle and the surrounding area. At Tynemouth, on the pier out by the lighthouse, he told me he loved me. He said how he had never realised how much he could feel, that he'd never been in love before, how our love was unstoppable! It's our place! Icon, Coins, Zoom! I looked up the What Three Words reference! How appropriate! Digby the Icon! Us making lots of money, Coins and Zoom I don't know, maybe that'll mean something in the future! It's a special place for me. Somewhere I go when

I need reassurance. Anyhow, we settled and the church did well on the back of our marriage. Everything snowballed once there was a fine, young married couple in charge. We made plans to open a couple of other branches in Oxford and Cambridge. The church transformed into a full on business. The more successful we were, the more distant Digby became. Then it started. The cheating. One girl after the other. Church helpers, university students, even one married member of the congregation for fuck's sake." The edges of Alura's mouth turned down. She sighed heavily. "There was a pause when I got ill; stomach cancer. Probably caused by the stress. We were close then, we prayed and I came through." Alura was far away. "Now he's back to his tricks. He never gets caught, for whatever reason those girls never out him. Maybe he threatens them, he's got a real temper after all. I don't know, but he's like Will O the bloody Wisp. I've lost count of how many affairs, Tariq."

"Why do you stay with him? Divorce would entitle you to half the assets and then you could start a new life with someone else. You're still young." Tariq was open.

"Good question. Maybe I'm hoping he'll change, maybe we know too much or maybe I love him?"

If Tariq were honest, a relationship like this was alien to him. He was suddenly grateful for the straightforward relationship he and his girlfriend had. He checked his watch.

"Anyway, I'll finish my story one day. I don't want to keep you."

"Sorry, I've taken an early lunch hour. Why now? Why does this latest infidelity bother you?"

"Again, good question. This one's different. He's distracted by her. She's occupying a place I never have. He wants her in a way he's never wanted me...he calls her name in his sleep. She's got under his skin." Alura stretched out her neck.

"This one could be true love?" Tariq reasoned with brutal

honesty.

"Maybe, it happened once before, some time ago. It's terrifying when the person you love falls in love with someone else. I saw it happening right before my eyes. That time she was a young graduate volunteer, they'd go off for weekends supposedly seeking out premises to set up a new church." She paused and examined her fingers. "Tariq, I can't take it again. I can ignore the odd fling but if he's got feelings, that's the killer. You need to find out when they meet, where they go and what they do."

Nodding Tariq handed over his folder of terms and conditions.

"Take a read of this, I'm sure I can help you. I only work evenings and weekends but that seems to be the time your husband's playing around. I can collate details of his movements for you and take photographs of anyone he meets in an open, public space."

Alura had a quick glance and nodded.

"Yes, I need evidence."

Tariq finished his tea. Standing up they mirrored each other. Hands shaken, Alura left first. Having waited a few minutes, Tariq walked out, giving the barista a nod. Across the road, he spotted his new client pulling her Burberry umbrella down and jumping into a cab.

'My first private investigation. Mrs Honeyfield looks like she can afford my prices. This could really help me get that deposit together for a flat.' The rain was lashing down and his collar was soaked within a minute of leaving Blake's. A trickle of warm rain ran down his back. *'God I wish I could get a cab, but if we want a place of our own it's all about sacrifice…as long as I keep this dark I'll be okay.'*

3 December 2019, Bri's flat, Durham.

Bri

Tuesday morning, hair blow dried, nails painted, Bri stood before her white Brimnes wardrobe and opened its doors. A cacophony of colour shouted out. Odd shoes fell onto the floor, she picked up a silver ballet pump and a red kitten heel. *'Why do I suddenly care about work clothes?'* She had relived Digby's kiss over and over. Her heart raced at the thought of seeing him again. As soon as she got back, she had furiously researched his pastoral timetable and had noted that he was giving the assemblies that morning. *'A bit of fun is all I need, nothing serious, if they're no longer a couple then no one needs to get hurt. No sex for over a year has made me hungry.'*

She picked out an outfit more suitable for the pub than four hours of teaching teenagers maths and sprayed on extra Calvin Klein cologne.

Later that morning, St Wolbodo's School, Durham.

Filing into the hall students were as despondent as they were disorderly. Moans and mutterings were shushed out by stern looking senior managers and ambitious young teachers. The school hall was still as dark as ever with the only improvement being the addition of some spotlights. School secretary, Pat Davies, had no idea how to work these so just one was shining onto Digby Honeyfield's holy head, giving his sandy coloured hair an almost radioactive glow. Bri could feel her throat tense up. Immediately she relaxed as Digby sent her an enormous grin. Eyes fixed on her he put his fingers through his hair, he stepped to the side of the lectern black polo neck tight over his chest, dark grey jeans ever tighter. She could imagine him whispering how he could not resist her. The sound of her phone vibrating jolted her back. Students were still streaming in so she slipped out of the walnut clad hall to answer the caller.

"Brianna Francis?"

"Speaking!"

"PC Tariq Azzara here, we've found an item of your property in Newcastle…"

"My purse!"

"Exactly if you come to Forth Banks station with two forms of photo ID we can set about getting it back to you. Just ask for me, Tariq Azzara."

'Thank God!' Bri breathed and rushed to rejoin the assembly. The students resigned themselves to twenty minutes of listening and Digby dominated the stage. The cross above his head seemed Damoclesian.

"How do we know things?" He threw the question and his arms out.

Silence.

"Come on, how do we know stuff?"

"It's on Google." A voice suggested and a few students sniggered.

"Yeah, great answer! Zat's so true! We can see facts, on our phones, online and even in books!" A muffle of laughter spread through the hall. "But how do we know about things we can't see, things we can't feel? How do we know about…" everyone hung on his words, and as he finished his sentence his eyes found Bri's, "love?"

Eventually the talk to introduce different kinds of love was over and everyone filed out.

By breaktime Bri was ready for caffeine like every other teacher who had been on their feet dealing with thirty recalcitrant teenagers for two hours. She rushed to the staffroom, hoping that she may also catch Digby.

The staffroom coffee area was swarming. The hot water machine was broken so too many people were staring at a suddenly very small looking kettle. Tuts and groans did not speed up the water boiling. Bri was at the back of the colony and had rightly predicted that she would not be getting a hot drink. A voice purred in her ear.

"Fancy getting out to a proper coffee shop?"

"Sure…I've got a free next but I'm not sure if I'm technically allowed to leave the building."

"With me it's fine, Cathal has given me senior management privileges."

He raised his eyebrow and shifted his blue eyes to the staffroom door. She could see the glint of the car keys in his fist. Before she knew it she had eased herself into the leather seated comfort of the convertible Mercedes. She relaxed and began to blend into her surroundings.

"There's a kind of cheap vulgarity to their desperation!" Bri remarked now that she was no longer one of those dependent on the kettle for a moment of respite from the demands of the teaching day. "It feels quite naughty to be skipping school!"

Digby laughed "You're an adult in need of caffeine. You're not teaching, let's go!"

The car swung out of the car park and within a few minutes was at the Radisson hotel. Together they strolled into the lounge. Bri was tingling.

"Nice hotel this one!" Bri looked around her.

"It's fine isn't it, I stay here after school events when it's too late to get home."

'Too late to get home? There was no problem driving me to Durham yesterday evening.' Bri's brow dropped. "Isn't that a bit expensive?"

"Cathal sorts it out."

"Oh, the police found my purse! We shall be reunited by the end of the day!"

"That's lucky!"

"I know right! But thank you for looking after me, I appreciate that Digby."

Bri wondered why hotels still had such garish carpets, always in a maroon colour with huge swirls of pattern or in this case something resembling petals. Her musings were interrupted.

"I'm always happy to look after you Bri…we could look after each other."

"Digby, you're still technically married, I don't do affairs. A very ex friend of mine knows exactly what I think about cheats. It never turns out well for anyone." Her voice was firm, she checked the time on her phone. She stood up, he followed her.

Back in the car Digby paused and looked into the distance.

"I have feelings for you Bri. They're outside of my control. I've never been in love before." His hands were gripping the black leather steering wheel. She felt cold, her stomach was heavy.

"In love?"

"Yes! With you!"

"What rubbish!" Bri was no fool but she admired his efforts.

"I should explain, my ex-wife, she's not well. We no longer have a relationship; it's been like that for a few years now. She has episodes, she needs help, it's like that book, Jane Eyre…let's hope she doesn't burn the house down!"

Bri felt slightly nauseous, unsure if it was caused by Digby's confession or his quip. The basic, breeze block wall of the hotel car park loomed before them and reminded her of her greyscale life.

"Come on Digby, this is the North East not some romantic novel. No one can fall in love with someone they don't know! Let's get back to school! Come on!"

"You know what, Bri, I shall prove my love to you!"

"Go on then!"

As the car crunched over the gravel, the automatic windscreen wipers jumped into action as drizzle began to seep down from the slate grey sky.

CHAPTER 8 - FRIDAY THE THIRTEENTH

Friday, 13 December 2019, Oxford.

Tianna

Friday the thirteenth. Oxford city centre was the hub for clubbing for freshers finishing their first term. Joel and Tianna were out with a huge group, which included their mutual friend, Louisa James and her entire cheerleading team. Bubbling they all queued to get into Fever. However being a Friday close to Christmas the locals were out in force too, hence the clubs were overflowing. After an hour of waiting a small splinter group decided to get some drinks at the house of one of the cheerleaders, a second year student called Octavia. Piling in from the local supermarket, they helped each other to drinks and settled to chat. Octavia put some Christmas music on.

A typical student house over in Walton Street had been a lucky find for Octavia and her friends. Their house took the first two floors and on the third level was a separate flat. The front room was dominated by a large, navy sofa which Octavia had covered with a cream throw in an attempt to cosy up the space. The burnt orange shag pile carpet was clumped in places with mysterious spillages accumulated over the past fifteen years. A huge, clumsy analogue TV was balanced precariously on a Regency style, reproduction yew cabinet with a broken door. Homely cushions donated by proud parents were scattered around in the hope of creating some ambiance. The beer stains on them gave testament to a successful first term of partying. Exams were done and everyone could relax. Excitement electrified them.

"Love this city. Love my course. Love my mates." Louisa sipped a glass of rosé. "I feel like nothing can go wrong!" "Which is exactly when it does!" Tianna reasoned and she took a Corona from their bright orange carrier bag. Louisa eased herself back onto the sofa and threw a cushion at her friend playfully.

"That's a bit of a downer. If we could see into the future, we could avoid all dramas!"

Octavia's housemate, Maria, jumped in.

"Divination! Let's get the tarot cards and find out then! You first Lou!"

Tianna felt her chest tighten as Maria shuffled a deck of larger than normal cards and fanned the cards into a line. Louisa gave a scoff,

"What a load of rubbish!"

"No! Come on! Pick out four!"

Gingerly Louisa made her selection. Tianna could not help herself; she was fixated. Maria had a swig of her drink and began her witching.

"Here we go, ooh lovers and it's not inverted! Could be a sign of things to come!"

The lovers' card was bright purple and pink, with Adam and Eve style imagery, Tianna thought to herself, '*I shouldn't be here! Pastor once said of all things we should keep away from the occult.*' She thought back to her times in church. Her hands were clammy.

Louisa chirped, "Oh not so shabby!"

Octavia added, "Future's shaping up then Isa!"

Another card was flipped; a jester style figure, it was the hanged man, upright. Tianna's heart was racing. Maria explained,

"Nice one, this means you're ready to let go! Self surrender! Break patterns of the past!"

Louisa seemed impressed. Octavia signalled her approval, "Great idea!"

Maria turned the next card, it was the devil, reversed. Tianna could not hold in a scream of shock. The room exploded in laughter. Maria was crying with mirth.

"God Tianna! It's not the actual devil! It's just a way to find out people's secrets! Chill out, this card actually means Louisa's ready to overcome the pride deep down within herself! Ask no questions!"

Tianna was trembling. Having been brought up in a Christian family she was beyond uncomfortable. She noticed Joel glance her way. He took her hand,

"Are you alright?" he whispered gently. She gave a small shake of the head, just for him. He squeezed her hand.

Octavia caught Louisa's stare, "Secrets, eh?"

The next card was death, Tianna could no longer bear it.

"Can we stop now? It's black magic, I don't like it!" She stood up and turned to leave the room Maria took a gulp of beer, almost inhaling it, she scoffed,

"Tianna's getting shook!"

Everyone laughed apart from Joel who went to follow Tianna.

Maria called out, "Ti, let's do your cards!"

"Nah she won't want that will she!" Joel replied as he went over to his girlfriend.

"Come on Tianna don't be boring, it's just jokes!" Maria was not giving up.

"Yeah, she's not into it so leave it! And you, don't you dare call her boring!" Joel jabbed his finger in Maria's direction.

Rolling her eyes, Maria said under her breath, "She's so lame."

"Hey that's bang out! I heard that! Apologise and just leave her alone!" Joel stood, cheeks shaking.

"Fine! Sorry Ti but learn to live a little will you!" Maria stomped to the kitchen to get some more wine from the fridge. The others sighed and chatted amongst themselves for a few moments, then started to gather themselves up to try a second time to get into the clubs.

Tianna moved out to the hall and Joel followed.

"Thank you!" She gave him a cuddle.

"Ignore them, they're just being dumbasses. I get it, I was brought up Catholic, not as strict as your family, but that Dia de Finados used to terrify me...that's the day of the dead, it just felt so supernatural!"

The others shuffled out of the lounge one by one like a waddle of penguins.

"Just leave everything as it is, we'll finish up back here!" Maria instructed and soon the group were all standing together in the hall almost ready to go. Being by the door, Tianna could see into the lounge. Empty, with just a night light plugged in. The soft orange light soothed the room which was stark and ugly by day.

In an instant an almighty crash cracked through the lounge and the sound of glass breaking filled the air. Tianna could not comprehend what could be happening. The group were immediately silenced and Maria turned on the main light. The room was covered in broken glass but no windows were broken, nothing else was out of place. Stooping to pick up a piece, Maria held up the stem of a wine glass. It had somehow shattered all over the room.

"Wh…what?"

Basic science told everyone that even if the glass had toppled from the small coffee table, onto its side, that the thick shag pile carpet would have cushioned its fall. The wide expanse of fragments gave the impression the glass had somehow exploded by itself. They were dumbfounded. Silently Octavia went to get the vacuum cleaner as Maria and the others stood like statues and just stared. In the hush Tianna felt a weight on her chest.

'Our Father in heaven,
hallowed be Your name,
Your kingdom come,
Your will be done,
on earth as in heaven…'
Tianna was sure she had been cursed.

Saturday, 14 December 2019, Radisson Hotel, Durham.

Bri

Determination to resist and actually doing so, should be mutually inclusive. However, for Bri, very quickly they became mutually exclusive; the first somehow justified the failure of the second. A sequence of events that were, in the hypnotic words of Digby, 'unstoppable' had led her to a weekend saver rate standard room in the Radisson.

"At least I tried so it's not like it's my fault," Bri said out loud as she peered at herself in the bathroom mirror of her last minute hotel room. The complimentary, clear plastic toothbrush was a relief, her overnight stay had not been planned. The bathroom was small and functional, she wrapped a huge white fluffy towel around herself as she exited the shower.

Friday, 13 December 2019, the night before, La Spaghettata, Durham.

Noëmi

The evening of Friday 13 December had started without the slightest portent of adultery.

The senior staff from St Wolbodo's were meeting at La Spaghettata for an end of term Christmas meal. The restaurant was buzzing with Christmas celebrations; merry university students squeezed onto long tables enjoying the carafes of wine and jugs of beer. Smells of garlic, olive oil and tomato from delicious pasta and pizza dishes filled the air. Noëmi and Bri had been invited along by Cathal Shelmerdine, the head teacher, because of their work with the school charity, The End Noma Campaign. The group would include Frank and of course Digby. Sitting in the glow of twinkling fairy lights and soft candles Noëmi had saved a place for Frank. Coatless and shivering, Bri arrived, a waft of icy air following.

"Bri you must be freezing!"

Bri was dressed in a black jumpsuit with a jewelled neckline. The rhinestones caught the candlelight and illuminated her face. Her lips were plump and soft and her hair fell gently from her messy bun.

"Oh Noëmi stop fussing, I'm not one of your babies, I'm a grown up, now where's that waiter we need a couple of shots before the great and the good get here!"

Bri looked around her. Noëmi gulped some water. At that moment she smelt fresh cologne and the crisp cotton of a freshly ironed shirt. Frank had arrived, a bottle of red in hand, he gave her the longest hug and the much desired drink.

"I love that you've gate-crashed, now the evening will be bearable until…when do you have to leave? Give me a nudge as I'll be off then too! Not being abandoned like that last time! Shocking!"

He shoved his chair close to hers, lowered his head and began to divulge the latest school gossip. Before too much had been dissected, Digby made his entrance. Open collared in a white shirt, soft brown caramel leather jacket and indigo jeans, he was effortless. He drew his chair up in between the head teacher and Bri. Noëmi watched as their interactions grew more animated as the drinks flowed.

"Shouldn't you be wearing a dog collar? And isn't drinking a sin?" Noëmi half joked as she poured herself some more wine.

"Ah Noëmi, Jesus turned the water into wine, remember? And the dog collar gets so itchy, touch there! Feel 'ow rough my neck is!" Half inhaling her drink she knew she had no intention of going anywhere near the man but Bri quickly obliged, softly rubbing his skin.

"You need some cream on that!" Bri commented. Digby whispered in Bri's ear and she snorted out her wine.

"Sorry guys, yeah, sorry about that," She mopped the table around her. "I'll just go and sort myself out."

"Let me give you a hand," and Digby followed, not taking his eyes off Noëmi as he left the table.

"St Wobo's never fails to disappoint in its cheapness!" Frank sighed.

"Frank, he's married and Bri definitely knows better than to be flirting her ass off like that!"

"Judgy! Anyway she's his second choice. Never a good look." Frank examined the rim of his wine glass in the candlelight.

"Sorry?"

"It's you he's really interested in."

Shuddering, she thought back to the hen do and wished she had ignored Digby. She felt nauseous. The song Joe le Taxi ran around her head.

"Shut up Frank! You really just push it too far sometimes! I need the loo." She stomped off, marching down the dark sticky stairs, only to encounter Bri touching up her make-up.

"Bri, you know he's married!"

"We're just having a laugh! Nothing's going on! Don't jump to conclusions!"

"Bri! You were the one who pulled up Evan! You tried your damndest to stop her! That meant everything! Don't be fooled by Digby! He's a cheating love rat!"

"God! I'm just having a laugh! …Just like you did!"

Noëmi slammed the cubicle door, she heard Bri leave the toilets. By the time she was back with the group, Digby and Bri had moved away to get more drinks and were giggling conspiratorially together. Rolling her eyes she turned back and helped herself to more wine from the bottle on the table. Before Frank could open his mouth she hissed,

"And don't say it's my hormones!"

Frank may have been smiling as he poked a piece of tortellini with his fork,

Noëmi sighed. "Just look at Bri and the preacher!"

"Who? Dig-Bri?" Frank smirked as he shipped the two together. Looking around she saw them still flirting together at the bar. Christmas spirit and free drinks prevailed until the head teacher left. He disliked being out in public near the school, for fear of being spotted by a student or parent. Frank claimed to have witnessed a parent accost the head teacher in The Shakespeare pub one evening after work. The story had now been embellished, by a bored school secretary, Pat Davies, into a fully-fledged head butting incident. Now having to pay for drinks, other members of staff drifted off leaving Frank, Noëmi and Dig-Bri. Finishing their wine, they got up to leave as their table was needed for a group of students who were bubbling in the bar area. Frank's husband, Val, was picking him up and they had invited Noëmi back to their place for a nightcap. As they waited for him, outside the restaurant, crowds of students and party goers hurried along, giving off shrieks and choruses of Christmas anthems. The cobbled streets were dark with just the glow from garish holly and Santa shaped lights; all sparkling red, gold and green. Val's car pulled up, Bri turned, shivering. Noëmi felt the pulsating warmth from Val's electric Kia. Knowing that Frank had bought Val a novelty fleece for his birthday that she could borrow, Noëmi did not hesitate,

"Bri, take my coat, you must be freezing!"

Grateful, a shivering hand snatched the faux fur coat as Noëmi jumped into the purring car. In the front mirror she could see Bri walking off with Digby. Frank sighed,

"Something's brewing!"

"Qualcosa bolle in pentola." Val and Noëmi said at the same time.

14 December 2019, Radisson Hotel, Durham.

Bri

Bri heard him softly calling her name. *'Whoa, I had no idea a guy could be so insatiable.'* Catching her smile in the mirror as she opened the door to go to him, she thought to herself, *'After all he's gone through, he deserves some happiness.'*

Digby lay propped up on one arm as he reached the other out to Bri.

"You know I've never slept with someone on the first...er night...I guess...it wasn't really a date was it...not with the head teacher next to me, staring at my boobs, all evening!"

"You're the best..."

Soon they were in another embrace, out of breath, skin sweaty and hearts beating.

"It really helps zat you understand Bri. I've never met anyone who was prepared to take me on with all my Rochester baggage." He stroked her tummy.

"Ha, is she stuck in the attic then! Seriously, why can't she get help and be out of your life? I don't really remember her from the awards evening."

Bri could only picture them arriving, Digby's wife, Alura had looked stylish in black wide legged trousers and a cream silky shirt, her red hair had bobbed smartly around her collar. If Bri were honest Alura had not seemed 'ill' but then she reminded herself that so much can remain hidden.

"I've got specialists in London working on her case. And actually, I need to get back to be sure she's taken her medication."

"Oh! I was hoping we could be together until check out time, then get breakfast together…it's not included with the room, we could go to Flat White café…"

Sulkily, Bri pulled out of his arms and sat up, knees to chest. Digby moved his finger up and down her spine, she felt a frisson, he continued.

"We're at the start, we've got time to organise ourselves. For me it's like I've been hit by a train. A love at first sight train!"

He extended his fingers through Bri's dark brown hair and pulled her round and kissed her. She did not resist.

CHAPTER 9 - RIGHTFUL OWNER

14 December 2019, Jesmond, Newcastle.

Noëmi

2pm and a soft knock on the door. Relieved as the babies were sleeping, Noëmi opened the door wide. Bri plus borrowed coat.

"Ah Bri, is my phone in the pocket?"

"No, don't think so!" Bri felt the coat.

"Damn I can't find it, I must've left it at Frank's. Have you got time for a coffee?"

"Sure, I'm shopping in town after this so no probs."

The new McKenzie house was taking shape; warm, bright and homely. Primary coloured toys burst out of every corner, sunlight streamed through the windows and the kitchen was busy with cooking. Noëmi hung up the faux fur coat and ushered Bri onto a kitchen stool as she then went to put the coffee on. Mellow Magic played softly in the background. The women were relaxed.

"What did you do after we left the restaurant?" Bri asked.

"Went back with Frank and Val for a nightcap or two, got a taxi back here about 3am! So I feel totally rubbish, today's a struggle, plus I lost my phone so I've got to sort all that out." Pausing as she poured the cafetiere, "You?"

Bri looked over her shoulder, "Yeah, Digby walked me home then I got an early night. We sorted some of the details for the noma evening so all good."

Bri gave a long yawn.

Noëmi had suspected that things had progressed well beyond charity event organisation.

"Did Digby go home to Newcastle then?"

"Oh yes of course. Although I think things aren't great, he says they're in the middle of a divorce, so it's going to be a tricky Christmas. He's waiting for all the paperwork to come through!"

"What?" she pushed a red and white striped mug in front of Bri. The coffee was still steaming.

"Anyway, none of our business really, he was just telling me about it!"

"Interesting. As it happens, Bri, I actually know his wife, I'm not sure she knows anything about this divorce! She seems to think he's cheating."

Noëmi watched as Bri's face paled.

Bri
'Lying git. Telling me he needed to get his wife's medication sorted. In the end it seems it was just me!' That lunchtime, Bri had rushed to the chemist to get the morning after pill. In order to avoid one night

stands she had come off her contraception. *'I thought this was going somewhere, bloody men.'* She bit her lip.

'Stand by your man' by Tammy Wynette, trilled out of the radio.

"Bri can I borrow your phone a sec to call mine, thanks…Marcus! Yes!… oh wow you've got it! Please thank him, that's brilliant. I love you!"

"Found your phone?" Bri took her mobile back.

"Yes, someone handed it in and they contacted Marcus! I turned off my location finder when I was getting those weird text messages earlier this year. Actually, what happened with Evan St-John-Jones in the end? I really appreciate how you were the gatekeeper of my relationship when that woman was pursuing Marcus."

Bri rolled her eyes and sipped her coffee.

"Evan's crazy, and you know I'll always have your back. She was disgusting to be after Marcus like that. The pain she caused is unforgivable. She's volunteering now for a homeless charity in London. Ironically, she's changing for the better although she's living with some rich bloke so it's a bit easy to be virtue signalling and playing Mother Theresa when you don't need to worry about the bills. Not sure she could get a proper job at the moment… after all that business. She says she's sorry for what happened, or at least sorry for herself."

"You know Bri I don't actually feel anything about Evan. Sorry is an important word, though. It does mean something." Noëmi glanced at the pictures on the fridge and shut her eyes.

"You're so lucky Noëmi." Bri's gaze took in the cosy kitchen which displayed all the love that could be had in the world. The fridge was covered in Polaroids of Bruno and Emmanuelle with little **'I love you'** notes stuck in between; messages the parents had left for one another. Rotas for domestic and parenting duties gave testament to the care that they had for each other. Bri pointed at the cooking schedule.

"You see that, the meal prep rota, it just shows how much you look after each other. How you don't take each other for granted. It's not about fancy weekends away, flash cars, it's about that! How much you love each other, it's there! That's what I want!"

Noëmi looked down, "But Bri you just need to look in the right places! Digby Honeyfield is definitely not the right place; he's a charming but unreliable man."

"Yeah, he's charming as you know right? He said he almost got with you after the hen do! I don't really remember much from that night but good job you didn't, you'd not want to risk all this!" Bri's hand swept round the kitchen to display what she meant.

"No! No! That's not true! He's lying, we had a chat! That was it!" Noëmi was nauseous and sweating suddenly.

"Sure! Whatever you say." Finishing her coffee Bri smirked. "Anyhow, Noëmi there's nothing going on between me and Digby! Yeah, we had a laugh and a bit of a flirt but that's it! Just because I have a giggle with someone doesn't mean I'm shagging them!"

"Bri I'm sorry, you're right, talking to someone does not mean anything!"

Noëmi was emphatic. A few moments of silence and Bri sighed as she gathered up her black leather handbag.

"Thanks for coffee. I'm thinking of trying online dating again." Bri stood up.

"That's the spirit!"

Walking to the door, Bri put on her lavender North Face puffer and zipped it up tight. She kissed Noëmi on the cheek and put her foot on the doorstep. Bri's phone buzzed as she set on her way.

'Hello, beautiful. Hope you enjoyed last night as much as I did. When are we getting together again?'

Her face curled into a smirk. *'It was a full on night, Digby certainly knows how to keep a woman satisfied!'*

14 December 2019, Newcastle Royal Victoria Infirmary (RVI).

Marcus

Between bleeps and huddle announcements Marcus began his Saturday shift in the emergency department. Walking in he was almost knocked sideways by patients sprinting to the emergency dental treatment queue. He watched as two young men aggressively outran a mum struggling with a crying toddler and he sighed. Turning around, he went over to the line to put the young mum into her rightful place and resumed his progress to the admissions desk. His first job was to review some X-rays.

"Artefacts everywhere! Honestly, who takes an OPG with the patient wearing sunglasses?" He groaned.

Saturdays also featured the Friday night FOOSH (fall on outstretched hand) crowd who began drifting in from late morning onwards, once the anaesthesia of partying had worn off. Marcus noted that a good number of wrist and elbow X-rays would be needed and bleeped the radiography team to warn them.

He moved to the triage desk and checked the list to see how many patients were waiting.

"There he is! That's him! Dr Marcus!"

Marcus swung round as a young man at the A&E reception pointed at him. The receptionist on the front desk looked over her glasses asking.

"Have you lost a phone? This gentleman recognised you from the screen lock photo!"

The dark haired young man was eager to please and explained.

"Oliver, I work at the Radisson in Durham."

Pausing Marcus hugged his clipboard, "Oh hello, how's the shoulder?"

"Alright mate, totally fine now and back on the bike. How are the twins?"

"Amazing. And little Rudi?" Marcus smiled.

"Wow, impressed you remember that! This mobile was left in the bathroom of one of the rooms! I saw it was you on the lock screen photo!" Oliver seemed determined to talk.

Marcus shook himself, "Maybe my wife has lost her phone? I left before she woke up."

The receptionist was professional, "What type of phone does she have?"

"Even better I can give you the number so you can ring it!" Marcus moved to the desk and wrote down Noëmi's mobile number. Within seconds the lost phone was ringing.

Oliver looked curiously at Marcus and asked,

"An attractive woman in a leopard fur coat? We got them on CCTV."

"That's her! Yep, she was out in Durham last night!"

"That's your wife?" Oliver scratched his head.

"Well this is her phone and she wears a leopard coat, actually it's a cheetah print, so I'm no Sherlock Holmes but I think it must be!" Marcus watched as Oliver put his head down and pursed his lips.

"I'm so sorry. You seem like a good man. I hope it all works out for you…and the twins…God, six months old…" Before Marcus could answer, Oliver was on his way, shaking his head. Marcus shrugged and stared at the phone. *'Everyone seems so antsy today!'*

A second later it rang again. "Hey N! How's your head? Wondering where your phone is? A patient I treated three months ago found it and recognised me and handed it in…Sure! I love you too."

CHAPTER 10 - CHRISTMAS CHEER?

Monday, 16 December 2019, Newcastle.

Tianna

Arriving home for Christmas Tianna was jubilant. Her first term had been a triumph of academic challenge and endless socialising. She yanked her case across Newcastle Central Station. Echoing tannoy announcements heralded the departure of trains and a brass band was playing Christmas carols. She pulled her coat tight; the almost one hundred and fifty year old station invited the bitterest of winds. However, Tianna was insulated by the best result from her first term at university; she and Joel were definitely in love. Tianna had made plans to move their relationship on and was visiting her well woman clinic the next day to organise contraception. She mused about what to buy Joel for Christmas; *'Polo cologne? Plus the latest Newcastle football jersey or a festival ticket? I've got my birthday money I can use to get him a special present.'*

Tianna continued to daydream, Joel would be travelling back to Newcastle towards the end of the week once he had completed a paramedic work placement at the John Radcliffe Hospital. Before she knew it a shiny young woman jolted her from her reverie.

"Hey! It's nearly Happy Christmas!" Her accent was American, maybe Texan? "And this is when we celebrate Christ's birth!"

"Amen!" replied Tianna automatically, memories of sitting in church, throughout her youth, played in her head. *'He likes Polo, blue or green?'*

"You know the Lord!" Her new pixie cropped acquaintance jumped like a Mexican bean. Make up free, her skin was clear and eyes were bright blue.

'Those have to be contacts?' thought Tianna as she replied. "Yeah, I used to go to church with my family!"

Moving forward, the young girl followed,

"Hey, I'm Keziah, I'd love to invite you to one of our group meetings! It's a new church, the Newcastle Church of Glory!" Keziah gave Tianna a small card. **Keziah Deevon, Newcastle Church of Glory Outreach Team #savingsinners**

"Sure, why not!" Tianna needed to get on and continued through the station concourse.

"Oh you've made me so happy! Let me take your number!"

Having come this far, Tianna felt too embarrassed to decline the wholesome looking new friend she had just made and the pair exchanged numbers. Within minutes the texts began.

'Tianna sooooooo lovely to meet you! I'll see you outside Newcastle Green on Wednesday at 7pm and we can go to the New CoG together. It's just great to have a new buddy like you! Agape Keziah :)'

'Hey Tianna, you rock! Can't wait to introduce you to everyone!'

Being hyper aware of potential risks of meeting up with anyone whom she did not know, Tianna persuaded Louisa to accompany her.

"If it makes you happy!" her friend had replied nonchalantly.

18 December 2019, Newcastle Church of Glory.

Tianna

Wednesday arrived and the girls met up at Tianna's former school. Her alma mater was barely recognisable from its daytime drabness. The Newcastle Church of Glory (New CoG) rented the hall each week as it did not have a dedicated building. However, believers had a 'vision' for an actual church complex, as per the architect's plans, which were on the New CoG website. In the meantime, reminders were given that the New CoG members were really the 'church' and it was joked that maybe a generous benefactor would be saved by one of them. In the meantime, the 'need' for a building exerted pressure on members to recruit and to give. Regular messages with how to transfer to the New CoG 'vision fund', were sent out. Buildingless, in the meantime, the ministry team had transformed the soporific space of Tianna's old school hall into a vibrant venue. Tianna walked into the 'church' and felt her phone vibrate. She looked down at her screen. The selfie she had taken with Joel at her college Christmas formal pinged into her newsfeed.

'Changed my profile picture because I just adore my girlfriend.'

Floating, she sent back a love heart emoji and turned her phone to silent. Tianna relaxed and checked the time; she could call him in an hour or so.

"I need to be back by nine to pack; I'm off to Austria, skiing, at 5am tomorrow, ugh so early. God I could just fall asleep, this term has exhausted me!" Louisa whispered. Indeed, she resembled a dozy sloth and moved as slowly. In contrast Tianna, was fidgeting awkwardly as they chose their place. Chatter ran through the hall as it filled with the happiest and sparkliest of worshippers.

"Tianna! Yes!" cried Keziah who appeared ninja-like at her side. "It's so, so good to see you!"

"Hi Keziah, this is my mate, Louisa."

Said mate was inquiring, "Hey Keziah, do you know Tianna from uni then?"

The fresh faced Keziah ruffled her hands through her pixie crop and gave a white toothed grin, "Aw no, but Tianna's a special friend through church. This is so exciting! Digby Honeyfield's preaching tonight, he knows the Lord's words like no one else! And he's a perfect witness of God's blessings! I'll see you at the end of the celebration!" Hugs were exchanged between the girls.

"How do you know Keziah then?"

"I met her the other day at the train station, she invited me along…" Tianna did not meet Louisa's eye.

"You're not even friends? She acts like she's known you forever! And what's all that friend through church crap?"

"Louisa stop!" Tianna snapped. In the next moment a full rock band of smiling, denim clad twentysomethings took to the stage with microphones and electric guitars. Dry ice, spotlights and a hologram of the Cross adorned the stage. Suddenly, the drums kicked in and the rifts strummed out.

"Hallelujah, His name be praised…" This group could sing. Tianna's fellow worshippers jumped to their feet, hands raised and eyes shut. She relaxed, this was not dissimilar to her childhood church, although the gospel choir had been replaced by the edgy rock ensemble. She checked the time and thought about when she could call Joel, then looked around her.

A voice spoke over the singing, "What does God want you to do...Praise His name...Praise His name!"

'Should I stand up and join in like everyone else?' Tianna felt her skin get clammy. Before she could decide, a preacher, evidently in charge, strolled out onto stage in a black t-shirt and dark grey jeans. Next to her, she felt Louisa jolt with laughter. *'Why's she laughing, we're in church, this is God's house!'* Tianna gazed before her. She felt the preacher's eyes upon her as he lifted his hands to Heaven. *'That must be Digby Honeyfield.'*

"Oh Lord! Praise Your name! Bring Your love to us Lord!"

The preacher was praying. Tianna's throat was tight. The service hushed, fellow worshipers murmured praises to God. Tianna wondered if she should do the same. Digby Honeyfield was presiding idol-like on stage, Bible readings were given by devoted followers of God and or Digby. Moments of quiet contemplation followed. Then Digby took his rightful place, centre stage.

"Just as Moses had to deliver his people, God sent His faithful to deliver zee world from sin." Tianna gave a start.

"Deliver us!" Digby raised his hands to the ceiling and melodramatically dropped to his knees. Tianna recalled the Christmas concert in Year 9 when boys from her class had got up into the lighting rig and dropped Skittles onto the school orchestra. She sniggered as she recalled the sounds of the sweets pinging off the brass section. *'Was that really five years ago?'*

"Deliver us!" Digby called out.

Distracted, Tianna hummed the tune from The Prince of Egypt in her head.

"And those who reject Him will know his vengeance!"

Tianna shuddered.

"Those who hear His word but ignore it will be damned! Gehenna exists and those who do not repent will spend eternity in its fire." Rev Honeyfield began to bang his fist on the lectern as he spoke, "zee liars, murders and sexually immoral!"

Tianna shuddered. The reverend's eyes were upon her. He was talking about her. His X-ray eyes could see the contraceptive implant in her arm. He knew she was planning to sleep with Joel. He could read her mind; all her sexual fantasies. This was a message from God. She was an evil sinner. She would be spending eternity in hell with murderers and rapists. Her heart raced.

"Repent now and turn to our church! Your only chance for redemption! You will not escape judgement! No one escapes His wrath!"

Gehenna was real; God had abandoned her. Tianna gasped out loud.

"Lord forgive me!"

The assembled worshippers began to pray. The stage emptied, ready for private prayer. Louisa whispered,

"Oh God, what a load of utter crap and has Rev Testosterone on legs, got a shuttlecock down the front of his trousers or what?"

Louisa pulled her phone out and started scrolling. Face unflinching Tianna ignored her as her mind filled with her latest downfall. *The wages of sin is death! God has punished me for planning to be immoral! I'm a sinner! I need to repent.'*

The spirit of something lifted her to her feet. Slowly she moved to the front of Digby's congregation and knelt before him. The icon. The last time she had been in an actual church was for

Marcus and Noëmi's wedding. *'Even then my head was full of impure thoughts, fantasising about Joel. I'm so evil.'*

Reverend Honeyfield put his hand on her head.

"We pray for our sister, hear her prayer. Fill her heart with righteousness, cast out her sin."

His firm hand left her and he was then praying for the next sinner, prostrate before the chosen one. Tianna's skin felt cold. She stood up. Keziah had followed and was right there.

"Well done for coming into the fold! I'm now your prayer manager; a kind of soul mate! The Church of Glory will set you free! Praise the Lord!"

"Praise the Lord!" Tianna's head was spinning. Stumbling, she felt Keziah grab her.

"Don't worry it's the power of the spirit! Praise God!"

"I've not eaten today…" Tianna all but mumbled as she was guided from the prayer queue into a chair. Keziah stood behind, holding Tianna's shoulders. Her thin hawk talons clutched her prey.

Alura materialised beside the girls and gave Tianna a contact form to complete, plus a pen. Beneath the section for entering personal details, there was a detachable direct debit donation form asking for ten per cent of all income. **'Student loans included.'**

Louisa

Tracking Tianna's pilgrimage to the altar for prayer, Louisa gave a start.

'She's still struggling with all that Kit stuff. I really thought Oxford and Joel had helped her move on, but she must have been papering over the cracks.'

Louisa moved respectfully through the rows of the prayerful to reach her friend. Alura and Keziah were giving simpering looks.

"Is she alright?" Louisa was concerned.

"I'm Alura Honeyfield, wife of Reverend Digby, isn't Tianna's decision to come to God amazing! God performs miracles, he cured me of the big C!" Her soft hands shook Louisa's. Alura's face was plump, her lips dewy and her eyes bright. Her look was fawning.
"She already goes to a church with her family, she doesn't need any more churches!" Louisa snapped.

"Bless you! Do you know her from her old church then?" Alura asked.

"No, we're both at Oxford together."

"Oxford? I used to work in Oxford!"

"Great, but is Tianna alright? She looks delirious!"

Keziah released Tianna who slumped forward. Alura collected the direct debit form and the pen. She then continued.

"It's the work of the spirit! Sin takes its toll! The battle is constant within us! Good versus evil and all that. So much sin in the world; sexual immorality, adultery, murder! Anything can happen to women! Always getting themselves killed." Alura said.

"What? Getting *themselves* killed?" Louisa was confused by the bizarre monologue.

"As sinners we're all separated from God because of sin! Adam and Eve ate that apple remember and kicked the whole thing off! Humans have to pay God back for their sin! Everything's a transaction. When someone takes your most precious thing then you should take their most precious thing! *An eye for an eye, a tooth for a tooth*, Leviticus, chapter 24, verse 20! Look it up!"

Louisa's spine shivered at her words.

Alura turned to Tianna who was now sitting with her head between her knees.

"Now there's no going back. You'll need to get baptised Tianna. We'll be in touch to get prayer and Bible study sessions started!" With a final squeeze of Tianna's trembling hand, the divine counsellor was gone.

"We need to go, this place is freaking me out. You're shaking!" Louisa was firm.

Mute, Tianna gave her a nod. Together they left.

Tianna

The texts began. Incessant messages of support and affirmation from people she did not know. The very next evening just Tianna was invited to the Honeyfields for a Bible study group. She tried to decline but Keziah would not stop messaging her.

'I can't say no!'

Keziah assured her it was 'totally a joy and the Lord's work' to come all the way to meet her and accompany her to the meeting. Soon the two girls were heading into Newcastle city centre as the scripture meeting would take place at the Honeyfield's home.

* * *

The buildings were quiet and hidden in the darkness, only lazy streetlights guided the girls on their way. As they walked along the dank, dark town centre street towards the preacher's apartment, Tianna got a text from Joel.

'Busy will text later xxx' she quickly replied.

"Who's that?"

"Oh, just a friend." Tianna was walking faster all of a sudden.

"Sorry, I didn't mean to be nosey. It's just best not to have close relationships, you know boyfriends and so on, when you're preparing for baptism. Rev Honeyfield can explain." Keziah was chirpy even in the delivery of devastation.

"Sure, yeah, no worries." Throat now strangling her, Tianna's heart was bouncing in her chest. There was no going back.

The preacher's apartment was right in the city centre, on the second floor of a converted nineteenth century building opposite Central Arcade. The location was Newcastle's finest; prime and exclusive. An ornate and original Victorian staircase in wrought iron led to an ultra-modern flat with wooden flooring and smooth white walls. The outer appearance of the converted bank did not match the opulent interior. As they arrived, Tianna was welcomed by a large group of strangers who were all around her age.

"Hi Tianna, lovely to meet you!",

"Tianna, great to see you!",

"Tianna how are you?",

"So good to meet you Tianna!",

"Hey Tianna, we're going to get on I can tell!",

"Praise God for you Tianna!",

"Tianna I think you're amazing, God has a plan for you!"

Everything was about Tianna. Everywhere were smiling people. Everyone was watching Tianna. Her phone buzzed, she knew it was Joel. Hand in her pocket she flicked her phone onto silent. Still it vibrated.

Keziah led her to the reception room of the Honeyfield flat, which was by contrast a humble place. A woven, faded, oatmeal carpet, heavy sand coloured, velvet curtains and mismatched chairs all in drab shades of brown. A grandfather clock ticked in one corner, boxes of Bibles were strewn around and a huge wooden cross was suspended over the fireplace. No ornaments or pictures, apart from a photograph of Digby and Alura on their wedding day. The reverend and his wife rejoiced in the most deferential of lives it would seem. Amidst perpetual greetings and concerned check-ins, the group settled to read God's word. Tianna was perched awkwardly on a bean bag, Keziah at her side. Tianna had the Bible she was given from primary school at the ready. Realising how ungrown up it was she tried to hide the brightly decorated front cover. Tianna noticed that everyone else's Bibles were well thumbed with highlighted passages and post-it notes on almost every page. Reverend Digby appeared as if from nowhere and settled on a chair. He was casually dressed in a bottle green sweater and a pair of indigo denim jeans. His dog-collar was interrupted by designer stubble and he had a diamond earring in his left ear. All voices hushed as he closed his eyes and was deep in prayer. Slightly swaying he began muttering in some kind of gibberish. Tianna gasped, was this a seance? Reading her mind Keziah whispered,

"He's praying in tongues." Keziah stared Medusa-like back at her. Tianna was petrified. Head exploding. Her phone vibrated.

Soon Digby was conscious again. "My brothers and sisters in Christ, Amen!"

Amens followed, Tianna found herself joining in.

"Welcome to you all but especially to our sister Tianna who's soon to be baptised as a full member of zee church!"

More 'amens' and a few 'praise the Lords' followed. *'When did I say I'd get baptised?'* Tianna's mouth was dry.

"Now shall we share our outreach successes? God said zat we must make disciples of all zee nations and baptise them in the name of the Father, the Son and the Holy Spirit. Teach them to obey all God has told us. Praise God! Matthew 28 verse 19 we all know this so who has brought souls to zee Lord?"

Amidst even more amens, various group members shared stories of happy new recruits whose lives were now transformed because they were part of Digby's church. Tianna felt shaky, at what point would she become a recruiter rather than a recruitee? Prayers followed.

Digby then began a sermon about 'spiritual nourishment' and the duty to 'give financially'.

A series of amens followed. Tianna's phone vibrated.

Time for tea, or orange squash and biscuits. Digby's wife, Alura brought out trays of basic, humble supplies. Digby smiled at his wife and gave her hand a squeeze. Tianna was struck by how wholesome the couple were, *'This is what devoted Christian marriage looks like!'* Believers sat crossed legged, enthusiastically sharing Bible verses and smiles. Tianna was overwhelmed by their righteousness. Keziah sat close.

"So Tianna we need a date for baptism!"

Tianna's heart jumped. "Sure, I need to check in with my family. I'll need them there…and my boyfriend."

"Right! Why don't you bring him along to the next meeting!" Keziah's white teeth remained fixed in the happiest of grins. Tianna closed her eyes. 'Bunch of fucking weirdos' is exactly what Joel would say post prayer group.

"Sure, great idea! Where's the loo?" She felt physically sick. Memories of the previous year's Christmas party flashed into her mind. *'Why are there now problems when everything was going so well?'*

"Just by the front door." The teeth were still gleaming.

Tianna stumbled out of the room and turned towards what she thought was the main hallway. A large magenta, hessian curtain had been drawn across. Pulling it, she found a door which led into an open plan living area with designer kitchen cabinets, marble worktops, silver trimmings and opulent furnishings. Soft music was playing, the burgundy leather sofa had some work papers scattered over it. Next to these was a fresh glass of what looked like champagne. *'That orange label, Louisa had some for her birthday, Veuve Clicquot, expensive.'* The contrast between this and the puritanical front room made Tianna gasp and she jolted the door shut. Turning, she made it to the toilet by the front door. The small cloakroom was simple with a hanging tapestry of the Ten Commandments and a small statue of the virgin Mary. Returning to the room she met Keziah's now slightly fierce eye.

"Did you find it? We're only allowed in this room and the toilet. Mrs Honeyfield is a top lawyer, she works so hard! God worked a miracle in her life! She was totally cured of cancer. Their testimony about how they prayed and how God answered is mind blowing! The tumour shrank and then disappeared! The doctors couldn't believe it! Only God could do that and only believers could receive that! It's inspired Reverend Digby; he works with many charities, so he needs a private space for prayer where no one is to enter." Keziah, the mortal Gorgon, could turn anyone to stone.

"Sure, yes!"

Tianna's phone vibrated.

CHAPTER 11 - CHEAP SHOTS

20 December 2019, Newcastle.

Joel

Friday evening arrived. Having made it back to Newcastle Joel was racing. A huge bunch of red roses in his arms, he charged across the station concourse on his way to meet her. She was there!

"Tianna!" He ran and hugged her! She giggled with delight, and they kissed. "I'm the luckiest guy on earth because we're together at uni and at home! Ti, these last four months have blown me away. I just love you so much!" Joel gave her the tightest embrace.

Tianna was suddenly serious. "Can you come with me somewhere now?"

"Oh yeah, are we off to Spoons? First, I need to dump my stuff. Will your parents mind if I crash in one of the spare rooms or are your brothers home? Ah maybe I'll have to crash in your room? Ha, ha can you imagine!" Joel squeezed her tight, then stopped to rearrange his rucksack. Tianna was still silent, he continued,

"Straight to Spoons it is then for some cheap shots! I've got my laptop, we'll need to watch my rucksack, don't want it nicked!"

Standing at the station entrance Tianna dropped her head,

"I want you to come to a Bible study meeting with me, it would mean a lot."

The sound of taxis, trains and tannoys was all he heard. Neither spoke until finally he replied, "Right…sure, how long's it gonna last?"

"You need to give this a chance. It's important." She was earnest.

* * *

Tianna

Tianna's prediction was spot on. Having sat silent and stern-faced on a bean bag for the duration of the meeting, Joel had finished by telling Keziah that 'the Newcastle Church of Glory is probably a front for money laundering and drug running'. Prayers were said for him.

Leaving the Honeyfields, Joel yanked his case down the road.

"What a bunch of fucking weirdos. So fucking fake! That so-called vicar is a fat fraud. It's like those American cults! I saw that on Louis Theroux."

Following him, Tianna, nourished by Digby's doggerel, was aghast,

"Jesus is the only way to Heaven, it says this in John chapter 14, verse 6, I am the way and the truth and the life. No one comes to the Father except through me."

She could remember a verse by heart, she was beginning to fit in.

"We're never going there again Tianna!" Joel strode ahead like an angry bull.

"You can't tell me what I can do!"

Stopping, he turned to her, "This is insane! Those people are so phoney, fine, go to church but like a normal person! This is sucking you in! That reverend is just a joke, a con artist! Jesus Christ, can you not see it?"

"Shut up! Don't blaspheme! Don't take Jesus' name in vain! Never do that!"

Tianna began to cry hot tears of frustration. Joel looked heavenwards and exhaled.

"I'm sorry Ti! But this is not what I signed up for! These people are too extreme. They're not good for you! They're all just another version of Kit! Come on, let's go for a drink and have a chat."

"Don't mention him! That's a cheap shot! I want to go home." Tianna dug her heels in like a mule. In silence they walked to her parents' home. Tianna went straight upstairs to her room.

Joel

Tianna's embarrassed father, Anthony, drove an unflinching Joel to his home in Durham. Joel thanked him.

"Could you please give these to Tianna?" He handed the red roses to Anthony.

And like a ball of wool tumbling down the stairs, Tianna and Joel were unravelling. Fleeing up his own set of stairs, he paced his room. Hollow disappointment gnawed at him. Finally, he got a message:

'Joel, we're better as friends. I think we should cool things off. Tianna.'

'Ti please no! Can we talk? I need to see you - I really love you - J xxx'

Shaking, he waited for a reply that never came. Slipping into darkness, he tried to clutch her hand, but she kept falling. Her tear stained face screamed at him, he tried to call her name but there was nothing. Sweating, he curled into a ball and sobbed.

* * *

Tianna

Within minutes Keziah had arrived at the McKenzie house. Thinking this new friend could help, Marianna, Tianna's mother, invited her in. She raced to Tianna's room. Having sat on the bed next to her tearful new recruit, Keziah looked at Tianna's phone and gave a sigh,

"Just so toxic, so controlling, don't reply Tianna, you cannot be unequally yoked. The day you get married to a believer, you will be pure. The whiteness of your dress will be a statement of what a dedicated believer you are. This is what you deserve."

Keziah opened her Bible to illustrate her point with a fitting verse.

Tianna had begun to realise that all members of the Newcastle Church of Glory spoke in non negotiable statements. Therefore, despite the huge lump in her throat, Tianna had been persuaded that finishing with her non believer boyfriend was for the best. A further stream of desperate texts from Joel were ignored. That weekend, Joel's distressed visits to her parents' home left Anthony in despair. Both men hid their tears. Tianna would listen to no one except Keziah, New CoG recruits and of course Digby Honeyfield.

* * *

21 December 2019, Sarai Bianchi's flat.

Donnie

Sarai Bianchi was a petite, dark haired Vietnamese woman with bright eyes and a kind mouth. At the age of thirty-nine she was at a tipping point in her life. After the death of her husband, Luca, Sarai had given birth to their daughter Lucia. She coped well with motherhood and in September 2018 she returned to work as an administration assistant at St Wolbodo's school. However she found the separation, when leaving her precious baby with a childminder, traumatic. Therefore, after one month and without warning, she suddenly resigned. Life without an income was tough. The old lie of being poor but happy was just a lie.

Donnie McAllister, Noëmi's father, was always happy to take Sarai shopping each week. He was a fit man with a full head of chestnut hair and Scottish blue eyes; he appeared younger than his fifty-two years. If he were honest, he enjoyed the company of someone who was, at times, as equally melancholy as he. Arriving outside her place in Durham, he jumped out of his Red Renault and sprinted to her building. The communal doorway of the Sixties style block shielded him from the bitter breeze. Buzzing the intercom, he bolted back to open the car, dodging the ice heavy sleet.

"Ahhhh!!!" Wrapped in a bright yellow raincoat and red tights, Lucia giggled as she ran towards Donnie. Grabbing her, Donnie swung the little toddler high in the air. Lucia gave a high pitched scream of delight as she kicked her legs. *Just like N! How I miss those days!'*

"Hold on, Lucia's car seat has got some work files on it. I'll just shove those in the boot." Sarai was plodding, head down to the car. Lucia's coat scrunched as he passed the squirming toddler back to her mother.

"Are you alright? You look tired."

Taking Lucia back again to strap her into the car seat, he then turned to Sarai. Everything about her was lifeless; like an empty eyed, shop mannequin. Donnie put his hands on her shoulders.

"I remember now. Three years."

Sarai nodded and crumpled into his arms.

"Shhh, Luca could not have been more loved or more in love."

Finally, she pulled away. Donnie's shoulder was wet. Without speaking they drove to the hypermarket. Sarai stared out of the window, Lucia slept and Donnie carried Manon in his thoughts. The car radio played soft rock anthems and rain greyed the sky. Silently they parked up and got a now grumpy Lucia out of her warm seat into the hard damp supermarket trolley, with its jerky wheels. Donnie took his list out and they went in together.

Sarai

"Fruit and veg." He mused out loud. Sarai padded next to him grabbing things that she needed and flinging them into their shared trolley. As they turned into the next aisle a voice cried out.

"Look Millie, it's Lucia! Give your friend a wave!"

Sarai caught sight of two uber trendy women with children of a similar age to her daughter, *'They must be mothers from Lucia's new play group. She's making friends already!'* Sarai was walking on air. Everyone was smiling.

"Hello! Do your children go to Mini Marvels? Lucia's just started there!"

A shiny woman in a navy fur trimmed puffer coat, put her French tipped fingers through her long auburn hair and replied in a soft, slightly far back voice.

"Yah! This is Millie and I'm Jules! Isn't it a super set up! Mills

111

has started to recognise words already when we have story time together!"

'Story time! I need to do this! Can Lucia recognise any words? God I don't think so!'

"And this is Willow and I'm India, Mini Marvels is just fab, Willow recognised Lucia immediately, she loves her!"

Sarai was also keen to make friends, Jules and India seemed perfect. Donnie meandered behind, no doubt happy for the mothers to share their stories. She had told him how keen she was to be part of the crowd 'for Lucia's sake, as friends are important'.

"I'm Sarai, Lucia's totally exhausted when she gets home! I think it's so good for her to socialise."

Sarai felt a lump in her throat as she recalled the moment that week, she had received a phone call about Lucia pushing a child. *'I'm not sharing that, I hope Donnie doesn't say anything!'* He had popped round to lend her a toddler bed that day. When he arrived, he had found her sobbing and eating ice cream after the phone call from Mini Marvels.

India was wearing a trendy green parka coat and suede, fur lined boots. She had short, dark curly hair and expensive looking earrings. Sarai thought to herself, *'I need to work on my yummy mummy image.'*

Jules continued, "Such an amazing nursery, mind you I was totally scared on Friday when I picked up Millie. The lead educator came straight my way, I was shaking, what's my baby done? I thought,"

Sarai felt suddenly brighter! *'Yes! Their children are not as perfect as they seem!'*, but Jules finished off,

"…and then she said to me that Millie had been chosen as

student of the week as she was so kind to the new starters. In fact, she said she's not met a more polite child and that Millie really knows her stuff! Phew!"

Sarai felt her throat tighten as she tried to block out the detailed description she had been fed by this lead 'educator', of how Lucia had 'bullied' another child. More exchanges about the wonderful educational prowess of Mini Marvels followed and the group wished each other well. They parted company. Deflated Sarai continued filling the trolley.

"Student of the week!" Donnie scoffed.

"Their children are so perfect." Sarai mumbled to Donnie.

"Yeah and so is Lucia." His smile was wry, she could tell he knew what she was thinking.

"But their girls are reading already…"

"Reading? Really?"

"… and they don't push other children."

Donnie stopped, "Then they need to learn to stand up for themselves! Sarai, they're not even three! They should be playing and exploring. Lucia's doing fine."

"Fine isn't good enough!"

"Sarai relax!"

"What do you know! She needs to keep up! It's a competitive world!"

"I *have* raised a child who's a kind, loving person, she also did pretty well academically and when she was nearly two and a half she used to eat sand and pushed many a child over to get what she wanted, so trust me, Lucia's fine!"

They eventually headed to the checkouts.

"I was thinking of trying to cook a pho this weekend if you want to come over with Lucia and teach me." Donnie said to Sarai.

She did not answer. Sarai had spotted her new friends and deliberately joined the queue behind them, keen to restart the conversation. If she were honest, she was lonely and did not want Lucia to feel the same. Before she could make any conversation, she heard India comment;

"Sarai's husband doesn't look that bad, of course he's older, durr, but he doesn't look as desperate as the usual catalogue bride shopper."

"Male order! Geddit?" Jules quipped.

Sarai stared at Donnie. He had evidently heard the comments.

"They're all the same! Although he looks like he might've been able to get sex without buying a wife!" Jules the perfect added.

'My God, how dare she think that! She's basically saying I'm a prostitute and Donnie's a sex tourist. How dare they say these things!'

Before she knew it things got worse.

"Do you think it'll last?"

"I mean he looks a bit shy and introverted."

Face flushing Sarai took a breath, "Donnie, can you just walk to another till with Lucia please."

He implored Sarai, "Don't worry about me, but it's a terrible slight on you and all women. I'm happy to step in but I think you want to say your piece." He duly pushed the trolley away but could still listen into the women's conversation.

Sarai moved in front of her new friends and stared them in the eye. They gave a jump back.

"Luca, my husband and Lucia's father, died before Lucia was born. He never met his only child. That man over there is my friend and we're not married but even if we were, how dare you make assumptions about us, based on my race and his age. That's a cheap shot. How dare you give out that disgusting racial hatred. How dare you assume that it couldn't be a love match!"

India and Jules were visibly mortified; hands to mouths, jaws hanging open, eyes full of regret.

"I'm so sorry, I didn't think…"

"That I could hear you! You should never say anything about anyone that you would not say in front of them!"

"It's just…"

"Stop, don't say it! There's no justification for what you said!" She clenched her hands. Donnie went straight to her and stood protectively at her side.

Jules was flapping and called over, "Listen, Sarai, let's arrange a coffee and we can talk, we're truly sorry, we were very wrong." Awkwardly packing away their shopping like it was an Olympic event, Jules and India beat the world record and could not get away fast enough. In the queue opposite, Lucia kicked her legs and pointed at Donnie. His countenance now bright red he fixed his jaw.

"Why don't you come back to mine. I'll cook. It's a tough day for you. I remember well, it's too big."

The pair quickened their step to get their chores completed. Sitting back in the car Donnie turned to her, with a wry grin on his face.

"And actually, what's the issue with my age?!"

Sarai mumbled something in Vietnamese and burst out laughing. Donnie rolled his eyes at her amusement. The early evening sparkled on the black puddles and the horizon brightened.

A miserable grey Christmas followed for Sarai. Although surrounded by good friends, Sarai was missing Luca viscerally. As Lucia grew, she resembled the father she would never meet in every way. Time was not a healer, time merely helped Sarai to become used to her loneliness. She found comfort in attending her local church, St Oswald's and listening to the services led by Attila Varga. Every now and then Digby Honeyfield would give the sermon but Sarai found his monologues oppressive and upsetting so she began to leave early if he was speaking.

* * *

In contrast, Tianna blocked all thoughts of Joel from her mind. She listened endlessly to Digby Honeyfield's sermons that had been uploaded onto the church's website. She spoke in absolutes and quoted God's word, just like the other church members. Spending time in her room, learning scripture passages off by heart, she studied her Bible hard. Her goal was to have a well thumbed Bible with highlighted sections, folded down page corners and post it notes. Tianna made sure she memorised all the page numbers of where chapters began as she felt embarrassed in meetings when she had to use the table of contents and 'better' believers did not. In contrast to discussing her usual post Christmas sales wish list, she announced that she would be donating the money gifted to her to the Newcastle Church of Glory. Everyone tried to reason with her but nothing worked. For his part Joel gave the perfume he had bought for Tianna to his mother, telling her so. Joel's mother, Penelope put the perfume to one side and did not open it, in vain hope. Working at RVI each day with Tianna's brother, Marcus, Penelope would cry. Marcus would comfort her. In spite of their own Christian beliefs, the McKenzies and the Riveras were rocked to the core. Dark days had come.

PART TWO - REACTIONS

Il ne faut pas toucher aux idoles: la dorure en reste aux mains

Madame Bovary, Gustave Flaubert.

CHAPTER 12 - NEW BEGINNINGS

Boxing Day, 26 December 2019.

Noëmi

The airport was full of people with purpose. Everyone was heading for exciting destinations. New York, Rome and Tokyo, all sounded exotic unlike home. Amidst the bustle, chatter and announcements, no one noticed six month old Bruno and Emmanuelle screaming in unison as Noëmi and Marcus rummaged to get their bottles from the carry-on luggage. Noëmi gave up and extracted Bruno from the double buggy and began to surreptitiously breastfeed him as she stood in the slow moving check in queue. Then once he was latched on, she grabbed a bottle and balanced it with her leg so that Emmanuelle could drink.

"I'll swap half way through." She announced.

Marcus looked something between impressed and confused. With their passports and boarding cards perched on the hood of the buggy, Marcus took charge of pushing that and the trolley piled with luggage and car seats.

"Is this a holiday?" She was not being sarcastic.

"Not as we know it! One day we'll have a honeymoon! Bali or Barbados!"

The McKenzie family were en route to their best friends' wedding that would take place on New Year's Eve in the snow kingdom of Niseko. Located in Hokkaido, Japan, the ski resort was a favourite of Yumi's family. A winter wedding in the snow would take place for just the close family and best man, Marcus and maid of honour, Noëmi. Then back in the UK a larger celebration would be hosted by Guy's family in the summer of 2020. A long journey lay ahead for the four and they were fifteen minutes in.

After flying from Newcastle to Sapporo via London Heathrow and Tokyo Haneda, the four took a shuttle to Niseko. Breathtaking scenery awaited them as they drove towards the Green Leaf hotel in Niseko. The mountains were snowy capped and magnificent against the shimmering blue sky. Fir trees poked out from the thickest powder snow that sparkled diamond like in the sun. Fresh air woke them from their jet lagged stupor as they unloaded and were welcomed into the modern yet atmospheric hotel. The Green Leaf Hotel lay deep in the countryside in the stylish resort of Niseko. Shuttles ran every half hour into the main village where bars and restaurants were plentiful. The wedding would take place at the Niseko Highland Chapel, a small church five minutes from the hotel. This intimate building with its traditional wooden structure and Victorian style roof, would accommodate the celebration of the love with its bells ringing out over the snowy paradise. First the group would settle and enjoy the pre wedding celebrations in the hotel. By the third day the jetlag was beginning to wear off and the friends could enjoy drinks by the open fire looking out onto the snowy landscape. Egg nog was served and a reindeer sleigh arrived to amuse older children. Excitement ran through their veins as they all prepared for the wedding.

The afternoon before, Guy and Marcus were in high spirits. Together they sat in hot green waters of the outside onsen, amongst the smooth grey rocks and snow laden firs.

"Will there be a translator for my speech?" Marcus asked as he studied the steam rising into the freezing air.

"Ah no! What a shame!"

"Yeah, well maybe I'll behave this time so as not to jeopardise the nuptials and let rip for the UK affair!"

"Perfect, my mum will love that!" Guy quipped.

Equally excited, Yumi and Noëmi bathed in the female hot spring.

"It's a precious thing your love. All around me relationships are falling apart, you give me faith!" Noëmi examined her shrivelled hand, the water felt too good.

"Tianna and Joel? That's so sad, they're the cutest couple." Yumi agreed. "Maybe we can try and patch things up for them?"

Noëmi began to daydream about heroically changing lives and reigniting lost love.

And so Guy and Yumi's immediate family plus Marcus and Noëmi, gathered to play their role in sealing the love of this beautiful couple. Yumi wore a white silk shiromuku, decorated with crystals, with a white faux fur wrap around her shoulders. She opted not for the bridal hood but instead to wear white flowers in her hair. Guy was sophisticated in his traditional kuro montsuki, decorated with the Watanabe crest. Marcus and Noëmi also wore traditional kimonos as did the rest of the guests.

Celebrations continued back at the hotel and Guy bonded with the family, all of whom were impressed with his ever improving Japanese language skills. Marcus felt quite left out,

"Everyone but me speaks another language!"

"Yeah, medical jargon doesn't quite count even though none of us can understand it!" Yumi agreed.

In the small private dining room, the large window gave out onto a balcony where they assembled for fireworks that lit up the mountains on that final December night. No one was cold as love and fine wine warmed their souls. Dancing and karaoke then filled the night as the babies slept in their buggy. Nothing was more perfect. Mr and Mrs Castle were officially bonded in marriage and neither could stop smiling.

CHAPTER 13 - TIANNA

Tianna

Having withdrawn from her family and actively avoiding her friends, the only people Tianna McKenzie had time for were her Newcastle Church of Glory confidants and of course the Honeyfields. Digby spoke at length about saving souls and how they hoped to set up a branch in Oxford, her student town. Imagining that she could be a founding member set Tianna on fire. She had been chosen by Digby and the Lord. *'I need to be the best believer ever!'* Tianna worked even harder.

Christmas holidays over, Tianna was back in Oxford and was anxious about the need to deliver members for the new church. Alura's words ran through her mind. *'Tianna you can be that difference! Imagine how God will reward you! Maybe he'll send you a perfect believer husband and you can be as happy as Rev Digby and me!'* Tianna knew the order of things: Prayer, silence, study, time, altruism, confession. 'PSSTAC' as Digby called it in meetings. 'Pisstake', Joel had renamed it after the meeting he had attended.

Tianna had read her Bible passages and emailed her confessions and prayer requests to Alura Honeyfield. Wringing her hands, Tianna was stressed. *'I'm not saving souls. I see students every day who are going to hell and I do nothing. I've not recruited one soul for The Church of Glory. Why does God hate me so much?'* She burrowed through her

Bible for a message from God. No luck. *'I'm sinning! I need to work harder for the Newcastle Church of Glory.'* Pacing, she resolved to take things into her own hands. Grabbing a pile of Reverend Honeyfield's leaflets, she pulled on her Primark puffer and shot out of her room. Tianna headed out to the city centre.

The late afternoon shoppers were scurrying, heads down, to get out of the miserable January drizzle. Standing outside the Westgate Centre on the corner of Castle Street, Tianna held out her flyers. As people passed, she approached them telling them of the church that would save them from the 'fiery furnaces of hell'.

"Let me talk to you about a new church!"

The shoppers brushed past her. A few seemingly embarrassed passers-by said, 'No thank you'. More than one person told her to 'Fuck off!'

Becoming bedraggled by the rain, she looked at her feet. *'Don't give up, Reverend Digby never gave up and he's just like Christ!'*

The swoosh of a city centre bus hailed a splash of muddy puddle on her cream coat. Tianna stood tall. She spoke out loud, "The cowardly, the unbelieving, the vile, the murderers, the sexually immoral, those who practice magic arts, the idolaters and all liars, they will be consigned to the fiery lake of burning sulphur. This is the second death. The Church of Glory saves you from evil!"

A woman pushing a buggy tutted loudly, "Weirdo!"

A couple of young lads stopped in front of her and began jeering. From the corner of her eye, Tianna spotted some familiar figures walking her way. *'Louisa and Joel! Oh my God! Who's that girl with them?'* Quickly she began to study her leaflets.

"Tianna! What the actual fuck are you doing?" Louisa snatched a leaflet and started to read it. Joel and the girl walked on without looking.

"What's all this?"

"You don't get it, we're all going to hell and only the Church of Glory can save us. If I don't tell people, then I'm killing them and I'm worse than the devil!" Tianna's voice was hoarse from her attempts to rescue the unsaved.

"No, no you're not allowed to do stuff like this. You need licences and shit or you'll be arrested for harassment! I don't think God would approve of that!" Louisa's eyes gave no escape.

"No, I should be saving people from going to hell by sharing God's word."

"Where did you get that idea? It's 2020, not the fucking crusades!"

"Keziah told me it's my final chance..." Tianna tried to push past Louisa to reach passing shoppers.

Louisa looked Tianna in the eye, "God never gives up on people, there are never final chances, love is all forgiveness."

"Satan is trying to destroy the Newcastle Church of Glory, and it's my last chance, if I can't prove to Digby how committed I am then I can never be saved, the devil will have me!"

"No, you need to calm the fuck down! Digby's an arsehole!" Louisa screeched like a bat. "You need to get back to reality. Right, come with me now before you get arrested!" Louisa took the leaflets, stuffed them in the nearest bin. Glaring, she linked arms with Tianna and began to march her back to New College. Mouselike, Tianna offered no resistance.

Having trooped back in silence, the girls arrived at Tianna's room. Louisa gave curt instructions which Tianna followed robotically. Tea was made and Louisa spoke at length about

Tianna getting help. Curled in a ball on her bed, Tianna uttered only five words,

"Who was that with Joel?"

Louisa spoke softly. "A good friend of his from his school, St Wobo's, Stephanie. He told you all about what happened to her. Noëmi used to teach them both. She's at Cambridge, she's come to visit because she's a bit down, just split up with her boyfriend from home. And also Joel's upset, isn't he, because you've turned into some kind of nut job!"

Tianna's mind raced. "Just like Noëmi and Marcus, school friends, university…they'll fall in love." She coiled up on her bed, head on Joel's face, staring into space. Images of Joel kissing this pretty, lilac haired, denim jacket wearing best friend intruded into her headspace. Tianna began to weep silent tears.

"Tianna you're not okay, I think I need to call someone." Louisa got her phone and sent some messages.

'Dad, can you get Marcus to call me. Everything's fine but it's about his sister. Love Isa xxx'

Gently she held Tianna. Eventually falling asleep together on the bed, Louisa kept Tianna safe.

* * *

Having driven through the night, Marcus and his father Anthony arrived at Tianna's college. It was almost midnight. Banging on the porter's lodge, they waited as groups of merry students weaved along the street. Marcus recognised one of the security team who was chuffed to see him. Having shared new photos and old memories, the porter took them to Tianna's room. Scooping up his child, Anthony thanked Louisa with all his heart. She explained the circumstances in which she had found Tianna, dishevelled, delirious and in danger. They escorted Louisa back to her college and began their journey back to Newcastle. Driving through the dark of night Anthony took his daughter home.

* * *

Pastor Malachai Owuo, always dark suited with the same cranberry tie, was a solid man in every sense. A reverend since the age of thirty and now in his late sixties, he had known Marianna since her childhood. Sombre, he arrived at the McKenzie home. accompanied by his wife Eunice who was bedecked, as ever, in one of her best floral dresses. They were welcomed with the fondest of embraces. Together they talked with Tianna and gave Marianna comfort. Pastor Malachai knew everything of God's love, His forgiveness and His never ending compassion. Tianna began to understand that a relationship with God should be based on love and not fear. Trusting her beloved Pastor, Tianna opened her heart and was given good advice.

"Carry Jesus in your heart Tianna. God will never abandon you. Forgiveness is eternal. Live your life but stay close to those you trust."

CHAPTER 14 - NIGHTMARES

January 2020, Jesmond, Newcastle.

Tianna

Surprisingly early, one morning, Tianna arrived on her sister in law's doorstep.

Having offloaded one of the infants into her arms, Noëmi grabbed the second.

"Only ever have children with no teeth!"

Giving a soft laugh, Tianna cuddled her nephew close. Bruno's cheeks were burning like little hot cakes, warm dribble began to soak into her shoulder. The front room curtains were still closed, a pile of washing on the arm of the sofa and changing mats laid out, it was easy for Tianna to see how Noëmi was overwhelmed.

"Do you get postnatal depression?" Tianna seemed to only think in absolutes.

"Mmm maybe, although depression is not really the word, it's the change of lifestyle. For me the attack has been hard to deal with. I get flashbacks. I can hear the car, I feel myself slipping further away. The trauma consultant, Alex James calling me, then I wake up at 3am… every night…"

"The witching hour…I like Alex. He's Louisa's dad."

"Marcus must be exhausted, either it's me or one of the kids screaming. How he works I don't know, I feel so guilty. He never moans, not even a flinch, nothing!"

Tianna knew exactly why her brother never complained, that night in the hospital she had seen fear in its purest form. Placing Bruno on his playmat to kick out, he began to whinge so Tianna cuddled him again.

"What about you Ti? How are you doing?"

"Better, but I feel such a failure. Pastor Malachai has made me realise the Church of Glory is a cult, the first thing I had to do was to sign that I'd donate a minimum of ten percent of anything I ever received. Keziah kept checking up on me, stalking me, controlling me…God it sounds so stupid, telling me that I'd go to hell forever…the leaders would send me messages asking me how many souls I'd brought to the church. Telling me I wasn't a true Christian if I didn't recruit, there was no escape…I've ruined everything. Joel and I were getting on so well…I could see in his eyes how much he loved me…I could feel it." Tianna's head dropped. Putting her arm around her, Noëmi brought her comfort.

"Listen, I messed everything up with your brother when I finished our relationship when we went to uni and then he messed everything up with me when we were getting back together, but we made it. Focus on your recovery, one step at a time."

Noëmi

With Tianna still in her embrace, Noëmi had not said to her sister-in-law that sometimes nightmares of Marcus' 22nd birthday party woke her at 3am too.

Sunday, 1 March 2015, almost five years earlier. Oxford.

Noëmi was studying at Cambridge and had visited Oxford for a varsity football tournament. Having been in touch to let Marcus know about her trip, she had hoped that he was single and that they would re-connect. To her dismay Marcus had let her know that he was in a relationship with a fellow medical student, Sophie. Noëmi had met his new girlfriend on the team terraces, where it became apparent that the women had nothing but their interest in Marcus in common. Nervous, she had linked up with Marcus' twenty year old brother, Jayden, for support. Jayden had suggested she join him at a house party that evening that Marcus was throwing for his twenty-second birthday. A mixture of curiosity and entitlement prompted her to agree.

Walking up towards the front door of the small, terraced house in the Jericho area of Oxford, she stopped. The sound of music and laughter was already upon them. Jayden was busy texting.

"Jay no, I'm not feeling too good." Nervously she held her bottle quite literally.

"Come on, Noëmi, he'll be made up, you've not seen each other properly like forever…yeah it'll be like old times!"

'You have no idea what our old times were like, it was physical, intense and it was pure, utter love.'

The door was on the latch and the party was already in full swing. **'Drunk in Love'** by Beyonce, belted out. A laser threw green and red pulses across the front room, lighting up the animated faces of the ten or so people already dancing. Jayden weaved his way through the groups of students to find his brother. Knowing no one else, Noëmi could only follow. Her heart throbbed louder than the base as she spotted Marcus. In a tight black t-shirt, mid blue denim jeans and white trainers; he was on point. Hair was softly curled, he was back to his sixth form style.

'Maybe he doesn't see me?' She smoothed out her short black lace dress and arranged her hair so it was falling over her shoulders.

"Yesss! My bro, literally my bro!" Marcus rushed and hugged Jayden as tightly as a mother would her child. A tear pricked her eye. As Marcus released from the embrace, he gave a start.

"Noëmi!"

Aware he had only expected to see her at the matches that afternoon, she knew he had not mentioned his party to her. Technically she was not invited. She filled the silence.

"Sorry to gate crash! Jay said … happy birthday." She flung her gift and bottle in his direction. Sophie swooped in like an eagle and put her arms around Marcus' waist and ducked under his arm so that his arm went naturally around her shoulder. Searing jealousy stabbed Noëmi's heart. Sophie was ski sun tanned and toned. Wearing a beige and white, striped jumpsuit, her hair cascaded in soft, blonde curls down her back. She was perfection.

"Did you win?" Sophie asked Noëmi who opened her mouth to attempt a response, only to be drowned out as more friends swamped the birthday boy. Noëmi found herself pushed to the other side of the room. Feeling clammy she could feel her pulse quicken, she sat on the frayed arm of a dark green velour sofa and caught her breath. She turned her body, to avoid the sight of Sophie and Marcus glued together. A reflux of vomit shot into her mouth.

"Why have I not seen you around before? Now that I'm a postgrad, I thought I knew everyone at Oxford!" A far back voice interrupted her thoughts. Before her stood a mop of auburn hair, a chiselled jaw and piercing hazel eyes, dressed in an Oxford blue rowing hoodie.

"Oh I'm quite literally batting for the other team! You know the other place!"

"Right!" He walked away.

'I mean Cambridge you idiot, but that worked. I can't even pretend to enjoy a conversation.' Her throat was acidic and dry so with a sigh, she made her way to the kitchen and helped herself to a beer. Marcus and Sophie appeared, *'Of course they're inseparable. My worst nightmares are following me like the furies.'*

As she took a swig of her Corona, she caught Marcus' eye but he looked away. As he did Sophie leant in for a kiss. A quick embrace took place right before her. *'Sophie, Charlotte, gross moron, Marcus McKenzie's next girlfriend…'* Her beer choked. Falling forward it propelled from her mouth. Coughing she doubled over. In an instant she felt a hand slap her back, she knew its touch. Gently he moved her long hair out of the way. As his hands brushed her neck, he lingered on the silver heart necklace. She gasped at the reminder of his touch. Manoeuvred by the firm, kind hands onto a kitchen chair she put her head to her knees.

"Okay?" The tone of his voice brought back so many memories.

Without looking she nodded and then shook her head.

"It went the wrong way," she gasped as he knelt beside her. *'Everything just goes the wrong way.'*

"Dr McKenzie's bedside manner is like no other!" Sophie joked, laughter followed. Marcus did not react. The group behind began to chat, Marcus kept his hand on her back.

"Thanks, sorry…I need to go." She took her phone out.

"Already? Where are you staying?" He asked.

"Ha! Bunking down with Jay in a cheap hotel." She looked round at him.

Marcus frowned.

"There's four of us in the room. I know Sophie offered but…yeah, that Premier Inn room was calling me…I thought I'd get back first to get a bit of the bed!"

Wiping her mouth, she put her shoulders back and stood up. The kitchen was clearing, Sophie called out she was off to dance. Noëmi stood alone with Marcus.

"Does she know that we were together for a year?"

"Nope, she knows I was with someone before uni but she's not worked out it was you."

"Story of my life, why would anyone think someone like you would be with me?"

"Stop! And she keeps calling it a crush, she's not worked out how I felt, I keep that for myself." He was intent.

"Same. I guess it's no one else's business."

"It might be to the person I end up with one day." His eyes met hers. "Are you seeing anyone?"

"No." She took a breath and lowered her head. "My last…my only relationship was us. It's all been a bit of a fail." As she laughed it off, she knew exactly what he would understand. She did not have casual relationships. His face filled with a mix of surprise and conflict. He put his shoulders back,

"N…it's just…"

"Sorry I didn't mean to weird you out…"

A cacophony of noise overwhelmed them. Charlie hurtled in and grabbed Marcus.

"Come on birthday boy! Truth, dare or drink! Let's learn your secrets!"

Amid jeers and cheers Marcus was pulled into the front room. Following, Noëmi felt her palms get sweaty and she sought out Jayden, who pointed at his brother with his bottle, "Look he doesn't want to give anything up! He's always been like that! I shared a room with him when he was studying for his A levels and he hardly spoke. Spent all his time texting you as I recall!"

In her mind she could see every one of those messages. Her heart was thumping. Marcus was being manhandled reluctantly to the middle of the room.

Charlie took the floor, "Yeah we all know where the bottle will stop right!" He spun it and immediately put his foot on it to make it finish opposite Marcus. Some cheered, others carried on chatting unimpressed with the childish antics.

"Alrighty, who's got a question for the birthday boy? Maybe the best of three hey? He looks like he wants to slope off! Marcus if you don't answer it's the bottle of wine in one!"

"Who do you want to kiss?" A voice shouted!

Sophie gave a screech, "Me, obviously!" Marcus grimaced and tried to pull away. Noëmi saw him look down.

"No answer, right, drink!" Charlie was amused, Marcus had the wine bottle thrust to his mouth. Unable to keep up, half of it poured down his face.

Noëmi felt her heart in her throat. *'He didn't say Sophie.'*

"Okay, right, next question. Marcus! Marry, shag, avoid."

Sophie squeaked, "Me for all of them!" Everyone laughed.

"We need answers or it's the bottle!"

Silent, more wine covered Marcus' face as the bottle was shoved into his mouth.

"God he's a tough nut to crack, okay final question, violins please, have you ever been in love?" Charlie rolled his eyes dramatically. Spluttering, Marcus wiped his mouth and coughed, everyone laughed some more. Searching, his eyes met Noëmi's.

"Yes."

Neither of them looked away. She put her hand to her mouth. Marcus put his hand to his mouth to wipe the wine away. Still he held her gaze.

Charlie pointed and yelled, "You need to finish that bottle! That was pretty boring, who's next? Sophie, what about you?"

With a squeal Sophie jumped with delight at the prospect of being the centre of attention.

Moving to the kitchen Marcus wiped his mouth with a tea towel, leaning over the sink he caught his breath. A few party goers pushed past him to get to the garden for air or a smoke. Noëmi went and stood in the doorway of the tiny galley kitchen.

"I've not passed the party animal module yet, not even after three and a half years! More practice is obviously required!" He did not look at her.

"Water?" Gratefully he took it. She checked behind and could see Sophie in the middle of the party spinning the bottle.

"It wasn't a crush." She was defiant. *'It was so good.'* Physically and emotionally both had reached their peak together as one and they knew it.

"N, it's just weird you being here. I'm not sure it works." Marcus was wringing his hands.

"It's weird you being with Sophie."

"N, you should know that…it's nothing like us…but now I'm

with Sophie, I find it easier not to think about the past..."

'Tell him how you feel, say sorry for what you did, the love was real.'

"Sure. We're grown-ups now, right Marcus?" she stuttered.

She could see his reflection in the underlit window as he remained motionless at the grubby sink. After a few moments he sounded resentful.

"Why did you never give us a chance?"

"I wanted you to be free..."

"Oh don't put that on me! You left me. Do you have any idea what these years have been like? How long it's taken me to get over you?"

"Y...yes I do!"

"And this year, finally I've met someone who's good for me. I start getting myself together and you turn up!" His voice was strained. "Don't mess with my head, Noëmi."

He slammed the glass down and tried to move past her. Suddenly Jayden was upon them. Marcus turned his back and put his hands on his head.

"Ah bro, you're rubbish at spin the bottle, far too honest! Everyone just makes crazy shit up!" Jayden grabbed a lager and opened it on the back of a kitchen chair. Raucous laughter machine gunned out of the lounge, Marcus spun round. Noëmi grabbed his arm.

"M, I'm sorry, I'm glad things are working out for you. I just want to be friends."

"Friends! Really?" He gave a sigh and dropped his head as he left the kitchen. She glanced through to the lounge as she left; Sophie was chatting animatedly with the Oxford rowing postgrad and a serious looking Marcus was drinking with his friends. He did not see her leave.

3am, Monday, 2 March, 2015, Budget Hotel, Oxford.

Lying in darkness on the hardest mattress in the cheapest hotel room they could find, the silence overwhelmed her. It was now Marcus' birthday. Hot tears were unstoppable. Jayden, Marcus' brother, and a couple of others piled back in from the party. Curling into a ball, she willed herself not to sob out loud. Jayden flopped down next to her and gave a big sigh. Three of them lay down on the bed all still in their clothes and the fourth member of the group resigned themselves to the floor with a pile of coats for a pillow.

"How was the rest of the party?" A sober Noëmi asked Marcus' brother.

"Yeah alright, Marcus was his usual miserable self, he went into one of his moods and sloped off to bed early!"

"What with Sophie?"

"Ha no! She's still up! Party animal! She just loves to be the centre of attention! God knows how those two are together!"

"Shut up you lot I'm knackered." The voice from the floor spoke.

January 2020, Jesmond, Newcastle.

Noëmi grew cold at the memories. However the painful encounter was the first step to their reconciliation. During the university years they had visited briefly but always in a group. Their contact had faded as Sophie came into his life. His new girlfriend had discouraged him from friendships outside of their Oxford group. That day Marcus had indeed been thrown by the feelings that seeing Noëmi had rekindled. Whilst he had forever held her in his heart, he had lost hope. From that moment he started to yearn. He longed for her. Although he continued to believe that Noëmi was only keen to be friends, Marcus was drawn to her as a butterfly to nectar. He kept in more regular contact and made sure he went to her graduation. However Sophie had time bonded his availability and whisked him away to her parents' place in Norfolk before he could spend any proper time with Noëmi. For her part she replayed his words in her mind and decided on Oxford for her PGCE. Ultimately the laws of attraction could not be denied.

On the coffee table, Noëmi's phone pinged. Jolted back to reality she glanced over at it and rolled her eyes.

"Who's that?" Tianna asked.

"Yeah, just a friend whose husband is a lying cheat and get this, he's a vicar!"

"What!"

"I know. Sounds awful but I can't face her, so I'm not replying for a bit."

Tianna looked at the phone all lit up. Tianna read out the name, "Alura?" Her voice was curious.

"Alura! Yeah, her husband, Digby, he's the pastoral leader now linked to our school. What a joke!"

Tianna began to shake, "That's them! The Church of Glory! Them! They're the leaders! The Honeyfields! Noëmi, it's the same people!"

Comparing notes the two women were incredulous.

Later that day…

Noëmi

Barely had Marcus walked into his home after a ten hour shift, when he got the full Honeyfield rundown. Noëmi spoke like a woman possessed; chasing Marcus around the kitchen as he tried to unpack his rucksack.

"That's a weird coincidence, but whatever their methods, Tianna was vulnerable. She's the perfect profile for a cult; bright, insecure, God fearing." He yawned. "Digby's a bit of an ass in many ways but I'm gob smacked that he thinks it's okay to sleep around especially when he's a vicar! Just proves how fake he is!"

"It's the worst thing…" Noëmi grabbed his arm as he washed out his flask. Marcus was emphatic.

"Tianna's doing fine now, we need to focus on her really. Plus I'm at the last hurdle for getting my foundation programme done, thank God!" He sighed as he gave the lid a final rinse. "I've nearly caught up! It's been a nightmare, so busy."

Noëmi shook her head, "I think we need to look into him, something's not right."

Marcus swung round and stared directly at his wife. "N, are you even listening! No! Don't start meddling! Remember what happened last time?"

"We found out John Dyer was a…"

"No, N! Just leave things alone! Ti's away from that church now. Digby's not our problem! I've got my final assessments, it's full on!" Drying his hands, he grabbed his rucksack. "Anyhow, Tianna's all that matters. I can't tell you how upset I am that this has wrecked her first term at uni and her relationship with Joel!" He stormed out of the kitchen.

Oblivious to his agitation, Noëmi was obsessed by Digby's double life. *'Should I get evidence for Alura? No, she's been through so much! But if she already has suspicions then I'll just help her prove he's a cheat? Show the world what he is!'* The faint sound of a baby crying jolted Noëmi back to the present.

CHAPTER 15 - VENUE

Noëmi

Alura popped in to see Noëmi more often than anticipated. Their surprise friendship grew; Alura confided in Noëmi who felt ever more sorry for Alura.

Each time, over coffee, the news never varied; Digby was definitely cheating. Alura's soft face would crumple and her cheek dimples would disappear as she grew dejected. Sobbing bitter tears, she would clutch Noëmi's hand and repeat,

"That woman is taking everything that's precious to me!"

Seemingly blameless in Alura's eyes, Digby was, once again, 'getting away with it'. Alura began to ask how she could get 'the pain to just disappear'. Noëmi was worried yet her mind was more purposefully engaged in playing detective. *This time I'll be cautious, just dabble, see what Digby's all about. I owe this to Tianna and to Alura!'* Thus Noëmi bargained with herself. *'It'll be a triumph when I bring him down.'*

* * *

Not being at school, limited Noëmi's knowledge of the day to day occurrences at St Wolbodo's but she would keep in touch by checking her emails. Now, more than ever, she became fixated. *'Who's Digby having an affair with?'* Her babies were becoming routined so the afternoon nap was the usual time for her deep dive. Soon she was driving the babies round the block so they could fall asleep quicker.

One time the school alerts delivered a particularly juicy prize. An all staff email:

'Noma evening. The school charity group is organising a glittering evening of fundraising on 18 June 2020 at the Radisson in Durham. Prizes, raffle, live music, dinner, dancing.'

She took a deep breath, "Everyone together! Event of the year! The Digby Honeyfield show!"

More emails followed. One to her.

'Noëmi, hope you and Marcus can make the event, giving you lots of notice. Can M speak like he did at the awards evening? Bri'

Although on maternity leave, she was cc'd into other emails for information. One was to the staff charity committee.

'Digby and I will visit the venue on Friday 17 January about 8pm to check out its evening vibe. Let me know if any of you want to join. Kind regards Bri.'

'What? An 8pm meeting? Is Bri seeing Digby? Has she been lying to me?' She could no longer resist.

'Hey Bri, yes I'd love to join. Thanks, Noëmi.'

'Time to spoil that little party.'

Having calculated bedtime and travel time, she persuaded her father to babysit. Biting her lip, she thought about her priorities and bristled. *'I'll be in and out. Get the info for Alura. This time I'm not going to be an idiot and hide things from M!'*

Quickly she texted.

'Popping out to a noma charity meeting on Fri, Dad babysitting. They want you to be the speaker at the event in July #famous!'

'Sure can do. Why do you want to go all the way to Durham for a mtg? Don't go! Stay with the kids!'

Although she was no longer hiding things, she chose to ignore his advice.

17 January 2020, Radisson Hotel, Durham.

Noëmi

Barely had her father arrived and Noëmi was out the door.

Conveniently located in Durham city centre, The Radisson overlooked the River Wear. Running over the Pennyferry Bridge, to get to the front entrance, Noëmi pulled up as a pain shot through her leg. *'Damn, I thought that fracture ache was a thing of the past.'* Slowing up to a limp she hobbled to the steps that led up to the main door. Shifting from foot to foot, she waited.

Cold hands slapped over her eyes.

"Agghhh! Get off!" With a shriek, her heart jumped in her ribcage. "Stop! No! Who is this?"

Warm breath whispered into her neck.

"Guess!"

Her heart thumped, she knew exactly who it was.

"Get off me!" Her neck was being pulled backwards. He was strong. Reluctantly he slid his hands from her eyes and draped

141

them over her shoulders. Leaning in he was hugging her from behind. She spun round.

"Let me go!"

Still standing with his arms over her shoulders Digby grinned, lizard-like teeth were right in her face. Playfully he patted her nose with his right index finger. Wriggling free she brushed herself down and glared at him. With a smirk he stood to the side and gestured at her to enter the hotel.

"How dare you! You can't put your hands on me! That's assault!"

"Sue me then! Don't over react! Come on, Bri's running late. Let's go to zee bar, what do you want to drink?"

"Water! I'm driving."

Burning up she was incensed. *'He touched me!'*

Oliver Legatt

Oliver was patrolling reception. Nothing unusual for a Friday evening, the usual Durham guests; businessmen leaving from conferences, parents arriving for a long weekend to see their student children and couples escaping on minibreaks. He checked the main entrance and gave a start, the lady in the faux fur coat. *'She's back! With that man again!'* Following with half an eye he observed them enter and go straight to the bar. The pair appeared tense. Somehow drawn to them he moved their way, gave his colleague a nod and stood to the side. Many couples were probably using the hotel for affairs, it was a given, no questions asked, but these two raised Oliver's hackles. *'I really liked her husband, Dr McKenzie. She's wearing her wedding ring. Have they no shame?'*

Digby went across and ordered drinks at the bar. A bottle of Sancerre rosé on ice plus a sparkling water. "

How many wine glasses sir?"

"Just the two, thank you."

Oliver felt hot. He tidied the counter top as he listened into the conversation.

"Here for the weekend?"

"No, only this evening, we need to get a feel of whether zis is right for us." He tried the wine and gave a nod. "Can I pop that on a tab?"

Wiping the counter the barman smiled. "Certainly sir, no problem for our regulars."

Digby gestured acknowledgement and sauntered back to Noëmi.

Noëmi

"And how's my wife's new best friend?"

He poured the wine. Thinking how easy this was, Noëmi went straight for him.

"Are you cheating on her?"

"Excuse me?"

"She's really upset. She knows something's going on." She stared at him.

"No, why would I do that? I'm married and a church leader. I don't cheat!"

In a whisper she hissed, "Don't give me that! When I met you that evening, you made it clear what you were after!"

Digby's lips curled. "If you've changed your mind, that's fine by me!"

Noëmi sneered at him. "You're deluded."

"You think? I suggested you get to know my wife. Nothing inappropriate with that. Women are such fantasists!" He sipped his wine. Piped piano music filled the silence. The sound of glass on glass shrieked through the bar as she slammed her drink down. Everyone looked around.

"How dare you! Is it Bri?"

Digby leaned into her.

"Listen. My wife's a highly complex person, probably best not to believe everything she says. Bri's my colleague, we're working our butts off to get this event organised whilst you play 'appy families."

"But after all Alura's been through! How could you? She's had cancer!"

Digby sneered a look of contempt. Sitting back in his armchair, he threw out his hand,

"So what do you think of this place for zee dinner? It'll be a black tie event, I'm hoping we'll get a chunky discount, given zat it's a charity do."

Undefeated, Noëmi went for a second line of attack.

"And your church is confusing young people. Someone I know has been really messed up by the methods used by you and your so-called prayer partners. It's a cult!"

"Now that's a very serious accusation. Lives are transformed through our church. Never condemn anyone for their religious commitment! That's zee unforgivable sin!"

As he spat his reply, he grabbed her arm and twisted it back. His hand was locked on with such force that his fingers pressed into her bone.

"You're hurting me!" She snatched her arm back from him. She shoved her face up close to his and hissed. "And what's all this praying for a church building? Getting money off vulnerable people."

"Zat's none of your business. Giving is in zee Bible, it's a huge part of believing!"

"Rubbish! How are these donations spent? Who checks your accounts? And why is there no building for that London church after all those years?"

"What are you implying? You should know that it never ends well for those who speak out against our church."

His nostrils flared, Digby's face was up against hers. He stared just as he had stared at Alura; cold, venomous, contemptuous. His phone pinged, his eyes shifted. Finally, he spoke,

"Bri's late as ever, she's gone straight to the banqueting department. Let's go!"

Digby pointed towards the ballroom and the pair left to join their last minute colleague.

Tariq

Rushing from the Radisson lobby into the toilets, Tariq collided with the wash basin. He splashed water over his face and felt his heart pounding.

"No! Not her. I just don't get it. I must be wrong."

He peered into the underlit, art deco mirror and saw his eyes were bloodshot. *'She must have a twin sister or something, this just makes no sense. Those babies are what, six months old. How on earth does she even have time for an affair?'*

Staring at his reflection Tariq wondered what hornets' nest he was disturbing. The rose diffuser and soft background music were making him feel nauseous. Maybe this was all quite innocent. He began to breathe.

"Yes, if I capture them both leaving separately then it's just a meeting."

He rushed out and careered into a staff member coming into the toilets.

"I need to…go, sorry!"

Tariq charged through the lobby. A voice was following him.

"Sir! Sir!" The call was suddenly louder, "Excuse me!"

Tariq stopped.

"Your phone!"

He recognised the security guard.

"Thank you and sorry for just now…"

"No worries, I'm Ollie, I work here. Are you alright mate?"

The two men stood opposite each other as Digby sauntered past on his way to the toilet. Tariq's eyes followed his target.

"Do you know him?" Oliver was like a hawk..

"Not really, I'm just trying to get information on him…I'm investigating…insurance fraud."

"Nice one, give me your details I'll send you some stuff. I've seen what he's up to!"

Narrowing his eyes, Oliver took the small business card Tariq proffered. Oliver then added, as he gave a wink.

"He's a cheating bastard, messing about with married women!"

Tariq felt acid rise to his throat and turned to leave. Going through the main doors, he went towards the car park, checking the pictures he had taken on his phone. They were all of this couple; messing about on the steps of the hotel, playing peekaboo, his arms around her, relaxing with a drink together. Zooming in on the faces he wanted to be sure. His phone pinged.

'He's out and says he's not back until the early hours. Make sure you find out what he's up to. Some crap about a school charity meeting. I pay for results.'

Tariq sighed, he wished he could unsee everything.

Noëmi

Late as ever, Bri swept into the conference facilities. Upon noticing them, her face became one huge grin.

'And that smile is definitely not for me.'

As the banqueting manager went over the possible room set ups, Noëmi sensed that she was the only one listening. The energy between her colleagues was palpable.

'Good God I think he and Bri are a thing!'

The facilities were magnificent and the numbers could be flexed right up until the last minute. The hotel manager was delighted to work on charity event pricings and would help sell tickets. Primary arrangements made, they thanked the hotel representative, gathered their belongings and began to walk towards the main exit. Digby strode ahead and Bri went to the toilet. Trailing somewhat as she put her coat back on, Noëmi could feel her breasts getting tight. The ten O'clock feed was still programmed in her body.

Tariq

Teeth chattering, Tariq was in his small sky blue Corsa in the hotel car park. Waiting to capture Digby leaving, he spotted movement in the darkness. The night black Mercedes convertible was also in his sights. He heard giggling and muffled sounds of a couple chatting. Through the blackness Tariq could see the sandy glow of Digby's hair and that he was with a dark haired companion, who could only have been Noëmi. Craning his neck he could see they had stopped, they were kissing and then they jumped into the car. The purr of the Mercedes broke the silence. They were gone. Tariq put his head in his hands.

Noëmi

"Excuse me!"

Busy texting in the hotel foyer, Noëmi turned to see the security guard had run after her, with their bill. Digby and Bri were already gone.

"Good evening, I'm Oliver, hotel security, your party has a bar account to pay."

"I'm so sorry! I thought my colleague had settled that!" Noëmi went bright red and began fumbling in her handbag. "Here, let me sort that out!"

They walked to the bar and the card machine was put her way by the waiter, who gave Oliver a look. A few awkward moments.

"Thank you, can I put a tip on that? Ten per cent?"

"Certainly…and there we go," Oliver looked at the card, "Mrs McKenzie, thank you very much… This is a bit forward but you're not related to the doctor at RVI are you?"

"Yes! That's my husband! He works in the emergency department! How do you know him?"

"He treated me when I got knocked off my bike. Your husband really is the best! Remember that!" Oliver held her gaze.

"Of course!" Guilt at going against Marcus' advice swept over her. Why was she here and not with her babies? Tears pricked her eyes. Bri and Digby were gone. She rushed to get home.

Once back in Newcastle, she threw herself through the door; her breasts were ready to explode. Her father was cradling one of the babies as the other began to whinge. Without speaking he passed her the infant and went to fetch the other one. Tending the infant she settled on the sofa.

"Dad I'm so sorry, I think I'm going a bit crazy."

And for many reasons she cried inconsolably.

CHAPTER 16 - IN PLAIN SIGHT

17 January 2020, late that evening, Radisson Hotel, Durham.

Tariq

Drumming his fingers on the dashboard, Tariq went over his options, *'Say I didn't see him at all and send her nothing. Forget the money. Or show her the truth? The camera never lies, as they say, she deserves to know that her husband is a cheat. Or say he was with someone but I didn't see them…but that's proof of nothing.'*

A text popped up from Alura.

'He's not answering his phone. Do you know where he is and most importantly who he's with? £500 tonight for pictures.'

Tariq's throat got lumpy and he scrolled through his photos. His girlfriend sent a message.

'A full structural survey on the flat is £600, I just don't think we can do that this month, we'll have to forget it.'

Selecting the best photos from that evening, Tariq pressed send. He followed up with a note of his bank details.

18 January 2020, early that morning, Jesmond, Newcastle.

Noëmi

Having settled the babies, Noëmi pounced on Marcus when he got home from his night shift. Having told him how much she loved him, over and over again, he finally had to admit.

"N, sorry, I'm so knackered. Come to bed when B and E nap but you'll have to wake me up."

He rolled over and was asleep in seconds.

Paddy Freeman's Park, Jesmond, Newcastle.

A morning of chores and a brisk pram walk to the park, Noëmi was reflective.

'I can't take on Digby Honeyfield, he's in a league of his own. I need to focus on Tianna.' Her phone lit up.

'And again, the cheating bastard never came home last night.'

With a sigh, she replied, **'Alura I'm so sorry to hear that, let me know you're okay!'**

And then Noëmi sent another message.

'Bri what happened to you last night? I got abandoned at the hotel with the bill.'

'Oh sorry, we can put it on expenses.'

'Err no I don't think charity donations should be used to cover our drinks!'

Bri sent a thumbs up.

'What did you do after you left?'

'Digby dropped me home and I had an early night, #boring!'

'Digby's wife says he never went home.'

After a few awkward seconds Bri replied.

'Do you think we should call the police?'

'Bri you're lying. Digby's married. He's a cheating pig! Keep away from him!'

A message from Alura interrupted their stream.

'Dagli amici mi guardi Dio, dai nemici mi guardo io.'

She knew the translation: *'God guards me from my friends; I guard myself from my enemies.'*

'Alura r u ok?'

'I'm not good, I'm taking some pills. You've been a wonderful friend.'

'Alura no! I'm coming over!'

Dialling Alura's number, Noëmi got no reply.

Bri's flat, Durham.

Bri

Lying in her bed, Bri put her phone on her bedside table. Digby grabbed her into his arms. She noticed soft golden hairs on his forearms.

"How about a weekend away sometime?" He nuzzled into her neck.

"Oh yeah, where are you thinking?"

"Oxford or Cambridge? We're looking at setting up churches in the university towns, so I have a reason to be visiting those."

"A cover story? Of course I keep forgetting, you're married and I'm just a dirty, little secret."

Bri pulled herself up and looked down at him.

"Baby don't be like that, you know she's sick. I 'ave to be careful because of her mental state." Digby groaned. "I seem to be surrounded by nutters." He stroked her peachy skin. Bri's phone rang.

"Noëmi? …What? I don't know where Digby is… I'm not sure but I can look for his number in my emails…I have no idea but I'll let you know if I come up with anything. Bye"

Putting the mobile down, she scowled at Digby.

"Your wife's sending goodbye messages and talking about taking pills."

Digby sank backwards, shut his eyes and put his hand to his forehead.

"Fucking lunatic. Right, I need to deal with this. Bri I'll text you later but choose a nice hotel in Cambridge for our weekend away. Sorry my love."

Out of the bed, clothes on, keys grabbed and Digby was gone. Bri flung herself back onto her pillow and gave a cry of frustration.

"What am I doing? Affairs with married men is the one thing I've always vowed I'd never do!"

She sent Noëmi a message and glanced at the time. *'One more hour of dozing and then I'll go to the chemist.'* Having been awake all night with Digby, Bri fell into a long, deep sleep and never made it to the pharmacy.

Paddy Freeman's Park, Jesmond, Newcastle.

Noëmi

Sitting on a bench, she looked across the park. Memories of lying on the grass with Marcus flooded her head. Testing each other before exams, sharing jokes and confiding dreams. The swings were emptying as lunchtime approached and a skyline of terraced houses, rustling trees and lone dog walkers filled her view.

'I need to check on Alura. I want to go to Marcus.'

Bruno and Emmanuelle began to whinge in their double buggy, they were getting tired. Gathering her stuff, she manoeuvred the buggy through the heavy iron gate and out of the dog free area. Picking up her mobile she tried Alura again. No reply.

"Damn I'll have to go to her."

She set off for Alura's house in the city centre, cursing her luck. Turning out of the park the babies were falling asleep. Her phone pinged.

'I've messaged Digby, he's on his way, Bri x'

'Wow Bri, what a miracle that you tracked down Alura's HUSBAND!'

Giving a cry she turned on her heel and heaved the double buggy back towards her home. Finally, having settled the babies for their nap, she slipped into bed with Marcus. He was warm, his skin was soft.

"How long have we got?" He asked sleepily.

"Probably five minutes knowing our luck, thirty if a nap miracle occurs."

He turned over and smiled,

"These days, a lot can happen in five minutes!"

The babies were tired. Marcus and Noëmi held each other tightly.

"Alura thinks Digby's cheating."

She pulled the pale blue, cotton duvet cover into a cocoon around them.

"Ugh, I don't want to hear his name and why do you hang around with Alura? You've got nothing in common...I hope."

Marcus stroked her cheek and moved some of her hair out of her face.

"I feel sorry for her. She had cancer!"

"God that's awful, what type?"

"You're so medical! She's cured!"

"Wow, that's good but she must still be on some kind of treatment?"

"No I don't think so, she describes it as a miracle!"

"Divine intervention via medicine I think you'll find! But still she's a bit odd."

"You can't say that! She's a victim! He's a rat! How do people get away with it?" She brushed his lips with her finger.

"What cheating?"

"Yes! Hiding a relationship in plain sight?"

"Like we did? Obviously not cheating but getting away with no one finding us out!" Marcus stretched his arms out behind his head, "like after that concert in Year 13."

Noëmi thought back.

22 March 2011, nine years before, Newcastle Green Academy.

Noëmi

March only delivered miserable, grey skies. An early start with double maths was not brightening things up for Noëmi. Sauntering to sixth form along street after street of Thirties semis, she daydreamed of getting the results for Cambridge. Imagined success was interrupted by the breathless gasps of her friend Ruby running to catch her.

"Noëmi, how was the concert?" Ruby was at her side.

"Yeah gr…"

"Did you see Marcus McKenzie? Apparently, Kai's brother saw him there packing on the PDA with a girl!" Ruby caught her breath.

"Oh a girl! How does Kai's brother know Marcus McKenzie?" Noëmi kept on moving.

"From football, but never mind that! What do you know? You do work with him and stuff, has he mentioned anyone?"

They walked through the Newcastle Green Academy main gates.

"In what way?"

"In a girlfriend way stupid!"

"To me?" She took her Blackberry Bold out of her pocket and began to fiddle with it.

"Anyway, apparently he was at the concert with a petite, dark haired girl, she was wearing a baseball hat and they were *all* over each other!"

"Maybe it was me!"

"Ha! Yeah, hilarious but not possible, she was really pretty and looked a load of fun."

Noëmi bit her tongue.

"Clearly not me then. Ruby, I hear Mars One is looking for volunteers for that one way trip to the Red Planet, you should look into it."

Ruby was furiously texting on her phone, "What?"

"Nothing." Noëmi felt her throat get tight and her heart beat faster. As they walked to the canteen, Marcus was already there chatting with his friends. He looked over at Noëmi, smiled then averted his gaze. Ruby led the way to join their group. Noëmi hung well back. *'He's with his friends.'*

"I hear you're an Enrique fan, Marcus, bit of a surprise there!" Ruby pushed her chest out, flicked her hair and stood in front of him.

"It was alright! Not been to the Metro Radio Arena before, it was a fun night!" His hands clenched the sky blue melamine table he was sitting on.

"More than alright, who were you with?"

Marcus laughed, ignored her question and turned to his friends who were all nonchalantly scrolling on their phones. Noëmi felt her pulse quicken.

'If she pushes it I know he won't lie.'

Like a fly buzzing at a glass pane, Ruby was not giving up.

"I hear from Kai's brother you enjoyed yourself!"

"I always enjoy myself Ruby!"

"Who's the lucky girl then?"

Marcus was not giving up either, "Ruby, I see all sorts of lucky people!" Swinging his feet off the chair he stood up. The bell went. His friends all fist bumped each other to say goodbye, as they reluctantly pulled themselves up.

"Noëmi we've got maths now, let's go!" He called over Ruby's shoulder.

Ruby turned and hissed at Noëmi,

"For God's sake get some info will you? This is killing me!"

"Sure!   I'll   try."
Marcus and Noëmi left the sixth form social area. As they got away from the group Marcus grinned as they walked towards their class.

"Busted!"

"Nope! She even knows I was there, she's not even flinched that I could have been that lucky girl!"

"Such a lucky girl!"

"Oh for goodness' sake!" She pushed through the double doors letting them swing back into Marcus who caught them and then her up. Checking around them as they turned into the maths corridor, he pulled her to one side by the lockers and kissed her.

18 January 2020, Jesmond, Newcastle.

Back to reality, Noëmi shook her head.

"No, the best one ever has to be our contraception appointment with the GP."

Marcus burst out laughing. "We kinda failed there!"

On cue, Bruno and Emmanuelle began to whimper and then the volume increased.

Noëmi was not the only one to have a clear memory of that particular day. Following their A Level results, a fellow sixth former had put up a poll on social media to get everyone to choose a girlfriend for Marcus McKenzie. Her friend Ruby had found the whole incident hilarious.

20 August 2011, post A level result celebrations, Ruby's house, Newcastle.

Dr Barraclough, Ruby's mother

Ruby's jet lagged mother padded sleepily through the lounge, opened the curtains and looked over her daughter's shoulder.

"What are you laughing at?"

"Mum no! You'll get all uppity!" Ruby pulled her iPad to her chest.

"Go on, what is it?"

She stood behind her daughter, holding the back of the beige leather sofa. Ruby gave a guffaw, adjusted herself, pulled a soft cream throw over her knees and showed her mum the iPad.

"Which of these two girls do you think that guy, there, should be with?" She sniggered as she pointed the three out to her mother.

'I remember those two.'

"Who are they all?" Dr Barraclough kept her cards hidden.

"You know Charlotte, everyone thinks she's hot. That's Noëmi she's a geek, gets bullied the whole time and that's Marcus McKenzie, everyone wants to get with him but he's always single, I dunno maybe he's gay."

Ruby's mum sighed, "Kissing Charlotte like that in the middle of a party doesn't look very gay."

"Yeah, true but nothing happened."

"Isn't that our hallway?"

Ruby bristled and pulled the iPad away. "No! Don't be silly, mum, it's not only you that has a house full of Laura Ashley stuff!"

Luckily for Ruby her mother was in her own thoughts. *'I remember Noëmi and Marcus well from when they came into my surgery last autumn, I wonder what's been happening there.'*

September 2010, High Heaton medical practice.
Dr Barraclough, Ruby's mother
'That's polite to knock, people usually just barge in!'

"Come in!"

Sitting at her desk she checked the clock as her patient walked in. *'Two hours until I go home...who's that with her?'*

"Hello Noëmi, take a seat."

"Dr Barraclough, how are you?"

"A GP's life is quite stressful, Noëmi, but thank you for asking. And you are..?"

"I'm Marcus, Noëmi's boyfriend." Marcus shook the doctor's hand and smiled as he pulled up a chair.

'He's all ease and confidence and she's a bag of nerves! Opposites attract it would seem.'

"What are you planning for uni?"

"Maths."

"And you?" She glanced at Marcus.

"Medicine… hopefully, how did you find it?"

The doctor's face lit up "Great choice, good luck! Are you at Newcastle Green too?"

Nodding he looked across at Noëmi.

"My daughter's in your year, I wish she'd done the subjects for medicine…I think she's doing art just to annoy me." The doctor sighed as she continued to read her screen. "Don't worry, you know I can't discuss patients. I'd get struck off! Excellent, now as I understand we're reviewing your medication after six months…let me see, the combined pill…that's helped with the period pain and got you through your exams?" Dr Barraclough shifted her eyes from her screen.

"Yes, but now I'm using it for contraception." Noëmi fidgeted on her chair.

Dr Barraclough turned back to her computer. Her eyes glared onto the screen as she typed.

Relaxing, Noëmi and Marcus took each other's hand.

"I understand why you've brought your young man along with you." Dr Barraclough turned and smiled warmly at the pair.

"We thought we should have everything properly explained." Marcus spoke up.

"Indeed, very sensible. Given the tendency for casual relationships and so on amongst your age group…"

She saw the two look stunned.

"We're in a serious relationship!" Noëmi managed.

"What's the and so on?" Marcus quipped.

"The world is not a very idealistic place, people get tempted, you know especially at sixth form and university…hormones are out of control!" Dr Barraclough moved her gaze from the attractive form of Marcus to what she considered was a rather plain looking Noëmi.

"No, we have plans." Marcus protested.

"I'm sorry it's just my job to be pragmatic."

Noëmi

Consultation over, the pair escaped to the fresh autumn breeze, Marcus turned to Noëmi.

"Whose mum is she?"

"Ruby's, her mum's a GP; uses her maiden name. Plus I spotted a family photo!"

Marcus gave a scoff. "That gossip about us would absolutely kill Ruby!"

"Ha! It's our own secret! I saw you looking at me in maths the other day!"

"No one else noticed! You were cute trying to work out that differentiation!"

Turning into a busy road, they put pace into their step.

August 2011, Ruby's house, Newcastle.

Dr Barraclough, Ruby's mother
Dr Barraclough shook her head and returned to the conversation with her daughter.

"The 'geek' as you so unkindly call her, is the best match for that young man. He's off to do medicine right?"

Ruby swung her feet off the soft sofa and stared at her mum,

"Yeah how did you know?"

"Parents talk!" Dr Barraclough lied.

"Whatever, he'd never go with her, he's too good for her!" Ruby slouched back into the leather again with the iPad.

Her mother threw her arms above her and her voice exploded.

"Ruby! No wonder women are subjugated, put down and abused when their own sisterhood can't stand up for them! How dare you say any woman is not good enough for a man! For the sake of womankind, sort yourself out!"

Enraged she slammed the door, the ornaments and bookshelves shook.

Ruby
'Calm down mommy!' Ruby thought as she shared a social media feature with her friend Charlotte,

'Change your life in a week! Seven days and seven ways to get that man!'

CHAPTER 17 - STRESS

February 2020, Northumbria Police HQ.

Guy

The main Northumbria police headquarters was situated in Wallsend. Now based here, Guy, Tariq and the rest of their colleagues worked in an open plan office sprawled across one floor of the ten year old building. Being a band higher than his mentee, Guy had a sort of partition to demarcate his area. He had nicknamed it "the cubby hole". Guy was an organised man and his area was immaculate, with neatly aligned files, potted houseplants and a silver framed picture of Yumi smiling out to all who passed by. On one side of the partition, was Tariq's desk and on Guy's side a dog basket for Rolo. A schedule for Rolo's duties was pinned just above this dog bed. Someone in the office had used a biro to cross out Rolo from the heading and had written 'Scooby Doo' instead.

Back from his idyllic honeymoon at the Sugar Bay Hotel, Barbados, Guy was plunged into Monday morning reality. However, with Rolo at his side and a spring in his step nothing would dampen his mood. As he walked in, Guy did a double take. Tariq Azzara sat fidgeting at his desk. Guy checked the time.

"Good morning! You're early Riqqi! What's going on?"

Avoiding eye contact, Tariq was now burrowing, rabbit-like, through some files.

"Yeah, I had some personal stuff to get done. We're trying to buy a flat, being kicked out of our rental in four weeks so it's a bit stressful…and everything's so expensive."

"Mmm that's not going to happen quickly mate, what will you do if you don't get that sale sorted?"

Tariq grimaced, "Move in with my parents. That'll be a step back. I might be better off in one of the cells!"

Guy grinned and put his rucksack down to get his laptop out. He saw Tariq tidying his papers away and caught sight of the header of a letter, **SAS - Surveillance Azzara Style**.

"What's that? You got relatives who are Enquiry Agents? Our favourite people!"

Fumbling Tariq was jittery and he stuffed his papers away.

"No, no…just an old…"

The two men looked at each other. Tariq cast his eyes down.

"Riqqi, mate, you know, if you need to, you can talk to me." Guy side eyed his colleague who was staring down at his hands. "Let me just say that if you want to get some extra work, it must be approved by the Chief Inspector, and this is reviewed annually through the Performance Development Review (PDR) process. Private investigations are not permitted…plus I don't think you can use a known acronym, like SAS…"

"Yeah, I know that! It's just some old papers."

Tariq scrambled his final documents away. Rolo gave a woof.

"Can that dog not just shut up!"

A clammy Tariq stormed off in the direction of the toilets.

Tariq

The irony was not lost on Tariq that he was back in the men's bathroom when the email from Oliver, security guard at the Radisson hotel, pinged through. He doom scrolled through the images.

"No, no, no, why?"

Guy

Before Guy could gather his thoughts about his colleague's odd behaviour, he had a call to make. Guy bounced impatiently and Rolo sat up in hope. Finally, Marcus picked up.

"Come on, come on, yes! Guess what? The best news ever!" Guy was screaming.

Marcus had worked out what was coming as Yumi had not been drinking since before Christmas. Guy gave him no chance to talk.

"We're having a baby!"

"Man! Awesome! Congratulations, Rolo will be a great mum!"

"Shut up! It's the best news, right?"

"Mate, that's so good. I'm chuffed for you both! You found out on your honeymoon?"

"No, just before the wedding, finally now Yumi's three months I can tell you! Everything's perfect, we're so happy!"

"Such good news, make sure she tells N at the same time!"

"She knows, don't worry! Twenty-second of August is D Day! If it's a boy he'll be Matsu, known as Matt, and if it's a girl, she'll be Mia, because that's pretty and works in both languages. So exciting. We tried to make a name up with the letters from our names, like Donnie did, but all we got was Guymi or Imyug!"

"Matt or Mia are sound choices then!"

"We should celebrate! Pub later?!"

"Definitely and I want those hotel details! We fancy Barbados when we finally get a honeymoon. Man, I can't wait to meet that little *new Castle* in September!"

Guy had no reply for a few seconds. "You and Joel both love making the worst jokes, you two must really get on. But yeah cheers!"

"Ah it's the *fort* that counts…"

"No! Enough!"

Later that day, Pitcher and Piano, Newcastle.

Guy

The day's work done, Guy settled in the bar, he checked his inbox to see when their first pregnancy appointment would be. He immediately noticed an email from Laura, his ex-girlfriend. Messages from Laura had filtered through every month or so since his engagement to Yumi. They came via text, social media and email. As the wedding date approached, they increased to weekly communications. Then she began sending pictures of her with Guy from their time together at university; freshers' parties, formal dinners and raucous house gatherings. Memories flooded back of genuinely good times. Yumi was aware of these communications and dealt with it in a dignified manner. Then the photos became more personal. Guy kept no secrets from his wife but Yumi had no interest in seeing some of the more 'coupled up' pictures of him and Laura together; kissing, lying in bed together and where they were sharing a look of love. As he was aware of exactly why the relationship had run its course, Guy did not respond to Laura. After the wedding the communications had tailed off. This email was a surprise.

It was marked urgent. He clicked it open.

Guy, I hope you're well and I wish you all the best for your married life. I was not sure whether to contact you as I'm ill. I've been diagnosed with stage 4 bone cancer and I'm really not sure how long I've got left. My treatment is now palliative. I would like to see you one last time to say goodbye.

Laura x

Guy broke down and wept.

Marcus

Rushing to meet up with Guy, Marcus was a free man. *'No work, no domestic duties, no worries! Time to celebrate with my best friend! I think at this moment it's okay to love the pub more than anything in the world.'* Spotting Guy at the bar, he weaved his way over to him. Guy was wiping his eyes and without a word, showed him the message. Marcus had never met Laura but knew about the irritation her messages had been causing Yumi, now he realised why Laura had been so persistent.

"Mate this is tough."

Marcus nodded to the bartender and ordered their drinks. Guy was staring at his phone.

"Yeah, I mean it's been nearly eight years since it finished and I know that relationship would never have been right for me but we were each other's whole university experience. If she had been the one I'd have fought for her, not gone travelling, anything. That's how I feel about Yumi, I'd do anything for her, for us. But the thought of Laura suffering like this is absolutely killing me. I still care that she's happy."

"There's a lot going on here; shock, grief and genuine affection.

But remember you can't confuse these emotions with any other."

"No of course, but to be losing someone who was such a part of my life…"

Marcus wondered what he would feel if he received such a message from Sophie. He understood. Together the men discussed how best to deal with the heart wrenching situation.

It was agreed that Guy would visit Laura before she got more ill. That way the right things could be said with some control over emotions. Marcus helped Guy write the message back to Laura. She quickly pinged back to confirm a date.

CHAPTER 18 - ME, ME, ME

February 2020, Oxford.

Tianna

Tianna's phone had been switched off as part of a digital detox. Pastor Malachai had spent time with Tianna and she had been banned from any contact with the Newcastle Church of Glory. Once therapy had been arranged, it had been decided that she was well enough to return to Oxford. Louisa agreed to check in with Tianna and with the McKenzie family each day.

The grey drizzle of late February sulked all day long. The two friends sat on a faded elephant grey sofa in the glow and crackling of a real fire. The old transistor radio played Seventies hits in the background and the coffee machine hissed away. Tianna broke their silence.

"I love this coffee shop, my brother used to come here…he told me the brownies are to die for…Louisa I'm so grateful to you."

Louisa rolled her eyes and blew on her cappuccino.

"Sure. How's the counselling going?"

"It's helping, but I've been thinking the whole time about Joel.

It was his birthday…his twenty-first…"

Tianna stared out of the window as if she hoped he would somehow appear.

"Yeah, Joel and I went to see Parasite, got pizza at Pilgrims and did some shots in the college bar. Just low key. I'm not gonna lie, he's been in a bad way."

She bit into her white chocolate brownie. **'Take a Chance on Me'** by Abba thudded in the background.

"He's not sent me a Valentine's card." Tianna's voice was thin.

With another eye roll, Louisa flopped back into her seat.

"How did you get into Oxford when you're this thick! He's hurt. The only message you're likely to get is that he hopes you never feel the way he does right now. That would be generous! He's hurting like I've never seen anyone hurting."

Pain seared through Tianna's body.

"Do you and Joel like each other?"

Tianna's gaze did not move from the grubby window. Louisa gave an empty laugh,

"Now you're emphasising my point! You actually know we've always just been mates! I've got him to join cheerleading, keeping him busy and all that. Look, I know what you're going to ask. Yes, that girl on his course is still hanging around trying to impress him but he's not interested and he's not seeing anyone…and he doesn't want to be involved in your recovery. It sounds harsh but he can't be. You need to decide what life you want, uninfluenced by anyone else. Find out who you are. He can't see you whilst you sort yourself out, plus you do his head in…let's face it this isn't the first time…"

Slowly Tianna understood.

"I know I need to get better. But I …"

"Tianna shut up about yourself for one minute will you! And how are you, Louisa?"

She said sarcastically.

Tianna understood some more.

Louisa leant forward, she gave a nervous laugh.

"Right, you can help me now. I'm seeing someone. We're serious. I think I'm actually falling in love."

"Oh that's amazing, who is he, Louisa?"

"Yep! Big sigh! You nailed it, that's my problem."

Louisa exhaled and averted her gaze out of the window. "Everything just got greyer."

"I don't get it?"

Louisa swung around, silky blonde ponytail following.

"Tianna I've got a girlfriend! Octavia and I are way more than friends. As you've just proven, coming out to my friends and family is just going to be excruciating. Can you imagine my very upper middle class parents? I'm not sure I can do it. I thought you could help me," Louisa played with her milk froth.

Now Tianna understood everything.

"Sorry Louisa. You have to realise it's just their current assumptions that like them you'll follow the girl meets boy path. I'm sure their future expectations are for you to be happy, right?"

Louisa nodded.

"Then just open up to them. Tell them how you feel."

"I need you to help me when the time comes. Sow some seeds with your brother. I know he and dad are close. He can drop some hints and guide dad through this."

It seemed Louisa already had a plan. Tianna took her friend's hand and squeezed it tightly.

"What, get Marcus to hand out the rainbow wristbands at RVI? Look it's really unfair of you to assume that they won't be alright with this. Plus it's wrong to tell Marcus before your dad. Give your parents a chance!"

In the background, **'January'** by Pilot played out.

"And don't you think there's only one month of the year they should really play this song!" Tianna said.

Louisa beamed, "And the old Tianna is back in the building!"

* * *

Louisa

Finishing their drinks the girls went their own ways. Having borrowed the books she needed from her department library, Louisa rushed to meet Octavia. They had first noticed each other at a freshers' evening at The Jolly Farmers where New College students had been invited to find out more about Pride events in Oxford. Curious and open minded Louisa had gone along with a view to helping. Having spent her teenage years as a bookworm, furiously studying and playing sport, romance had never been a priority. Louisa had been quite proud of how many boys were interested in dating her and suddenly wondered why none of them had tempted her. Now Oxford was giving her time to explore her heart. Glancing around the pub she spotted Octavia, small, brown eyed with shoulder length black hair, dressed in jeans and a rainbow t-shirt. Octavia seemed to buzz with energy. Watching Octavia as she organised the information stand, Louisa found herself moving that way. Heart beating she felt her hand shaking as she picked up one of the flyers.

"Are you here for the entz or the cause? You know this is the only gay pub in Oxford?"

"Interesting but I guess that makes Pride important in Oxford then?"

"You've got it! I'm Octavia, medicine, second year."

"Louisa, medicine, first year! You can help me!"

"Sure no probs and you can help me!"

And so they got to know each other. Louisa found herself desperate to impress 'Tavi' and sought her out at every opportunity. Over the Christmas break Louisa was skiing and found herself recalling their moments together. Messaging one evening, they swapped to video chat. In a heart to heart, they confessed their mutual attraction and Louisa went to visit Octavia for the New Year when they officially became girlfriends. Louisa could not have been happier but she had avoided revealing their relationship to her family; *'They'll never accept it.'*

CHAPTER 19 - NO CRIB

February 2020, Durham.

Sarai

Having given up her job the previous year, Sarai Bianchi had decided to see if she could manage by living simply. However the costs of raising a child far exceeded her expectations. Despite a careful financial planning session with Donnie McAllister, Noëmi's father, Sarai did not seek the help to which she was entitled. She remained convinced that exposing her lack of money would mean that social services would take Lucia away. Over the ensuing year, Sarai was increasingly excellent at hiding her troubles.

Soon Sarai was using her savings to live. She was too embarrassed to seek help from anyone, including her late husband's father in Italy. Therefore, by early 2020 things were getting desperate. To afford the basics for her daughter, Lucia, she started going to a loan shop where the APR was over twenty per cent. Her debts spiralled out of control and by the end of that February Sarai had no money to pay her rent.

Pacing her kitchen Sarai knew exactly who it was when her doorbell rang out constantly. Bursting into tears, Sarai hugged

Lucia who howled. Sarai's head was ready to explode. She put Lucia into her high chair and gingerly she went to the door and looked through the peephole; on her doorstep was her landlord; a sullen buy-to-let property magnate.

"Open this door now!" Fists banged on the wood.

Shaking Sarai could only acquiesce.

"What gives you the right to live here rent free? Do you know how many people are queuing to get a place in this area? I could let this flat ten times over at twice the price. You make me sick!"

She could see the rage. The landlord pushed past her and gave big sighs of exasperation. A silk paisley scarf around the neck, the coat was dark blue navy cashmere well cut and heavy. Beads of rain sat on his shoulders. Sarai stared; his eyes were bulging, fingers poking and spit spraying.

"Your rent is two months in arrears! I'm not a charity. You need to pay up!"

"I…I can't." She had moved and was standing behind Lucia's high chair, holding her child's shoulders. Sarai's throat was paralysed as she then listened to a barrage of racist abuse, her tears fell and Lucia howled even louder.

"We're here to serve you notice. You have one week!" A letter was flung down onto the small melamine table. "You need to be out by 9am next Friday. Bailiffs will be round to take what they can to recoup money owed."

At that moment all sets of eyes cast themselves around the flat to see nothing of value. The furniture was basic mismatched chairs and an old melamine table. A few toys added the only touch of colour. There was not even a television. Sarai's most expensive purchase of late had been a large bag of prawns as these were Lucia's favourite. Her landlord shook his head, said no more and left.

Jesmond, Newcastle.

Sarai appeared on Noëmi's doorstep with Lucia that same evening.

"Sarai, what? Come in! It's so late and it's freezing! Are you okay?" Noëmi scooped up a yawning Lucia.

"No, we will soon be homeless."

Noëmi brought them into the warm, made tea and listened to her story.

"The agent said my landlords are good people, well respected in the community, but that is not how they have been with me. There's no heart. They called me a 'foreign freeloader' and that they needed to get rid of my smell. Those were the least bad things they said." She wiped a tear away.

"That's a hate crime, racism. You should report it. Don't worry, we'll help you Sarai,"

However, she realised they did not have the space to accommodate them in their two bedroom, terraced home. Suddenly an idea sprang into her head, dashing to the kitchen she phoned her father.

Sarai remained in the lounge, with Lucia on her lap and she rocked her back and forth to soothe her. Noëmi reappeared smiling.

"Sarai, we have a plan. Obviously, we need to talk to the housing association but that can take a few weeks. They'll no doubt put you and Lucia into emergency accommodation but that'll be one room with a shared bathroom; a kind of bed and breakfast arrangement, plus it could be anywhere in the UK. My father has very kindly offered for you to go and stay with him until you're sorted. You would have my old room and Lucia could have the box room. I think we should explain everything to Lucia's grandfather in Italy, he'll be upset if he cannot help you. Will you let me do that?"

Reluctantly Sarai nodded and the plan was set into motion. Lucia's grandfather immediately sent money to his daughter in law when he heard of her troubles.

* * *

Noëmi's childhood home in High Heaton, was a typical 1930's three bedroom semi-detached. Donnie kept his house immaculately but he preferred company to silence so he was delighted to help Sarai.

High Heaton, Newcastle.

Donnie

The next day Sarai turned up with two suitcases and Lucia in a buggy. Donnie welcomed her in. He had got Noëmi's old child bed out of the loft and set it up in the box room. The first night was extremely awkward as Sarai kept apologising and thanking Donnie profusely; almost bowing to him. Her behaviour made Donnie uncomfortable. She appeared to get anxious if Lucia made a sound or touched anything and began saying,

"We cause too much stress."

By the next morning Sarai announced that she had decided to move out.

"Donnie I'm grateful but thank you very much, I cannot stay."

Donnie put the kettle down.

"Oh why's that Sarai?"

"We make too much noise and too much mess."

He spun round and opened his arms.

"Sarai, I like noise, I hate quiet, the silence has been killing me. True I like things tidy, it's my OCD, but we'll figure that out! I raised Noëmi so I love having you both here, make yourselves at home."

Therefore, Donnie could only watch as Sarai did just that. Donnie returned from work to find all sorts of Vietnamese dishes being cooked.

"Where do you get this stuff?" He asked as he looked at the fresh green coconuts, morning glory and dried octopus.

"There's a network, we help each other out."

Sarai did not look at Donnie. He smiled to himself and watched Sarai busying herself with Lucia.

* * *

Early March 2020, Newcastle.

Sarai

Lucia's grandfather was beside himself. To reassure him, Sarai had set up a video call and Noëmi was translating. The babies napped and toddler Lucia watched Peppa Pig. Sarai and Noëmi sat together in the Zoom waiting room waiting for Roberto Bianchi, father of Sarai's late husband Luca. Eventually Roberto appeared and waved at the pair.

"Sei muto!" Sarai called out with a smile.

"And you've just called your father in law dumb!" Noëmi said with a grin.

"This is why I need you here!"

"Roberto, accendi il tuo suono per favore!" Noëmi helped with the Italian.

"Mi scusi!"

Hearing her grandfather's voice, Lucia rushed to the screen and waved furiously.

Roberto, wiping a tear of joy, waved back. Sarai's throat was lumpy. Roberto continued to talk, with Noëmi translating for her friend.

"Sarai, I was shocked to hear of your money problems. Every morning, like you, I wake to realise Luca's not here. I miss him terribly. Regret weighs heavy when you get old. Therefore, I propose to offer you a trust fund from which you will always have an income for Lucia. I have bought a villa for you not far from me in Rome, it is perfect as it is close to a very good school for Lucia. There we can help you rebuild your lives."

They thanked Roberto who continued.

"We are experiencing a pandemic in Italy now. Lockdowns are being imposed, but when the time is right, I will organise transport to bring you to Italy. You will not fly. Train and boat are the safest ways for my precious family to travel."

The call ended with virtual hugs. Aware of the rise of Covid-19 in Italy the women knew that Sarai would be in the UK for at least the next month.

"What do you think?" Noëmi asked as she closed her laptop.

"Not sure, I was scared he would suggest this."

"What do you mean?"

Sarai gave a sigh, "I know he means well, but moving to Italy? As you know, I speak no Italian. Plus Lucia's settled here. Durham is where I met and lived with Luca, it's a special place for us."

"You don't need to decide now, Sarai, just give it time. How's it living with dad? Does he drive you crazy?"

Sarai was pensive and spoke without affectation,

"No, no, not at all. We understand each other…we suit each other. He makes me laugh and I've not laughed for a long time."

CHAPTER 20 - LOCKDOWN

25 March 2020 - one day before lockdown. Oxford.

Tianna

Having recovered fully, Tianna had been signed off from her therapist. She had reflected on her vulnerabilities and set herself targets. Routine helped, she knew what she wanted.

Covid 19 meant the country was facing new challenges. Lockdown loomed on the horizon and reluctantly, she had decided to return to her parents' house in High Heaton.

"One day to get back to Newcastle."

Tianna frantically looked up the train times, fended off a constant stream of **'OMG lockdown!'** texts and packed her case. Taking a quick glance around her room she breathed.

"Time to go home!"

She slammed the door shut and locked it with a firm click. Stepping out of New College she passed the Harry Potter tree and felt her throat tighten.

"Joel!"

How they had laughed that first day when they took the selfie under the tree. She felt his arm around her shoulders, his touch told her all she needed to know about his feelings for her. She felt her eyes sting. Her mind floated to the open mic the previous evening.

24 March 2020, The Jericho Pub, Oxford.

Tianna was second up. The Jericho pub was a popular live music venue and a good number of students were there. Indeed, the room was packed and although she had performed to nearly one hundred people at Marcus and Noëmi's wedding, this evening she felt terrified. *'That day the room was full of love...Joel...maybe he's come...I put it on my newsfeed.'* She scanned the room. *'Louisa's here, he must be with her, but... no.'*

Her head dropped. A squeak of feedback and the guitarist left the stage with a wave. Tianna was next. Nervously she walked to the spot.

"Now we have Tianna who's a student here at Oxford, so clever and talented! Tell us about your song Tianna."

"Hi, thank you, it's a cover of a song my grandma used to play, like the whole time."

"Great, a bit of an oldie and is it dedicated to her?"

"No, it's for someone I'm missing right now. Actually, I'm really missing him."

"Tianna, you're breaking our hearts already, the stage is yours!"

The MC gave the space up and Tianna was alone. Her backing track began and she sang a stripped back acoustic version of Bread's **'Lost without your love'**. Her grandmother Raeni would belt the song out and Tianna would join in. Tonight the words were from her heart and dedicated to Joel.

25 March 2020, New College, Oxford.

She shook herself back to reality. Head up she pulled her case along the gravel path and through the stone archway, past the porters' lodge. Fumbling in her pocket she clenched her phone and then could not resist clicking onto Joel's social media.

'The parents are frontline healthcare workers so can't go home. I'm locking down on my ownsome lonesome #abandoned #lonelylockdown #billynomates'

Tears sprang to her eyes. Tianna tugged her case with determination and set off for the train station. Her mind was racing. Checking her phone she mapped her route. The March wind bit into her face. Around her everyone was rushing to prepare for the unknown time they would need to be in isolation. Toilet rolls, pasta and long life milk were disappearing off the supermarket shelves. Yoga mats, wine and Netflix were now essentials.

'Will people die from this illness? Pandemics wipe out entire populations. Healthcare workers are most at risk.'

She pulled her jacket collar up around her neck. Suddenly she stopped. She changed direction.

Joel

Hearing the doorbell Joel put his bowl of Frosties to one side.

'Hopefully the one thing I need to get me through lockdown!' he said to himself as he darted from his sofa, *'New weights!'*

He swung the door open, "Tianna!" He gasped.

She stood silently on the doorstep. Joel could not help himself.

"Here we go again. Don't tell me you've come to apologise?"

Tianna burst out laughing and into tears. Joel opened his arms to her. For a few moments they were still as they held each other.

"Can I lockdown with you?" she looked up at him.

"What?"

"I want to stay with you, lockdown with you." Her eyes found her feet.

"But it's just me here. Jaz and Craig have gone home. If that old Rev Honey Fuck-up-everyone's-life finds out, the hounds of hell may eat you up or something."

"I'm done with all that. I'm better now. Louisa told you everything. I was hoping we could … not be friends. Unless…" His arms now cupped her shoulders, she stammered, "…there's someone else…"

Joel gave a hollow laugh,

"Yeah, let me just text them all to check if they mind you're here! God it's been tough Tianna, really tough. I hate how much you've hurt me…again. It's your fucking hobby or what?"

Nodding, she whispered, "I've hated every minute of not being with you."

"It's taken me time to get to where I can cope…it's been so fucking hard Tianna. I don't know if I could risk being this hurt again…"

Her eyes gazed up at him, like a spaniel desperate for their owner's love.

Joel moved to hold her gently by her arms, "…but Tianna, if you come back to me now, I want you to stay with me. I need to know where I stand. You know exactly how I feel about you. On my side nothing's changed. The last three months I've been living with the fear that all the future held was me looking for someone like you. Knowing they'd never quite be the one because they're not you."

His gaze was intent.

"You and me, Joel, I feel exactly the same…and I want us to be together again." Tianna's voice was decided. Quickly she texted.

'Mum I'm locking down in Oxford. I can bubble with other students xxx'

Swiftly, she walked past Joel into his flat. Looking around on the sofa she saw his spiderman duvet, with the hollow of his shape. *'I just love him.'* She remarked the discarded bowl of cereal and some neat piles of lecture notes. Her whole body felt warm. She caught glimpses of Michaelmas term house parties, shared cups of tea and uncontrollable laughter. *'This is home.'*

Joel's flat was a typical breeze block, Sixties, university build. The small lounge was lit at both ends by rectangular windows, covered with thin, ready-made curtains in a Wedgewood blue. The room echoed due to the lack of carpet and was starkly furnished with a dull grey sofa and sturdy melamine tables. Tianna busied herself, setting up her laptop and books at one end of the lounge. As she settled in, the whole place seemed immediately warmer and brighter. Joel felt a frisson as he watched her frown as she tried to work out where to plug in her laptop. Her shoulder length, dark curly hair fell softly around her face, her brown eyes glistened and she bit her lip as she concentrated. He moved to help her.

"What if we annoy each other?" Joel took his Frosties' bowl away.

"That won't happen." Computer connected, she stood admiring her workstation.

"I'll cook us dinner, enchiladas, spicy, I know you!"

Excitement ran through him. Dashing to the kitchen he went to his food cupboard, pleased that he had stocked up. Usually there was nothing but the de rigueur pasta plus sauce, protein powder and the odd tin of tuna. His mother had convinced him it was not selfish to get some stock in for lockdown.

Tianna

She shook her head and smiled. Her phone pinged, it was Marcus.

'Hey Ti. Mum's getting frantic, are you staying in college?'

'No, locking down with friends. Tell mum not to worry x'

'The fact that both my friend's flatmates have gone home need never bother mum.'

Walking into Joel's bedroom to offload her case she opened the curtains and the window. A small shaft of early spring tried to smile out of the clouds. She began moving clothes into his wardrobe. Having put her toiletries all over his chest of drawers, she smoothed down the bed. Spiderman was spinning out his web. Seeing her offload, Joel gave a laugh,

"You're moving in here? I'll change the sheets but where am I supposed to sleep? Craig and Jaz's rooms are total pits, I'm the tidy one."

Without looking at him she replied,

"You're staying right here…with me…and I'll have the side of the bed with you in it!"

"Tianna you've just recovered from a breakdown, this is not the time to be rushing things."

"Think about where we were and what we decided before I lost the plot. I know exactly who I am and what I want in life. You're beyond respectful. I would never mess with you. Trust me."

"Right but we take it easy eh?"

Standing awkwardly, they were silent. His phone pinged, he spoke too quickly.

"Louisa's just sent me a vid…my God! You won the open mic last night…"

Soon Tianna could hear her own voice, *"No, it's for someone I'm missing right now. Actually, I'm really missing him."*

Joel pulled the neck of his t-shirt as he watched her performance. Tianna fiddled with her suitcase handle, glancing side eyed at Joel every few seconds. He moved in front of her and she took his hand.

"I meant every word I've been so lost without you." She softly whispered to him.

"My God, Tianna…oh…saudades."

"Saudades?"

"Portuguese. It's the sad feeling, like you've lost your love forever…Tianna you're so precious to me."

Sometimes other languages had words that English could never express.

"Joel…"

"Sorry, it's just a bit of hay fever."

"Joel it's March…"

Giggling and falling back together, they kissed like the first time. The pair then spent the first two days of lockdown secure in each other's arms. Tianna applied the same enthusiasm as she had to her New Cog study meetings to making up with Joel. Now they were complete. In their bubble the pair felt the pure joy of each other.

* * *

Newcastle Royal Victoria Infirmary (RVI).

Marcus

Covid-19 swept through the country. The daily news delivered warnings and forebodings as the country hunkered down. Key workers became the media's daily stars and demands for reports from the frontline were never ending. Emergency departments were particularly tantalising to television journalists. Trauma Consultant, Alex James fended most of them off with a terse, 'We're working leave us alone!' strapline. Things became trickier when charity fundraising humbled everyone into thanking the patient public. Having been made aware of a young local lad who was sleeping in a tent to raise money for the NHS, Alex granted the media the chance to film in his department. Having been given special permissions and told exactly what could be shown, the TV crew arrived one morning.

Alex James viewed the arrival of cameras with pursed lips.

"What a waste of precious resources!" He muttered as the news team donned their PPE.

Most staff were too exhausted to care and got on with their jobs. Marcus was running to resus as the crew began their job. Homing in on the 'attractive' young doctor, the camera operator was forever on his back; practically following Marcus to the toilet. Reluctantly, after much pestering, Marcus gave an interview to an eager young news reporter.

"What's your message to the public in Newcastle!" The smiling presenter asked.

"Stay home and stay safe!" Marcus was on his way to the next patient.

"Listen to Dr McKenzie and follow those Covid rules! Back to the studio!"

Before the day was out, Marcus literally became the Newcastle RVI poster boy, representing NHS workers in the fight against Covid-19. The production company used his image everywhere, on their website and to announce NHS reports on the local news. Soon Dr Marcus McKenzie was a minor celebrity in Newcastle.

His phone lit up.

'Nice job!'

'Looking fit!'

'Awesome mate!'

Everyone loved him.

* * *

Accommodating the two person limit, the A&E staff room now had a booking sheet. Marcus waited for Esme to leave before entering. Sitting at a distance on the Sixties style armchairs he and Penelope Rivera were on their break.

"Ha! Everyone loves you now don't they!" Penelope grinned.

"Don't! It's so cringey. You know me. I hate all that!"

Sitting back he gazed out of the window.

"Why do I have a feeling that this so-called fame will come back to bite me?"

Penelope shrugged her shoulders and took her drink. Unscrewing the bottle top she leant back and gave a cry as she spilt orange juice on her scrubs, having forgotten she was wearing a visor. Marcus doubled over with laughter. Penelope shot her colleague a dark look.

"I'm sure your babies are more mature than you Dr McKenzie."

She wiped the juice from her visor with purple paper towel.

"Oh Pen, that's made the PPE wearing worth it! Your face was a picture!"

Penelope threw the soggy paper towel at Marcus who skilfully dodged it so that it landed in the bin. With a self-satisfied smirk, he then began writing on a large, enveloped package.

"What are you doing there?" She asked.

"You know Alex said we could give away these old student copies of Gray's Anatomy, well Tianna said she'd love one."

"Great idea, after all, anatomy doesn't change, does it? Men's brains are always going to be smaller than women's."

Marcus grinned at his friend and pulled out his mobile. He frowned as he copied the address his sister had texted to him.

Penelope

Penelope glanced out of the window at the empty town. Birds had taken over the abandoned streets. Nothing moved. Ambulance sirens continued in the background and she quickly finished her juice. The emergency department was already overwhelmed. Patients were even waiting in wheelchairs, given the log jam in getting beds, especially as the Covid pathway had to be separate from regular admissions. Nothing straightforward. With a sigh she knew her break was almost over. Her eyes moved to Marcus' neat felt tipped writing on the brown jiffy bag.

"Marcus, are you sending one to Joel too?" She raised her eyebrows.

"No but I can if you want?"

"...but that's Joel's address!"

He stopped and checked his phone.

"No, Tianna just texted this address to me, she's locked down with friends!"

"Eh? I'll check."

The pair stared at each other. Both suddenly texted on their phones.

Penelope's pinged back first.

'Ok Mum, Craig & Jaz have gone home. Yes I'm with Tianna. We've locked down together just the two of us as we're seeing each other again. Tbh we're keeping our relationship under the radar. Don't worry, everything's good - it's perfect x'

Marcus

A message also appeared on Marcus' device.

'There's a bubble at Joel's, his flatmate Craig has gone home so there's a room. We're all being v careful not to catch Covid x'

Scratching his head, he explained to Penelope.

"Mmm it seems there's a few of them at the flat. At least they've managed to keep their friendship after all that happened, shame they were so good together."

Penelope seemed suddenly perky and repositioning her visor, she jumped up to get back to her shift.

"Friendship yes, tão bons amigos!"

CHAPTER 21 - MCKENZIES ASSEMBLE…
VIRTUALLY

Sunday, 5 April 2020, Zoom.

Tianna

Waking up she could feel his chest rise and fall as he slept. She felt his skin on hers, their bodies together like magnets; they were safe and warm. *'I could stay like this forever.'* Reluctantly she pulled herself out of his arms. He wriggled, rolled over and hugged his pillow. No longer wrapped up in Joel, she felt a shiver. She grabbed her dressing gown from the floor beside the bed and put it on. Stretching, she sneaked open a corner of the curtain to bring some daylight. *'Actually, I can't wait to see the fam.'*

Pillow propped behind her, Tianna then carefully arranged her laptop on her knees as she sat up in bed. *'Time to join the first virtual McKenzies assemble!'*

She entered the Zoom waiting room.

"Hey Ti!" Marcus grinned at her blank screen.

"Of course you're first! And have you all forgotten what time zone students are in? Ten am! It's a bit early!" Biting her lip she remembered her text, **'There's a bubble at Joel's, his flatmate**

Craig has gone home so there's a room. *So what if the bubble is just me and Joel, and the second part's true even if I'm not in that room!'*

"Anything goes in lockdown, there's no rules. Joel's always saying how messy Craig's room is. I want to see if you've transformed that space! Turn your camera on!"

She looked across at Joel dozing next to her. His olive skin glowed on the white sheet, the duvet barely covered his torso. *'He looks just delicious!'* she giggled to herself.

"Yeah, maybe in a minute!"

Sleepily Joel rolled over and snuggled into her waist. His arms flopped around her as he gently snoozed.

"You're still in bed aren't you!" Marcus laughed.

"So what if I am! I bet you've been up since 6am with my gorgeous niece and nephew! God knows how you had any part in producing them!"

"Yeah, they're perfect aren't they! But no chance of sleeping through those two! They're the loudest family members! Even louder than you!"

"Three big brothers, I had to make myself heard!"

She felt warm as she saw the nine month olds crawling around like the Rugrats characters she loved as a child. Family members then pinged into the call. Smiling McKenzies were everywhere. Matriarch Marianna sat proudly in front of her screen overseeing her realm. Underlings Raeni and Anthony were on either side of her.

"And you all thought I'd struggle with the technology!" Marianna was smug.

"Good job Mum!" Isaiah beamed at them all. "Great body count on this call too; saving me loads of time not having to talk to everyone individually!"

He put a rainbow up as his background. Not to be outdone Jayden gave everyone a wave and changed his background to bright coloured balloons.

"Oh Bruno likes that!" Noëmi held up a giggling twin to the screen.

"Oh my God, too cute!" Tianna cried.

Hearing this, Joel pulled himself up. Stretching, he put his arm around Tianna's shoulders and peered into the laptop. Tianna motioned at him to be silent and clicked onto the screen to change the view from gallery to single person so that she could show him the cute baby close up. However, as she did this she accidentally changed her settings.

"He's so gorgeous!" she cried, resting her head on Joel's chest. Tumbleweed silence followed, punctuated only by Bruno's squeals of excitement. The whole McKenzie family took in bare chested Joel and silky dressing gowned Tianna, snuggled tightly together in bed on a Sunday morning. Shreya and Jalissa each gave a cry of horror and Marcus gasped,

"Ti, your camera's on!"

"The fuck!" was Tianna's reply.

More tumbleweed as a panicked Joel dived off screen; thereby only to confirm to everyone that it was indeed his bed they were in, as pillows and duvet edges cascaded around them. Tianna fumbled furiously with her keyboard.

"I'm losing my Wi-Fi signal," and Tianna was gone.

Marianna gave a long sigh.

Isaiah collapsed into hysterical laughter and Jayden put a peach emoji in the chat.

Noëmi remarked "You can really tell Joel works out!"

Marcus gave her a look and a nudge to be quiet. The remaining McKenzies glanced at their family members in their little boxes. Anthony rubbed his jaw as Marianna remained motionless. Raeni peered into the screen.

Jayden was brave. "So much better than a wedding speech!"

Isaiah was crying, "Hey Mum, are Jay and I your favourite children now?"

Marianna was unflinching.

"In fairness, Mum, you've never been anything but accepting of…" as his mother's face darkened, Jayden quickly became silent.

"Have I said anything to anyone yet? Have I accepted, as you say, anything yet? And none of you should be using language like that!"

Each remaining McKenzie sat up to attention, Marianna was addressing them. In the meantime, baby Emmanuelle pointed at the screen and squealed with delight.

"Gaaaa!"

Everyone was silent. Eyes went between them.

"Oh my she recognises you Marianna! Gran!"

Marianna burst into tears and Anthony hugged her. The McKenzie parents left the Zoom call.

A few moments after the inaugural family Zoom debacle Marianna called Noëmi.

"You don't need to remind me of the irony that I'm choosing to talk to you."

Noëmi moved from the toy covered sofa to take the call in the kitchen.

Marcus

At the same moment the familiar sound of Tianna wailing filled Marcus' ears as he answered his mobile. Finally, Tianna drew breath and spoke,

"Dad's face…"

"Hey Ti, he totally adores you and everyone loves Joel…"

Marcus put Bruno back on his playmat.

"What can I tell them? Think of something! I know we were just studying together! That worked for you two!"

"There's not really anything to say, Ti, best have a chat with dad when you can next see him. They just want to make sure you're safe. I guess you've thought everything through…"

He gave Emmanuelle a teething ring.

"Oh God can you even begin to imagine how I feel?"

Marcus had to admit this trumped absolutely everything in the history of McKenzie sibling embarrassing blunders.

"Tianna you smashed it this time!" He moved to get an escaping baby.

"I knew you'd be just so smug! At least I'm a better age than you were! But now you two sitting there with your picture perfect children! That gets you off the hook every time!"

"Ti don't get pregnant!"

Both his babies looked round as they heard his voice raise.

"Honestly you're no help, just leave me alone!" Tianna hung up.

Noëmi walked back into the lounge a few minutes later and scooped up a commando crawling Emmanuelle.

"Your mum's worried Ti's gone from one extreme to the other."

Marcus sighed. "Ah no, they're serious! Tianna's eighteen. Joel's trustworthy, not a player. It's not really anyone's business."

She popped her daughter onto a play mat, in front of a neon yellow octopus soother.

"I think she's hoping we can show them the way!"

He flopped onto the sofa and winced as a Sassy Light Up Rainbow Reel dug into his lower back. At once, the babies crawled off in different directions.

"I'm not sure our way was the best, six awful years of missing each other. I do wonder if Joel and Tianna realise how lucky they are."

Noëmi picked up one crawling baby after the other and sat next to Marcus. He gave her a long kiss. Turning Emmanuelle to face her she looked at her giggling child as she bounced her up and down.

"I'm thinking parenting gets harder the older they get, not easier!"

A video call buzzed into Marcus' phone.

"Are you alright Dad?"

Anthony gave a hollow laugh. "Joel just called to reassure me about his 'intentions' regarding my daughter! I mean what century is this?"

Marcus raised his eyebrows and thought about the speech he had prepared, aged eighteen, in case Donnie had ever found out about his relationship with Noëmi.

His father continued. "I told him life isn't a Disney film, but I appreciate the sentiment. One thing though he does seem to be extremely committed to Tianna from what he was saying. I hope they make it, he's a fine young man."

"Joel's the best. Is mum still upset?"

"You know Marcus she'll be fine. I guess we have to be realistic about relationships these days. I think it's harder for you all; different pressures, but we too were young and in love, like all of you, and we managed to get things in the right order!"

"Ah Dad!" Marcus had never thought of his parents as humans, let alone youngsters in love. They had known each other since they were sixteen. On Fridays there was a church social. Anthony would pick Marianna up and bring her flowers. On the last Friday of the month, after payday, he still brought her those same roses. Anthony smiled knowingly at his eldest son.

"I'm just so absolutely delighted that they're back together and Tianna's returned to her old feisty self!"

Giving him a thumbs up, "Amen to that Dad!"

CHAPTER 22 - OFFLOADING

Northumbria Police HQ.

Tariq

Grey skies, grey tarmac, grey faces. The sunroof of Tariq's Corsa was leaking and the Wallsend drizzle was seeping in.

'Sunroof, the irony. No way can I afford to get that repaired.'

His mind wandered to the day ahead. Each case he investigated seemed to plunge lower into the moral vacuum of humanity. He shut a folder concerning a woman stealing her blind grandfather's pension. *'I had no idea how awful people can be.'*

He sighed as he saw her Mercedes draw into the car park of the Northumbria police headquarters. A suede booted pair of legs emerged as Alura lifted herself out of the car and began towards him. She knocked on the window and Tariq leant across to open it.

"Hold on!" Tariq grabbed a plastic Wilko bag and laid it over the seat. "Seat's a bit wet!"

He pointed at the sunroof.

"Thanks, you see my horrible husband would've just let me sit down on the damp seat. I think we have to keep apart because of lockdown?"

"Of course, sorry!" Feeling sweaty Tariq cursed himself. *'The lockdown rules.'*

"Right, what have you got for me?"

Tariq pulled a black briefcase onto the passenger seat. Opening it he passed her the copies of the photos he had received from the hotel security guard. They showed Digby arriving and leaving on various occasions, accompanied by a dark haired woman. Alura's face aged in an instant. She put her hand on the car to steady herself.

Tariq felt wretched. "I've sent everything to you electronically as well. Alura, that's my job done now. You have the evidence you wanted for the time frame requested. I'm sorry to say I need to terminate our contract. I'd just like to add that you don't deserve this and your husband doesn't deserve you."

With a hollow laugh Alura quipped, "Oh yes he does!"

Tariq felt a shudder of unease. Alura burst into tears.

Embarrassed Tariq asked, "Do you want a minute?"

Alura nodded. Tariq turned away and gazed out over the car park. Presently Alura had composed herself.

"Never mind, I understand, I'll pay you off and then we're done. Can I ask why?"

Tariq stretched his neck, "Yeah, it's against the rules of my contract. I actually didn't realise, I was just trying to make some cash to get myself and my partner onto the property ladder."

Alura smiled "Right. Give up on me like everyone else."

"It's really not like that. I could lose my job!"

Taking a breath, Alura straightened herself up. Smart in every sense, she was immaculate with her hair softly curled, statement gold jewellery and a red silk shirt that was popping out at the neck of her dark navy woollen coat.

"You don't need to worry. I'm not going to drop you in it. Not after you've helped me so much." Waiting, she watched Tariq as he shut his leather case and grabbed it from the seat.

"Thank you, I'll send you a receipt. I need to go to a meeting." He pointed at the main building.

"Yes, me too." She went to offer a hand but retracted it. "Ooops! Not allowed!"

Tariq started to walk towards the police headquarters. The damp wind caught his neck and his coat was blown open. He became aware of Alura following him. As they reached the main doors, he turned and said firmly.

"Sorry, this is a secure area."

"Yes, I know." Alura walked past him and swiped into the building. Stopping to sign the visitors' book, she said something that made the guards laugh and was on her way to the lifts.

Heart pounding Tariq ran to the visitors' book. The guards looked round as he gave a yelp.

Alura Honeyfield, Chief Crown Prosecutor for the North East. Meeting with the Chief Superintendent.

* * *

Newcastle Royal Victoria Infirmary (RVI).

Marcus

Walking through the RVI staff car park Marcus checked his phone. The wind bit his face. He pulled his black North Face puffer tighter. A familiar voice caught him up.

"Freezing for April! Did you have a good weekend?"

He side eyed Penelope who was balancing a number of holdalls on her body.

"Ah Pen! Let me help you offload a few things!" He grabbed her heaviest bags and she thanked him.

"Anything else you want to offload Pen?"

Drawing her coat around herself, she gave him a quizzical look.

Marcus could not wait, "You knew didn't you!"

"Knew what?" They stopped and she gave him a confused look as she rearranged her bright blue flask and matching lunch box in her Sainsbury's hessian holdall.

"Tianna's back with Joel! Just the two of them in that flat, how cosy!"

Penelope's colour rose and she fiddled with her load. "Perhaps, he might've said something about them being together! I can't quite remember!"

"Pen! Why didn't you tell me? You've been so damn chirpy all this time! You knew!" Marcus grinned.

They regained their step across the car park.

"They're very settled. She turned up on the first day of lockdown and hasn't left. He completely adores her. Your fussy old family don't need to worry." Pen pulled her arms in as the wind bit their faces.

"Tianna's determined. I bet she planned it all! Joel will need to stand up for himself!"

"Like I said, they're good for each other."

They reached the major trauma centre on the third level of the Victoria wing. Marcus turned to his friend, "Then what does that make us, Pen? We must be related in some way through this! Like you're my great aunt twice removed or something!"

She shot a dark, disparaging look,

"Great aunt!!! Estás aqui estás a comer! It means if you don't behave I'll slap you!"

And off she marched. Marcus felt the chill of a Brazilian curse run through his veins.

'Pen actually scares me sometimes!'

CHAPTER 23 - WORK FROM HOME

High Heaton, Newcastle.

Donnie

Lockdown rumbled on. Tales of people on illegal strolls too many metres from their homes dominated the news. Working from home meant the morning commute for many was one minute down the stairs. One such morning a sleepy eyed Donnie wandered into his kitchen to get a cup of tea. Sarai was sitting feeding Lucia a rusk. He noticed his new housemate flinch and sit up as he entered. *'She really needs to relax, it's making me feel most awkward.'*

A searing pain flashed through his foot.

"Bloody hell! What was that?" He looked down to see a Duplo floating red panda beneath his heel.

"Don't you dare use language like that in front of Lucia!" Sarai was fierce. Donnie fell back against the table as Sarai launched into him. The toddler glanced, bright eyed, between the pair.

"Sorry, it was just a shock. I didn't think…"

"Didn't think or didn't care? If you don't want us here, we'll go!"

Sarai stood up and fiddled awkwardly with her dressing gown.

"No, no Sarai, calm down, I just need to get used to remembering Lucia's here!"

"uddy!" giggled Lucia, as she banged her spoon on her high chair. "Uddy ell…uddy ell!"

Donnie burst out laughing. His shoulders shook.

"See what you've done and don't tell me to calm down! Soon I'll be gone!" She turned her back on him.

With a deep sigh, he made his tea. Deciding to make amends, he sat down at the breakfast table with them. Given that Lucia's toys had invaded every square inch of living space, Sarai was evidently not going anywhere despite her threats. Bit by bit Sarai was moving a few possessions into the main living area. He looked down to see a large, silver framed wedding photo of Sarai and Luca, on the pine table.

"You should put that up in the lounge."

Sarai gave a nod but did not meet his eye.

"Sorry." She mumbled.

"I'm sorry too."

Only Lucia's burbling filled the heavy silence. Eventually he finished his tea and finally spoke.

"I understand from Noëmi he was a fine man."

Sarai lowered her head. "The best."

"Thank God you weren't on that plane too, imagine…"

"Just shut up!" She yelled.

Donnie jolted backwards, he knocked his cup over. Sarai snatched the rolling cup away from the edge of the table and moved to the sink.

"What?"

"You don't understand, you have no clue."

Donnie flexed his neck. "I'm not sure that's fair Sarai."

She turned. Her fired eyes stared him out. "I wish I'd been there. I wish I'd died with him. He was alone. I should've been there! Every night I imagine him facing those moments without me."

"Sarai I'm so sorry, I didn't mean…"

"You could say goodbye. I couldn't."

Eyes to the ceiling he sighed. She was his equal in all things terrible. There was no contest.

"Neither option is preferred. The terror in her eyes as we said goodbye. The doctors had given her just enough pain killer to keep her comfortable but also the right amount to keep her awake and lucid. She was so weak, she knew it was the end. This was it. We would not see each other again. She tried to hide her fear for me… but all she didn't want to say was there…in her eyes…and I couldn't make her better…it keeps me awake at night."

Sarai dropped her head. "I just can't get over the fact I couldn't be there for him. I couldn't save him. It absolutely kills me."

Reaching out, Donnie touched her arm. "I know. I couldn't make her better and that completely kills me too. If I could've taken her place…"

Only Sarai could understand. Sitting for a while, neither spoke. Lucia continued to chatter and thump her small biscuit covered hands on her high chair tray.

Friday, 17 April 2020.

Donnie

Donnie's birthday was only to be marked by doorstep deliveries and masked waves from a two metre distance. Sarai decided things should be otherwise. This morning Donnie descended to a closed kitchen door. Sarai intercepted and took his hand in hers, telling him to shut his eyes. Lucia jumped with delight behind them. Donnie felt her soft hand in his.

"Su..pwise!" Lucia yelled.

Donnie opened his eyes to a breakfast table of balloons, streamers and champagne.

Sarai was grinning with delight at his shock. She handed over a smartly packaged gift.

"Sarai, thank you! That's wonderful!" Donnie exclaimed as he opened up a beautiful shirt in soft white linen, covered in intertwined crimson, azure and pale pink flowers.

"It's for all our summer parties!" She joked. Donnie gave her a hug and a kiss on the cheek. Shyly she turned away and busied herself with breakfast. Admiring the shirt, he then opened the card that she had given him.

Happy Birthday to my favourite housemate!

Tôi là tôi nhiều hơn khi tôi ở bên bạn. (I'm much more me when I'm with you).

Love and hugs Sarai xxx

Donnie glanced over at her just as she looked his way. They both averted their gaze quickly.

Jesmond, Newcastle.

Marcus

Marcus viewed the Donnie-Sarai living arrangement with amusement. Lying on the sofa watching the rugby on catch up, he turned to Noëmi, as she arrived home with the babies.

"Your dad's asked me to help Sarai get her paintings out of the basement at her old flat. He wondered if we had space to store them."

"Sure, no problem! Lockdown's going well for those two. Dad seems happy, the distraction is good for him."

"What happens if they fall out? Whilst they're both the gentlest of people they stand their ground." He flicked to the football scores.

"I think she's in charge already, dad stood on a Duplo piece and swore. She told him off and made him apologise!"

"That's just hilarious, Lucia will soon have a whole new vocabulary."

Marcus got up and went to the fridge to decide what to cook.

"I think he's enjoying having Lucia around, he was always such a fun dad when I was little, he knows how to bring up a happy child."

"I'll be intrigued to see how it pans out. We've got the stuff for a curry, are you okay with that?"

"Sounds good...pans out? I'm not sure what you mean." She walked out to hang up her coat.

Marcus shrugged his shoulders and smiled to himself as he grabbed the ingredients for dinner.

CHAPTER 24 - CLICK ON THE LINK

Noëmi

NOMA ZOOM CALL PRESENTATION
Noma charity information event: Thursday 18 June 2020 -
19:30 to 21:00 UTC

Agenda:
Introduction: Jesse O'Donnell - Executive Director, End
Noma Campaign
Newcastle Meets Sokoto: Marcus McKenzie - Junior Doctor,
Newcastle RVI
St Wolbodo's Mission to End Noma: Reverend Digby
Honeyfield, Newcastle Church of Glory
Vote of thanks: Alex James - Consultant, Newcastle RVI
Fun quiz: Bri Francis & Noëmi McKenzie - End Noma
volunteers, St Wolbodo's
Q&A: Guy Castle - Detective Sergeant, Northumbria Police
**Join us with a glass of wine / a cold beer (next year we'll
meet in person!)**

Click here to join the presentation

With the in person event cancelled, the stakeholders had organised an online information evening to raise awareness about the neglected disease, noma. Registration numbers were good and the presentations were ready.

Half an hour before the event, the various organisers met online to run through the timings.

Bri was first there, unaware her camera was on she was using the screen reflection to adjust her messy bun and touch up her make-up. Excited to see her, Noëmi sent her friend a private message.

'Bri how's things? I've not heard from you in ages! I hear you've been off work a bit! x'

'Hey! I'm ok, I've got a stomach problem. Lockdown's a bit lonely!'

'M can help if you need any medical advice. Can we meet for a walk soon? We're allowed to do that at least!'

Bri was online but did not reply.

Next Jesse popped up. Ignoring everyone else he went straight to his person of interest.

"Hey Noëmi! Back from the dead! I was completely shitting myself in case you didn't make it. I lost it and had to go to my mum's for a week. She fed me soup and comforted me. I cried buckets."

Alex James had a wry smile. Marcus turned his camera and mic off, he turned to his wife and said, "Why can't he just resign? Five fucking years he's been in charge, surely he needs a break."

Diplomatic as ever, Noëmi moved, with her laptop, next to Marcus so they were snuggled close together on her screen.

"Hey Jesse, how are you? Yep my guardian angel Alex James wouldn't let me through the pearly gates so I decided to hang around on earth a little longer." Never did she miss an opportunity to thank Alex.

Noëmi saw a message ping through on Marcus' phone from Guy,

'Jesse! If there was a prize for trying.'

Marcus replied,

'Four weeks in Nigeria with him raving constantly about my future wife.'

"Hello everyone." Digby's voice was thin. "Sorry my camera's playing up."

An awkward silence followed.

"St Wobo's skimping on the tech then!" Guy quipped.

"Giving it that Sokoto vibe, when the generator stops working it's just darkness!"

Jesse adjusted his background settings to put up a picture of the noma hospital.

Marcus was back on screen, "Hey everyone, thanks for your time, I'm in charge of the slides, please put your cameras on so everyone can see the presenter; makes it more personal. Noëmi will keep an eye on the chat."

"Hey, Mrs McKenzie, what's this fun quiz?" Alex chipped in.

"Mmm, an opportunity to find out more about aspects of the work. It's not too competitive! Oh yes, people are entering the waiting room!"

The meeting began. Jesse gave the context, Marcus detailed his experience of working in Nigeria in the main keynote and then Digby took the floor.

Alura

Digby began his presentation, camera off. Alura gave a huff and moved from her burgundy sofa to his side. She leaned across and turned on his camera. Up they popped onto the screen as he went through his slides on the commitment of St Wolbodo's to fundraise for the End Noma Campaign. Alura had an adoring smile for her husband throughout his speech. Then she decided to be heard.

"And can I just add my approval to the work St Wolbodo's is doing to raise funds and awareness. My husband and I look forward to visiting the project when our church mission sends their volunteers."

Jesse gave a start and scratched his head.

Noëmi

Taking control from the Honeyfields, Noëmi passed control to Alex James.

"Right, I just, can I…thank you to all our presenters…the work of the End Noma Campaign…is so life changing…yes…it's just amazing…thank you." And Alex was done. He looked pale and confused.

'Is Alex okay?' Noëmi noticed Guy had texted Marcus.

'Maybe not. That's not his usual vibe, he's normally a full on speaker. He's the Zoom king.'

Bri messaged Noëmi,

'Not feeling good, have to leave, sorry x'

Bri left the meeting.

Noëmi shrugged her shoulders, "Quiz time everyone! I'll put a link in the chat and you just join with your mobiles when you get the code…" And she was off. As she played quizmaster, Tianna pinged her.

'Why r u working with that Rev Creepyf*ck?'

Tariq

Watching the presentation, mainly to support Guy, Tariq peered inquisitively into the screen.

'Noëmi's playing a dangerous game. I need to block it from my mind. The Honeyfields look a picture of happiness, planning a trip to Nigeria. Bri Francis, it was her wallet I returned. Life's a series of coincidences.'

As he waited for Guy's Q&A he checked his email. Alura had messaged him on his work email.

'Tariq, I need more details. My husband's a cheat, he needs to be revealed, humiliated, taken down. You've come this far and you wouldn't want Guy Castle to find out about your moonlighting. I think you're right, you would lose your job.'

Glancing at his girlfriend sleeping soundly next to him, Tariq felt his blood pressure rise.

'She's a manipulative bully. How close is she to Guy?' He chose not to reply and absent mindedly watched the Zoom session. Shutting his laptop he prepared for another sleepless night, *'…work, money, house, bills, Alura.'*

Donnie

Turning off his laptop, Donnie gave a yawn and a stretch. Next to him Sarai slumped in her kitchen chair and gave a sardonic laugh,

"Nice of Ông Ba Bị and Bà kẹ to show up!"

His look asked his question.

She sighed, "The bogeyman and bogeywoman, the Vietnamese versions. Never mention them to Lucia, they terrify her. But my Durham version was that racist landlord, Honeyfield." She gestured towards the now turned off screen.

"That vicar! He's working at N's school! He was the landlord that made you homeless?" Donnie was now also pointing at the computer.

Some Vietnamese curse came out of her mouth, "Said they needed to get rid of the smell and a load of other stuff, racist stuff." Her chair scraped as she stood up.

"We should report all that to Guy!"

"I'm not sure, some of my paintings are in their cellar. I want them back."

"But they can't get away with a hate crime!"

"Like the police care! Every day there's some kind of micro aggression, looks, tuts, assumptions."

"He should *not* get away with it!" Donnie thumped the table. Sarai shook her head and went to the cooker to make milk tea for them both. Sighing, he moved next to her.

"I love this stuff, it helps me sleep!" He worked in unison with her. "Maybe it's good you were made homeless by that dreadful man! You brighten this place up!"

Opening the fridge, Donnie looked at his stock of all sorts of new foods. He wondered about life in Vietnam and pondered on visiting and whether Sarai would be keen to take a trip. He passed her the milk.

"You need to learn how to enjoy yourself Donnie! Milk tea isn't exactly hardcore!"

Pulling her hair up, she twisted it into a top knot, put a clip in it and shut the fridge door with her foot.

CHAPTER 25 - ISABELLE

Friday, 19 June 2020, Newcastle Royal Victoria Infirmary (RVI).

Alex James

RVI was at the forefront of the Covid19 pandemic. Alex James was leading the emergency department (ED) which was managing all patients admitted with Covid symptoms and breathing difficulties. Arriving at the patient care centre hub, he reassessed the layout of his department with his team which included Dr Marcus McKenzie.

"We're moving all non-Covid cases to the minor injuries wing. Major trauma needs access to resus and to the high dependency unit, but we need to keep a separate pathway for our Covid patients. We're allocating two HDU wards to Covid and one to major trauma. Each time we huddle we need to review the numbers in each and be ready to change our strategy in an instant. Deep cleaning services have been doubled and are available within thirty minutes. We cannot allow any patient group to be at risk from the other in any way. Apart from the human cost, hospital acquired infections would be catastrophic for us as a trust." Briefing over, the staff disbanded and got on with their duties. Marcus was writing Penelope's name on her visor and she did the same for him as Alex moved past their station.

"Thanks for your help last night Alex with the noma event." Marcus called out.

Alex fixed his eyes on his colleague.

"How well do we know each other? I completely flunked it!" Alex sighed and gazed at the front desk littered with request forms for oxygen cylinders, pages of the latest government advice, packets of wipes and boxes of gloves in various sizes. He already knew how difficult the day ahead would be.

"I owe you an explanation. Let's take a break, it's quiet here for now, I'll take the code red bleep."

He led Marcus to his office and the two men sat before each other in their visors, protective glasses and plastic overalls. Marcus lightened the mood.

"Feeling like a boil in the bag chicken!"

Alex gave a wry smile, "And I'm a boil in the bag turkey. Marcus, remember I told you I was an expert witness once? I saw your eyes light up at the thought of another way to help or was it another way to be clever?"

"Hopefully both!"

Alex smiled warmly through the plastic and sighed. "It was a few years back in London when I was leading the ED at Kings. One of my research projects was on accidental drowning, and I was brought in to advise the coroner on a case."

Turning his head to stare out of the window, he paused. The bright blue sky belied his mood.

"Five years ago, late 2015, in Oxford, a twenty-six year old woman was found drowned in the bath. Isabelle Williams, I can't ever forget her name. It would seem to be a simple case of accidental death and unfortunately we've all seen this kind of thing before. However, the police found inconsistencies. Her blood alcohol level was high but she had no history of substance abuse and was described as a church going, teetotaller. We never truly know another person, you may say. Yet the one overriding fact to show foul play was the medical evidence. I refer to the coroner's report of the displacement of both the humeri. Both posteriorly dislocated, small avulsion fractures on the glenoid. As you know anterior dislocation is not uncommon even if it does take some force but posterior dislocations only account for five per cent of cases. However, to have both the right and the left humerus bones posteriorly dislocated takes such a force there's no way that could have happened without her being held down in that bath. The coroner argued that shoulder injuries can come when the body thrashes around in the bath; similar to electrocution or an epileptic fit. Yet never have I ever been aware of a case where this has happened. Also, for that posterior dislocation the arm must be abducted and internally rotated, if she was thrashing in a narrow bath, how could she have got into such a position. I argued this in the preliminary hearings in the coroner's court but the verdict was accidental drowning, with the alcohol level being a contributory factor. Her cardiac arrest, no doubt caused by hypoxia from drowning, was deemed to be the result of an undiagnosed heart condition. Case closed. No one listened. I demanded a review by the CPS, but they claimed to have no evidence of a third party, also stating that the crime scene had been contaminated by the emergency services. In my experience, first responders have always respected that possibility, but this was the reason given by the regional head of the CPS at the time."

Alex turned to Marcus, who was hanging on his every word.

"I had to take a few days off work, the only time in my life I've felt that kind of stress. I know that judgement is wrong. I couldn't get her out of my mind. Having three daughters, I was haunted by the case. I devoured information in the media, it's really not healthy and I don't advise it. The more I coloured in my patient the more wretched I felt at not getting justice for her. Anyway, I come to my point, thank you for bearing with me Marcus. I mentioned she was a church goer. Isabelle had graduated five years earlier and moved to London to make something of her life. Young, lonely, vulnerable she had got involved with the London Church of Glory. As I dug deeper, I became suspicious of this church. They go for shy, intelligent, young professionals whom they can mould into their believers to go out and evangelise. The London Church of Glory was run solely by Digby Honeyfield. That's not a name in a million so when I got to the meeting, I knew it was him. Finally seeing him I was shocked. Whilst there's no evidence to suggest he had anything to do with Isabelle's death, it's no coincidence that she died the same week she left the church. According to her sister she was about to make a public statement regarding the church. She had instructed lawyers to investigate the church's practices given how she was groomed and controlled. Whatever the opinions of others, I know two things, that Isabelle's death was no accident and Digby Honeyfield's cult is in some way the cause."

He felt good to have said his piece. Marcus was staring ahead.

"My sister Tianna got sucked into his so called church; the new one he's set up in Newcastle."

"My God!" Alex leant forward. His PPE scrunched as he put his elbows on the smart dark oak desk.

"Yeah, luckily the episode was short lived but she had a breakdown at Christmas from it. Again, she's the classic target, bright, lacking in confidence, fears doing the wrong thing. Your daughter saved her, did Louisa not tell you?"

"No! Isa did what?" Alex was halfway across his desk.

"When Louisa asked for my number that time, Tianna was obsessed, brainwashed, she was in a catatonic state. Louisa literally marched her off the streets of Oxford and called us up to bring her home. Sorry I thought you knew. I dread to think what would've happened without Louisa." Marcus rubbed his chin.

"The pandemic has sucked the life from us all, I literally fall asleep on the way home. I have no time for my family. I must speak with Isa." Alex put his hands firmly on his desk.

"She's our heroine." Marcus gave a faint smile. "Digby Honeyfield is definitely not anyone my family want to spend time with after all that. Noëmi's friendly with his wife, I think she feels sorry for her. Apparently, there's rumours that Digby's having an affair."

"To be honest, nothing would surprise me with that church lot. Bunch of arrogant hypocrites. Each time they seem to get away with it, men like that."

"But would he have known you were involved in the coroner's report?"

"Oh yes, I was very vocal especially as my evidence was withheld as my testimony was given in camera. Therefore, the details I've just shared with you are not public knowledge. However, I gave my views quite straightforwardly when I was interviewed on TV disagreeing with the verdict. The hospital board remained ambiguous, neither backing me nor admonishing me. If Honeyfield followed the story in the press he would know exactly who I am, my account was well reported. I imagine he would've cared about one of his flock. Plus she had put in a formal complaint to the police." Alex's view became faraway. "I know something happened to that poor girl and I lay my whole career on it. I still wake up some nights with a recurring dream where I'm screaming but no sound is coming out." Alex shook his head and stood up to face the window. "It just feels like whoever did this got away with it."

* * *

Finally home from work, Alex James sat on his patio, quietly drinking a glass of malbec. The evening sun glinted on the horizon and the garden flowers brightened his mood, antirrhinums, dahlias and lavender. Birdsong soothed his mood. Life was still there in the chaos of the pandemic. He reached for his mobile and called Louisa.

"Isa! Did you feel your ears burning today?"

"Dad?"

"I've been hearing about all you did for Tianna McKenzie, you extracted her from the cult. Horrible man, that Honeyfield person."

He sipped his wine.

"Yeah Dad, that was a while ago."

"Well done my darling."
"Dad, there's a couple of things…"

"Money?"

She laughed, "Kind of, I got a fine for breaking Covid restrictions. Don't be mad I went to see my girlfriend and got caught away from my household."

"You're not really allowed to see your girlfriends! How much is it?"
"A hundred pounds…sorry Dad…"

"I can help you with that!"
"…but Dad I said I went to see my girlfriend…Octavia."

There was silence. "Oh…your girlfriend…sorry Isa, I'm not

quite understanding what you mean."

He heard her take a deep breath, "Dad I'm in a relationship with a girl called Octavia. It's been six months now. My first relationship. I think I'm in love."

Alex was silent as he comprehended finally. "Oh...six months...and this is the first we hear!"

"I couldn't tell you..."

"Isa, that's wonderful, I'm so glad you're happy. You should've said! We look forward to meeting her!"

He heard some little sobs on the other end of the call.

CHAPTER 26 - GINA

Friday, 19 June 2020, Heaton Leisure Centre, Newcastle.

Donnie

For the past ten years, Friday nights had been reserved for badminton. The Heaton Leisure Centre club could always rely on Donnie McAllister. Members came and went, but Donnie and a core group of about five fellow players were dependable.

The rule of six meant the club could only play in small groups and this Friday Donnie had been allocated a place. As he was helping put the nets away, one of the newer players approached him. The echoes and squeaks of the draughty sports hall were suddenly softened by her gentle voice.

"Donnie, have you got a sec?"

Gina stood before him. A tall, athletic woman of fifty with short soft blonde hair and sparkling blue eyes. Having just spent a week in Mallorca cycling, her legs were tanned and supple. In spite of a two hour session she smelt fresh and was smart in a white t-shirt and shorts, edged with navy piping. She indicated with her head for him to move to one side for a private conversation.

"Certainly Gina, how can I help?" Donnie wondered if there was a problem with the rota or the club website page.

"This is a bit forward, and nothing I've done before but I wondered if you'd like to go out for a drink?" Gina fumbled with her racket and went bright red as she asked.

"Ah...well...yes! Of course!" Donnie was equally burnt up by now.

"How about tomorrow then?" Gina gave him an enormous smile.

"Yes, wonderful! I'll pick you up at about seven if that works!"

The pair exchanged details.

Arriving home, Donnie sat at the kitchen table and spent ten minutes composing an email on his laptop. Behind him, Sarai was preparing a pho with homemade noodles for them to share. Closing his emails, he rang his daughter.

"N! Are you sitting down? ... okay... I'm going on a date! ... I hope the babies can't hear that language! ... Hold on, Sarai's just dropped something... Right everything's sorted here now!... Gina...A fairly new member of the badminton club... No, she asked me!... about fifty, I know she's got a daughter at university, she's divorced and started playing to meet new people...mmm...I don't know, it just seemed rude to say 'no'...she seems very nice...pleasant...N, that's not fair you can't compare my date to a floral cushion!"

Behind him Sarai gave a burst of laughter. Donnie ignored them both.

"I thought you'd be glad I was making an effort! How many times have you encouraged me to try and get out?...Tomorrow...not sure...a drink...maybe a meal...what do you suggest?... N, that's not very nice and badminton rackets can be very interesting by the way…No of course I don't need anything like that and no I'm not going to do that!…Yes, I'll let you know how it goes!"

With a sigh Donnie hung up. In the corner of his eye, he noticed Sarai stirring her broth. She said nothing. His mind wandered to Manon and the excitement he felt with her. Remembering how, even after so many years together, he would watch the clock until he could leave work and get back to her. Recalling their physical connection, he began to get lost in his memories. *'Stop! There's no comparison. It's not fair on another woman. Time to look forward. The Gods have smiled upon me! See how it goes with Gina. Finally I'm taking a chance!'*

Sarai had taken the stairs.

Saturday, 20 June 2020.

The evening of the date arrived. Parking outside Gina's house, Donnie was all nerves. He smoothed out his shirt, used some breath freshener and checked his reflection in the car mirror. Making his way to her door, he held tightly onto the flowers he had bought for her. Gina opened the door before he could knock and grinned, he was impressed. She had styled her hair and was wearing tight jeans and a sparkly top.

"You look lovely!" Donnie was genuinely charming.

"So do you! Nice shirt!"

"Yes it's from Woven in Durham, a couple of my friends recommended that place so I picked up a few pieces from there last year!"

She touched the pale blue shirt, decorated with a delicate, floral print in dark navy and rose pink.

"Soft, but strong, just how I like my men!" She let her hand linger on his arm.

Donnie felt himself burn up and gave a small cough,

"It's not Covid!"

They drove to Shiremoor House Farm, a rustic pub, for a drink and a light snack.

"I've not been before but I've heard good things!" Donnie enthused.

'Even before Covid I've hardly been out. I hope this place is good enough!'

Settling in at a table near the bar, the lights were low and the mood was good. Gina told him she was in marketing, enjoyed evenings with her girlfriends and visiting Spain where she had a holiday home. This bolt hole was all hers and something she was glad to hold onto after her divorce as she had put so much into refurbishing the place. She explained that she and her husband had grown apart as their two children grew up. Donnie felt strange hearing about two people falling out of love. *'Why on earth did they let that happen?'* Having explained his background, Gina looked shocked when he told her this was the first date he had ever been on since Manon's passing in December 2006.

"It's nearly fourteen years!"

"Thirteen and a half!" Donnie nodded, "I know, it's been tough."

For a moment they were silent, both comprehending the magnitude of this moment in different ways.

"If I'm honest Donnie, I feel a bit like your late wife is like an untouchable saint staring down on us! It's a bit spooky!" She sipped her prosecco.

He loosened his collar and thought for a moment, *'I don't like her talking about Manon like that, not at all, but I understand she can't for one moment imagine how I've been feeling, it's nobody's fault.'*

"Let's choose some food! Tell me more about your house in Spain!"

They chatted away discussing families, the badminton club and work. Donnie was enjoying himself. Gina was a classy woman, intelligent, sensitive and fun. Around 10pm, then began the drive home.

"It's not late, fancy a nightcap?" Gina asked.

"Sure! Your place or mine?"

"Maybe yours, my son's home for the weekend!"

"Right!"

With a dolphin wide grin, Donnie re-routed the car. He was chuffed as he was evidently someone Gina wished to spend time with. Arriving at Donnie's home, he ushered her into the lounge. Gina gave a start.

"Hello!"

Sarai smiled up at them. She was sitting on Donnie's familiar slate, grey sofa, right in the middle seat. Like a cat in the sun. Sarai may have been smirking. Donnie noticed immediately that Sarai was dressed in a stylish, tight fitting powder blue dress that she had last worn when she went out to Noëmi and Marcus' housewarming back in October 2018. He remembered telling her how good she looked that evening when he arrived to babysit Lucia for her. Tonight, as she curled her feet underneath herself to settle in, he noticed her hair was shiny and brushed carefully over her shoulders. *'No ponytail and dressing gown tonight then, Sarai!'* He could smell her perfume.

"Oh Gina, sorry, this is Sarai, she and her daughter, Lucia, live with me!"

"I had no idea!" Gina had a face of stone.

"Let me get us all a drink, what do you fancy, we've got everything!" Donnie had been shopping just in case and was proud to be so well prepared.

Sarai

Sarai adjusted her legs and called out to Donnie, "White wine please!"

The women glanced at each other. Gina moved to sit in one of the two armchairs. Her eyes took in the whole room.

"Where's your husband?" Gina asked as she pointed to Luca in the wedding picture.

"He died three and a half years ago."

"I'm sorry…and is that Donnie's late wife?"

Sarai nodded and wondered what Gina thought of the whole set up, even she could see to an outsider it was overwhelming.

"What do you do?" Gina asked cautiously.

"I'm a homemaker, you?"

Gina pursed her lips, "I work in marketing, for a software company in Newcastle."

"Alexa, play Eighties hits everywhere," Sarai called out and the music started.

The three sat together and small talk passed between them; songs they liked, weather for the next day, state of Newcastle town centre and shops that were closing. Eventually it was time to take Gina home.

"Lovely to meet you!" Sarai called out from the sofa, as Gina left.

Donnie

Pulling up outside Gina's front door, Donnie was impressed by her smart house on the new housing estate nearby. Evidently Gina was self-sufficient and financially secure.

"Thank you for this evening." Gina held his gaze, Donnie swallowed hard. Getting out he showed her to her front door.

"I enjoyed spending time with you." Gina put her hand on Donnie's shoulder. He froze. Nodding he muttered,

"Yes, it's been a pleasant evening!"

Her eyes did not move from his. She was still, as if on pause, waiting. Her body moved into his. Her head tilted and her lips looked for his.

Embarrassed, he turned away, "Right, see you at badminton."

Head dropping, Gina sighed out her frustration. "Yes, see you next Friday! We're scheduled together!"

Gina turned her key and was gone.

Driving home Donnie was confused. *'Everything about her is right and I feel nothing. Am I some kind of mournful, emotional eunuch now? There's no bloody hope!'*

Getting back to his house, he exhaled deeply as he returned to his kitchen where Sarai was now perched in her usual chair. Donnie grabbed a beer, reclined himself over two chairs and undid the second button of his shirt. His brow furrowed, he sighed and with a half-smile gave Sarai a look.

"Sarai, I don't think I've ever seen you sit on that sofa before. You're always busy, always on the go, there's always something to do!"

"It's Saturday, I felt like relaxing!" She was coy as she finished her wine.

"Relaxing? In that dress?" Donnie did not hide his surprise. *'I bet N put her up to that!'*

"You could've worn the shirt I gave you!"

"Ah no I don't think so!"

"She's perfect! Did you kiss her?" Sarai asked, examining her wine glass.

"That's none of your business, but no I didn't, she wanted to, but, I don't know, I wasn't feeling it. And it's not because I think Manon's looking down on me! You know my therapy has served me well." Donnie ran his hand through his hair. He was far away, "Maybe you're the person who understands this but for years I couldn't move on even though I knew Manon would want me to. You see I kept thinking what if I meet someone, I even fall in love and…and then Manon comes back, what would I do? That would not be fair on anyone. I was stuck in a limbo. Yet now I accept that she's never coming back. What we had was perfect, we truly loved each other, she could not have been more loved and neither could I. But that's in the past. It was and it was everything, but I know if the positions were reversed all I would want would be for Manon to live her life and be loved again. So I know what she wants for me."

Sarai nodded, "I understand, Luca and I had that same love. I'd do anything for him to come back, sometimes I think maybe he escaped and lost his memory, maybe I should go look for him but then I remember the DNA evidence that Guy showed me. When she's old enough I'll take Lucia to his final resting place so that together we can accept that he's gone. For now I'll live the life he wanted me to live, loving his daughter, keeping his memory alive for her, but I too need to close that door. It's so hard."

Remembering the moment he had taken Noëmi to see her mother at rest, he understood. Donnie took her hand, "I know, Sarai, it just takes time, but rest assured that Luca died as a truly beloved man. Not everyone has that in life. Your love made him the man he was."

She looked on the verge of tears. They sat for a moment and then she spoke.

"Why didn't you tell her I live here? You had all evening together!"

"Sarai, it was just an evening of small talk, nothing real, nothing personal, nothing intimate. You're a full on part of my life now aren't you! Baggage I think they call it! I don't know, maybe I don't want other people interfering with you and me. And besides, she already thinks I'm a bit weird about Manon, so I can't even begin to explain about you!"

"If I'm a problem I can go!" Sarai adjusted her dress as she fidgeted on the chair.

"No, Sarai, stop, I don't want you to! I like having you here."

"Funny way to show it!"

"Sarai!"

With a huff, Sarai took herself off to bed, Donnie rolled his eyes and called his daughter.

"Is it too late? Yeah, fine… no we didn't!...The Shiremoor…we had a steak…back to mine…no we didn't!…Sarai was in the lounge anyway and did you put her up to that?...Just coincidence then! Sarai never sits down!...no it didn't matter…stop it, that wasn't an option there's no way I'd be taking anyone upstairs on a first date!...no, I wasn't feeling it…is there something wrong with me, N? She's nice looking, we have things in common, she's financially stable, got grown up children…I hope I've not hurt her, I just can't get physical with someone when there's no connection…I don't know it's going to take time…bye, love you, thanks for listening."

Donnie glanced round at his kitchen and saw Sarai's frosted pink hair clip, its diamante edging catching the light. He could picture her putting her hair up and down. Suddenly he burst out laughing as he remembered the moment he had seen her resolutely sitting, like a smug, immovable cat, right in the middle of the sofa, earlier that evening.

"Ah I'm sure it was N's doing! Those two are in cahoots!"

CHAPTER 27 - LOOKING FORWARD

Monday, 22 June 2020.

Monday morning Guy's in-box was filling up.

Guy

Hope lockdown key worker duties are not too onerous. I'm working from home which is a novelty but actually quite pleasant given that Sarai and Lucia have moved in. Indeed this brings me to my point. I need to report a hate crime. Here are the details:

Victim: Sarai Bianchi

Perpetrator: Rev Digby Honeyfield & wife

Date: 28 February 2020

Background: Sarai was renting a flat in Durham when she fell into rent arrears. Without serving the proper notice her landlord evicted her and Lucia and de facto made them homeless. She was threatened with bailiffs and not offered any support. During his visit to evict the family this

landlord made some heinous, awful racist comments to her, of which Sarai can give you the details in a statement.

Thank you for looking into this.

Donnie McAllister

From his cubby hole, Guy leaned out to locate Tariq. As he moved, Rolo's eyes tracked him in hope. He kept on checking and was surprised that his colleague was so long from his desk. Eventually he saw him, heading his way, sweaty and holding his abdomen.

"Riqqi! What's going on? Have you eaten something?"

"Yeah, stomach's playing up." Tariq was distracted.

"Right, I've got a hate crime for you and how's your contract law? I'll forward the email now. The complainant is a friend of mine so I have to declare a conflict of interest."

"Again! Do you know everyone in Tyneside?"

Guy nodded, "Right, it's that vicar from the noma Zoom conference the other day. Accused of a racial hate crime, him and his wife. Can you interview the pair of them and the alleged victim? It's all in the email message I've just forwarded to you."

Turning on his heel, Tariq rushed back to the bathroom.

"Get some Imodium!" Guy called out. He watched his colleague go and began to think about Reverend Digby Honeyfield. Within a minute, his mobile rang, he listened and then spoke in a low voice,

"Don't worry, Mimi, I'm sure it's going to be fine; I'll ask Marcus." Nodding he clicked off the call and mentally calculated the number of weeks left in this pregnancy.

Guy sat and played a quick game of solitaire on his phone.

Everything was chaos. *'I can't face any more loss. We're seven months into this pregnancy and every day I feel like that bloke walking a tightrope across the Grand Canyon. I've never been scared of anything and now I'm scared of everything. I wonder how Laura's coping. How does anyone face being told they can't be cured?'*

He stopped his game and messaged Marcus.

'Mate, can you call Yumi when you get a chance? She had a spot of bleeding and she's terrified. Also are there any specialists or new treatments you know of for bone cancer?'

'I could get some of the uni crowd to help me start a fundraiser to get her the best treatment. Maybe there's some new drug in development here or in the US or Japan?'

Marcus replied straight away.

'I'll talk to Yumi right now. There's a pathway where Yumi can be seen. The non-Covid treatment is still open. Don't forget that. Also, one of us can take Rolo if that helps ease things for you. I'll definitely look into the specialists for you. Medicine is making advances the whole time so stay optimistic. We love you bro."

Tuesday, 23 June 2020, Donnie's house.

Donnie

Soon Covid restrictions would permit a gathering of thirty outdoors and Donnie was delighted; he could now advance a special plan. He bounced downstairs and found exactly what he had hoped for, Sarai in the kitchen preparing Lucia for her day. Cheerios were being spat out everywhere as Lucia ate breakfast. He walked towards the pair and felt a soggy cereal ring underfoot. It stuck to his big toe. Pulling his dressing gown tightly around himself, he grinned.

"Sarai! I hear someone's nearly forty! We should plan something!"

"Ngọt mật chết ruồi!" She held his gaze.

Now used to this routine, he paused to allow her the effect she desired and then asked,

"Translation please!"

"You catch more flies with honey than vinegar!"

"Translation please!"

"By being nice to me, you obviously think that you'll gain something!"

"And any other meaning? Sarai?"

"No of course not!" She quickly went to the sink.

Donnie sat and fiddled with Lucia's sippy cup.

"Okay, you're right. I thought we could take advantage of the event and have people over in the garden to celebrate. We can have up to thirty! Of course, you can make up the guest list! I hope to be on it!"

Sarai shook her head, "No, I don't like any fuss. We can do a meal together, six of us inside maybe?"

"Ah come on! You're only forty once! Plus the twins are nearly one and Lucia's almost three, it's a triple celebration!"

"And Guy's birthday was the same day as mine!"

"A quadruple celebration!"

CHAPTER 28 - UNQUIET

Saturday, 27 June 2020, 120 Walton Street, Oxford.

Louisa

The pandemic meant that university accommodation closed as soon as the term was over. With Oxford university setting a deadline for students to be out by the last weekend of June. Louisa was not ready to return home and moved in with her girlfriend Octavia, reasoning that they were already bubbled. Six visitors were allowed to meet inside and out. With the university experience curtailed, Octavia and her Walton Street housemates found all sorts of distractions with which to amuse themselves.

The Walton Street six were sitting around one Saturday evening in late June. They were bored of their board games; Cluedo, Scrabble, Pictionary had been turned into every drinking game possible. Suddenly inspired, Maria, one of Octavia's housemates, grabbed a litre of vodka and a family size value bottle of coke and filled their glasses. She flipped the Scrabble board and arranged twenty-six letters of the alphabet into a circle. Finishing her drink she slammed her glass upside down into the middle of her board. Now Louisa saw she had set up a kind of Ouija board. Maria said in a low growl,

"Let's contact the dead!"

Louisa shuddered. She did not like these dark games that Maria played. How she wished for Tianna to be there to stop this. She swallowed hard.

"Nah let's watch a film, choose a horror, why don't you?"

Yet the other housemates were keen on Maria's games.

"We're all filmed out, this'll be jokes!" Louisa could hear Maria everywhere.

Maria instructed them all to put a finger on the upside down glass and shut their eyes. Giggling, they did so.

"Is there anybody there?" Maria laughed.

Nothing.

"Oh spirits of the dead talk to us!"

Louisa felt sweaty.

Nothing.

"Unquiet spirits tell us your name!"

The glass moved and they opened their eyes: it had stopped at the letter *I*.

Shrieks and accusations of moving the glass flooded Louisa's ears; she was feeling shaky.

Fingers back in place Maria called again to the dead. The glass stopped at *S*.

"Is?" Murmured Maria.

Back to it Maria called "Desperate soul, tell us your name!"

The glass shook and moved violently to *A*.

The group gasped and pulled their fingers off the glass!

"Isa?" Maria called out.

Louisa screamed. "That's my pet name! Only dad and Octavia use it!"

In a move all five year olds would be proud of, she kicked the home made Ouija board off the coffee table with both feet. Screaming like an unquiet spirit, she jumped off her chair which fell to the ground.

"Chill out, it's only Bex pissing about!" Maria began retrieving the plastic letters from the orange shag pile.

Bex was ghost white. "No, I did nothing!"

"Then Joe or Rhys trying to spook you!"

Both boys shook their heads, their anime eyes staring with shock.

Louisa gave a cry, grabbed her bag and flew for the door. Octavia was right behind her,

"Isa! Calm yourself! Wait!"

She could hear their echoes of laughter.

"I'm never going in there again!" Louisa was fumbling for her phone. Catching her up, Octavia held her girlfriend and let her sob her terrified heart out. Standing outside the large Victorian villa in the deserted street, Louisa's trembling fingers texted Tianna.

'Can Octavia & me bunk down at Joel's place until we head back up north?'

'Sure, no worries, that'll be fun'

'Tianna, God bless you! I really love you! Pray for me xxx'

Tianna sent an eyeroll emoji, **'I don't do sarcasm!'**

* * *

Blake's Coffee Shop, Newcastle.

Tariq

Back at Blake's, Tariq sat at a table separated from the next by a large perspex board. Tapping his fingers, he ordered an Americano with the app and checked his messages.

'There in a sec!'

'Time to get this sorted!'

His hand shook as he put his phone down, he flexed his neck. And there she was. Caramel raincoat, Burberry scarf, electric blue jumpsuit, flaming curls. Her hair style and her clothing made her look older than her years but her face was childlike, innocent and unwrinkled. Marching across to his table, she met his eye.

"Tariq, any more information?" Her face was slightly fuzzy through the finger smeared plastic screen which was not the most expensive.

"Alura, we need to finish this. There's now an allegation of a hate crime committed by you and your husband. It's being investigated by my unit. I have a conflict of interest!"

"So?"

"So I can no longer help you! We're done, no more contacting me and no more threats!"

"Bit harsh, I paid you for a job." Alura examined her fingers.

"This is getting too close to home. I'm losing my shit literally! Did I give you my supply of police headed paper by mistake? I can't find it and the serial numbers are registered to me!"

"No you only gave me photographs, devastating ones at that!" Alura dropped her head.

He rolled his eyes, "And whilst we're at it, I had no idea you were CPS! Why didn't you tell me?" He hissed.

"You never asked!" She poked her face towards the plastic screen.

"That's unfair. It's done, you've got your evidence, now back off and let me do my job, which will involve interviewing you and your husband about a hate crime allegation!" Tariq got up to leave as his coffee arrived.

"Fine, have it your way. I'm happy to pay for the photos. All I wanted was to prove to myself that he was cheating. To actually see it with my own eyes gives me closure. He's been gaslighting me the whole time. You can't imagine how it feels. I've given up everything for him."

Alura quietly began to cry. Her eyes were red and her mascara began to weep down her face like muddy rain in a gully. She grabbed a napkin and wiped her nose. Her bottom lip trembled,

"I just want to move on." She collapsed in front of him like Lot's wife, turned into a pillar of salt. Her shoulders shook as she began to sob loudly. A few glances from other customers made Tariq sweaty, *'I feel so bad for her but I wish she'd shut up, everyone will think I'm some kind of arsehole.'*

"Look I've got a couple more photos with dates from the hotel in Durham, let me send you those then you've got everything." As the words left his mouth, he cursed himself. *'What the hell have I just done?'*

"That's wonderful, I can really nail the old bastard. He'll have no idea, you know revenge served cold and all that! Can you send the pictures now then I'd say we're done!"

Fumbling, Tariq grabbed his phone and prevaricated for a few minutes.

Alura watched and said under her breath, "How long does it fucking take?"

"Sorry I don't seem to be able to find them…"

"Oh I'm sure you will, I had a long lunch with your superintendent the other day, we're as thick as thieves but we wouldn't want him to find out about your little hobby!"

"Oh there we go, can I airdrop them to you?"

Alura smiled, "Sure, now with regard to the hate crime allegation you can tell your unit that the CPS will find no evidence of a crime and that there'll be no prosecution." Stretching her hands out she raised herself up from the table.

"Yes but I need to…!"

"I'll cover it, stop panicking! Honestly, it's now me helping you! Some kind of dark, symbiotic arrangement. Anytime you want to scratch each other's backs just call me up!"

"Sorry I'm engaged and I don't…"

Laughter peeled through the small plastic booth. "Oh take a joke, Tariq, honestly, like I'd go for you!" And off she flounced.

Sweaty, Tariq sat back down, loosened his collar and tried to work out if he'd done anything illegal.

* * *

Saturday, 4 July 2020, Oxford.

The chaos of Covid was devastating for university students; lectures online, the student experience shut down and anxiety levels rocketing. However small bubbles of optimism popped up in this sea of misery. A couple of these pockets of air were the flourishing relationships of Joel and Tianna, JoTi, along with that of Octavia and Louisa, TavIsa. The Oxford Brookes term would finish one week later than Oxford's, so they all huddled at Joel's flat. Not risking another fine, the four stayed under the radar of the local WhatsApp group. Curtains twitched more than ever with neighbours eager to out those who flouted lockdown rules. The only remaining official resident was Joel and he was sent out to buy the necessary student supplies.

Anthony

Finally the time came for the respective fathers to pick up their offspring, Anthony offered to bring Joel back with Tianna. Marcus had told Guy that one of them could take Rolo for a while. That person turned out to be a somewhat surprised Alex, given the size of his garden and his love of dogs. Thus Alex, plus Rolo, set off to collect Louisa and the two cars drew up outside the breezeblock flat around the same time. Rolo was panting at the window of Alex's green Land Rover Discovery.

"I'm not sure that car's big enough!" Anthony joked to his friend. Alex laughed as he let the spaniel out.

"Shall we see if they're doing any drugs!" Alex pointed to Rolo. Arriving in Oxford had obviously brought out a mischievous side to the former St John's student.

"Honestly, you doctor types are all the same!"

Alex grinned and the men stretched their legs, maintaining the two metre distance. The neat row of 'recycling' trophies displayed in the front window of the student flat was their next talking point.

"Not sure how they can afford Grey Goose," Anthony mused.

"That Hendricks gin isn't cheap either! No sign of a text book anywhere!" Alex quipped. They got to the door and saw a plague style homemade sign.

'We're all so negative!' A large red cross and an emoji of the Coronavirus followed.

"People are actually dying! As a medical student Louisa should be respectful of that!" Alex pursed his lips.

Sluggishly the four pulled out bags that the fathers loaded into cars. With most of the bags extracted, they all decided to go and check that everything was gone. Walking around the flat it became very obvious that only two of the three bedrooms had recently been used as the third was piled with items stored by the new tenants.

Realisation of how obvious this was evidently flooded over Tianna.

"Oh they dropped all that off this morning." She tried.

"No they didn't!" Her father replied as he opened the hall cupboard to check it was empty.

"That sofa's really uncomfortable to sleep on…" She gestured towards the lounge.

"No it isn't. No one sleeps there!" He glanced at the meter readings and noted them down.

She refused to look at her father. The last bits of rubbish were thrown out and the trophies finally made it to the recycling bin. The four students hugged each other goodbye. Louisa and Octavia had the longest farewell. Octavia would be returning to London where her family lived. Alex and Anthony spoke amongst themselves.

"We're much more accepting as parents than our parents were." Alex commented to Anthony. Reflecting on what Alex meant, Anthony felt reassured by Alex's openness. Anthony was simply struggling with Tianna being an adult. He saw Joel putting one duvet in the car.

"I know. They have much more freedom. I'm not sure that would be for me!" He knew the lifestyle Tianna was enjoying would have horrified his parents.

"It's good that things are more open. I do feel if they were in trouble they'd talk to us. We didn't have that. I remember once my wife, Cathy, had a very short lived pregnancy scare when we were students. Funny that, calling it a scare given how much we love our daughters. We had no one to talk to but ourselves. Being there for them, that's important."

Anthony nodded. "Yes but they need to be able to cope when things go wrong. I'm not sure they're as confident as they think." A whole raft of memories of Tianna's ups and downs over the past two years cascaded through his head.

Tianna turned to him. Her dark eyes shone and her smile was warmer than the summer breeze.

"All ready Dad!"

How he loved her.

As they set off, Joel gave a sigh and commented,

"This term's been exhausting!"

Anthony wondered how sitting around with the odd online lecture could be such hard work. He noticed a grin pass between his daughter and her boyfriend. He pursed his lips and then could tell Tianna was checking if he had noticed. They drove on, Joel was soon asleep in the back of the car. With a mute Tianna at his side he took his opportunity.

"Ten months since you and Joel have been together."

"Seven months if you take out the three month break up."

"You're well suited."

"I know it's hard to talk about…because you'll think we're being unrealistic, but we are planning a whole future together. We're compatible and we give each other space. All I know Dad is that he really loves me and I love him. That's all I know. He's kind and funny…plus he'll never let me down, so don't worry."

"That's wonderful Tianna, don't ever take that love for granted. Always make that effort to be the best person you can be for each other."

"Oh yes Dad, I will. I've watched you with mum, I know how to be tender and loving. That's important as we have to nurture each other."

Enough said. Joy filled his heart.

Alex

Alex's journey began in the opposite direction of his home. Louisa needed to collect some things from Octavia's house which was now empty of students. Although Covid tests had been done, Octavia did not share a car with Alex as he was on the front line. Arriving at the Walton Street address, Louisa was biting her nails. Alex gave a shudder. *'It was this road, I can't remember which number, but Isabelle lived right here!'*

"Dad, can you go in there for me?" Louisa stared at the front door.

"Isa, how am I supposed to know what's yours?"

He noticed his daughter freeze. Reluctantly she headed inside. After a few minutes, Alex decided to get Rolo out. The dog had a pee at the front gate. Deciding to give his daughter a hand, he took the spaniel to the front door Rolo dug in and refused to cross the threshold. Alex pulled but no Rolo would not move. Instead, he lay down, fixed his paws and whimpered. Alex gave an exasperated pull but Rolo tugged harder back, whole body shaking; he would not be budged.

"How strange, what's the problem with a student house! You're supposed to be a police dog hunting out contraband, scared of nothing! Catching criminals!"

Charging from the house, Louisa reappeared with two black bin bags of 'stuff'. Rolo bounced back to the car.

"Let's go!" She yelled.

CHAPTER 29 - GOODBYE

Saturday, 4 July 2020, London.

Guy

Also making a trip that day was Guy. With more than four months having passed since he had the devastating news about Laura, he had been forced to postpone their meeting due to lockdown. He trembled at the thought of how ill she would now be. Having no personal experience of death, he was floored by her terminal diagnosis and yet resolved to see her.

Guy travelled to his sister's place in London, without telling her the reason for the trip. Yumi had decided not to accompany him as they both felt that this was something they wished to keep separate from their relationship. Guy had agreed to meet Laura at Richmond Park. Laura loved deer and they had never been there before. That was important as they agreed that this would be the place where he could remember her. Arriving early the weather was chilly for July. As he walked from the car park, he texted Yumi to tell her he had arrived. She wished him well. He felt reassured he was doing the right thing. Guy sat on a bench and looked at the beauty of nature; vast oaks, chestnut trees and the summer green of rushes and grasses stretched out before him.

Soon Laura was walking slowly towards him. He jumped up and rushed over to her. She collapsed into his arms.

"I'm sorry, I told myself not to cry."

"Shhh Laura, it's natural," Guy was also now quietly weeping.

They sat on the bench for a while and then began to walk.

"My God, how are you coping?"

"Really, I have good days and bad. My managers have been very good, I get flexi hours and obviously I'm working from home. I'm on an eighty percent contract now. Sorry, can we sit down?" They sat close to each other and he held her hand.

"Guy, it's good for us to see each other whilst I'm well enough. Thank you. I just wanted to thank you for the time we had together. It was perfect. For me it was love. You are the love of my life."

He shut his eyes. Marcus had told him to be careful what he said.

"You mattered to me too Laura. We had so much fun at Durham! We made each other happy then."

Laura's head lowered. "Could we not try again?"

"Laura, I think you need to focus on time with your family. It's going to be devastating for them. As it is for us all. You know I'm married to Yumi. Nothing's going to change that."

She turned to him. Her eyes were the same as the ones that had met his across the room during the first formal in college. She had the same youthful glow. Her hair was slightly shorter but still it sat softly at her shoulders. She looked good. Life was so cruel, she did not appear to be dying. Nodding, she gave a cough.

"Sorry it's the drugs. I hope you'll have the happiness that we had. Remember when we slept together that first time?"

He smiled. "First love eh?"

"Yeah! For me you're the one."

Guy felt his throat tighten. It would be so easy to just tell her what she wanted to hear. No one would know. She could die happy and he would feel like a better man. Yet he knew that this was wrong. The words from our mouths imprint on our souls. He remained silent.

"Right, so there's nothing more to say is there? But Guy please! Could you not just try? One more time? The two of us?"

"Laura, that's not the way my life's going." He could not tell her about Yumi being pregnant.

"Your life? Yes at least you have that to look forward to."

Guy felt pain.

"Laura I'm so sorry. You were an important part of my life. That was our time. We should cherish those memories when we were young together. Now we both need to accept where we are."

"It just hurts so much! Why her? What's this Yumi got that I don't?"

Refusing to cause her any more pain, Guy was pragmatic. "It's just she's the one my life's moved on with. It's been nearly eight years Laura."

He could not tell her that the feelings he had for Yumi were stronger than those he had ever felt before. That would be cruel. The visceral need he had for Yumi was about her personality, her tenderness and it was intensely physical. How she made him feel he wanted to make her feel. However, Guy also knew that he and Laura had been torn apart by her lack of care for their relationship, it became almost indifference. In spite of his desperate efforts to rekindle their closeness at that time, it had become a functional pairing. For Guy this was not enough.

"Just remember me as your first love."

He nodded and held her. She began to sob. Eventually they both knew it was time to go. Guy managed to avoid her attempts to kiss him and only broke down again once she had left. Wretched could not even come close to how he felt.

* * *

Getting back to his sister's flat he was morose. Settling himself before his drive home, questions flew through his head. Motionless, he sat with a mug of tea as his sister dealt with an irritable toddler.

"Make sure you use a coaster. Who were you meeting today then?"

Finally he gave up his secret. "Laura."

"What the? Does Yumi know?"

He nodded. "I had to say goodbye to her." He began to sob and his sister put the toddler in his bouncy chair and her arms around him.

"What do you mean? Is she going somewhere?"

"She's ill, Poppy, Laura's got stage four cancer. It's terminal. There's nothing they can do. I've said my goodbyes. It's the worst thing I've ever had to do, I can't bear it."

"Oh my God! I had no idea. I've been so wrapped up in babydom!" Gently she rocked her little brother.

CHAPTER 30 - SARAI'S BIRTHDAY

Sunday, 5 July 2020, High Heaton, Newcastle.

Donnie

Having decided to keep the numbers to the maximum minimum, plans were shared.

Bring your own glasses and cutlery, keep a safe distance and sanitise hands at any and every opportunity.

The day before the barbecue, Joel and Tianna were arriving back in Newcastle at the end of their first year of university. The event would also mark the first time Joel and Tianna would be together at a family event since their relationship was spectacularly revealed via Zoom.

Bouncing down the stairs Donnie was wearing the shirt Sarai had gifted him, he was excited. Anxiously he checked that everything was in order. *'Today must be perfect!'* Bottles of wine and champagne in the fridge, gazebo up and food ready to barbecue. He checked his list and the timings he had planned.

At midday, Lucia's little friends, Willow and Millie visited for the first hour with their yummy mummies India and Jules. Both still embarrassed by their gossip, they filled every silence with enthusiastic comments about Donnie's garden and Sarai's food.

Soon Vietnamese spring rolls, chicken nuggets and strawberry mini milks devoured, it was time for them to light Lucia's birthday candles. The three toddlers gathered around the caterpillar cake. It was as if they too were of the order of Lepidoptera with their bright eyes and busy little limbs. Donnie and Sarai sang Happy Birthday. Lucia giggled and took a deep breath. Before anyone knew it, Millie had shoved the birthday girl out of the way and was going for the candle blow out. Lucia jolted to the floor and burst into tears. Willow on the flank, launched in to snatch the antennae off the cake. She shoved them into her mouth. India and Jules cried out in shared horror.

"Mills never behaves like that!"
"Nor does Wills!"

Donnie quipped, "Seeing that I now know how the world will end!"

Once again apologies were profuse although Donnie was momentarily bothered that the women were trying to blame the 'environment'. Eventually Lucia had her moment, cake was shared and party bags grabbed. Time for the toddlers to go and for the adult afternoon to begin. Watching the nursery mums leave through the side gate, Donnie and Sarai waited until they were gone and burst into fits of laughter.

"One day they'll all be butterflies I suppose!" Donnie mused as he wiped tears of laughter from his eyes.

Sarai was already on her way back to the kitchen. He raced behind to catch her up. *'I don't want her seeing her birthday cake! Everything needs to be a surprise!'* Slipstreaming to undertake her, Donnie took Sarai's hand and told her to shut her eyes. Opening one of the drawers of his kitchen dresser, he pulled out a couple of thoughtfully wrapped boxes.

"These are for you! Happy birthday! Sorry! Happy fortieth birthday!"

Sarai sat open mouthed. Evidently, she was not expecting a gift. Donnie was chuffed. He watched as she opened the presents and was delighted as she gasped with delight.

"That bracelet! How did you even know?"

"Oh I just guessed!" Donnie lied.

Spending lockdown together they had fallen into a routine. He worked from home in the front room as Sarai took care of Lucia. After lunch they took a walk all together and in the evening Donnie would use the spin bike in the garage whilst Sarai put her daughter to bed. Once dinner was done, they would watch a film or series together. During the intermissions he had noticed how she sat up as the charm bracelet was advertised. Once he had noticed her googling the item and the cost of the charms. He saw that she liked the cherub charm so he had added that. He guessed that this was about Lucia being her greatest achievement. He felt the same about his daughter. Donnie knew that with no spare cash, Sarai would never buy anything like this for herself, everything went on Lucia. When Noëmi had been growing up it was the same for Manon. Sarai jumped to give him a hug. Neither rushed to release the other. She felt warm and soft; he was conscious of her touch. *I'm getting all emotional in my middle age!'*

Marcus

McKenzies began to arrive. They were swarming everywhere. Marcus, baby on hip, opened the side gate of Donnie's house and spotted Tianna approaching with Joel. At that moment the cacophony that was brothers Jayden and Isaiah arriving, surrounded them. The two middle siblings seized Joel and their sister by their arms and hauled them round the side of the house, joking, teasing and mucking around.

Many McKenzies sat in the McAllister garden. Over the years Donnie had transformed the space into a beautiful flower haven, with rose bushes, bougainvillaea and rhododendrons. It had helped him cope with his struggles. A hot afternoon, everyone relaxed with the smell of the barbecue and Eighties music playing out from a brand new gazebo. Anthony was in a novelty apron and helping Donnie, barbecue burgers and chicken. Sarai had moved the large dining table outside and covered it with fine dishes; salads, fried potatoes, breads and dips. Warmed by hearty food and longed for family, everyone settled in.

Rolo bounded through the side gate followed by Yumi and Guy, arms full of drinks and gifts. Now that Yumi was better, Rolo was back with his devoted master. Seeing the spaniel, Lucia gave a giggle of delight. Bruno and Emmanuelle attempted to toddle towards the dog, falling down like skittles in their excitement. Marcus gave a longing sigh. Not having seen one another physically, the group were keen to be close but pandemic guidance advised caution, so hugs were not shared. Marcus being on the frontline kept a careful distance from everyone. Seeing Guy arrive, he found it hard.

"Man, I need a hug so bad!"

"You and Noëmi really are such huggers!" Yumi side eyed Noëmi.

"Oh my Yumi, just stop!"

Guy and Marcus exchanged confused looks.

"Noëmi loves a hug!" Yumi said under her breath. Noëmi gave Yumi a look and stomped off to check on the babies. Yumi rolled her eyes and followed her friend.

"What's got those two?"

"Oh it's some banter from the hen do that's still doing the rounds. Yumi says Noëmi was over friendly to that Honeyfield vicar when they met him. Obviously they didn't know who he was. He speaks French so Noëmi loves all that!"

Marcus was stunned. "She never said anything! I guess we're so busy with feeds, naps and nappies...bet you can't wait!"

"Actually, I'm that excited! ...It's just the Laura thing that's depressing me. I got an update that her X-rays were showing deterioration."

"As I assured you, I'm in touch with our oncology specialist and as soon as they get back to me, I'll let you know. They have new experimental treatments and Laura would be a suitable candidate, stage four, palliative care and only twenty-nine. Unfortunately, bone cancer can happen in younger people but X-rays are not the best modality, surely she must be having whole body bone scans? For now, Covid's putting everything back a bit."

"Mate, I really appreciate your help. Dr Google just gives horror stories." Guy was faraway.

"Stay off the internet! If you could get me her consultant details; where she's being treated then I'll be able to put them in touch."

"God, Marcus, you have no idea how grateful I am. Yumi's been brilliant about this. It's casting a shadow, I can't deny that."

"Take heart. The wife of that Honeyfield bloke was cured of cancer. It's hailed as a miracle and probably the only good thing you'll hear about that vicar and his church. Both are pretty sinister. Not only did Tianna get brainwashed, but it also turns out a former member of his congregation from the London church died in suspicious circumstances about five years ago."

"Yeah, but people die Marcus, as you well know, many a time it's just coincidence. A church would have many members, many older people so..." Guy was morose.

"No this was a young twenty something. Ask Alex! He was the expert witness for the coroner. He found inconsistencies with the injuries but the CPS didn't think it warranted an investigation."

"That's sad but unfortunately people die…Laura's only twenty-nine."

"She had just left the church and was preparing to make a statement about it!"

"Weird, there must be a case file, I'd love to see that!" Guy's mood picked up.

"Can you request things like that?"

"Everyone can request coroner's reports, the case file I'd have to go through my superintendent. The preacher is worth keeping an eye on now that he's on our patch. He's also accused of a hate crime as when he evicted Sarai, he bombarded her with racist abuse. There's never just one thing."

Presently Marcus sat down with Joel on the dark green swing seat. Marcus saw Joel looking at Tianna with such love as she ran to catch one of the beginning to toddle twins. Noëmi charged to get the other. Marcus watched Noëmi running bare foot on the grass. Giggling, hair flowing and dress skimming her lithe body. It was the floral dress that she had worn to Val's birthday three years earlier.

"You know Joel, when you've got something special, hold onto it with everything you've got."

Joel smiled as he looked at Marcus who shut his eyes, *'I wish I'd fought harder for her.'*

Suddenly Marcus' mother Marianna was upon them.

"Avoiding me then Joel?"

Joel's mouth opened, but it was Marianna who spoke. "We're delighted you and Tianna are back together. Look at her! She's blossoming! Just take care of her, don't hurt her!" And just like that she left.

Guy

Guy was perplexed, Digby Honeyfield's name was coming up far too often for his liking, hate crimes, brainwashing and now a mysterious death. *'I need to keep an eye on this man.'*

He strolled over to the drinks table and grabbed a beer. He moved over to the main table where Donnie was busy trying to shield the birthday cake from Sarai.

"We got your email Donnie, it's all in hand, I've got my best copper on it."

He then helped Donnie with the candles and tapped his wine glass to get everyone's attention.

"Time to make sure Sarai knows just how much she means to us all!"

In a flash, the whole group was singing Happy Birthday. Noëmi refilled her wine glass and called out.

"Is this an offence, Guy? Singing in public?"

Donnie

Before Guy could reply, Donnie continued.

"Happy Birthday Sarai, I must be the only person who's actually enjoying lockdown with you and Lucia bounding around the house!" He gestured to Sarai who was wearing her powder blue dress again. Donnie's lips twitched at the memory of her strategically positioned on the sofa and Gina's face.

"Here's to Sarai! Happy birthday and I hope you'll always stick around to make me smile!"

An emboldened Noëmi next shouted across the garden.

"So Dad, tell us, who else makes you smile, maybe Gina?"

Donnie went bright red and knocked back the rest of his glass of merlot.

"N! Not now! Honestly, we don't need to advertise…"

Too late, Anthony was grinning from ear to ear.

"Oh what's this Donnie! Lockdown love?"

To Donnie's horror the whole garden went quiet and every eye turned onto him. **Voulez-vous** by Abba was grooving in the background.

"No, I went on a date, that's all! No big news!"

"Oh but it is!" Guy joined in.

"Alright I suppose so, it's the first one since…aye…nearly fourteen years."

The silence was now poignant. The laughter and jokes stopped. The music faded. Only the sound of a wood pigeon could be heard. Time stood still.

"Wow, amazing man." Jayden sounded choked.

No one else had any words. Donnie had come far and broke the silence.

"Just talking as you younger ones call it, a drink in the pub! Nothing more so you lot can stop speculating!" He wagged his finger at them all. Embarrassed, he looked around for his barbecue tongs.

"No Donnie, that's good, no need to rush anything, right?" Isaiah sounded moved. He had grown up with Donnie, who had been like a second father to him. "I hope she treats you right."

"Yeah, she'd better be good enough for you!" Tianna stood up as if ready to go into bare armed combat with this woman. Donnie had always had time for the youngest McKenzie as she grew up.

"No, it's like a comedy film, I'm not really getting anything right. Out of practice I guess!" His attempt to laugh it off, just pulled on every heartstring of everyone present. He tried to avoid all their puppy-like eyes. Searching the garden, he wanted to find Sarai but he noticed she had already moved well away from the group and was slipping back into the kitchen.

Noëmi

Feeling hot, Noëmi felt a bit dizzy with the wine and the sun and went to the drinks table to pour a glass of water.

"Honestly N, you really embarrassed your dad! And I don't think it's Gina who makes him smile!" Marcus gave her an old fashioned look.

"It's just me being clumsy. Sometimes I think the knock on my head affected my judgement. I feel terrible." She gulped some water and felt a lump in her throat as she thought of her father so lonely for all those years and she ran over to hug him.

* * *

Manon's birthday, 7 July.

Noëmi

A couple of days later, Donnie and Noëmi were back together to mark Manon's birthday. Over time it became less painful but this was the first year that Noëmi would remember her mother as a mother herself. They sat in Donnie's garden, just the two of them.

"Last year you woke up for this day but I'm not sure you knew what day it was!"

"Mum's looking over me!"

Donnie was thoughtful.

"Maybe some angels are N, but mum's gone. Her love and all that she gave us lives on but she's not here."

Wanting to scream that he was wrong, Noëmi paused. *'Finally he's found the acceptance he needs.'*

"It's brutal but if I don't speak the truth I'm left in limbo. I'll never stop loving her, wishing for her and remembering her but she's not here anymore."

Donnie took her hand and they walked around his garden,

"She loved flowers, always hoping bougainvillaea would grow in our Scottish climate up in Kenmore! I persuaded her heathers and ferns held more potential! She sulked, like you sulk. Italian blood. Luckily roses grow everywhere and that was our flower. This Santoro rosa was taken from your grandparents' villa, they cultivated it." Donnie gestured to the flaming pink to burnt orange rose that stood gloriously before them.

"It was her favourite!"

Holding tight, they comforted each other.

"She would be so proud of you N. You know how much Bruno and Mani (Emmanuelle) would have loved her too. Life's cruel but we must live our best lives for her now."

CHAPTER 31 - A SIGN

Friday, 10 July 2020, High Heaton, Newcastle.

Sarai

As the weather improved, Donnie's badminton club moved outdoors and therefore the numbers could increase. Soon the whole group could practise at the same time. One evening as he watered his plants, Donnie's phone lit up with a message. Sarai heard it ping and looked at the handset.

'Hello how are you? Shall I pick you up for training tomorrow? It's on my way, Gina x'

Drying her hands she took the phone to Donnie. Silently she stood before Donnie who was adjusting his hose nozzle.

"Who is it? If it's a message can you just read it out?"

"I think it's private."

Donnie was confused,

"I'm sure it's fine Sarai, unless it's M15 giving me instructions for my next job!" He grinned at his own joke. Sarai read the message, "and there's a lower case x at the end which is usually the sign for a…"

"Yes alright!" Donnie snapped. He gave a huff and went to turn off his hose.

"Food's ready in five." Sarai put his phone on a patio chair and returned inside.

Lucia was already sitting up at the table, playing with her cutlery. Donnie joined them and washed his hands carefully. Silently they all moved around the kitchen in perfect unison, handing each other what they needed; their timing was perfect. Donnie broke the silence.

"A lift can't do any harm can it? I don't want to hurt her feelings. I'll message her back…"

"Sure."

"How should I sign it off? You know, finish it?"

"Depends how you feel, a kiss is always a kiss."

"I'll put a smiley face. There we go!" He pressed send.

"I spoke to Lucia's grandfather again this morning. I can now access the trust fund he set up for myself and Lucia, so I can pay you rent now."

"I don't want any rent, I've paid off my mortgage last year, it's fine Sarai, save for Lucia's future."
"I could rent my own place, it'd be smaller than here but…"

"No, everything works perfectly don't you think? Us together? I love helping with Lucia."

At speed he changed the subject, "I notice she's keen on those scooters. Like the one her little friend Millie had, I think we should get her one. A good quality one, plus a helmet for safety. I'll look online."

"He really wants us to move to Italy."

"What? Sorry, who?"

"Roberto, I didn't tell you before but he thinks it'd be good for Lucia to be near family and seeing as I have none…"

"But she's thriving here! Plus the language, she's already learning English and Vietnamese! It'd be too much to add Italian! Soon you can get your art business going again! There's definitely a market here in the UK!"

Donnie began to pace the kitchen. He moved a couple of cups from one side of the sink to the other and back again. Sarai was pensive, then resolved.

"With Covid it's probably not a good idea to share a car space with Gina, it could be dangerous."

Stopping Donnie threw out his arms.

"But I've said yes, it's too awkward now to change things! I'll wear a mask!"

"You should tell her to wear one too…at all times!"

"Great idea! I'll do that!"

Sarai wiped the pasta sauce off Lucia's face and the smile off Gina's.

* * *

The next evening, Gina duly arrived in a brand new rose gold Range Rover Evoque. She bounced down the drive in a tight white badminton top and shorts, her hair flicked in sync. "Gina's here!" Sarai called out as Donnie bounded down the stairs.

"Okay! One sec. Nice car Gina!"

"Yes, I got an upgrade from my company! I wasn't going to say no!" She shouted down the hallway as he rushed to hunt out a water bottle from the kitchen cupboard.

The women stood at the front door, Gina a dazzling vision of sporty perfection on the doorstep and Sarai in old jeans and black t-shirt, guarding the entrance like one of the Horae. She had put on gold dangly earrings as 'yummy mummies' always wore an accessory or two.

"Hello Sarai, how's home making?"

"Wonderful and you?" Sarai offered Gina a mask.

"Busy working from home! Secured my bonus today as I had a big presentation which went swimmingly. Yes! Now it's good to get out finally and do some exercise; thrash out that tension! I can feel my body seizing up from sitting around all day!" Gina was nothing but enthusiastic. She obliged and took a pale blue face covering. "Do you get time to exercise? It's important we keep up our activity as we reach middle age."

Sarai pursed her lips. An awkward silence followed. Luckily a delivery van pulled up and hauled a large package to the front gate. The driver called out:

"Delivery for McAllister!" He took a picture of the box by the gate and drove off. Moments later, Donnie bounded up the hallway like an excited puppy.

"Ah I love surprises!"

Sarai saw Gina's face light up. Yet as he flew past her and sprinted to the gate, her smile was lost. With gusto, he manoeuvred the delivery into the hallway. His eyes made conspiratorial contact with Sarai's,

"Hide that until later!" he whispered. He sanitised his hands, grabbed his sports bag and put on his mask.

"Well hello and goodbye!" He joked between the pair. Gina turned, flicked her hair and zapped her car keys. A stylish ping filled the street. Sarai slammed the front door shut.

Lucia sat at the kitchen table, putting primary coloured cups into a large tower. Sarai watched as her face concentrated on reaching as high as she could. The package caught her eye and she went to examine it. Addressed to Donnie, the outer box clearly showed a hot pink scooter with a matching helmet. Taking a breath, Sarai imagined her daughter's face. She pushed the box into the front room from where Donnie was usually working and shut the door. *'He wants to surprise her and see her joy when she opens it!'*

The house was tastefully furnished with Donnie's touch showing through. Family pictures of himself with Manon and Noëmi filled the walls. Thoughtfully he had made space for hers of Luca and those of Lucia. He and his late wife, Manon, had collected decorative glass and an electric blue, blown glass flame adorned the dresser in the kitchen. One day, seeing Lucia's eye on it, he had taken the toddler and sat with her to allow her to touch and feel it; she was enchanted. He had explained to Sarai that Manon had chosen it in Venice.

Sarai went through her evening routine. Lucia was fractious and started screaming as Sarai washed her hair. 'Keep yourself calm and your child will follow,' Donnie had advised in the past. She soothed Lucia and soon her daughter was relaxed and asleep. The house was silent. *'When will he be back?'* She wondered what she was feeling.

Donnie was dropped back by Gina, just before midnight. Lying in Noëmi's old bed, Sarai knew badminton finished at ten so she pondered why a fifteen minute journey had taken two hours. She heard laughter and the chatter of two people enjoying themselves, then Donnie's key. She listened, he was alone, he used the bathroom and shut his door. Exhaling sharply, she lay in her bed. In the half-light she could see some of Noëmi's childhood possessions. She gave a start as she caught sight of a 1960's Bonomi blonde, walking doll who seemed to resemble Gina but without the badminton racket. Turning her head, she noticed Noëmi's olive green, chalk painted bookcase, and sitting on its shelf, an exquisite leather bound book, embossed with gold, **Il mio primo libro di fiabe italiane**. She reached for it and flicked it open.

'Alla nostra carissima figlia, Noëmi. Divertiti ad imparare questa bellissima lingua!

Tutto il nostro amore mamma e papà'

'To our dearest daughter, Noëmi. Enjoy learning this beautiful language. All our love Mamma and Papa.'

Sarai felt the soft leather and saw small finger marks all over the book.

'It's a sign! Italy will be the best place for Lucia and me to live. Family is everything.'

CHAPTER 32 - LOWLIFE

Sunday, 12 July 2020.

Guy

'All units, domestic disturbance, distress reported, high priority, urgent response required. Grey Street.'

"Unit 6, Castle and Azzara, Status five!" Guy glanced over at Tariq, "Lowlife alert, here we go! Stab vest in place?"

"Yes and you?"
"Yes! Remember protocol for taser use, basically just don't."

"Acknowledged."

Sirens, blue lights flashing, they knew there was a danger to life. Running up the staircase, to the front door they pounded on it! "Police, open up!"

They could hear there were residents inside. Without delay, a man came to the door.

"Police, step aside!"

The man indicated for them to come in. The pair were going in anyway and entered the kitchen to find a flame haired woman sitting at the table and clutching at her wrist. Guy could see she was quietly weeping. Tariq gave a sharp intake of breath.

"Having been alerted due to cries of distress, we need to ascertain the individuals in the property. Do we have your permission to search? You understand we do not need that permission but it's reasonable for me to establish if you are co-operative."

"Yes, no problem it's just myself and my wife here but you're free to check." The man spoke softly. Guy knew the voice and was sure he recognised him.

"Thank you sir, Tariq, can you check the other rooms. Entry and non disturbance protocols. Respect for property."

With a nod, Tariq was off.

"Can I take your names please."

"Digby Honeyfield and my wife Alura Honeyfield."

Guy felt the hairs on his neck and he turned to the woman, her arms were covered in cuts and smeared in what looked like dark red, watery paint. Guy could smell the metal of blood. A large kitchen knife was on the floor.

"You need medical assistance. I'll call for help."

"No! I'm fine!" She insisted.

"I can't ignore this. Unit 6 requesting an ambulance at Apartment 7, Bank Buildings, Grey Street, domestic disturbance, female, lacerations to upper body."

He assessed her quickly and passed her a towel, one wound seemed deeper than the others. Next Guy visually checked Digby who had no obvious injuries, just hands covered in blood.

Tariq returned, "No one else in the property, no sign of forced entry or exit, everything as would be expected. Noted for the record."

Guy glanced at his colleague who seemed jittery, *'He'll need to get used to the blood.'*

Quickly Guy addressed Digby who was now sitting with his arms prone before him.

"Digby Honeyfield, I'm arresting you on suspicion of causing actual bodily harm. You do not have to say anything, but it may harm your defence if you do not mention when questioned something which you later rely on in court. Anything you do say may be given in evidence."

Without a word Digby nodded and lowered his head, Alura started to sob and tried to wipe her tears with her shoulders given her injured arms. Guy got on with recording the evidence as the ambulance arrived and Alura was taken to RVI for treatment. As she was led away by paramedics, she called out,

"Digby...Digby please..."

Guy noticed that Digby did not respond, nor did he glance her way. Without complaint or resistance, Digby then accompanied Guy and Tariq to the police station.

* * *

Tariq

Newcastle City Centre police station was receiving a new detainee. Feeling his pulse quicken, Tariq flustered over the check-in process. Grabbing a pen, he searched for the forms. At his side, Guy radioed in the details to RVI emergency department and dispatched one of his colleagues to interview Alura Honeyfield at her hospital bedside.

"Don't forget to register the form number on the database."

Guy reminded him.

With a lump in his throat, he gave a nod. Tariq's fingers shook as he logged on. *'Do I have a conflict of interest? Am I making all this invalid?'* He dropped the computer mouse. Leaning forward he put his head in his hands.

Guy

"Tariq, you're not well, take a break and let me do this one."

Guy waved his mentee off and turned his attention to Digby who was sitting staring into space. Quickly with a supporting police officer, they ushered Digby into a holding room. The reverend was lost as he sat at the plastic wood, melanin table, in the drab, grey pebble dashed room. Digby's hair was Sif like in the late sun that peeped through the high, thin windows. A plastic cup of water was given to him and Guy checked that he felt well before starting the recording.

"Reverend Digby Honeyfield, thank you for your cooperation. Location Newcastle Central Station, interview room four, in attendance DS Guy Castle and PC Finlay Turton. Time 10pm. Reverend, are you happy for us to address you as Digby?"

"Yes, yes…"

"In reference to the crime scene report, noted on file, Digby, can you explain how your wife got injured?"

"We had an argument."

"Go on…"

Digby exhaled loudly.

"We run a church, zee Newcastle Church of Glory. Each Sunday we 'ave a big meeting with a fairly high tech approach to worship so lots of videos, sound systems and so on. Now with being online that translates pretty decently…"

Digby continued to explain exactly what had happened previously.

Sunday, 12 July 2020, earlier that evening.

Digby

Entering the virtual church that evening, website worshippers could feel the onslaught of love from all sides and slides. The online comments buzzed.

"Hey great to see you!"

"Wonderful you're virtually here brother!"

"Awesome to be with you again, my best believer buddy!"

The chat was moving like the Spirit. It was as if the Texas Bible belt had tightened itself around Newcastle. The young congregation were indistinguishable from one another. Wholesome, devoted and donating. Hallelujah, Amen and God Bless masqueraded as conversation. Digby took control and visited different break out rooms to join the prayer huddles. Alura sat po faced in a box in the corner of the screen, fiddling with the presentation controls. Eventually the worshippers were brought together as one for the virtual service. Digby rallied his troops, the cause was the same, to love New CoG with every breath, with every word and with every donation. Sighing out loud, Alura was evidently bored by the spectacle,

"How many times do I have to sit through this drivel?"

Ignoring her comment, Digby concluded his sermon. Now the congregation were boxed in prayerful meditation. Aligned in gallery view, key church figures were praying. Holiness abounded. Suddenly a pre-recorded video blasted onto everyone's screen.

'Friends, you may know Digby as your leader but I know him as my husband, although really I know him as my cheating husband. An adulterer, a fake and a sex obsessed

git. Take a look, here's the evidence, just untrance yourselves for a moment and see him here going into the hotel, time after time with his mistress. The coat says it all cheater!'

"Pun queen, that's me!" Alura gave a snort of laughter as the scales fell from everyone's eyes and the pictures scrolled through onto each and every worshipper's screen.

'God bless you all! Lots of love Bertha!' was Mrs Honeyfield's final message.

* * *

Guy

Listening to Digby recount the events, Guy swallowed hard and thought about his spaniel Rolo being redeployed to another force to prevent a smirk that was desperate to creep all over his face. He wished he had seen the moment when Digby was taken down. *'His wife's got some front to do that! Maximum coverage! No one likes a love rat.'*

Digby cleared his throat.

"Zee meeting was terminated. Shocked, I escaped to the kitchen and poured a glass of red. Eventually she made an appearance. We started to argue about her big reveal, then I turned, picked up the knife to frighten her a bit and we started to fight. I cut her accidentally with zee knife."

"Can you tell me exactly what happened? Take it slowly." Guy drew a basic plan of the kitchen.

"She came in, started 'aving a go about me being unfaithful and I picked up zee knife to frighten her and we tussled with each other and she got cut by accident."

"Where were you standing when you picked up the knife?"

"I was sitting drinking wine."

"And then?"

"She came in, I grabbed zee knife and we began a fight."

"Again I need more detail."

"That's it! Wine, knife, strife. I've confessed, what's the problem?"

"Was the knife already on the table?"

"No, we keep them in the knife block over by zee kettle. They're Enso, top quality; Japanese."

"But you said you were sitting!"

Digby rubbed his chin and his hair darkened as the sun lowered. He was silent.

Guy studied the statement given by the neighbour who had called the police.

'The couple argued for around ten minutes, the woman's voice was particularly strident. The man sounded like he was either being sarcastic or trying to calm her down as he was not out of control, although I could not make out the words. After a moment of silence only he spoke in fairly controlled tones and I did hear him say 'No, stop!' Then she started to scream uncontrollably and I was truly scared as I've not heard that kind of cry before...'

Maybe Digby was more manipulative than anyone realised?

"Can you tell me about the argument when your wife entered the kitchen and you were drinking wine?"

"She wanted to know if I was cheating, when it started and whether it was serious. I answered her questions."

"The neighbour said she heard your wife lose control, can you tell me about that."

Digby sighed and examined his fingernails, which were a delicate shell like pink.

"She asked if I was in love, so I told her…" he finally met Guy's stare, "that I was and not with her!"

"You said you wanted to frighten her, why?"

"To stop her screaming?"

"Right, but that didn't work…"

"Yes we started fighting."

"Can you show me?"

Digby stood up and gave a simple performance that a five year old child could have delivered, then held his hands open,

"I'm sorry, I didn't mean to hurt her. It was accidental."

"Right, one final thing, who's Bertha?"

"It's a pet name we 'ave or rather we 'ad them for each other."

Guy had no desire to find out what Alura called Digby in long forgotten moments of tenderness.

"Okay thank you Digby. We'll be reviewing the evidence, I understand the video that she played in the service is being prepared for us now. We'll need to come back to you for more information but this gives us a starting point."

Guy left Digby with his fellow officer and went to find Tariq who was swivelling in his chair in the main office. Rolo jumped up to greet his master as Guy thumped down into a faux leather chair which jolted upright as he did so. He opened his emails.

The slurry of communications made him groan, then one caught his attention.

'Guy, just to let you know I'm still at RVI as Mrs Honeyfield is awaiting a mental health assessment. She refuses to press charges but we can still go ahead anyway if the evidence confirms an assault. RVI Consultant Alex James is going to call you with his report.'

"A call I actually want to receive!"

And as if voice activated, Guy's computer began beckoning another video chat.

"How's things, Alex?"

"Guy, manic, we're all Covid now, no beds for anything else. Two pathways in our department but soon if a major trauma comes in we'll be struggling. Staff are at breaking point."

"Any support we can offer in terms of manpower let us know, I know the Chief superintendent is looking at that. But what about Mrs Honeyfield?"

"She refuses to say anything other than that she and her husband had a tussle and she got hurt. However, I must tell you those wounds look self-inflicted. The expensive, silk designer shirt was undamaged and she kicked up a storm when we had to cut it off her. Wounds are very superficial, shallow and uniform. Only on her hands and wrists; on areas she could easily reach. No evidence of defence injuries, hands and face unaffected. None of this is consistent with a fight. If this goes further the lawyers will need to get her mental health assessed before putting her through a trial. I also think you need to dig a bit deeper into the background of our esteemed reverend. Trouble seems to follow him like a shadow. I'll email my report over to you once I get a minute. Sorry I have to go, we need to get to resus."

And Alex was gone.

Guy called out to Tariq, "Did you hear all that!" Then he sat back and flung Digby's statement on his desk. He pursed his lips.

"Someone's lying."

Scowling at his computer Guy clicked through the rest of his messages.

"Here it is! The video! The big reveal, I'm actually going to enjoy this!"

'Friends, you may know Digby as your leader…'

Settling in, Guy's lips were twitching. Then his face darkened. With a shriek Guy catapulted forward. Hand on his mouth he shook his head,

"No, no, no…"

Groaning with prolonged agony, Guy was suddenly sweating. As his heartbeat calmed, he began to hear muffled hiccoughs. From behind the toughened plastic screen, he peered to scan the office. Work from home meant that it was empty apart from himself and Tariq, two metres away at a light oak desk. Surrounded by a number of files, empty coffee cups and a picture of his girlfriend, Tariq was hunched, his back jerking every now and then. Then his chair darted backwards and Tariq fell forward, knocking over a frosted blue paperweight he had been given for completing his first trainee year. The thud made Rolo jump up. Guy waited. No doubt sensing the gravity of Guy's stare, Tariq pushed a folder towards his boss and whispered.

"Guy, I need to talk to you, I've got myself in a mess."

CHAPTER 33 - TELL ME IT'S NOT TRUE!

Monday, 13 July 2020.

Guy

Guy was beside himself. He had not slept. Everything was dark. Worry weighed him down.

'Laura, a doctor friend of mine can put your consultant in touch with a centre that can offer a new treatment. It's getting good results. Msg me your specialist's details. Thx Guy.'

Checking his phone, Guy huffed. *'Why hasn't she replied?'* Messages from Laura began to fade. He wondered how she was. He found it hard to comprehend that she would die so young. Life was brutal. He began to feel his pulse racing. Deciding he wanted to talk to her one last time and with no reply from her personal number, he messaged his mother.

'Mum, what's the name of Laura's accountancy firm in London?'

'Reeves, Dicken and Demarillac.'

He quickly looked up the number and called the main

switchboard.

"RDD, how can I help you?"

"Laura Randall please."

"Can I ask who's calling?"

"Guy Castle."

A few moments and he was through to another office.

"Major Accounts, how can I help?"

"Please could I talk to Laura Randall?"

"Right, what's it regarding?"

"I'm a friend, Guy Castle."

"I'm afraid Laura's not working here anymore."

"Oh my God!"

"Sorry, Mr Castle, is there something else we can help you with?"

Guy was desperate. Never had he faced loss. Life had always been as it should. Happy and straightforward. He messaged his sister.

'Poppy, what's happened to Laura? I can't get hold of her. I feel dreadful. I can't bear to think of her suffering. I'm scared x'

'Guy just stay calm. I'll get back to you, Pops xxx'

Guy spoke to Yumi and explained all that he felt.

"I know it's guilt because I couldn't love her the way she wants me to, but I can't bear to think of her not being alive."

Yumi understood. Guy was a good man.

Within the hour Poppy rang her brother.

"Guy…"

"Tell me it's not true!" His voice was pure theatre.

"Yeah, it's not true." Poppy's voice was flat.

"She's not dead?"

"Not even close. Alive and kicking…ass, I imagine from what I knew of her!"

"Poppy, that's not funny."

"And neither is lying to your former partner that you've got a terminal illness. For fuck's sake think of all the people actually dying of cancer will you, well not you but that fuckwit ex-girlfriend of yours!"

"Sorry?"

"She lied to you! She never had cancer! She's now moving to the US with that RDD firm! She's absolutely fine! I asked her parents! Nothing! She was just trying to get you back or get back at you maybe? She's planning a new life in New York now!"

* * *

If Guy were cynical he had Yumi to help him not to be.

"She was just desperate. Not saying I understand why she would do that but she was just scheming, going for the prize!"

Guy thought long and hard. He rang his mother. He could not comprehend why Laura would act in this way. Maybe everyone was trying to spare him pain? Maybe this was a double bluff? As a detective he examined information from all angles.

"Mum, is what Poppy told me true?"

Giving long sighs, his mother replied, "Yes I'm afraid Laura's had some mental health issues. She never had cancer. She hijacked her father's story, he's now in a hospice. Horrible woman, what a thing to do. Let's hope therapists in the US are ready for her. Do you want her contact details to let her know how you feel about her lies?"

"No it's okay Mum, the woman I once knew is gone and I've said goodbye to her. I'm done."

He blocked her number from his phone.

* * *

Quayside, Newcastle.

Guy

Upset, Guy called Marcus to see if he was free for a drink by the river. Amazingly he was and the two friends met to talk. Walking along the Quayside, they strolled in the evening sunshine. Joggers, cyclists and skateboarders dodged past them as they ambled along with Rolo. Pubs had table service outside so they knew they could catch a drink at the end of the walk. Sitting outside the Pitcher and Piano, Guy updated Marcus on Laura.

"No! I can't believe that! When I was training we had a patient once who did the same, shaved his entire body. With patient confidentiality the GP couldn't do anything when his wife came in for anti-depressants. All he could do was tell her to accompany her husband to his appointments. Eventually the truth came out."

"What kind of a person would do that? She's not the girl I once knew. And the worst thing, her horrible deception has cast a shadow over our whole pregnancy. It's unforgivable! Why do people lie like that?"

They sat at a bench and gazed out at the water. The river was expansive and its dark waters were agitated.

"Marcus, everything's too much. I can't believe what Laura did to me. I've got problems at work, Tariq's been moonlighting. I just don't know who I can trust anymore!" He omitted to mention the video and the pictures that Tariq had shown him. Pictures he never wanted to see. Marcus sighed.

Guy continued. "I mean how do *you* know who you can trust? I mean really trust?"

Marcus replied.

"I know, for me it's only N, really, oh and my family, and you and Yumi. Yeah Alex, Pen, Madhav and Esme at work too. I can trust all these people…Joel yes definitely him…Donnie, of course, Frank and Val have my back so them too. And of course Sarai, she's solid."

Noting his friend's serene face, Guy wondered how Marcus could be so affable. Was the police force making him cynical? Marcus could see only the good in people. They finished their drinks and strolled back to Guy's car. They stopped outside Marcus' small, terraced house with its bright yellow front door and matching flower boxes. Geraniums, marigolds and petunias burst out in a shout of colour. Noëmi was Donnie's daughter.

'I'm his friend, I have to tell him.' Guy cleared his throat but Marcus was already talking.

"Thanks for the lift, mate, I'm that excited, on Wednesday it's our three year anniversary of N and I getting back together! And this year it's the ten year anniversary of us falling in love. I have to block out the years apart, it's too difficult, I was so lost. Can you believe, ten years of true love! I hope lockdown will be over soon so I can take N away for the night! Every day I love her more!"

Forlorn attempt to do the 'right thing' abandoned Guy leant across and opened the car door. The men fell into a bear hug and Marcus disappeared into the sunny front door. Guy groaned. Parking up outside his and Yumi's flat, he noticed that Marcus had left his Bathing Ape hoodie.

'He was so excited to get that in Sapporo!'

Guy recalled queuing together in the snow. Warmed by the memories of their friendship he was conflicted.

Another disturbed night followed for Guy. People lied, people cheated. Having to choose between hurting his friend and defending the truth, he was conflicted. Finally, being a man of principles he decided to confront Noëmi directly.

Tuesday, 14 July 2020, Jesmond, Newcastle.

Noëmi

Sitting in their small garden Noëmi sighed with contentment. *'Promotion! Strong, self-aware woman juggling career and family!'* A cup of tea in her hand, finally she could relax. She had been selected as the new Head of Sixth Form at St Wolbodo's school. Her mind raced with her interview performance. *'That answer I gave about promoting allied healthcare courses was a real game changer.'*

Infant gurgles of delight were interrupted by the persistent drilling of the local woodpecker. A song thrush repeated his pretty tune and a light breeze swirled in the high trees. Assembled on a multicoloured blanket Bruno and Emmanuelle bashed bright, shiny, jingling, 'educational', plastic toys at each other. Summer warmth breathed on them. Life was good. She shut her eyes.

"Have you got a minute?" She recognised his voice coming through the side gate.

"Guy! Hello! Two metres remember, don't break the law!" Grinning, she jumped up, delighted to have adult company.

"Of course." He seemed so serious.

"I wish I could give you an enormous hug!" Noëmi put her arms around herself to demonstrate how hard she wanted to hold him.

Guy was unsmiling, "Yeah you like all that don't you."

"Of course! I'm Italian!"

'Why's he so moody? He must be dealing with a difficult case.'

Chips off the block, Bruno and Emmanuelle giggled and lifted their arms to Guy who knelt to pat their heads. Unable to resist, he cuddled both the babies. Noëmi felt warm.

"Tough day?"

"Yeah you could say that." Without making eye contact, Guy started pacing.

"Guy, sit down, you're making me nervous. Do you want a cuppa?"

"Noëmi, we need to talk." Guy fixed his jaw, he avoided her stare. "How could you?"

"Guy?"

"Have you thought about Marcus? What will all this do to him?" Fists clenched, he leant against the fence panel and lowered his head.

Noëmi backed away, heart racing, palms sweating.

"G…Guy?"

A deep breath and eyes wiped, Noëmi held her children close as Guy walked past her.

"Guy what's wrong?"

She could feel her face crumbling. Her throat was choking her. Bruno pulled her hair.

Guy put his hands to his head.

"Why? He's the best person and after all that happened…how could you?"

"I know but I'm young…I need to have more in my life!"

Bruno, whose gaze had not left Guy, began to wail. Emmanuelle joined her brother in a high pitched scream. Noëmi shook. Guy walked to the end of the garden and stood statue-like at the end. Without looking round he spat out "You're unbelievable!" And walked out.

Quivering, she knelt with the babies and consoled them, her own eyes filling with tears.

Comforting herself, Noëmi moved to the kitchen and texted Marcus.

'Guy's so angry with me for taking the promotion :(I feel horrible x'

'??? He's just stressed! He's had that Laura stuff to deal with plus he's investigating some kind of cheating case. You need to progress in your career #partnership! x'

Noëmi's hand was shaking as she put her mobile down. She paced the room, the toddlers were holding onto the furniture and trying to balance. Out of the corner of her eye she noticed Emmanuelle rocking on the stainless steel kitchen bin. Falling, catching, hearts beating. Having dived to the floor to save her child, she enveloped her and cried bitter tears, *'Guy wouldn't look at me!'*

Before she could make sense of anything her mobile went, it was Sarai. She was talking at speed.

"Noëmi, it's your father, he's been admitted to RVI with Covid. He's in good spirits and conscious but having difficulty breathing. I have to isolate now with Lucia, I've got a number the ambulance team gave me, I'll text it to you."

Everything was too much, she began to sob.

CHAPTER 34 - NONON AND MAËMI

Noëmi

Hospital rules meant that those with Covid were not allowed visitors in hospital. They were accommodated in separate wards and only permitted to communicate with the outside world via their mobiles. Having received the devastating news, Noëmi messaged Marcus who was working on the Covid pathway. Next she rang her father.

"Mr McAllister's phone!" A nurse answered.

She explained who she was and was passed to her father.

"N! Don't worry…" He wheezed. "I'm fine…" A long pause. "Damn Covid…" Another pause as he caught his breath, "…Sarai…may need…help. Shopping and so on?"

The nurse came back on the line.

"His stats are fine, he needs to rest. We're not ventilating as that may reduce his lung strength. He'll get oxygen if he needs it. In comparison with other patients, he's doing very well. He just needs rest."

Marcus messaged her back.

'N don't worry, he's good. I'm checking whenever I can. It's busy here! xxx'

Everything that anchored her was unravelling. Her father ill in hospital and Guy's contempt. Marcus was exhausted and the children exhausted her. Reminders of her mother lying in her hospital bed haunted her. Lonely and afraid, she prayed,

"Dad please don't die, please!"

* * *

Late November 2006, Perthshire, Scotland.

Noëmi

Little Noëmi sat alone outside the ward on a hard plastic chair. She was thirteen, awkward and scared. No one had fully explained to her exactly why her mother had suddenly been taken to hospital.

Her mother Manon was a primary school teacher, full of energy and smiles. Her father Donnie worked for a transport company, Highland Vehicle Company, in their logistics department. **HVC for your HGV** was their strapline. The family's routine was very much fixed. Noëmi's mother would meet her from school and they would discuss their days as they took the bus back from Aberfeldy to their home in Kenmore. Once home they would settle in their bright kitchen, chatting, catching up on school work and preparing food together. Her father, Donnie, would return home around 6pm and the very first thing he would always do would be to embrace her mother. Not a quick hug or a rushed peck on the cheek, a long meaningful caress. Noëmi would watch as he stroked her mother's hair and gazed at her with a love she did not really understand. Her mother would respond similarly. *'Grown ups are weird!'*

One day as they arrived home, Noëmi noticed that her mother just went and sat on the sofa. The following day she did that again and by the third day she took herself to bed. Feeling lonely she waited for her father who immediately insisted that Manon see a doctor. The week after Manon was in hospital.

Noëmi read up on leukaemia and found out as much as she could. There were comings and goings, hospital appointments, telephone calls and lonely trips on the bus to and from school. Her grandparents arrived from Leeds and Italy. Now she understood things were more serious than anticipated.

Outside the ward, she waited on the hard chair and tried to read the book they were studying in English.

'And at home by the fire, whenever you look up there I shall be—and whenever I look up, there will be you.' (Far From the Madding Crowd by Thomas Hardy).

She opened the large envelope of school work that had been sent to her, whilst she was off school. The teachers had made a grand effort. Worksheets and instructions from all her subjects were collated into one neat document. From her tutor group, a card, with a rose on the front, was also enclosed. She felt her hands begin to shake as she opened it.

Sorry your mum's not well xxx

Hope your mum's better soon!

Missing you, sending your mum lots of healing powers! x

Messages of hope. Her skin felt hot then cold. A nurse appeared at her side and spoke gently to her.

"Noëmi can you come this way? Your dad needs to talk to you."

Her throat was lumpy. Something was wrong. Stuffing the envelope and book into her school bag, she was led into a small side office off the ward where her mother was sleeping. Piles of papers had been hastily pushed to one side and two chairs were now next to each other. A box of tissues dominated the desk. Her heart began to race. Her father was standing looking out of the second floor window. He was trembling. The nurse indicated for Noëmi to sit down and scurried out, shutting the door with an ominous click. Noëmi could hear the echoing sounds of the hospital staff at work in the outside corridor. The odd shout and occasional laugh broke up the hum of mid-morning activity. Her father turned and sat next to her. His eyes were red, he took deep breaths.

"N, you know mum's not at all well. You understand what leukaemia does to someone?"

Noëmi nodded. She had researched it online when she heard the diagnosis.

"N, the doctors have been working hard but things are not going to plan. Mum's too sick."

Noëmi wanted to block her ears. Her father put his arms around her and she fell into him, beginning to cry. In a whisper he slowly explained,

"N, she's not going to make it…we don't know how long she's got but… it's days not weeks." They both held the other and sobbed. Neither could contain the tears. No more words were needed. After a while they both knew that everyone's pain would only increase.

Arrangements were made to move Manon to a hospice for palliative care. The advantages were that Donnie and Noëmi could stay with her in a special suite and the staff were experienced with helping families like theirs. The three received caring advice; Manon was advised to write letters whilst she was well enough and she composed three; one for her daughter, one for her parents and one for her husband. Doctors managed her physical pain and therapists prepared the three for the wait. Never before had Noëmi had to think about death. It was the stuff of books, the news and TV shows. Death was elsewhere. Death was faraway. Death was not real. Now she realised that death was her whole life.

After two weeks, Noëmi was told it was time to say her final goodbye to her mother. Kindly it was made clear that this would be the last chance as Manon was now sleeping most of the day. Buoyed up with drugs Manon was sat up and made ready by the nurses.

Entering the now familiar bedroom, Noëmi was to go in alone. She knew her father was close but it was her time with her mother. Amongst the fresh flowers, she noticed the fir tree ornament that she had given her mother for her 38th birthday in July. In fact all her little gifts were on that bedside table; the painted plate that said 'Mummy', the mug with a swallow on it, the London paperweight from the school trip to the theatre and the tartan beret from Edinburgh. Noëmi tried to swallow. Tears pricked her eyes. Upon seeing her daughter Manon bounced up and forward in the bed and smiled like bright sunshine.

There's a mistake! She's better! Look, she's so well! She's going to be okay!'

Noëmi ran and flung her arms around her,

"Mamma! I love you so much Mamma!"

The familiar laugh shook through her body,

"My little Noëmi! How I love you! My beautiful child!"

They smiled at each other. *'She's not going to die! The doctors were wrong! There's been a miracle! God heard my prayers!'*

Manon pointed to the small woodland ornament.

"Do you remember that time when we got lost in the forest? We'd been making up stories about two fairy spirits and how they lived in the tall fir trees! You gave them names!"

"Yes! Nonon and Maëmi!"

"Ah! You were so clever coming up with those names! But you know, I think we're a bit like those spirits! We have bits of each other in us!"

"Mamma I have your fun spirit!"

"And I have your kind soul, Noëmi. We need to remember and take comfort in that." Her mother grasped her hand.

"But Mamma you're better! You're going to be okay?"

"No, Noëmi I'm so sorry, I can't get better, I have to go, but remember we've had the best life together! I need you to live your best life and carry my love with you! Can you do that?"

Her throat was choking her, the tears unstoppable. She nodded. Her mother put her finger under Noëmi's chin and raised her face.

"Noëmi, I just need to ask one thing of you; look after dad, it's going to be too hard for him. Help him to find a path to happiness again. I can't bear to think of him sad."

"I promise I will Mamma."

"You know my heart is always with you and that I love you."

She clutched onto her mother and cried those tears that only come when your heart is truly breaking. Her mother lay back and stroked her daughter's soft hair. In time her breathing was shallow and they were peaceful, her mother was now sleeping. Noëmi watched her chest rise and fall. She stroked her hand and kissed her face. A knock at the door and her father entered quietly and came and just held her. No words. He just held her a while. A final kiss on her forehead and they left. She had said goodbye. Later that night Manon died in Donnie's arms.

The next morning they left the hospice with the small bag of Manon's possessions and some paperwork. A hospital car drove them home in silence to an even more silent house. Her mother's things were everywhere but she was gone. Noëmi sat in the bare wintered garden as the grey rain fell and she cried. She was sure her father was doing the same thing somewhere in the house. She prayed that her father would never die.

* * *

Sarai

Sarai had noticed Donnie's cough and his tiredness. It was she who had insisted he go to hospital. Now in isolation both she and her daughter Lucia were perfectly well. Watching her daughter run around Donnie's well stocked garden, Sarai paced up and down the patio, phone in hand. Her body trembled. The shock of losing Luca had made her afraid of everything. She was living the eternal separation that death was. Donnie offered her help and comfort. He understood. Here she was without him, she felt his absence.

'When I feel the panic he tells me to breathe and occupy myself with a small job or activity. I should tell the badminton club that he has Covid.'

Sarai searched for the club newsletter that was on the fridge door under the Isle of Skye magnet. She flicked through it and called the club secretary.

"Hello!"

Sarai recognised the voice. She felt deflated. *'It's Donnie who matters, not me.'*

"Gina, it's Donnie's house guest, Sarai."

"Hello! How's homemaking! It must be such a pain having him work from home the whole time!"

Sarai bit her lip and gave a scoff, "Oh yes! So true! Gina, I need

to let you know that Donnie's in hospital with Covid…"
Gina gave a scream.

"…he's fine, doing very well but they need to keep him in for a few days to check his lungs and make sure he fully recovers."

"Oh no! Can I talk to him?"

"Yes, just call his mobile, the nurses are managing his communications and they will get back to you. I've let his daughter know." Sarai felt her heart race. She was scared.

"Maybe I should take over being the point of contact? Would that help? You must be so busy!"

"Oh! …err…no…it's fine I can manage…"

"It's just with Donnie and I being so close…"

"I've given his daughter's details as next of kin…but he's doing well. No need for anyone to worry!"

"I'll phone the hospital now. Thank you for letting me know."

Gina ended the call. Sarai sat on the green swing seat. Lucia was pretending to water plants, just as she had seen Donnie do so many times. She ran from flower to flower with a hot pink watering can, decorated with big daisies. Her giggles filled the evening. Sarai thought of when she had found Donnie struggling to catch his breath. Sitting in his front room, sweating and beginning to cough. She remembered the pink scooter he had wrapped in bright, balloon birthday paper. He had been keeping it beside him, ready for Lucia's actual birthday the next day. She recalled his excitement.

'So close?' Suddenly Sarai was overwhelmed. She began to pray. *'Donnie please just get better! Don't die! Please!'*

CHAPTER 35 - BAILING OUT

14 July 2020, Newcastle Central Police station.

Digby

Lockdown offered some a place to hide and others a place in the spotlight. Suddenly obsessive about the law, Digby asked about his rights as he was bailed.

"Obviously I'm not permitted to live with my wife, so can I create a new bubble?"

Behind a perspex screen, PC Turton laboriously filled out a form by hand with a sticky Bic biro before answering.

"Indeed, you must not return to Mrs Honeyfield's address and you must inform us of your whereabouts, which must not be within 200 metres of your wife's abode."

Through the small window, he passed the form to Digby who completed it and returned the paperwork back to the officer.

"We will retain your passport here whilst you're on bail. You must check in everyday and if you have symptoms, you must do so online. Instructions are in this letter here."

And just like that the Newcastle Church of Glory suspended its services and Digby disappeared into the shadows.

Grey Street, Newcastle.

Alura

For her part Alura was similarly dispatched from RVI with instructions on checking in with her support worker who was monitoring her domestic situation and mental health. Transported by taxi to her home, she sat alone in her kitchen. Heavy silence overwhelmed her.

'He's gone, no, he's coming back, he's never gone before. He said he loved her. He said he loved her, his true love, his kindred spirit, his baby. Where is he?'

Alura paced her kitchen. She grabbed a glass of wine and her phone.

Jesmond, Newcastle.

Noëmi

Babies in bed, Noëmi was flopped on the sofa with Marcus. Neither could be bothered to move. Her phone buzzed impatiently.

"Don't answer that. Your dad's fine, I checked before I came home. Still on oxygen but fine." Her throat was lumpy. *'Dad will get better, dad will get better…'*

"Let me see who it is! Yumi's got to thirty-five weeks and is a nervous wreck with worry!"

"Don't stress, she calls me if she's worried! Pregnancy hotline!"

Noëmi scowled.

"Oh my God, you're jealous! Ha! I love it!"

She defiantly grabbed her mobile and answered.

"As long as it's not…" Marcus flopped sideways onto one of their once white linen cushions.

"Alura!" She saved Marcus from his gaffe. "What! No!..." she listened intently, poking Marcus as he rolled his eyes and pointed at his watch. Finally, the call ended.

"Digby's left her! She has no idea where he is!"

"That's good, no one should stay with a cheat. Plus you know he's accused of a hate crime against Sarai, the Honeyfield's were her landlords!"

"My God! That's unbelievable! Oh there's more, Alura's been at RVI, they had a fight and he attacked her! He's been arrested."

"What the?" Marcus sat up. "What happened? Is she okay?"

"Not sure, he was brandishing a kitchen knife. She sounds shocked. I'm worried about her!"

Shaking his head, he grabbed the remote and put the TV on. She wondered where Digby was and whether Bri was still involved with him; lockdown had stilted the conversation between herself and her friend. Bri was always strangely vague and never free to even meet for a walk. She messaged her friend.

'Bri, how's things? Digby's attacked his wife, thought you should know.'

Bri did not reply.

* * *

The big reveal had caused a schism in the Newcastle Church of Glory. The Grand Canyon sized gulf between those who believed Digby was a victim of a hate campaign and those who thought him a cheating fraud could not be bridged by the pastoral team. The church shut down. For those in denial, the Newcastle Church of Jehovah, New COJ, rose up Phoenix like from the New CoG ashes. For those for whom the scales had fallen from their eyes, there was social media. Tianna had blocked Keziah's number but Louisa had not had any need to. Her social media feeds still had algorithms to receive New CoG updates. Lying on her bed one sunny afternoon, contemplating revising the muscles of the leg, Louisa burst out laughing at a feed on her homepage.

'We urge you to pray for our dear leader who is a victim of a hate campaign by immoral women #jezebel #digbyisinnocent'

'Immoral women rock!' Louisa was enjoying this. In the comments, she clicked on the random picture of a pair of doves which was attached with the caption.

'Yeah here's the big reveal, he got caught out shagging away from home! Lol'

A link followed. Louisa clicked on it and saw the first part. Not bothering to watch the full video clip, she instantly shared it with her friends putting **LMFAO** next to it. As the clip played on she sat up in horror.

*"*Oh my God!"

She desperately tried to delete her share but it was no longer possible.

PART THREE – RESULTS

Tu seras pour moi unique au monde.
Je serai pour toi unique au monde…

Le Petit Prince, Antoine de Saint-Exupéry.

CHAPTER 36 - JEZEBEL

Wednesday, 15 July 2020.

Marcus

Lockdown continued and to offset the gloom, *cats going out more than their owners* memes flooded the internet. Life was magnified through the lens of separation and isolation. Social media came into its own. In a vain attempt to continue as normal, Marcus and Noëmi had plans to celebrate one of their many romantic anniversaries. However, her father's hospitalisation prompted them to defer to a quiet dinner at home that evening and they decided to celebrate in August when they could enjoy the 'eat out to help out' scheme.

This was the morning that Noëmi was due back to work to confirm the details of her new contract. Exceptional clearance had been given for her to attend socially distanced meetings at St Wolbodo's school. Thus the McKenzie family were experiencing the reality of being working partners with kids. For Marcus, no more strolling out of the door with an insulated cup of coffee; leaving the house was now a military operation.

They had carefully researched the childcare options and had settled on Busy Tykes nursery as it had a solid security system.

The gates required fingerprint recognition for staff to open them. Parents were recognised using facial identification software and a security guard was on duty at all times. With the children's bags packed with nappies, bottles and a change of clothes times two, the family were ready to go. Noëmi was applying her make-up in the hall mirror. Marcus had prepared the car seats. He stood at the front door and they went over their drill.

"The one who drops off texts the other to confirm that they're in the nursery. If the one not dropping off doesn't get a text, they ring the nursery to check."

Having been part of a team desperately trying to revive a two year old who had been mistakenly left in a car for eight hours, Marcus was particularly cautious. Pulse quickening, he distracted himself with the morning chores. Flashes of the forgotten toddler jumped into his mind. Unconscious and dangerously dehydrated, the tiny child was lost on the vast emergency department couch. Small blonde curls had brushed his hand as he inserted the nasogastric tube. Another team member was working on the intravenous tube. Suddenly all hearts stopped. Alex James grabbed the defibrillator and double checked the paediatric pads.

"Everyone clear! I'm clear! Shocking."

They waited. Nothing. *'Come on, come back. Please God!'* Marcus prayed. Alex repeated the process. Nothing. And again. Finally a faint heartbeat. His observations were the worst Marcus had seen. Respiratory rate was scoring poorly. Heart rate dropping. Blood pressure falling. The fluids needed to move quicker into the body. Where was hope?

"We won't forget the plan."

"Yes, no matter how busy or late we are, they come first!" Noëmi agreed.

Noëmi

As Marcus put the seats in the car, Bruno and Emmanuelle toddled around and threw things at each other. As he returned, he took her hand.

"Good luck today! I'm proud of you, N!"

"I love you! Today's a special day, hey?"

"The best day of my life take two!"

"And mine!"

They giggled. His arms around her were strong, he smelt good, she could feel his breath on her neck. Their quick embrace was interrupted by toddlers exploring new ways to harm themselves. They scooped them up as they both toddled towards the open front door.

"No sense of danger!"

She could hear the traffic as she shut the front door and she shuddered. *'Bad memories. Keep busy.'* She knelt down to finish preparing the babies. Noëmi was sanitising Bruno's hands when a message on her phone interrupted the morning chores. She stood and opened up the text, *'Tianna? Sweet! She's probably wishing me luck!'* Next she furrowed her brow, Tianna's message was to the point;

'N, what the actual fuck is this?'

Noëmi put her baby down and took a breath. Next she saw the link Louisa had shared to a news channel that Gen Z and Millennials used for pictures of baby sloths, chilli eating challenges and funny stories about life. She clicked. A video played out.

'Congreve was right when he said that hell hath no fury like a woman scorned! A Newcastle preacher has had his

cheating revealed to the world over Zoom! #weirdcovidtimes!'

She gave a yelp. Marcus was now holding Emmanuelle. He came and peered over her shoulder. A picture of Digby in full reverend mode was on her screen. His holy hands were raised. His pious eyes were shut.

"No way! Ha, it's our favourite preacher!" Marcus burst out laughing.

"Hilarious! What in *God's name* has happened to him then!" Noëmi was intrigued.

More Bible belt style pictures of Reverend Honeyfield in action flashed up. The accompanying mid Atlantic drawl explained.

'Digby Honeyfield is used to saving people from hell, but it seems his wife has just given him a one way ticket to the fiery furnace. Hell hath no fury like a woman on Zoom! During their online service last weekend, his wife used Zoom to out him to their loyal congregation as a love cheat. As the prayerful watched, she played a video which clearly captured pictures of him with his Jezebel! In a twist of the devil, it seems his mistress is the wife of the Newcastle RVI poster boy, Dr Marcus McKenzie! She didn't stay home and stay safe now did she!'

The images then changed. The cheetah coat going into the hotel, Digby with his hands on Noëmi's face, Digby and Noëmi laughing at the bar together, Noëmi in the coat, a back view of them entering a hotel bedroom. Each picture seemed to be on the screen for eternity. Anyone who knew Digby and Noëmi would clearly recognise them. The montage was peppered with added text; kinky gifs and racy emojis. She screamed like a bobcat. The children burst into tears. Marcus stood like a statue, staring.

"What the fuck? What is that?" He said.

She could only yelp. After a minute or so, he turned to face her. His silence unnerved her.

"That hotel, the Radisson, you left your phone there! Oliver, the security guard, brought it back to me!"

"No, I went for a meeting! For the school charity! That's all!"

"The meeting was in January, the phone was left in December after your Christmas meal with him!" Marcus turned away. His mouth quivered. He was angry.

"No, I went to Frank and Val's! Ask them! This has been faked somehow, I'm not involved with Digby!"

Marcus put his daughter down and sat on the sofa. Slowly he shook his head.

"The only time we've been apart is Guy's stag do…he came to that meeting when I was in Prague! To our house!"

"Marcus this is a mistake, someone's got the wrong idea, that's not me, of course those pictures in the bar, yes but that was the noma meeting! Ask Bri! Both times she was there too! I promise I've done nothing to hurt us!"

Their phones were buzzing away like fireflies. He grabbed his and put it on silent. She did the same. Sitting, thinking he was eerily quiet. The children gurgled and giggled behind them.

Finally, he spoke,

"N, I get it. I know you'd never cheat. I don't understand those pictures but it's true that images can be manipulated or faked; that happened to me, *remember*? I know you, I know us, you'd never do that to me, to the children. We had that misunderstanding before. I'll not get caught out this time…but you've meddled your way into…a big mess!"

"I went to a school meeting…for charity!"

"And I told you not to! Why on earth did you still go? Our children are way more important!"

Noëmi felt red with shame. She whispered.

"I was trying to get something on that man! For Tianna!"
"Exactly and look at what you've done! You've made an absolute fool of us…of me! Look at this stuff! They've named me!"

"What about me? I'm being outed as some kind of a horrible love cheat!"

"I know it's not true! Unlike you I'm not jumping to the first conclusion in spite of how it all looks! *Remember?*" He emphasised his final point. She knew he was referring to the time she had walked out when Evan was scheming.

"That's mean! And actually you did! *Remember?*" This time she was referring to when he assumed the texts to John Dyer were from her. He ignored her comment.

"N, this is so embarrassing! I'm representing the fight against Covid and I'm up for a speciality training position soon. What will everyone think? I have a reputation!"

"And I don't!" she thought on, "…and being called the RVI poster boy doesn't matter then?"

"Anyone could see this! You'd better think of how you're going to sort this mess out! Honestly sometimes you're just…so…useless!"

He stood up and gathered the children's bags. He gave a loud huff as he put his rucksack onto his shoulders. Without looking at her, he took the toddlers by the hand and started for the front door. Shaking his head, he left without a word. She heard the car. Trembling, she rewatched the clip and examined the pictures carefully. *'How on earth? I need dad!'* After a few minutes she rushed to the toilet and was violently sick.

Having sat for a while, she was still nauseous. On their white shelving unit, she noticed a picture of the four of them. Following her attack, it was the first one they had taken together with the babies after she had come round. Marcus' face was turned towards hers. He absolutely beamed. Love radiated from him to her as light from the sun. Similarly, she was gazing into his eyes with the same pure delight. Her hair had been brushed and the bandage around her head looked like a hippy hair band. Each was holding a baby, wrapped in colour coded blankets. Yellow for Bruno and white for Emmanuelle. *'Am I of sound mind?'* Holding back the tears, she finished getting herself ready but her eyes kept filling. As she prepared to leave, the post arrived with an official looking letter addressed to her. *'Must be my new contract!'* she breathed. Tearing it open, she gave a gasp. Formal looking papers, with a covering letter requesting her to study certain pages carefully. Flicking through the legal document from **Fisher, Seaford & sons, Solicitors since 1899,** her name jumped out in section eight.

Adultery cases only:

Mrs Alura Honeyfield vs Rev Digby Honeyfield

8.1 Name of person your spouse committed adultery with (co-respondent)

First name(s): Noëmi

Last name: McKenzie (née McAllister)

A fox-like scream filled the room. Angrily she threw her head back and stared at the ceiling which as ever gave no answers. *'God no, what the hell is happening. What an absolute mess.'* Resolving to call the lawyers, she stuffed the letter into her work bag and stomped out of the house.

CHAPTER 37 - WHAT HAVE YOU DONE?

Wednesday, 15 July 2020, Newcastle Royal Victoria Infirmary (RVI).

Marcus

The whole of RVI had been transformed into a Covid-19 response operation. Different pathways for patient care were efficient but they needed constant monitoring. PPE stocks were in short supply and clinicians were exhausted. Once trussed up in their gowns, aprons and visors, staff were at full pelt. Marcus was on the frontline. They received the most desperate patients and determined their care plans. Surgical theatres had been turned into treatment areas and almost all the beds in the hospital were for Covid patients. In the midst of the relentless onslaught of intubating patients and requesting chest X-rays, Marcus was sure to do one thing before anything else: he sent the text on his phone that the children were safely in nursery. He felt himself relax. He had sought permission to have his phone on him for this teething period and Alex had agreed.

St Wolbodo's, Durham.

Noëmi

Similarly, St Wolbodo's had been transformed by the Covid containment operation. Daily testing of masked students, teachers in PPE and smaller classes. Everyone was equally exhausted. Noëmi was experiencing this for the first time as her maternity leave was coming to an end. She had formally been offered the post of Head of Sixth Form and had come in specially to plan for that next step. She noted that the text from Marcus had arrived and she felt herself relax, *'Right time to work!'*

Towards the end of a long, socially distanced day, she flew out of the door to pick up Bruno and Emmanuelle. The Busy Tykes nursery manager had been quite clear in her terms; collect by 6pm, after that time the fine was a pound per minute per child and at 7pm social services would be phoned. Noëmi was on the train to the nursery, which was located just by the main station in Newcastle. Everything was going to plan, *'We can do this!'* She thought to herself.

Later that same day, 5.50pm, Busy Tykes Nursery, Newcastle.

Noëmi

Arriving at the nursery, she put a kick in her step. *'I've missed those two babies so much! I did well not to phone in and check every five minutes. I wonder if they settled!'*

She joined the queue of parents waiting to pick up. Mentally planning the logistics she looked around the reception area but could not see the twins' car seats. *'Marcus must have left them in the car. Not part of the plan!'* The lobby was decorated with scribbles and colourings done that week by various children along with photos of different milestone achievements such as stacking cup towers. She thought how well the children were safeguarded as no surnames or faces appeared on the artwork or pictures. Her turn came.

"Hello! Mrs McKenzie here for double trouble! Bruno and Emmanuelle!"

The receptionist had a huge sunshine name badge on her cardigan; Kim. Sitting with her spreadsheets before her at the main welcoming point, she was evidently employed just to do the administration. Initially she returned Noëmi's pure cheerfulness, but gradually her face darkened over as she checked the registers.

"Please step this way!" She got out of her seat and pulled her navy cardigan across herself as she indicated for Noëmi to enter a small office. *'Oh my! Maybe there's more paperwork to sign?'* Once in the office the receptionist shut the door.

"Mrs McKenzie, we were unaware that there were child protection orders in place, regarding the twins."
"Excuse me?" Noëmi was flustered.

"Social services paid us a visit. You've breached your rights, again!"

"Sorry?"

"...and the children have been taken into social care."

Head swaying, Noëmi fell forward and managed to grab onto a desk to steady herself.

"W…what?"

"The official said there are safeguarding concerns regarding your family unit. Apparently, you've taken one too many chances with the authorities!"

"What? Who? Did my husband come?" Confusion clouded her head.

"I don't know. We were served with papers by a safeguarding

officer from the local social services department…"

Noëmi burst into uncontrollable tears. Bending double Noëmi could not take in what she was hearing. She fumbled for her phone in her handbag. It fell from her hands and skidded across the office floor. She scrambled to get it. The receptionist stood over her as she crawled over the beige carpet tiles and then stumbled to get back on her feet.

"You need to move on, we have other parents to deal with." Kim's voice was curt.

"Someone took them?" Shaking, she clicked on Marcus' number.

"Social services, they had safeguarding papers!"

"I need to call my husband." Noëmi's voice was tearful and shrill.

Her hand trembled as she waited for him to answer. Finally, she heard his voice.

"Have you got them?" She could not catch her breath.

"What?"

"The kids, have you got them?"

"No, you're picking up!"

"I'm here, there's no car seats and the receptionist says social services came with a court order!"

She broke down, sobbing.

"I'm on my way!"

The receptionist had now dealt with all the other parents and came back into the office.

"We close in five minutes, Mrs McKenzie!"

Weeping, Noëmi turned to the woman who seemed suddenly nervous.

"Who took them?"

"Like I said, social services. Somebody representing a police officer or something!" Huffing she replied, "I can check the signing out register but I suggest you call the council!"

She flounced to the door and started turning off the lights. Everything was being powered down. The nursery nurses started leaving. Goodbyes and cries of 'have a good evening!' were being chirped out as staff members passed by Noëmi who was shaking in reception.

Marcus sped in, "What's going on?"

The receptionist, Kim, was now putting her jacket on as she simultaneously shut down her computer.

"I've explained to your wife! Social services came with some paperwork about you two and your violation of child protection rights!" She jabbed a finger in his direction. "They've been taken into care. Apparently, your wife was well aware of the conditions of the order!"

"I'm sorry but you must have confused us with another client! We don't have any orders or stuff like that! We're the parents of the new twins who started today! Where are they?" Marcus' voice was getting louder.

"Mr McKenzie, I would ask that you don't shout at me!" Kim neatly positioned her mouse next to her keyboard.

"I'm not but are you saying that Bruno and Emmanuelle are not here?"

"Yes!"

"Then where are they?"

"With social services! A representative came around four O'clock this afternoon to pick them up. They had papers!"

"No! That's not possible! God! What have you done?" His eyes were truly filled with fear, as he spoke, he leant in towards the receptionist. Noëmi began to scream. Marcus called 999 and reported the abduction of the twins. He then called Guy.

6pm, Northumbria Police HQ.

Guy

Guy was finishing his day with Tariq and Rolo at the cubby hole.

"Tariq. You got the email about your disciplinary regarding your moonlighting?" Guy was distracted, moving papers and clicking on his computer.

"Yeah, thank you for your support." Tariq's voice was small. He fiddled with his notebook.

"Hopefully get a good outcome but the Superintendent has a bad view of private investigators or *proceedings instigators* as he likes to call them!"

"How so?"

"He got caught playing away from home with one of the office staff. Tried to cover his tracks but his ex-wife was suspicious and in the end, she got a much bigger settlement because of evidence gathered by a PI!"

Tariq may have smiled. Marcus' call buzzed through to Guy's mobile.

"How was nursery then? Free for a quick pint later at your local to tell me how many cups they stacked? We could catch the end of Newcastle Tottenham maybe?"

Guy listened. His face suddenly dropped and he fell forward.

"God no! There must be some mix up! We'll be right there!"

6:15pm, Busy Tykes nursery, Newcastle.

Guy

Within minutes the emergency response unit had arrived at Busy Tykes nursery. Guy and Tariq jumped from their patrol car and charged in. Kim, the receptionist, was attempting to leave but Marcus was refusing to move from the doorway and blocked her path. Therefore, she had also called the police, stating that she was 'being threatened by a parent'. Next she phoned her line manager. Within minutes many confused people were in reception.

Guy met with the nursery owner and was able to hasten procedures given that he knew the McKenzies. Within minutes he escorted Marcus and Noëmi into the side office. They sat around one of the office desks. Holding both their hands, Guy was pale.

"This is serious. God, I'm so sorry to tell you this, but we're starting child abduction protocol times two..."

Noëmi began to shriek hysterically, Marcus held onto her. He was shaking his head,

"No, no, this isn't happening, it's day one, there's been a mix up, someone's taken them by mistake."

"The border agencies have been stepped up. This is a nationwide alert. We've checked with social services and all the enforcement agencies. Obviously the so called social services representative was just a fraudster. Apparently, the receptionist said it was a woman, maybe with an accomplice. We're getting the CCTV asap. You need to see if you recognise her." Guy held onto his friends. "Someone has taken them deliberately but I must say it's really unlikely this woman will harm them. These kinds of cases are usually rooted in deep grief. The children will be substitutes for her loss." As Guy spoke, he doubted everything he said. All his training had taught him child abduction was a race against time.

In the main office behind them, officers furiously gathered information from shocked nursery staff. The Busy Tykes manager spoke loudly about 'safety protocols', 'official ID badges' and 'appropriate safeguarding paperwork'. Guy chose action to keep them all, himself included, from utter panic. His skin crept as he ushered the pair back into the main office where officers were already checking the CCTV. The first pictures showed a chirpy looking Marcus dropping the children off. Guy's heartstrings tightened as he saw Marcus kiss each child in turn before handing them to a bright looking nursery assistant. Late afternoon, the nursery staff were seen preparing the one year olds and putting their belongings into their bags. The recording just caught Kim being handed some papers, taking the car seats and returning to wait in the foyer. In some kind of excruciating slow motion, Bruno was handed over first and taken away. Moments later the same happened to Emmanuelle. However due to the position of the camera, only the back view of the hat of the person taking the children was visible.

"State of the art security so the website says." Guy said under his breath.

As she watched, Noëmi reached out to the screen as if to try and grab them back. She gave an agonising cry each time. By now Marcus and Noëmi were hunched together, whispering, sobbing, attempting to calm and console each other. Guy gently asked them,

"Is there anyone who would want to hurt you in any way?"

"Honeyfield…" Noëmi was hyperventilating.

"Alura?" Marcus cried out.

Shaking her head, "No, she's my friend, she's too scared to go out! Digby attacked her with a knife!"

Family liaison officers were next on the scene, and they sped them back to the police headquarters in Wallsend. Guy escalated the alert to international, as this appeared to be a carefully planned operation. More CCTV was to be reviewed from neighbouring businesses. The next step was to examine the car park surveillance cameras for details of the car that transported the children. Fingerprints, statements and a list of registered users of the nursery had already been collated.

In the incident room, Tariq was cross checking the details of vehicles entering the car park and surrounding roads in the time period.

"Given that reveal, we've got the Honeyfields as prime suspects, but we need more than circumstantial evidence to bring them in." Guy said.

"There are sixty odd cars on the list. We'll check if they give us anything!"

Guy was pacing. "Time, Tariq! We're more than two hours behind the suspect. We've got to get a lead on this?"

CHAPTER 38 - REASON VS EMOTION

6:30pm, Jesmond, Newcastle.

Guy

As part of the protocol, Guy rushed to secure the family home before any media onslaught as the story broke. There was an eerie silence to the house which was bathed in sunbeams of summer twilight. Drawing all the curtains, he glanced around the front room with its sky blue sofa, white linen cushions and wicker toy baskets; the McKenzie vibe was stylish yet simple. Pictures of beloved babies, smiling family members and fun friends filled the walls in silver or white wood frames. A wedding photo of Marcus and Noëmi was the only thing on the mantelpiece. Guy saw himself and Yumi with the couple, in a large, framed picture of the four friends on a sleigh ride in Niseko. Memories of the trip took him back; how they had all laughed that holiday. Head down. Fists clenched he collected a few basic belongings that he thought would be useful.

Suddenly the atmosphere changed, the forensic team swooped in. Two men in white plastic suits, armed with suitcases of equipment began working through the house. A luminescent blood detector was set up and used to examine each room. Luminol would show up blood, Marcus knew what they were thinking. The men worked painstakingly. *'It's just another part of the procedure.'*

Standing by the familiar kitchen table, he grimaced as he saw the babies' breakfast bowls decorated with kittens and puppies. Guy reported back to his team and requested further resources to step up the investigation. With officers now in place at the property, Guy moved swiftly from the McKenzie house in Jesmond to his patrol car. As he did up his seatbelt a call came through. He sighed, "Superintendent Adrian Rumbelow".

Guy knew his superior officer was his first obstacle every time. He was not wrong.

"Start with what we know DS Castle! It may be children missing but here we need reason over emotion!"

"Babies! They're one year old babies!"

"Castle, we've got the background reports on the McKenzies. Their personal lives are a bloody mess! There's just been that big church cheating scandal, it's all over the internet. Plus the Honeyfields have been attacking each other with knives! Before we allocate any more manpower or resources to this case I need to check out the love triangle between that wimpy medic, his bored wife and the oversexed priest! There's definitely some link!"

"Watch it, these people are my friends! Their children have been abducted!" Guy was screeching.

"Sort your boundaries, Castle! Reason over emotion! Now you get those Honeyfields in for interrogation straight away. I'll tackle the parents! News blackout for the moment until we've had a go at these four dreadful excuses for human beings…"

"Stop! They're my friends!" Guy yelled.

The superintendent ignored him and thundered down the

phone,

"...then if that questioning comes back with nothing, we go public with an appeal! Get all the media prepared! The mother would be best but only if she's a crier. Pull at the nation's heart strings."

For the first time Guy wondered if this job was for him. Silently he cursed his boss as Horkos would all liars. He hurried back to Wallsend.

6:45pm, Northumbria Police HQ.

Guy

Shadows behind a frosted glass door. Quietly Guy entered. The family liaison room was sparse thanks to Covid-19. Red and green stickers demarcated two metre distances and advised where one could sit but now these were justifiably ignored. A flip chart in the corner was filled with buzz words from a recent online meeting: 'Helpless', 'Alone', 'Vulnerable', 'Scared', 'Victimised', 'Angry'...the list went on. Guy sat at the wobbly, plastic oak table, head down, he waited. Opposite him Marcus and Noëmi clung to one another. Their sobs were simultaneous and their tears ran together. No one needed to say anything, everyone knew there was no comfort. Again, Guy took their tear soaked hands in his.

"You need to be interviewed. I'll stay with you. Anything that has happened recently could be significant. Try to focus. Most mispers are found."

"Mispers?" Noëmi stammered.

"Missing persons."

"Found alive?"

Guy rubbed his jaw. "N, yes, we need to be positive here."

Stepping out from the family liaison room, Guy ran his fingers through his hair. The only motives were the purported 'affair' which put the Honeyfields in the field of view. He thought back to what he knew of them; Marcus had told him of a conversation between himself and Alex regarding a cold case. Previously he had contacted Alex for the exact details.

Instructing Tariq to commence the search at the Honeyfield penthouse, Guy remained at the police headquarters where he hunted back in his emails for the information. Guy set about asking the Oxford police force for the cold case files. Within minutes they had come through as a matter of high importance.

7pm, Grey Street, Newcastle.

Tariq

Within minutes Tariq was at the Honeyfield flat. Awaiting his team, he went from neighbour to neighbour. Finally, an executive working from home informed him that he had seen the Honeyfield Mercedes driving off, at midday. Tariq fumbled for his police radio.

"Guy, she's buggered off somewhere. Can I force entry."

"Damn not another misper. We need to get Digby Honeyfield back in now! I'm sending the search warrant through this very second, you have permission to force entry."

Tariq was now inside the Honeyfield penthouse where so many souls had been saved. The front room with its magnolia walls, rough sand coloured carpet and humble mismatched chairs in different shades of brown gave off the desired air of humility.

"Of course those Honeyfields are going for that vibe." He growled at the hypocrisy.

By contrast the other living areas were expensively furnished and atypical of a vicar and his wife. A bar, a huge flat screen television and an entertainment centre. Computers revealed a subscription to a soft pornography website and numerous bank accounts in both the Honeyfield's names.

Tariq swiftly reported everything back to Guy. Devices were seized and the area cordoned off. All units and officers were now solely focussed on finding Alura Honeyfield. However efficient the investigation thus far, the children had been missing for exactly three hours.

CHAPTER 39 - RAT

7:15pm, Northumbria Police HQ.

Superintendent Rumbelow

Superintendent Adrian Rumbelow was a solid detective. He had solved a car number plate racket by noticing mismatching screws on an impounded vehicle. Even more ingeniously, he had uncovered an insurance fraud at a local factory when one too many forklift trucks had gotten stolen. He was an unemotional man. 'A criminal is always a criminal' was his mantra. That violent robberies were on the rise and that women did not feel safe on the streets, did not perturb Superintendent Rumbelow.

'We can only do so much!' was his other favourite phrase. Having 'grafted' his way up the ladder he had little time for 'smart-arses' and today he was faced with too many of them.

Marcus

Covid had left the interrogation room little altered. The cups were now disposable and maybe the water in the accompanying jug was changed for each interview but nothing else. Unlike the archetypal prisoner with legs outstretched, Marcus sat hunched into himself, regretting ever having chosen to send his children to nursery. He slowly took out his mobile and with trembling hands he sent a text.

'Alex, sorry I can't work for a bit. Marcus.'

Guy had declared a conflict of interest but since Marcus had refused a solicitor, he was permitted to act as Marcus' support person. The pair sat.

"This is a waste of precious time…when are we doing the appeal?"

"After this."

Marcus took in the mould cornered linoleum, the cup ringed table and the air vent that looked blocked with insects.

"What are they doing about finding…Bru…" Marcus' head fell into his hands. Guy held his friend.

"Everyone's searching. Stay strong mate. He'll be looking to rile you, to get you to slip up."

"Slip up?"

"Sorry, he'll want to work out why anyone would target you both?"

Marcus was fiddling with his fingers, he sighed.

"That Honeyfield stuff…"

Guy put his hand on his friend's shoulder,

"We tried to stop all that getting out but once things are online…"

"It's fine she's not done anything!" Marcus defended his wife.

"Look even if she…"

"No! She's done nothing! How can you even think that she would? She would never betray me! I don't know what those pictures are but I know her. She always keeps her promise!" Marcus flicked Guy's arm away. Sitting back Guy put his hands to his head.

The superintendent marched in. His thin lips gave rat-like teeth.

"Can I offer you some water?"

Marcus shook his head.

"Start the recording, present Dr Marcus McKenzie, DS Guy Castle, Superintendent Adrian Rumbelow. According to your statement the last time you saw your children was around 7:15am on the morning of 15th July when you dropped them at nursery. Now we understand there have been some problems with your wife. What state would you say she was in?"

"She was upset…how is this helping find our children?"

"Upset? The neighbours have reported a woman screaming and raised voices around 7am just before you left your house."

Marcus exhaled, "I'd had a go at her because of the online report about Digby Honeyfield. What's happening with the search?"

"Tell me about the argument."

"I told her she'd made a fool of us. That she was useless." Regret flooded over him. Marcus refocussed. "We're wasting time!"

"That's a matter of opinion. Now let's look back at your relationship with your wife, we've uncovered a number of interesting titbits. Social media really is a detective's dream. Right, you met at school. You were the school crush we understand. She was not popular."

Feeling triggered, Marcus breathed deeply.

"That's my wife you're disrespecting."

He examined the superintendent; white nose hairs, sideburns from an age time forgot and yellowing teeth with brown interdent stains.

"You kept your relationship a secret, was she an embarrassment to you?"

Marcus noticed Guy flinch.

"Don't you dare talk about her like that! Our relationship in sixth form was only private because my church going family would never have approved of us having that type of relationship."

"So you used her for sex and dumped her before university so you could play the field?"

"No and no, she left me. How on earth is this relevant?"

"Or was it your behaviour at the A level celebration party that caused her to leave you?"

"No. Stop!"

"What was that social media post; Vote for Marcus McKenzie's next girlfriend, totally gorgeous Charlotte or…"

"Shut up, don't say anymore! Don't you dare! Say any more and you'll regret it! Do your job! Find our children!" Marcus' chair flew back as he stood up. Clenching his fists tightly only the table restrained him. He wondered how far he would have gone had it not been there.

Superintendent Rumbelow sneered at his prey,

"Temper, temper! Did she regret it? Are you punishing her Marcus?"

Clumsily Guy repositioned the chair and looked between the pair. His jaw was hanging in disbelief.

"We'll take a break. Pause the recording."

The superintendent flounced out.

Guy

Marcus was now sitting with his head in his hands. Guy touched his shoulder.

"I'm so sorry mate, I was wrong. I know she'd never hurt you. I love how you found each other."

Marcus laughed and wiped the tears from his eyes.

"Yeah, once I'd noticed her, I sought her out. She joined in Year 9 but we were on different sides of the year group. It was only in Year 10 when we started getting classes together. You know what she's like."

"A meeting of minds!"

"Not really, I fancied her like mad."

"Yeah, I get that!" Guy added with a cheeky smile.

"What?" Marcus leant forward.

"No, don't say it like that! I mean she's fit, good looking. I can definitely see why you fell for her!"

"Right… is that what you thought when you met her?"

"Yeah, so?"

"Then she's your type?"

"You're doing a superintendent there, twisting things. We all find lots of people attractive but it's about that…"

"Connection." They finished the sentence together.

"But Guy, something's happened. We need to be looking, they could be abandoned or hurt somewhere…"

"Mate, there are teams everywhere, it's a full scale thing."

And with a scrape of the door the superintendent returned to break his suspect. Superintendent Rumbelow regarded his 'criminal' over half rim spectacles. Guy had evidently had enough,

"Sir I'm not sure this is helping, can we discuss the media appeal?"

"Castle, you have no authority here. Hold your tongue! Now, Dr McKenzie, a year or so ago you were under investigation regarding your relationship with Evan St-John-Jones…"

"That was not a relationship! She stalked the hell out of me and almost got my entire family killed!"

"Dr McKenzie, the impression I'm getting is that you've not been very nice to your wife in the past."

The room fell silent. Marcus exhaled loudly. "You're right, I've been self-obsessed, proud and angry. I deserve nothing but contempt."

Superintendent Rumbelow jumped at him.

"So you admit it! You're a love rat! She's not much better! You suit each other! Now we've got this public *embarrassment* as you call it. To top everything, she's now been cited in the Honeyfield divorce papers! An even more public humiliation for Dr Perfect McKenzie!"

"What?"

"Yes, she's the other woman!"

"She's done nothing alright! I don't care what anyone says! I know her!" Visibly his whole body coiled up.

"Really? All this makes me sure that you want to punish your wife, steal the children from her! You're a smart man Dr McKenzie, Oxford, Junior Doctor, you'd know how to cover your tracks. Tell me how you did it. You must be proud of your work, it's immaculate, our teams are struggling to find them."

"What?"

"Yes! Well done! This proves you're cleverer than all of us put together, you love that about yourself. I hear you loved being clever, at Oxford, you had to be the best! You knew you could do better than her, that gross moron…"

"Shut up! Just shut up! You need to do your job and find our children!" Marcus lunged for the superintendent. Instantly Guy flung himself between them.

"Oh but I *am* doing my job! Interview terminated." The superintendent peered over Guy's arms which were clasped around Marcus' whole body. With a sneer on his lips, Superintendent Rumbelow left, mumbling something like 'horrible man' under his breath.

Guy was confused. '*Divorce papers? How on earth has she got into this mess? There has to be a connection.*'

CHAPTER 40 - WHO?

7:30pm, Northumbria Police HQ.

Superintendent Rumbelow

Superintendent Rumbelow strode ahead and marched into the next interrogation room. He noted Reverend Digby Honeyfield. Unlike the RVI poster boy, the preacher did not flinch as the superintendent sat down. Digby had been picked up earlier due to his connection to Noëmi. The recording started. Superintendent Rumbelow drummed his fingers.

"Et alors?" Digby was waiting.

"You're French? Digby Honeyfield sounds pretty British old boy!"

"My mother is French, my father British. They live just outside Paris. My middle name is Guillaume."

"D'accord!" The superintendent emphasised the final 'd' and his inability to pronounce French.

"Tell me about your wife."

"There's nothing to say." Digby was nonchalant.

"Reverend Honeyfield, you're on bail for a vicious attack on your wife."

"Attack? Are you sure?"

"The impression I get is that you've not been very nice to your wife!"

"Really? Some would say I've been a dutiful husband." Digby examined his fingernails and appeared bored.

"Firstly I need the details of where you were and whom you were with today."

"I was at my partner's place. I put the address on the bail form as previously requested. Mid-afternoon I went for a walk along zee River Wear; the path that leads down from the cathedral in Durham, it's quiet, peaceful. I needed to clear my head after this week; zee video incident, being arrested…plus my business has collapsed. My partner's not well, she's upset so I went out alone."

"And where was your mistress? Her babies are gone!"

Panic set on Digby's face, he met the officer's eye.

"I don't understand. What's 'appened?"

"Your partner? Mrs McKenzie?"

"Quoi?"

"Mrs McKenzie, your lover?"

"Pas du tout! Bri Francis is my girlfriend."

The superintendent gave Digby a sideways look. *'How does he get all these women?'*

"This love triangle, you, your wife, Mrs McKenzie…"

"Non, non, non…zat is all wrong, I 'ave never been involved with Madame McKenzie, not for want of trying I may add. I've been seeing Bri since December. Those pictures of me going into the hotel, I'm with her, not the McKenzie woman! How can you not see how different their hair is. Believe me as a man who studies the female form, whilst both women are a delight on the eye, they're quite different!"

The superintendent sat back in his seat. The evening was closing in and dust filled, orange light bathed the room. He tried to fathom what was going on.

"So your wife got her big reveal wrong!"

"En effet! She's deluded as usual." Digby rolled his eyes.

"…and now the McKenzie infants are missing…"

"Mon Dieu! C'est pas vrai!" Digby shut his eyes. For a minute he appeared to be praying. He reached for Superintendent Rumbelow who flicked his hand away. Digby was beseeching.

"Please, zis has nothing to do with me. I'm completely innocent!"

"What about your wife? Is she capable of kidnap?"

Reflective, Digby answered like a politician, "What is important is to find zee children! Rumours and stories are dreadful for my reputation. I am not responsible for anything and that's all that matters."

"But your wife? Could she be responsible?"

"I don't know! All I know is zat she is nothing to me."

"Interview terminated."

* * *

Guy

At the cubby hole, regrouping with Tariq, Guy was frantic. The two men clicked on their superior's latest message.

15 July 2020.
DS Castle,
Digby Honeyfield's playing games. No alibi for yesterday and he denies a relationship with the McKenzie woman. To complicate matters it seems he's been involved with a certain Bri Francis since December 2019. (As shown in those big reveal pictures). Get this woman in for questioning ASAP.

AR (Superintendent East)

"This is ludicrous, Bri Francis?" Guy gave an exasperated groan.

Tariq cried out, "Bri Francis! She came in to collect her driving licence! It was her in the photos! My God, Noëmi was never in hotel rooms with that man! The camera does lie!"

Guy felt cold. He recalled his contempt for Noëmi when he had thought the pictures to be her.

7:45pm, Newcastle Royal Victoria Infirmary (RVI).

Alex

Sitting in the RVI staff room on a break from his twelve hour shift, Alex James, Trauma Consultant, was having flashbacks. Since he had realised Digby Honeyfield was in Newcastle, Alex had been plagued by visions of Isabelle Williams. She was the former church member who had died in those terrible circumstances. Anxiety paralysed his mind. Brain fog. His forehead was sweating beneath his visor. Suddenly worried for all his daughters, he rang each one in turn.

"This is a surprise Dad! How's being a superhero today?" Louisa was bright.

"Everyone's losing it Isa. Marcus has just sent some bizarre message saying he can't work at the moment. I imagine it's just a mental health episode. No one understands the pressure we're under…damn Covid!"

A few moments of silence, then Louisa burst into tears.

"Hey, my darling, shhh it'll be okay, we're all just having a bit of a breakdown I think, everything's been too much for him, what happened last year, Covid…"

"Noëmi and Digby Honeyfuck?" Her sobs did not stop her ire.

"Louisa! I didn't pay thousands of pounds to a posh school for you to talk like that!"

"That vicar's a real weirdo. There's some rumour Noëmi's involved with him. It's all over the internet!"

"No! There's no way…I know that couple they're embarrassingly close, it's just not possible! That Honeyfield bloke has a dark history. I don't trust him…you know I was an expert witness in that Oxford drowning? It was put down as an accident and the CPS dismissed it as 'a woman getting herself killed!' those actual words Isa, can you believe it?"

"Getting herself killed…" Louisa was faraway.

Alex continued, "…but I know that the young woman was deliberately drowned. Science doesn't lie. She used to be a member of the Honeyfield church…"

"And I'm not sure they're big fans of science! He milks his wife's cancer recovery like it was a miracle from on high and not the hard work of doctors!"

"Oh is that right?" Alex was thinking. They both went silent.

She called out, "Dad, Mrs Honeyfield! She used to work for the

CPS…and she worked in Oxford, something's not right!"

"You say she had cancer…" Alex was breathless and he stood up suddenly. "I need to call Guy."

7:50pm Northumbria Police HQ.

Guy

Guy sped back to the family liaison room. As he turned into the corridor, he saw Superintendent Rumbelow heading that way too.

'No, you're not going for Noëmi!' Guy was right behind.

Noëmi was prone on the table, weeping. Marcus had his arms around her shoulders and was desperately trying to soothe her. The family liaison officer was sitting awkwardly two metres from her side calling out "Shhhh" the whole time. The Superintendent pulled a chair from under the table and shoved himself in front of Noëmi. She was sobbing the ugly tears of a childless mother. Flustered, he finally asked,

"…would you like some water? Here's a tissue!" Tariq knocked and entered. He moved close to Guy.

"One of the cars seen in the vicinity of the nursery around lunchtime is owned by an A.Burford." Tariq whispered. "That's her! Alura Honeyfield! Burford's her maiden name. A white Mercedes, registration number, DH4 AB, spotted just before midday."

The superintendent rolled his eyes, "Castle, Azzara stop gossiping like school kids in the corner there! We have an investigation…"

Guy's mobile rang, he took the call.

"Castle focus!" The superintendent growled.

Guy ignored him.

"Alex! What…yes, I'm listening…right…thank you!"

He clicked off the call.

"Where are they? Who's taken them?" Noëmi cried out. Her sobs echoed around the room that resembled a concrete tomb. Her visceral pain rendered everyone but Superintendent Rumbelow speechless, he stage whispered to Guy,

"This is simply perfect for the media appeal!"

Guy snapped back, "No! The news embargo stays in place until we've found the Honeyfield woman!"

Then he took over. With a loud scrape Guy dragged a chair and sat next to his superintendent.

"Castle…"

Guy cut over his superior and turned to Noëmi.

"Noëmi, the Honeyfields, can they be trusted?"

"No! Not at all! That church is a cult! They're both toxic."

"N, is there somewhere Alura likes to go?"

For the first time Noëmi looked up. Her eyes were bloodshot and puffy.

"H…has she got them?"

"N, maybe, is there anywhere you know of that's special to her, anywhere she would go when she feels all emotional?"

"No, no! She knows nothing about children, they need their tea, their nappies, their cuddles…" Tears streamed down her face. Guy was fearing for far more than the infants' basic comforts.

"But N, where's a special place for her? We've searched all the rental properties, she's not in any of them, is there anywhere she's mentioned? Anywhere at all? Think!"

For a few minutes she racked her brain. All at once Tariq cried out,

"Where he said he loved her! What Three Words! Icon, Coins, Zoom!"

In an instant, Guy and Tariq flew out of the family room. Superintendent Rumbelow could not move as fast. His familiar voice huffed as it followed them into the corridor.

"Castle, we need to re-group, this investigation is going backwards! I'm getting another team on it, you're dismissed from the case! You're now back on Covid walkers and indoor gatherings!"

"No, I'm not! We need to find Alura Honeyfield now!" Guy yelled back at his senior officer.

CHAPTER 41 - ICON, COINS, ZOOM

Guy

Before Superintendent Rumbelow could communicate any further with the 'maverick DS Castle', Guy was sprinting down the corridor. Together with Tariq he ran, half to apprehend the suspect and half to avoid the consequences of his impulsive defiance.

"We're like Starsky and Hutch!" Tariq panted as they started their patrol car.

"Who?" Guy asked.

"It's an old detective series, my mum used to watch it…"

"All this runs in the family, does it?"

The old coffee cups spilt their dregs as they cornered out of the car park. Tariq checked the location, he shrieked,

"No! The Spanish Battery!"

The car jolted as Guy accelerated and the radio bounced out of its holder. Seeing Tariq's hand move, Guy was terse.

"No blues and twos, we don't want any danger of her jumping…or worse…God, this is terrifying. Do we have an exact location?"

"From What Three Words, it's the Tynemouth lighthouse. It's notorious!"

8:30pm, Tynemouth Priory and Castle.

Arriving on the headland, they could make out the castle ruins, dark against the sky. The evening sun glinted on the horizon but a swift breeze denied its warmth. The jagged ramparts gave out to luscious lawns and in the distance was a lone figure walking along the sea buffer towards the Tynemouth lighthouse. Alura was before him, casual in a light coral coloured, button through, tea dress and bright, white trainers. Her hair was pulled into a short pony tail.

"Get Rolo on a lead. I'm going to talk to her. Organise the back up. Stay close to me!"

Guy was pulling off his uniform jacket and stab vest, he grabbed the Bathing Ape hoodie discarded in the car by Marcus. Another couple of walkers were enjoying the summer evening and surreptitiously Tariq cleared the area. Guy began towards her.

Approaching Alura, Guy was about to call her name. He froze. Two tiny figures were tottering next to her as she progressed along the pier. One stumbled and fell over. Alura picked up the howling child and brushed them down. At the end of the pier Guy could see a black, iron railing on one side and on the other a stone wall. Both of these dropped straight to the sea. The waves were lashing the sea wall and foam sprang as if the sea were alive with Nereids. He moved briskly and was soon just a few metres behind. Maybe sensing Guy's presence, Alura lifted the twins so that they were standing high on the sea wall. She was clutching each one by the hand. Up on the sea wall the twins jumped, pointed and screamed with delight when they saw the sea below.

'They're alive! God get them down from there!' Guy eased off.

Alura turned her head as he approached. She grabbed the children around their waists and pulled them down. She moved to the railings, knelt beside them and kissed their heads. Alura held tightly onto the squirming infants as they gazed out across the sea. The children grabbed the lowest of the iron bars and giggled. The waves were relentlessly slamming onto the rocks beneath the lighthouse. Slowly Alura lifted the twins into her arms. Clutching at their waists, laboriously she manoeuvred herself onto the sea wall. The babies were hanging like a pair of rag dolls.

Guy steadied his pace, sweat was on every inch of his body. Gingerly he took Rolo off the lead and allowed her to walk ahead. Emmanuelle squirmed and broke free from Alura's grasp. Slipping down, she flung herself on the spaniel. Bruno also squealed and pointed, kicking his legs. Emmanuelle was now only an arm's length from Guy. Alura sat herself up so that she was precariously balanced. Bruno was on her lap.

'I can't risk anything.'

Suddenly Alura spoke, "I've suffered. He's made me do bad things." Still, she did not meet his eye.

"We've all done bad things! We're all sinners."

"Some more than others!" Alura steadied herself on the balustrade, taking one arm off Bruno. At any moment they could slip into the sea. Whilst he knew back up was not far away, would there be time to rescue the child if they fell? Emmanuelle stroked Rolo.

"Maybe, but you can turn back from it!" Guy meant this quite literally.

"You sound like Digby. He's such a shit, this time he's left me." Her breathing was shallow like his. "No one wants me. I'm pointless." She kicked her legs. "Even these little ones prefer the dog! And I gave them sweets!"

"Be careful there!"

The waves lapped, the water was gloomy and unforgiving. She laughed.

"Drowning no longer scares me!" She manoeuvred herself round so that she was now sitting looking out to sea, her legs dangling over the side. His throat closed. His mouth was dry. Rolo yelped and moved towards Alura. Emmanuelle was at his side.

"This is Rolo!"

A look of pure joy took over Alura's face as she beckoned to the dog to come closer. Guy's heart pounded as he saw Alura lean right back; fingertips straining to reach the dog. She had just the one hand on little Bruno. Alura stroked the dog. Now she was no longer holding onto Bruno who was sitting, swaying, on her lap. Emmanuelle toddled towards Guy. He took her hand and passed her to Tariq.

'One safe. God, please help me.'

"If you come and sit with me, I swear I won't jump."

Mustering all his will power, Guy pulled his legs of lead and jelly to the edge and he sat down next to Alura. Without looking down, he fixed on the horizon, white horses darted between the inky waves. Feeling nothing between his head and his feet, gingerly he swung both legs over the sea. Gently Guy put his hands on Bruno as he bounced on Alura's lap.

"Digby's treated you terribly." Guy said softly. "Do you want to tell me about it?"

As she began, Guy reached and took Bruno into his arms.

Seemingly entranced, Alura gave the baby up. Guy clutched him tightly. Hot, soggy breath in his neck. Quietly he moved his legs back to the safe side.

"He fell in love with someone else. Isabelle." Alura selected a picture of herself with an attractive, dark haired woman. Together they were smiling. She held it up to Guy.

"Beautiful, isn't she?"

Guy's heart raced. *'Isabelle Williams?'*

"That's tough, but why did he kill her if he loved her?"

"I don't know, to shut her up, I guess. She was leaving the church, she could have ruined him!"

She scrolled some more and pulled her knees up to her chin. Precariously she balanced on the sea wall. To his side he could see Tariq opening his arms, ready to take Bruno. Guy passed the infant to safety. *'Thank God!'* His heart raced. Alura stared out to the waves.

"Yes, we know that the church has been a front for his crimes; embezzlement, defrauding charities, tax evasion and money laundering."

"You see he's a cheat in all ways. Never trust a word from that man's mouth! How do you think we paid for so many properties? He doesn't just know every trick in the book, he wrote the book! People give in the hope of miracles, cures and holy recompense for their suffering and endless misery. All that happens is that they remain just as unhappy and become poorer."

Desperate to get away from the edge, Guy leant back. *'If she goes she could take me with her.'*

"Would you help us convict Digby? Get him into prison?"

If she heard she was not listening.

"Water is so unforgiving." Her gaze remained on the horizon, the evening sun glistened on the wave tips. It was as if the whole ocean were alive with golden dolphins.

"They both need to join Isabelle. She's lovely; soft limbs, creamy skin, beautiful, dark cascading hair. He betrayed her…holding her down like that. Gold crucifix still around her plump neck. Waiting for that last air bubble."

Guy felt cold. Alura continued and held up a screenshot of Noëmi. Guy trembled.

"Now there's another one. Another Isabelle. Noëmi. She's got everything; a doctor husband, babies but it's not enough…she's stealing my husband too. Tariq showed me the photos of them sneaking around at hotels, pretending to be on charity business…and now he says he's in love. But he doesn't love me, who would love this?" Alura changed the picture to one of her. "He's never loved me and yet I love him."

"I feel for you Alura, what a dreadful husband. I bet he never went with you to any of your hospital appointments."

"What? What hospital visits?"

"When you had cancer."

Forlorn and lost, Alura put her arms around herself.

"Oh, no, no, it's not real! None of this is real! Digby's not left me! No, he's coming back for me! Here! He told me he loved me! It's our special place! Everything I've ever done is for him! Soon he'll be back! There's no way he'd leave me! We've always had each other!"

She began to rock. Seeing her flinch forward, Guy grabbed her waist, dug his heels into the ground and pushed back to stop her falling. Tariq charged towards them, screaming. Crashing to the ground, Guy thudded onto his back, as the officers lunged forward to secure the pair. Alura was restrained by the shoulders. She offered no resistance. Guy got to his knees, doubled over, blood pumping, muscles aching. He gave up a bear like cry. Slowly he got his breath and pulled himself up, away from the sea barricade. Guy met her eyes, his voice was shrill.

"Alura, Noëmi was never seeing Digby. You got it wrong! We all got it wrong!"

"But…Tariq saw them…he showed me pictures…"

"It was someone else! Digby's seeing someone else!" Tariq turned to her.

Alura stared ahead.

"…you didn't take the money?" She whispered back. Her eyes were glazed.

"No, it was wrong to accept that transfer. I need to be able to respect myself!" Tariq said.

"Cross the line and you never get that self respect back. All you see in the mirror is a grotesque monster." Alura said as she put her head in her hands.

"What line did you cross Alura? It's more than just the lies, isn't it? Exactly how far would you go?" Guy went for her. The children having been put close to death had fired him up. She remained silent, only the waves screamed back.

Finally, Alura uttered, "How far would I go? It's written in Leviticus, *'An eye for an eye, a tooth for a tooth'*. She took my husband so I took what was most precious to her! Hosea 13 says that those who rebel against their God, *'will fall by the sword; their little ones will be dashed to the ground, their pregnant women ripped open'*. So it should be!"

Alura's face was serene. Mustering all his self control, Guy leant forward and did his duty.

"Alura Honeyfield, I'm arresting you for the murder of Isabelle Williams and the abduction of Bruno and Emmanuelle McKenzie. You do not have to say anything. But it may harm your defence, if you do not mention when questioned something which you later rely on in court. Anything you do say may be given in evidence."

Alura put her hands together ready for the cuffs. Silent Alura sat in the back of one of the patrol cars flanked by Tariq and a female officer. As they drove off, Guy waited with the twins and the victim support unit. He immediately called Marcus.

9pm, Northumbria Police HQ.

Marcus

Intermittently, the family liaison officer was still calling out "Shhhh" as Noëmi shuddered with grief. Equally deranged Marcus was pacing, desperately trying to think where Alura could be. His phone rang. Before he could speak, Guy was yelling.

"We've got them! They're both safe! They're fine! Mate we've got them!" Marcus fell to his knees, Noëmi collapsed into him. Screams now turned to those of relief and disbelief. The good news rendered the parents even more hysterical. Guy turned to video chat so that they could see their children, safely strapped in police car seats. Tears of joy streamed down their faces. The support officer was pragmatic.

"Job done! We can all go home now can't we! My shift finished two hours ago!"

CHAPTER 42 - LEG GODT

Wednesday, 15 July, High Heaton, Newcastle.

Sarai

Later that evening Donnie was released from hospital. Unable to contact Noëmi, Sarai was unsure how to get him home. Patient transport was unavailable, taxis would not go near the Covid filled hospital and friends with cars were wary of even someone 'recovered' from the mysterious, killer disease. She had no choice but to call Gina who was there in a flash.

"Can I come with you?" Sarai asked in a small voice.

"You could be infectious, so I don't think so."

So there it was that Gina's smart Evoque purred to the driveway. After much animated opening of doors and offering of arms, she arrived with Donnie at her side.

"I'm very happy to look after you at mine, especially if they're still isolating!" Sarai heard Gina insist.

"No thank you, I'm fine, really, I just want to get home."

As his eyes caught Sarai's he gave her a wide smile. The trio stood at the door. Gina was dressed in a warm white track suit that skimmed her toned body well. Her hair was styled and the tanzanite from her expensive gold earrings caught the evening sunset. Suddenly Gina addressed Sarai.

"I hear you're moving to Italy!"

Sarai was dumbfounded.

"That'll be lovely for you to escape this awful climate! I'm so jealous!"

Gina threw her arms around as if copying some Italian stereotype.

"Take it easy, Donnie, and see you at badminton when you're ready. You could always come and watch!"

A little cutesy wave to Donnie with a bat of her eyelashes and reluctantly Gina sashayed away.

Donnie and Sarai moved inside. Lucia ran to hug Donnie and showed him her latest picture.

"Happy birthday!" Donnie croaked.

"You!" she pointed at a stick figure of a man in bed. "Mummy!" She pointed at a scribble without form. "Cry! Cry!" She pointed at the indistinguishable blob again and skipped off.

Sarai made tea and they sat at the kitchen table.

"Travel in Europe is opening up…obviously with quarantine restrictions. When we can book transport, Lucia and I can leave."

He guessed her thoughts.

"She asked me what your long term plans were, so I just told her what I knew." He sighed.

"What's that to do with her?" Sarai snapped.

"I don't know Sarai, she's one of those dusters and polishers."

"Sorry?"

"Ah, you know those people who like everything in little boxes, all neat and tidy." Donnie sounded exasperated.

"You like things tidy."

"Yes the house, that's my OCD, but not my actual feelings. There's nothing tidy about my emotions, Sarai!" He gave a cough. "I mean she seems to think relationships are like Lego blocks, all smooth, neat and structured. Just find a piece that fits the hole in her life and that'll do! My heart's not like that! Is yours?"

She put her arms around his shoulders and gave him a hug.

"Just take it easy Donnie. I need to try Noëmi, I've not been able to get her this evening. I know she was doing a trial run at work but I want to make sure she knows you're out and well."

"Don't worry. We can call her later." Donnie coughed.

Night was closing in and she watched the squirrels running up to raid Donnie's apple tree. *'Maybe I should be more daring like them!'*

He stood up and joined Sarai as she went to take Lucia upstairs. He had the final word.

"I know it's late but can we give Lucia her gift now? Together?"

Sarai smiled and turned to fetch the scooter. Donnie's voice was rasping.

"You know Sarai, Italy could be far too hot for Lucia. She's used to these northern temperatures. Plus the NHS is amazing, you don't get that anywhere else in the world!"

Lucia bounced with glee when she saw her gift. Donnie and Sarai gave gasps of delight as they saw her excitement.

"It's important they play well at this age! That's all they need! They learn through play! N was always absorbed in her imagination." Donnie was emphatic.

Sarai felt blessed. Donnie was back, she reached for him and he put his arm around her. She felt safe.

Lucia insisted on sleeping with the scooter and its matching helmet, next to her bed.

9:30pm. Newcastle Royal Victoria Infirmary (RVI).

Alex

Alex James was completing the daily Covid statistics when police officers arrived. They had blue lighted over a pair of one year old twins who needed to be examined as part of a police case. Dropping everything, he delegated his paperwork to Madhav, his second in command and headed to receive the infants.

His heart jumped. *'Bruno and Emmanuelle? What's going on?'* He looked down at the hastily written **SBAR** (**Situation-Background-Assessment-Recommendation**).

'Check overall health. Assess evidence of injury and abuse using child protection body map. Safeguarding protocols. Officer in attendance at all times.'

Sweat seeped from his brow. *'Good God! Are they having breakdowns? Are they being accused of neglect? Abuse? No, not possible. Cheating? Child abuse? What next?'*

Gingerly he began his examinations, then he stopped and turned to the officer.

"Bruno McKenzie, this child here, he's my godson. Is that a

conflict of interest?"

After a few moments and having checked with his colleague, the officer replied,

"No, not at all, apparently you're the best but we can get a second opinion if required."

Returning to his work, he noted Emmanuelle tottering happily around the hospital bed. On the couch, Bruno was becoming sleepy.

"Can I ask about the circumstances? It would help to know what alleged crime has been committed against the children?"

"Abduction."

"Right, so one of the parents took them without the other's permission?"

"It's best not to speculate Mr James, we just need to know if there's been any injury or abuse."

The officer sat on the hospital chair waiting. Alex was perturbed. *'My God, what's happening? Is it this cheating allegation that caused all this? What on earth goes on behind closed doors?'*

He meticulously continued his work, feeling clammy and nauseous. All at once a commotion was outside the bay. The curtain flapped. Voices were raised.

"You have to wait!" One of the officers on the other side of the curtain hissed.

"No step aside, let them in now! That's an order!"

Alex recognised Guy's voice. Before he knew it Marcus and Noëmi had charged into the treatment area. Scooping up their children, they cried out with relief. Soon the family of four were huddled together clutching, cuddling and sobbing. Guy moved past a dumbfounded Alex and fell into the hospital chair.

"Alex, mate, you have no idea! Absolute nightmare. Got any medicinal alcohol on that trolley? I need lots of it! By the way how did Newcastle get on against Tottenham? Did they play well? I missed it! Been a tad busy!"

PART FOUR – RECKONINGS

L'amour n'est pas un feu qu'on renferme en son âme.
Tout nous trahit, la voix, le silence, les yeux
Et les feux mal couverts n'en éclatent que mieux.

Andromaque, Jean Racine

CHAPTER 43 - MAVERICK

Northumbria Police HQ.

Guy

Guy stood outside the superintendent's office. The silence unsettled him.

'Definitely a deliberate ploy not to have chairs in this corridor. Failure to adhere to the commands of a senior officer could mean expulsion from the force.' Had he risked everything? Had he sacrificed his career and reputation on the altar of his pride? Was he just an impetuous, immature and arrogant hothead who was always right? 'Vainglorious' his Latin teacher had called him at school. He had laughed thinking the elderly teacher was from another era but now he saw the comment as prescient. Unusually, Guy felt small and uncomfortable.

Tariq was already in his disciplinary meeting. The superintendent had been considering the private investigation work that Tariq had attempted to start. Tariq exited the office and gave Guy a relieved look,

"He told me he hopes I'll be better at actual police work than I was in my attempts to be 'Norville Rogers'. He enjoyed explaining that he's Shaggy from Scooby Doo. I got a verbal warning."

Guy felt hot and rearranged his collar. He was next in. The superintendent's assistant opened the door. Guy stood to attention. All he heard was a long sigh. He felt his boss's eyes laser through him.

"DS Castle, you're quite the old public school boy aren't you? All jolly japes, chucking junket out of the window and sniggering at naughty puns. Now you've even got yourself your very own Timmy! Alma mater, some posh establishment with lovely grounds, no rough comprehensive for you! Then a bit of Durham uni, easy degree, a few essays on company law. Bit of sightseeing in Japan. Bit of volunteering, virtue signalling they call it now I believe. All of which leads you to a point where, you, the poster boy of privilege, decides he's going to fling on some superhero cape to single handedly hunt down a dangerous criminal. And then during the gathering of evidence, you recreate some tacky hospital soap opera in a place of legal jurisdiction."

The superintendent was more eloquent and imaginative than Guy had reckoned.

"It all just smacks of hubris."

Guy gave a start and said to himself, *'He knows that word?'*

"And I imagine your vanity makes you think I would not have such a word to hand? Tell me all the infractions that this act has committed?"

"Defiance of a command. Defiance to duty. Defiance to a senior officer. Endangerment to others…"

"Enough! You and PC Azzara with that dog! Running around like Freddie and Shaggy with Scooby Doo! It was all just plain wrong!" The superintendent huffed and turned to his notes.

"However…"

'Yes!' Guy could feel his lips curling into a smile.

"…you have succeeded in solving an extremely difficult case. You made the arrest for the abduction of the McKenzie twins, it would seem you and your sidekick, PC Azzara undoubtedly saved their lives. Those children coming to any harm would've been extremely embarrassing for our force."

"And their parents may have been upset too…"

"Castle, not the time. As I was saying, the victims were untraceable. You used the very skills we require of senior police officers. In addition, you arrested the same person for the murder of Isabelle Williams. Shockingly badly investigated by that other force at the time. Right so Castle, for thinking the Northumbria Police Department is some kind of place for your Mission Impossible fantasies, and I mean the old TV series not the Tom Cruise films, you get a verbal warning, like your little sidekick. Focus on doing the good work you've proven you can achieve and get out of my sight! Avoid me for a week or so until my ageing brain has forgotten all about this!"

"Thank you sir! That's great news!"

"That better not be a snide comment with some hidden meaning Castle!"

Guy was unsure whether the superintendent was now smiling but he did not hang around to find out. He sent Tariq a text.

'I got Mission Impossible, just saying!'

'Will be lodging a formal complaint about discrimination in analogies used in the delivery of verbal warnings.'

'Ok so not the Tom Cruise version, the Sixties TV series.'

'Good series, but I prefer Ironside. Still not quite Shaggy! I'm sure I've got a case!'

CHAPTER 44 - NDA

Wednesday, 22 July 2020, Zoom Meeting.

Noëmi

Assembled on a Teams call the necessary attendees had all returned their non-disclosure agreement forms in order not to risk the case. Each had to have their camera on and no recording was permitted.

Participants;

DS Guy Castle

PC Tariq Azzara

Dr Marcus McKenzie

Mrs Noëmi McKenzie

Mr Alex James

"Here we go again!" Guy quipped. "Have you two thought of moving to the Outer Hebrides or Shetland?" "That's a good series, Shetland, a high proportion of murders for the population though even for a TV series…" Tariq saw

Guy's amused expression and stopped. Putting on a serious face, he continued. "We're all aware that the information given here is not to be shared with anyone else."

Guy began. "I hope at the end of this session you feel psychologically safe within our culture of consultation, participation, empowerment and open communication…"

"He's just been on a training course." Tariq explained matter of factly.

Guy continued, "Anyway, let's refocus! Digby Honeyfield, quite a character, an intelligent man with a narcissistic personality disorder. Let's do our Poirot bit, eh Tariq? We can take you through what happened that day!"

Wednesday, 15 July 2020, Busy Tykes Nursery, Newcastle.
Kim, Receptionist

Having straightened out her desk, Kim neatly stacked her nursery registers into a box file ready for scanning. She double checked the attendance lists and did the hourly headcount. All present and correct. She signed off the infant numbers and placed the document into a lever arch file.

"I'm here to collect Bruno and Emmanuelle McKenzie."

Before her stood a vision of pure glamour. Vibrant henna red hair, Gucci sunglasses and a tightly cinched Burberry jacket. Being held up to her face was an official looking badge.

"CPS! Under section 46 of the Children's Act, 1989, we have child protection documents requiring their removal to a place of safety. You are obliged to co-operate. No court order is required."

The woman's French polished hands delivered a folder of documents, printed on Northumbria Police Department headed paper, which gave details of the need to safeguard the infants. Flustered Kim rang her manager. She indicated to her VIP visitor that she needed to listen for a moment. Nodding and noting, Kim's face became dark as she sought advice.

"Usually, papers from the council offices...they're stamped..."

"There's been a refurbishment and no one can find the official council stamp!"

"Right!" Kim hesitated between her phone and the documents. She then said, "Excuse me, I just need to call the parents so that they're aware of..."

"No! Never! Have you not completed your basic safeguarding training? In cases of suspected child endangerment, parents must never be alerted! There would be serious risk to the infants if those accused of harming them know of their whereabouts! Absolute confidence! Do I need to conduct an audit of your training whilst I'm here? I could shut this place down if it becomes apparent that the safeguarding certification is not up to date."

"Of course, I knew that!"

"You can call the police headquarters to check the serial number on the letter if you want! The lead officer is PC Azzara!"

"Yes, great idea! In the meantime, can one of us help you with the car seats?"

Kim rang the number.

'You've reached PC Tariq Azzara, I'm not available at the moment but please leave a message and I'll get back to you.'

Kim put the phone back down.

"That's all fine, can you complete the register and we'll prepare the infants for you, er Mrs...?"

The smart lady gave her name so quickly that Kim did not catch it. She tried asking again as the official looking woman completed the register, putting CPS in the personal identification column and PC Azzara's details in the next section. Therefore, having the paperwork in her hand and a verified police contact number, Kim felt all was in hand.

And so the children were taken on the semblance of authority. It would seem the more important you appear and the more you bark then the more you can bypass the rules. Their five hour excursion caused them no harm but much discomfort as Alura did not change their nappies or put on their jackets. She fed them sweets and gave them diet coke to drink. The one year olds were buzzing by the time they got to the Lighthouse.

Zoom Meeting.

Noëmi

Marcus grabbed tighter onto Noëmi who clung onto him equally hard.

"Thank God! But why us?"

"Alura wanted to literally make you suffer your worst nightmare. Having lost her most precious love, she wished to take yours from you. She put up with Digby's infidelities until the moment she knew he was falling in love. In 2014, a young woman, Isabelle Williams, joined the London Church of Glory. Vulnerable she was instantly groomed by our philandering reverend and they began an affair. During this time Alura was working for the CPS in London but then took on the lead in the Oxford jurisdiction. Alura reached out to Isabelle in so-called friendship and began to talk about being ill with cancer. Disillusioned, Isabelle broke up with Digby and decided to leave the church and she moved away. Alura came to her supposed rescue and offered her the flat in Walton Street, Oxford, at a cheap rent. Moving into that top floor flat she believed she was finally free from the past."

"The Jericho area, all those Victorian villas! It's lovely!" Marcus knew Oxford well.

"A new job with a prestigious law firm was just the ticket to freedom she had needed. Digby reconciled to duty as Alura told him her illness was terminal. Shortly afterwards in September 2015, Isabelle was found dead in the bath of her flat. The investigation was shockingly bad. If they'd done their homework, they'd have seen that the flat at 120 Walton Street was in the name of Alura."

"120 Walton Street!" Alex was incredulous, "Louisa's girlfriend rented a flat there!"

"Really? Wow six degrees of separation and all that! Digby was questioned and had told the investigators he'd been with Alura that night. In fact, he'd been with a new lover and had no idea where his wife had been. Digby gave Alura an alibi as he wanted to protect his church and his reputation."

Noëmi shut her eyes. She could only imagine the pain that Isabelle went through.

"Deep down Digby was wary of what his wife could do. We think he knew she had killed Isabelle. Whether he believed the cancer story or not, he found it useful for his deceptions. When he was interviewed, he thought only of himself. He's guilty of silence and coercive control. Alex, you also mentioned red flags concerning Alura, although you could not say why. I imagine it was something you read in her medical history but could not reveal. Since her arrest we've been able to make a request under the Data Protection Act to see her medical records. Alura never had cancer. I would never have believed anyone would lie like that until my ex-girlfriend did exactly the same thing. Unforgivable! Alura had no fertility problems and had been using contraception. She's perfectly healthy. For me there was another giveaway. Alura knew details about Isabelle's death that had not been revealed publicly as you gave your testimony in camera Alex."

Alex spoke next. "And Isabelle?"

"At the time there was no justice for her. Her heartbroken family planted trees and put up small plaques at her former university and schools. There's one at St Wolbodo's..."

"Oh my God yes! I've seen it! Outside the hall! She went there? Another six degrees of separation!" Noëmi cried.

"Indeed but she left in 2007 before you taught there. Now there won't be a trial as the Honeyfields have both pleaded guilty." Guy continued. "Digby, he'll get a custodial sentence for perjury, perverting the course of justice, fraud, embezzlement. And let's not forget the racism and his hate crime against Sarai. Alura has been detained under the Mental Health Act for assessment."

"...and is likely to be detained indefinitely and with a minimum twenty year term as the murder and the abductions were planned." Tariq informed them.

Gallery view showed all the participants visibly shaken. Noëmi felt a lump in her throat as Alex wiped his eyes. Tariq continued. "The nursery staff were negligent so they're facing an investigation. It's shut down, but no doubt will soon re-emerge with a new name. I guess you two are looking for other childcare options now?"

Marcus nodded, "Yeah definitely, not sure what though."

As the call was ending, Tariq spoke up.

"Noëmi, I feel ashamed. The photos I gave Alura caused her to target your family! I'm truly sorry."

Hanging his head, he sounded choked until comfort came his way.

"Tariq, you were the one who knew where to find our children! You saved them and helped get justice for Isabelle! Forget about the pictures, you didn't know it wasn't me!" Noëmi smiled warmly.

The call finished. Moments later Marcus' phone rang.

"Louisa? Yes, sure." He put her on loud speaker.

"Thank you for helping find the children!" Noëmi was bright in spite of baby Emmanuelle squeezing her nose with her newly found pincer grip.

"I'm the worst person. I shared that Digby reveal, that's how it got to you via Tianna, I'm so sorry."

"Louisa no worries it would've been worse for that to be behind my back! Plus, you didn't know it wasn't me!" Noëmi was on a roll!

CHAPTER 45 - FAREWELL

August 2020, Jesmond, Newcastle.

Noëmi

Marcus and Noëmi were inching their way along the road to recovery. Donnie visited as much as lockdowns would allow. One Sunday in early August he was at their house with Sarai and Lucia for lunch. The McKenzie lounge was ever more homely and furniture building skills had been acquired by both parents. Bright white Billy bookcases were squeezed full of toys and now pictures and ornaments were placed high out of the reach of sticky fingers. Sitting feeding her growing twins, Noëmi looked up at Sarai.

"Did you enrol Lucia for pre-school?"

"She's not going."

"Oh Sarai, why?"

"These places are not safe!" Sarai said simply.

They shared the silence. Both women shuddered with unspoken terror. Unable to contradict, Noëmi shut her eyes. Trembling, she soothed Bruno then released him from her arms. Having spotted the neighbour's fawn Abyssinian cat, he toddled out of the kitchen to the garden screaming.

"Gatta! Cat!" Lucia shouted as she ran out to play with Bruno and the quickly disappearing cat. Noëmi picked up Emmanuelle who was now restless.

"Noëmi, I've decided to move to Rome to live near Luca's father Roberto. It'll be good for him and Lucia; he's our closest relative now." Sarai finally admitted.

"And what would be good for you?"

Sarai ignored her determinedly. "First we will stay with him and his partner in Rome to get used to life there. He has already bought us a home."

"No, Sarai! You don't speak Italian and Roberto travels so much with work. Plus he's got the money to visit you here. Please stay!"

"It's what Luca would want for us. Roberto has moved heaven and earth to get our exceptional travel paperwork sorted. It's been his one focus. I've made up my mind!" Sarai sounded serious.

"But when can you leave? Flights are non-existent." Noëmi tried another strategy.

"Now we can travel to France, Roberto has found us a route to Rome. We need to settle everything in the next few days. Your father will get his house back!" Her voice was firm. They sat quietly as Noëmi fed Emmanuelle. The sound of Bruno and Lucia squealing with delight at the cat charging across the lawn, was all that punctuated the silence.

Suddenly, Noëmi hugged her friend. "I'll miss you."

Sarai sat stony faced, staring out at the garden.

16 August 2020, Newcastle Central Station.

Noëmi

Travel for specific purposes was permitted and by mid-August Sarai's plans were set. She was packed up; ready to leave for Rome. With a second lockdown looming, Sarai knew that she now had to mobilise. Therefore, she would first travel from Newcastle to London by train.

Newcastle's main station had systems to manage the pandemic; limited passenger numbers, one way systems and compulsory face masks. Walking from the fleet of four cars, the usual suspects gathered together on the station concourse for goodbye. Sarai's dear friends were subdued. Noëmi was standing near to her father trying not to cry. Donnie fussed over the arrangement of the bags in the luggage trolley. She could see he was getting agitated; *'No doubt he's worrying about Sarai and little Lucia getting on a ferry. He's watched too many episodes of **Seconds From Disaster.'***

The group moved towards the platform gates. Final checks made. Pictures taken. Hugs given. Tears held back. Smiles forced. Donnie was shifting his weight from foot to foot. He kept stepping forward and then back. Sarai got to the platform barrier where she had to say her final farewells before leaving for good.

"Is Lucia's food to hand? You'll need to get help with all these bags!" Donnie wittered on, going over to check once more and to rearrange things in her hand baggage. Sarai nodded, unable to talk. Each took turns to hug Sarai one last time. Noëmi was grimacing to avoid her tears falling.

"You're coming at Christmas? Yes? If we're back in lockdown, then just come as soon as you can?" She grasped her friend by the shoulders and pulled her into her arms.

Finally, Sarai turned to Donnie. Five months and seventeen days of living with Sarai were coming to an end. Without a word, Donnie moved forward and gave Lucia a pat on the head. Next, he gave Sarai the longest hug. Sarai was leaving. Head low, she glanced round at everyone as if in slow motion. She appeared resolved as she took Lucia by the hand to go through to the final ticket checkpoint. This was it.

Guy reflected on the almost four years that had passed since the day he had to tell Sarai the news about Luca. Frank, Val and Marcus were not fond of goodbyes and the accompanying feelings. Yumi was gently rocking, finding it hard to stand and although less emotionally affected than the others, she did not like the fact Sarai was leaving. It upset the natural order of things.

As Sarai walked away, clutching her daughter's hand, Donnie kept fidgeting and then he suddenly rushed forward towards Sarai. He pulled off his mask and shouted out,

"Sarai! Please don't go, stay here with me! Please stay with me!"

She scrambled straight for him.

"Donnie, you and me? Do you feel the same?"

"Sarai, yes! Yes I do!"

The others were speechless as Sarai fell into Donnie's arms. She yanked off her mask. Sarai and Donnie kissed each other with all the passion there was to be had in the world. Noëmi gasped loudly and steadied herself on the double pushchair. Nonchalantly, Marcus went to retrieve Lucia who was standing bewildered at the security barrier. The group moved away to give the pair some privacy and stared at one another. Behind their masks their mouths dropped open. No one was more stunned than Noëmi. Yumi put her phone in her pocket and swung around.

"He's young looking and fit for fifty-three. Not bad really, if I were single and nearer that age, I wouldn't say no."

Val and Guy both laughed.

"That's my dad, Yumi," Noëmi said flatly.

"Yeah so, just saying and that's what Sarai is, single and nearer his age Noëmi."

"Yes but...oh God, I'm so confused."

Looking across she could see her father and Sarai talking intently; he was stroking her hair as he held her in a strong embrace. She was clutching his shoulders, then touching his face. Deep in conversation, their eyes spoke nothing but love for each other. Next they were kissing and hugging again. Hands were everywhere.

"What are you saying fifty-three usually looks like then Yumi?" Frank asked indignantly.

"Fifty-three...depends on your attitude I guess Frankie, you're not bad either. N, those genes do bode well for you." Yumi replied. They laughed some more.

"No, everyone needs to stop this conversation, at flu jab time there was almost a murder in Boots when the assistant asked Frank if he was over sixty-five!" said Val.

"Honestly, I'm not sure what you find so funny Val, you're not that far behind!"

"Did I say I don't find you attractive? You know my older man!" Val put his arm around Frank.

"Yumi, how would you even think that way about my dad?" Noëmi had reflected a bit more.

"I don't, it's just right now I can see why she would like him.

He's got all his hair, which is a definite plus and his body is toned…"

"*His body is toned*. What is this all of a sudden? He's a grandfather by the way!" Noëmi was wide eyed.

"He plays all that badminton, have you ever been to one of his tournaments, Noëmi? Ah no of course not!" Yumi lifted her face defiantly.

"Yes, Yumi actually I did go to one once, it was somewhere in the Midlands…can't quite recall where…"

As they all squabbled playfully with each other about age, attractiveness and absence from sporting events, Marcus discreetly went over to Donnie and Sarai. They were still talking intently and holding each other.

"What's the decision then?" he asked gently.

Donnie did not look at Marcus, being too focussed on Sarai.

"I'm staying with Donnie." Sarai said, wiping her eyes.

"I'll let everyone know, take your time, we've got Lucia."

Marcus went over and told Noëmi the news first. "Sarai's not moving to Italy, she's staying here with your dad. N, I think the signs have been there for a while."

"Oh my!" Noëmi's face could not hide her shock.

Donnie

Since Gina had come into their lives, Donnie had begun to realise what his relationship with Sarai had become. Releasing from their embrace he had to reckon with her.

"Sarai, all this time I've been wanting to tell you how I feel about you! I just didn't know how, I thought you'd think I'd gone crazy!" He stroked her hair.

"Donnie, it's been so hard!"

Clutching each other, they both shared a gaze of pure joy. Donnie kissed her gently and smiled, eyes glistening,

"We should've had this conversation last night!"

"I tried!...I said it!...You and me. We laugh. We cry. We love. You make me me. I want to tell you that I love you."

He thought for a moment and realised.

"Is that what you were saying! In Vietnamese!"

He embraced her again and felt secure in her arms. He recalled the previous evening.

15 August 2020, the day before. High Heaton, Newcastle.

Bags packed, Donnie started putting them by the door. Lucia, now three years old, suddenly grabbed her mother's leg and began to whimper.

"She doesn't like suitcases after what happened earlier this year." Sarai was hauling one of the smaller cases into position.

"When Honeyfield evicted you?"

"Mmmm we were in a mess."

Donnie shut his eyes. *Why does she have to go?'* He walked to the kitchen and tidied anything away. Sarai followed him.

"I'll leave all the kitchen stuff, it'll be easier to buy new ones when we get to Rome."

His throat was tight.

"I'll keep it safe. When are you thinking of coming back to visit?"

She did not reply. Tears pricked his eyes as he looked at the different utensils she had added to his kitchen. How he loved to joke about all the new dishes and foods he had now tried. It was no longer funny. He saw her disappear to settle Lucia. He heard her take a shower and soon she was ready for bed in her old familiar dressing gown. They sat with a milk tea together and he checked their itinerary to Rome. As Donnie shut his laptop, he caught sight of Sarai looking his way. Eyes locking, then she turned away. She was a beautiful woman; petite with shoulder length dark hair, eyes of acorn brown and plump, plum coloured lips.

Sighing she broke the silence, "You and Gina will have the sofa to yourselves."

Donnie was quick. "I'm not sure about that! She asked about coming over to cook me dinner once you'd left but I told her there was no point! I told her that it was never going to work as I don't have those kinds of feelings for her."

"Oh! What was her reaction?" Sarai's eyes were bright.

"She called me pathetic!" Donnie replied.

Tea burst from Sarai's mouth. "Sorry! But she *is* the blueprint of your perfect partner!"

"No she's not! Sarai, listen to me, I've got to talk to you …"

Suddenly Lucia was screaming. Sarai jumped up.

"Night terrors! It's the suitcases!"

They both bounded up to the boxroom where Lucia was sleeping for her final night. Sarai cuddled her daughter and Donnie sat on the end of the bed.

"Not go! Not go!" Lucia sobbed as her eyelids gently flickered shut.

"She wants to stay!" Donnie's voice did not hide his hope.

Sarai tucked her daughter up and kissed her head. Lucia sucked her thumb and breathed deeply, with occasional little rasps from her crying. Donnie and Sarai stood together. She turned to face him, this time when their eyes met, she did not avoid his gaze. They stood before each other, he held her shoulders gently, she reciprocated by touching his arm softly. *'I want to kiss her so badly,'* Moments seemed like hours, *'Does she feel the same? She knows everything about me and there's nothing I don't know about her apart from whether we could just let ourselves love each other. I don't want to be friends. God, what if I blow this? She'll go to Italy and I'll never see her again. I could write her a letter?'*

"Donnie, I'm a bit scared if I'm honest."

He pulled her in for a hug. She began to cry. *'Oh God, I can't kiss her now when she's all vulnerable, it'd be like I'm taking advantage of her emotions. I'll have to write a letter.'*

They held each other. She quietly whispered words he could not understand.

"Bạn và tôi.

Chúng tôi cười.

Chúng tôi khóc.

Chúng tôi yêu.

Bạn làm cho tôi tôi.

Tôi muốn nói với bạn rằng tôi yêu bạn."

Later that evening, Gina had decided to try one final unprovoked attack. With the others asleep, Donnie sat at his kitchen table reliving his moments with Sarai. The spats, the jokes, the understanding. He could see her beaming smile and her lovely eyes. He could hear her laughter and how she called his name. He could feel his heart beat faster when she caught his gaze and when their hands brushed together. As Donnie mused on how to put his feelings for Sarai into the written word, Gina called him up.

"Donnie I'm so sorry about earlier, I didn't mean to be off hand, it's just I've invested time with you in the hope of a long term relationship!"

Donnie doodled on the paper before him.

"Gina, you need to know that's not going to happen. I respect you and I enjoy our friendship but that's all it is!"

She huffed, "If you don't have feelings for me does that mean you're still obsessed with your late wife?"

Sighing to himself, he knew he had to be honest. "Gina, I miss Manon with my whole being but she's no longer here. My love for her will never die, but finally I have moved on."

"Well then we could try?"

"The trouble is that I have feelings for someone else…"

"You useless waste of space! How dare you string me along! After all this time I've wasted getting to know you!"

Gina cut the call.

16 August 2020, Newcastle Central Station.

Noëmi

Eventually with their decisions made, the pair arranged for Val to tell Roberto about the change in plans. As everyone worked on the logistics of reversing all the shipments on their way to London, Donnie and Sarai were holding each other, oblivious to anyone else. Nothing mattered anymore.

Frank sighed and cast his arm to point out the row of grey steel ticket machines,

"I feel like this should be taking place somewhere more romantic, like Paris, not northern Britain!"

"And what's wrong with Newcastle? From what I remember the Gare du Nord anti trespass panels are not that picturesque." Noëmi snapped back, still in combat mode.

"N, look at them! It's all so full of drama and emotion! Kind of like a Robert Doisneau photograph right in front of us!"

She moved her eyes to her father and Sarai. They were like a pair of teenagers in love; kissing, sharing secret conversations and laughing at whispered jokes. He was stroking Sarai's hair with his right hand and her left hand was cupping his face, as their free hands were interlaced in a knot that was never to be undone. Noëmi had never seen her father like this; he had not kissed anyone for nearly fourteen years! Her eyes were child-like. Slowly she noticed Marcus with a cat like smirk all over his face as he knelt next to the double buggy, occupying their babies.

"What?" She scowled.

"I told you! How did you not see how perfect they are for each other!" He caught a falling sippy cup. "You could've meddled in that!"

"Who are you? Some kind of love guru all of a sudden!"

"It was when your dad asked me about how to sign off her birthday card; whether to put love."

"What did you say?"

"I told him, put what his heart feels and so he signed it…all my love!"

"And you didn't tell me!"

"I was busy and you were obsessed!"

"And it's taken them this long!" She was incredulous,

"Must run in families…but six months is better than six years I guess!"

* * *

Later that day Noëmi received a message from her father.

'Sorry about that N! All a bit embarrassing! I can explain, we just need a bit of time.'

Before they knew it, the North East had local restrictions and a second lockdown was looming for the UK. Noëmi had just finished a day of online teaching, in between caring for mischievous toddlers. Extracting a toilet brush from Bruno's tight grip, she watched the announcements on the evening news.

"Households can't mix. You won't be seeing your dad for a bit then! I'm sure he'll be fine holed up with Sarai!" Marcus quipped.

Nodding, she sighed. "Those two do love a lockdown, I wonder what's next? Oh God, are they using any contraception?"

CHAPTER 46 - IT WASN'T ME!

20 August 2020, Jesmond, Newcastle.

Noëmi

The summer holidays gave Noëmi time to focus on nothing but her family. However, she was increasingly unnerved that her friend, Bri Francis, had still not been in touch. Bri's relationship with Digby had been confirmed in his statement to police. Noëmi sent yet another text. Suddenly a reply.

'Noëmi, I need to talk to you, I'm sorry about all that happened.'

'Bri, no problemo, but you did know that it wasn't me in those photos!!!'

Finally, Bri called her friend for a long chat. Amidst tears and apologies, Bri was upfront.

"Noëmi, it's all a bit of a mess. My options were either to leave Digby or to stay."

Noëmi felt her heart drop to her feet.

"And you've chosen to…?"

"Leave him. When it started, I was lonely and it was a bit of fun, but we actually began to like each other. There was only one small irritation between us…he doesn't remember me from Yumi's hen do. It was only you he noticed."

Colour rising, Noëmi did not hide her anger. "I just chatted to him! I'm allowed to do that! Don't make all this about me! Well done to Digby for throwing in the golden apple of confusion to set women against each other! Think about what *he's* done!"

Bri continued. "I know. He never asked Alura where she was the night Isabelle was murdered. He desperately wanted to believe the accidental death verdict but deep down he knew what she was capable of… he never attacked her, she faked all that! Like the cancer!"

"That man's silence nearly killed my children! And he denied Isabelle justice! Just so he could keep swindling vulnerable people out of their hard earned cash!" Noëmi was spitting with rage.

"Digby takes full responsibility. Evil was unleashed and he was the catalyst." Bri continued her vain attempts to defend the man.

"Bri! How on earth can you stand up for that monster? Guilty as Alura is, he goaded her and flaunted his infidelities before her. His hands are also covered in Isabelle's blood!" She was incensed.

They were quiet for a bit.

"Yeah, I'm ridiculous."

"No! What was the attraction? He's a con artist and a cheat!" Noëmi was wary.

"Whoa Noëmi, stop! There's something else. Like you, I'm not great with contraception I guess…"

"What?"

"I've not seen anyone because of all the online lessons. My 'stomach problem' is the baby I'm expecting with Digby. I was about to tell you but I got scared in case there was a danger of the baby being taken into care. My lawyer's checked and I'm protected."

Noëmi felt a mix of rage towards Digby and confusion regarding Bri's blinkered devotion to the man.

"My children could be lying dead as Digby becomes a father!"

Bri began to cry.

"Whatever happens I need to protect this child. They've done nothing wrong."

Silence. Bri gave sighs in between small sobs. Images of the suffering inflicted by the Honeyfields filled Noëmi's mind. In her arms she felt the weight of her children. They were safe there. Gently their chests rose and fell as they drifted off to sleep; warm, soft, innocent. As she kissed their foreheads, she understood that to truly forgive was the most selfless thing that anyone could do.

* * *

Guy

Later that afternoon, Guy and Yumi popped round to the McKenzie house on the pretext of giving Noëmi and Marcus a printed copy of the next steps in the case. Outside in the garden Yumi, now nearly nine months pregnant, flopped onto a bright red bean bag and attempted to curl into a ball. Guy paced.

"You could've emailed this! You just want a chat with M don't you!" Noëmi perched on her bright blue bean bag, her hair fell softly forwards over her shoulders and gave golden glints in the afternoon light. Her smile beamed.

"Or was Yumi desperate to see you!" His voice did not cover his nervousness.

The babies made straight for Rolo. They all settled two metres apart. Sitting in the garden the quiet of Covid life continued. Not a plane in the sky. Just the chirps of birdsong and the hum of bees. Guy was weighed with guilt.

'Here, right on this spot, I was vile to her. Contempt is the lowest feeling you can have towards someone.'

"Tea anyone? Oh, forget that let's have some wine!" She skipped to the kitchen without an outward care. Marcus was playing with the children who toddled about like bowling pins.

Yumi was snoozing. Guy checked in with Marcus.

"How are you both doing?"

"Yeah good! Can I make a complaint about how the superintendent spoke about her?"

Guy took a breath, "I would say yes, definitely. I'm riled that she was bullied, she's the opposite of what he said."
"Yeah, it was bad, she still gets upset by it all. People don't realise that words are violence, hostility is hate and shunning makes people shy. We deal with it between ourselves."

Guy swallowed hard. Seeing Marcus charge to retrieve one of the toddlers, Guy slipped into the house, on the pretext of helping Noëmi.

"Hello hero!" Noëmi's eyes were shining. She always smiled. She always made that effort to make people feel good. Maybe her experiences had opened that generosity up in her? Burrowing in the fridge, her brow furrowed as she decided on the best wine. "Prosecco or rosé? Or rosé prosecco! We've got the essentials obviously!"

"Noëmi."

"Yes, Guy." The fridge door spoke. He waited. She looked round at him from behind the chrome.

"I know I've said sorry but it's not enough. I feel worse than dreadful."

She nodded, "I can tell you need to talk." Her free hand squeezed his. The relief was immense.

"I just believed what I saw. I didn't know what to think!" Guy fiddled with the fridge magnets,

Polaroids of happy McKenzie faces began to fall. With a hollow laugh she spoke,

"That I was having wild sex with Digby Honeyfield between nappy changes! I'm impressed that anyone thought I'd have the energy and disappointed that anyone thinks I'd do that to Marcus."

"I feel completely terrible. The horrible thing is that this apology is mostly to make me feel better. I honestly don't know why I didn't stick up for you! Marcus never doubted you." Guy began picking up photos.

"The pictures deceived the eye! To say sorry does mean everything Guy! Marcus didn't believe it! That's all that really matters. He was angry that I'd been so clumsy but hey you know me!" She shut the fridge with her foot. More pictures and fridge magnets cascaded off and the bottle of wine fell from her hands as she stumbled forward. Guy caught it and her. Steading her, he handed the prosecco back.

"Noëmi, you mean so much to me. We had a laugh when we met! Remember? I hardly knew anyone in Newcastle. Now because of you I've got you two, my best friends, and Yumi. Can you forgive me? Truly forgive me?"

"Yes! Honestly Guy, forget about it! I…"
"I can't."

"…get…"

"Enough of…"

"…you and…"

"…me."

They burst into giggles. Still hanging onto the bottle, she doubled over. Creased with laughter he could hardly breathe.

"I can't. Enough of me!" Guy repeated.

She straightened her sentence out too, "I get you and…I was going to add that you risked everything for us! Your career! The job that means everything to you! Thank you! At that moment you showed how much you love us!"

Hearing the hilarity, Marcus and Yumi joined them in the kitchen. Guy was scheming,

"Shhh! Let's break the law!" And the friends had a long group hug.

CHAPTER 47 - NEW CASTLE

21 August 2020, Jesmond, Newcastle.

Marcus

"Yumi's waters have gone!" Noëmi screamed.

Marcus stretched and pulled himself up to see the message.

"Yes! At least it's early morning so they probably have a good twelve hours until delivery. Not bad!" He flopped down only to hear crying in stereo via the baby monitor. "Welcome to parenting Guy and Yumi, just a few hours left of your chilled, sophisticated grown up life!" Together they got up and sorted out the toddlers.

With a full weekend off together, Marcus and Noëmi sat down at their French window for a well deserved, lazy breakfast. Scrambled eggs, avocados and bacon on toast, with freshly squeezed orange juice and Italian coffee. The morning was cotton fresh and warmed by the pair of squealing toddlers running around the patio. A knock at the door and Marcus went to it.

"Yumi! Shouldn't you be getting to the labour ward?" He remained open mouthed, as she pushed past him and Guy grinned behind her.

"Can you look after Rolo for a bit? Sorry about that!"

Rolo bounced past.

"Never a problem!" Noëmi's list of those to whom she was eternally and unconditionally grateful now included the spaniel Rolo.

Guy then stage whispered. "Anyhow, thought we could get some quick birthing tips!" Slapping Marcus on the back as he strolled past, Guy was excitement on legs.

"Mmm neither of us was actually there for our deliveries, if you think about it!"

The pair continued down the hallway. Yumi held her back as she sauntered bow legged into the kitchen.

"But your waters have gone! Yumi, you need to go to RVI! Now!" Marcus chased after her.

"Calm down Marcus, I've got loads of time! Baby's not due until tomorrow!" She positioned herself precariously on a kitchen stool. "This floor looks washable if the worst comes to the worst!" She gave Bruno and Emmanuelle a hug and flicked her hair back,

"We've got the works in the car! Snacks, earphones, cushions, Guy's even got his swim shorts in case it's a water birth! When we looked around there were these new pools...ooh...God...I really need the loo," She rubbed her pelvis and bent forward, breathing deeply.

"Yumi, has anyone examined you?" Noëmi was now wide eyed and open mouthed.

"No, the first labour takes, what, twelve hours or so. Don't want to be stuck in that hospital...ooh...ah...that's some pain and it's coming every damn minute..."

Marcus swung his head around, "What did you say?"

"Ah I've timed it, it kills for a minute then I get a minute off."

Jumping up, Marcus was agitated,

"Guy, you need to do something for me! Yumi, can you get to the front room?"

Guy was busy texting, "I'm just letting the family know there'll be news later today."

Marcus gave him a look and he stopped, took Yumi by the arm and followed Marcus' instructions. They helped Yumi lie down on one of the playmats and arranged some of their new linen cushions behind her head to support her. Moaning, Yumi was clearly now in pain.

"I'll talk you through it, but can you look and check if you can see the baby's head!"

"What?"

Guy furrowed his brow, bent down and removed her knickers for her. Suddenly he gave a start,

"Ah, it's never looked like that before! Marcus, I think you should check this out!"

Yumi gave a yelp and hissed,

"What the hell! No! Not your best mate checking out my vagina thank you very much!" Defiantly, she shoved her maternity dress between her thighs.

"Mimi, he's a doctor! It's not some guy from the pub!"

Yumi began to quietly moan then gave a cry, "Ahhh I need to push!"

Marcus grimaced at his options; talk Guy through the checks, Noëmi could help. What if they missed something? *'A precipitous labour increases the risk to mother and baby. I have to take responsibility if something goes wrong that can't be on their shoulders, it could only be on mine. Yumi will have to trust that as a doctor I respect her dignity.'*

Marcus ran to grab some gloves, and got into position,

"Yumi, I've done this so many times, just relax, it's really not personal!"

Noëmi gave a jump, "What! How many times?"

Yumi gingerly allowed Marcus to examine her. Carefully Marcus checked his patient, keeping as much of the dress pulled down as possible. Guy moved next to him and Yumi scowled at the pair the whole time, until another pain overwhelmed her.

"N, please call an ambulance. Yumi just breathe, really slowly, and tell me when you feel the pain again." With a calmness befitting of the Pope, Marcus was now an emergency doctor.

Yumi grabbed Guy's arm, "I need to push! Now! I can't hold it!"

'Ambulance come on!'

He felt around her abdomen. Her baby was on its way. Nothing was stopping her baby's determination to be born.

"Yumi, you're fully dilated and your baby's coming right now. You need to get ready to push!"

Guy's face blanched,

"What now! Here! I thought we had twelve hours or so! We need to pick up some massage oil."

"Guy, this baby's coming right now and right here!"

Marcus was checking as the head began crowning. Guy stuttered in a panicked voice,

"Do we need hot water, towels and shit, like in the movies?"

Marcus' eyes caught Noëmi's, he whispered,

"Is the ambulance on the way?"

Yumi never missed anything.

"Oh God, don't say we're just seconds from you and Tianna's boyfriend delivering…"

Yumi cried out half in agony, or maybe in fear of the imminent arrival of Joel, as another contraction took over her body.

"Yumi push hard, bear down! I just need to press here, to stop the baby coming out too quickly. Guy, support her!" Marcus pressed the perineum and then gently helped the tiny head out of Yumi. He looked at the squidgy, bright red, lifeless face. His whole soul shook, *'Oh God, you have to be okay.'*

Noëmi knelt down and held the two leg grabbing toddlers out of the way.

"And that's great, there the head's out, now pant, don't push,"

Marcus confirmed the cord was not around the baby's neck. *'All fine, just double check the shoulders.'* Sirens grew in volume; help was on its way. His confidence was rising.

"Final big push Yumi, you're doing brilliantly."

The baby slithered out with the last effort. Clearing the airway, Marcus held his own breath, waiting for the baby to take their first. An almighty, piercing scream gave everyone the good news.

"N, what's the time?"

"Nine forty-two!"

"Remember that! And you have a son!"

With no time to get a towel, the plump, squidgy boy was placed straight into Yumi's arms.

"Matsu!" Yumi howled with joy. Guy, still holding Yumi from behind, hugged her and their new baby.

Moments later Noëmi opened the door to the paramedics who got straight into action, checking Matsu and Yumi. Being a team from RVI, they recognised Marcus immediately and took an initial SBAR. Casually Marcus asked, "Is Joel working today?"

"Yeah, just finishing before he restarts uni. He's assisting on first response too, nearly came with us but he's just gone out to another emergency birth in a taxi!"

"Ah damn, so close!" Marcus teased, catching Yumi's eye as she was having her placenta delivered by the paramedics. Eventually, the new family were whisked off in the ambulance. As he left, a sobbing Guy hugged Marcus and Noëmi, assuring them that he would replace the front room playmat.

Marcus flopped into a seat, Noëmi joined him as the toddlers clambered all over them.

"How many births am I going to be at before I get to be *at* one of my own!" She sighed.

CHAPTER 48 - TEN YEARS

26 August 2020, Jesmond, Newcastle.

Noëmi

Walk to the park complete, babies fed, errands done. Having taken the day off work, Marcus made a birthday brunch for Noëmi and himself, smoked salmon, cream cheese on bagels with fresh coffee. Sitting at the kitchen table, he watched her open her gifts and together they admired Bruno and Emmanuelle playing with a set of large foam letters and numbers.

"A future genius!" Noëmi quipped as Bruno tried to ram the letter H into his mouth.

Marcus was suddenly silent. He did not react but stared ahead.

"Are you okay?" She could tell he was not.

"Yeah, sure." He drummed his fingers.

"Marcus…"

"Did you feel something?" He gave her a look that she knew too well.

"No, I was just flattered that some guy was flirting with me. Honestly that's it!" She took his hand. His wedding ring was one with his flesh. He turned his head and rubbed his jaw with his other hand.

"I meet women all day, every day. I know other women; I know them well. I work with them, they're my friends. I can see they're attractive, nice smiles, they work out, lovely hair. Without being up myself sometimes I can tell if they're interested, which is, as you say, flattering. But I don't need flattery. I never *feel* anything. I feel absolutely nothing at all. That's not me being some kind of saint. It's because of what I've got with you. You're the only person I've ever felt that kind of connection with, not just because we get on, because we're similar, because we love each other. What I mean is that pure physical attraction…"

"Yes, that's the same for me!" She squeezed his hand with both of hers.

"But N, I mean that visceral feeling in my gut that I can never get enough of you. Your touch, how you touch me, how you feel. And it grows as time goes on, I don't get used to you, I get more into you. But this thing scares me, that you could get your head turned by someone because he makes you feel…what? Desired? Clever?"

He put his free hand to her face and stroked her cheek with his finger.

"It wasn't like that, it wasn't physical, it wasn't attraction, it was just an ego thing. Maybe because of what happened at school. The John Dyer thing."

"The bullies proved themselves wrong. Every word they said, every silence, every hateful act."

She slipped herself onto his lap.

"It's ten years today since we got together and eleven years of knowing what we wanted! Remember that first time, you and me, that day, that pure sexual desire." She kissed him. "We found each other. The person who loves us as much as we love them." He caressed her neck, the silver heart necklace was always there.

She pointed to their children, "They're looking tired don't you think? Nap time?"

With a complicitous smile, they took the babies to their cots and themselves to bed.

Lying together they remembered when they first knew they had feelings for each other.

27 August 2009, eleven years earlier, Newcastle Green Academy.

Marcus and Noëmi

The moment had arrived; Newcastle Green Academy GCSE results' day. The school management's usual attempt to use smoke and mirrors to disguise their generally lacklustre results was itself worthy of an A star. Would today bring anything to repudiate reports that the management could do better?

The sports hall was arranged with mismatched tables where students would line up, depending on the first letter of their surname. Amidst the murmur of nervous students and even more nervous family members, occasional shrieks went up for surprises of both sorts; success and maybe a little less success. Ruby was already in tears before she had even got into line, let alone opened her envelope. Her mother, Dr Barraclough, rolled her eyes and gently pushed her daughter into her queue. The buzz fell away as Marcus and Noëmi huddled together in the M to O file. Marcus was moving from foot to foot. In front of him Noëmi was biting her nails. Having finished her right hand, she moved onto the left.

"We need at least six A* grades to be able to do the Oxbridge thing." Marcus stated what they both already knew. "And no duds, you can't hide them."

"No one in this school ever gets high grades." She gave a small cry as she bit too hard.

"You need to stop doing that!"

She sucked her finger which was bleeding.

"Remember we open each other's, but don't let them notice. No wind ups, got that?"

Marcus nodded.

Taking their envelopes, they thanked the school assistant politely and moved to the side of the hall. Out of the corner of his eye he could see his mother peering anxiously. Hiding their exchange, they took the other's results. They kept glancing at each other as they tore open the envelopes. Noëmi gave a choked laugh and started to flap her hands at her face. "You've done it, my God, everything A* only one A in English."

At the same time, he gave a scream, "N all A*s only one A in English too! You smashed it."

"Identical results!" Swapping back, they devoured the information.

They flung themselves into a hug. Tightly they held each other, not letting go, rocking side to side. As the dusty, stale trainer smelling hall transformed into the sweetest, sunniest place on earth, they both felt light as they saw nothing but each other. Life was beautiful.

Mrs Gomez, eyes sparkling, appeared at their sides.

"Congratulations you two! The best results ever in the history of

Newcastle Green, although you can't really compare GCSEs to 'O'Levels and we did get some solid results back in the day!"

Noëmi and Marcus released each other.

"Now we do have the raw marks if you want to know who came top in each exam!"

"No Miss, we're fine. Although maybe for maths?"

"You really don't want to find out that I beat you in your favourite subject Noëmi!"

Marcus gave her a playful knock with his shoulder. She bumped him back. Unable to wait any longer, their families were at their sides. As they looked at both sets of results, Marianna burst out sobbing, Anthony stood open-mouthed, Raeni danced and Donnie had to sit down. These two were to be feted, they had found the formula, their dreams were coming true. Phone calls to grandparents and lunch plans followed. Noëmi and Marcus walked away together. As they moved through the packed hall, their hands brushed each other's and they felt the force of the magnetism between them. Attraction confirmed, a mutual preoccupation with mouthwash and deodorant acquired, it was a matter of time.

26 August 2020.

He held her tight.

"That day!"

"What a day! It has to be our best memory, ten years!"

"Noëmi, you kept your promise. Our promise."

26 August 2010, ten years earlier, High Heaton, Jesmond.

Noëmi

After the beach visit for her birthday, Marcus opted to go home with Noëmi and her father in the small red Renault. Marianna sighed. The teenagers said this was so they could continue watching the Luther series on catch up. In truth they would have signed up for anything; even housework if it meant being with the other. Sitting together in the back, Donnie smiled at them and complained that he felt like a taxi driver.

"I hope I get a good review!"

"Ah, no little bottles of water! You lose a star Dad!"

She rested her head on Marcus' shoulder and he rested his on her head. Arriving back everyone was sandy and sticky. Donnie systematically unloaded the car and the seventeen year olds were first in taking turns to shower.

"Bathroom's free," Noëmi called out. A trail of shower gel foam bubbles showed her path across the hall to her room. Marcus bounded upstairs to have his turn.

"Towels are in the airing cupboard." She called out from behind her door.

A few minutes later he shouted back to her.

"N, how do you even turn it on?"

She remembered Marcus had never used the new digital shower her father had got fitted. She called for her father but he was not answering. *'This towel's huge, I'm decent.'* She went to the bathroom and knocked, he unlocked the door. Marcus stood in his towel, waiting. She showed him the settings. Turning as she finished explaining they looked silently at each other. Although covered in their towels, embarrassment burnt through them, quickly they averted their gaze. Leaving him to it, she got dressed, but for some reason chose her best outfit for an evening of sitting on the sofa.

Heart beating, she went downstairs. Hyperactive, she began to tidy up the leftover picnic in the kitchen. Eventually Marcus ran down the stairs, refreshed and sand free. Towel around his neck he had evidently wasted no time. They smiled self consciously at each other. Their nervous silence deafened her. The warm afternoon streamed onto the hob past the red gingham curtains. The faint sound of Donnie sorting himself out upstairs was all that could be heard. The distraction was welcome. Eventually Donnie dashed down and called out.

"I need to do the supermarket shop, get the car washed and get to the city centre too. Sorry Marcus, got N's grandparents arriving for the weekend tomorrow. I'll get pizza on the way home, but I won't be back for a good few hours. I've got some surprises to organise!" He gave his daughter a wink. "Certainly not before eight," he said, "at the earliest! You'll have to wait for the Pepperoni Passion!" And he left.

Noëmi opened the fridge. The cool air was a relief, every sense in her body was heightened.

"You know how he shops, lists and spreadsheets! Want a Pepsi?" Hunting past a bag of old potatoes, she groaned, "Damn there's only one, we'll have to share."

"And that's why he's gone shopping!" Marcus was still drying his softly curled hair.

"Yeah, alright Einstein." She gave him a look. Grabbing the can, it felt ice cold against her hand. He was busy arranging his hair, bending to look in the mirror on the kitchen wall, his t-shirt had ridden up as he stretched over. She quickly pressed the can onto his back. He swung round, "Ah that's freezing!"

He prised the can from her hand and went to retaliate. Giggling and going for his wrists she held him back. Pushing his hand forward, he moved closer. Now holding his shoulders, she shrieked as he fought to counterattack. They were close. Noëmi stopped. Marcus was still. She slipped her hands from his shoulders to around his neck. Naturally his arms hugged her around the waist. He dropped the drink. For a minute neither spoke. She felt him hold her tightly. She could feel his heartbeat. Noëmi was brave,

"Maybe I shouldn't say this but…" Her voice failed.

Marcus did not take his eyes from her and finished her sentence,

"I like you, I really like you…and not as a friend."

She gasped, "Same! I don't want to be friends!"

"I've felt this way for ages, N…" His voice was breathless. He was fidgety.

Her heart began to race,

"My God…my God, all this time…we've been falling in love!"

His face lit up with pure joy, his breath was warm, his touch was gentle.

She tilted her head back, "Do I get a birthday kiss?"

Leaning together they kissed. First kiss. Nothing was awkward. So naturally they fell together. As they finally released, she was short of breath. He stroked her hair.

"Over this last year…" She tried to speak.

"Yes, me too, the feelings just get stronger."

They kissed again even more feverishly.

Marcus held her face, "N, I don't want a friends with benefits thing, I want us to be a proper couple. Together. Us."

"Yes! Yes! You and me!" She whispered cupping his face.

"Oh my God, I've actually dreamt of this actual moment." He threw his head back. "I've been thinking when to say something, I thought maybe after the exams…"

"Another year of feeling like this? Oh God!"

Embracing again and again they were unable to resist the force of their attraction. Tightly they held onto each other to be as physically close as possible. Kissing, touching, giggling, then they were serious. She beckoned him to follow her upstairs.

"N, with the way we feel about each other, that's dangerous!"

She smiled. She was certain. As longed for romance replaced their firm friendship, they did not hesitate to advance. Conspiratorially, they confirmed consent and checked contraception. They were ready.

Marcus

Marcus felt like he had been hit by a tidal wave. Never had he wanted anything more. Friendship had turned into love; feelings he had never experienced before. Constantly he thought about her, always he wanted to be with her and more than anything he cared deeply for her. He knew it was no longer friendship as he was irresistibly and physically attracted to her like a sailor to the Sirens. Before long they were lying together on Noëmi's bed, skin on skin, no longer self conscious; they trusted each other completely. Stupefied by this new experience for them both they were overwhelmed by their physical compatibility and the intensity of their connection. Hearts racing, they were breathless. Plans for their future ran through his head.

"Don't let me go. Being here like this, with you. I'm fine but… sixth form…" she rested her head on his chest.

"Ah, can you imagine when everyone there finds out we're together? I love that! First day back, we'll walk into the common room together hand in hand." Marcus whispered, kissing the top of her head.

Noëmi looked up and began to smile. She touched his lips,

"Now you're scheming!" Suddenly she was bolt upright. "No, no!"

"N! What? Why are you worried about what people will think?" He sat up behind her and gently caressed her shoulders.

"I am…but it's not that, Marcus," she grabbed his hand and turned her body to his. "If your family finds out we're so much more than friends they'll stop you coming over. Your mum would absolutely freak out if she knew what we're doing! Beliefs and all that. I can't manage all this work, this Oxbridge stuff without you! No one else understands!"

"I can't do it without you either." Wanting her so much, he had put all those thoughts about his family's rules to the back of his mind.

"Then it's just for us, we'll tell no one else!"

They held each other tightly.

"Yes! We don't need to be deceitful to anyone, we just won't mention anything."

Resolved, they relaxed and made the most of their time together. Her room was bright and inviting; Marcus knew it well. She had upcycled her dressing table, chest of drawers and wardrobe into the popular shabby chic style, painting them duck egg. However, Noëmi always had her own play on things and she had overlaid a gold glitter paint which made the pieces stand out. Her curtains were gold flecked voile and she had draped them into an Italian style design before her small window which overlooked the back garden. Pictures and small ornaments distracted the eye and a corner was dedicated to her work. The plain oak desk was covered in papers and stood before a huge bookcase filled with academic works and fiction imprints.

In time, Noëmi looked at the clock,

"It's just before eight, we need to get ourselves together!" As she went to get up, he stretched and took her hand in his.

"N, this is the beginning for us. Remember all we've said to each other today. You mean absolutely everything to me."

Leaning to kiss him she replied, "My promise to you is that we'll always love each other and never hurt one another."

Slipstreaming downstairs, they made as if they had been watching television all evening. Donnie rushed in oblivious to their hypersensitivity,

"N! I've got it!"

Blackberry Bolds, shopping bags, sim cards, queues, chatter all fell into the background. Before long Donnie had settled with a beer and pizza. Marcus and Noëmi could not take their eyes off each other. Slipping out to the garden, as Donnie snoozed, they could hold each other in their arms again. Now everything made sense.

And so throughout their final A Level year Noëmi McAllister and Marcus McKenzie were a couple, hiding in plain sight. Their alma mater, Newcastle Green Academy described itself as a 'vibrant centre of excellence for all students'. In reality the management struggled with the behaviour of a minority and relied on the good will of the majority. Therefore any student 'getting it right' in terms of their conduct was left to fend for themselves academically. Noëmi and Marcus worked this out pretty quickly.

The final year of sixth form had a more flexible timetable for students preparing for university. So every other Friday afternoon they finished at midday. This helped the school free up space for the other year groups and also for the bi-weekly management detentions for students 'not getting it right'. With the final year sixth formers 'off site' or rather, out of the way, senior staff could collect up their defiant brood and set about correcting their behaviour. Marcus and Noëmi identified these Friday afternoons as opportunities to spend time together and omitted to mention to their parents that they finished early on those days.

'Jacketgate' uncovered. Friday, 24 June 2011.

Noëmi

One early finish Friday they could not keep secret from their parents was the one when they finished their last A Level exam. Further maths was an additional subject which they had both taken and it was one of the most gruelling. To celebrate, the families had decided to organise a barbecue for the young students and a few of their friends that evening. Although the second exam was in the afternoon, the pair had finished by 3pm and were home by 3:30pm, giving them a good two hours before Donnie would return. Once back at Noëmi's house the pair were lying together in Noëmi's bed when they heard the front door open and shut. Some toing and froing and then her father called up.

"N! How was the exam?"

His footsteps were rushing up the stairs. With skin freezing horror Marcus and Noëmi sat up and stared at each other. There was no time.

"Hold on Dad! I'm just changing!" She yelled. Her limbs entangled with Marcus' as they frantically tried to get out of bed.

"Well hurry up, I want to hear all about it!"

The footsteps began to descend the stairs. They breathed. The doorbell went. They heard Marcus' mother enter and start chatting about shopping. From the way their voices echoed their parents were at the bottom of the stairs.

"He's early! He's never early! Now you're mum's here! What do we do?" She whispered, heart racing.

Indeed, Donnie was usually as precise as an atomic clock. The portents were not good.

"I don't know!"

They began to get dressed and tried desperately to make no noise. They heard Donnie talk to Marianna,

"N's just getting changed." Then he yelled up again, "N! Come on! Marianna's here, she's waiting for Marcus to find out how it went!"

The young lovers were like a pair of startled deer.

"You stay here, I'll go and distract them, when it's quiet you get out!"

Noëmi checked her reflection, brushed her hair and jogged downstairs. At that moment Marianna was coming up to use the toilet as the downstairs one was being redecorated.

"How was the exam Noëmi?"

"Fine!" she squeaked.

"Where's Marcus?"

"On his way…I think!"

"His jacket's here!" Marianna pointed to the bottom of the

stairs. In silence all sets of eyes tracked to the hallway bannister where the Adidas jacket had been flung with the transparent pencil case and scientific calculator poking from its pockets.

"With all his exam stuff!"

"Oh really?…he must've left that here!"

"I can see that! How did he manage in the exams? Let's hope he won't be long!" She gave a sideways glance and went into the bathroom.

Marcus shot out of Noëmi's room and jumped, ninja-like, down the stairs, checking for Donnie. Luckily he was in the kitchen organising the food. Silently they opened the door and Marcus escaped as Noëmi spoke loudly to her father.

"Hey Dad, this is all amazing!"

"Marcus has left his jacket here!"

A text pinged through. **'Couldn't find my boxers. Check bathroom? Get them fast!'**

'Oh God!'

She ran up to see Marianna exit from using the toilet, without a word.

"The new towels are so fluffy." Noëmi filled the silence with the first thing she could think of as she dived into the bathroom. By the shower she saw Marcus' undershorts.

'Did she see those? She must recognise them?' Trembling, she grabbed the underwear and hid it in her room. Downstairs Marianna and Donnie were preparing food. Noëmi sauntered into the kitchen and stood awkwardly.

"Anyone want tea?" Noëmi's voice quivered.

"Thank you, that would be very welcome." Marianna turned to Donnie, "The bathroom is so modern now since you had that new shower fitted last year and you keep it so tidy Donnie. Not a thing out of place!" Marianna exclaimed.

Noëmi could not bring herself to look at Marianna. Fumbling over the mugs as she took them from the cupboard, one crashed to the floor.

"Careful, Noëmi, watch you don't slip up!" Marianna commented without looking up.

Anthony

Turning off the main road, Marcus' father, Anthony strolled along. Having also decided to take the afternoon off work, he was looking forward to spending time with his children. *'Growing up far too quickly'* he mused as he approached Donnie's house. With a start, he spotted Marcus texting on his phone as he tiptoed out of the McAllister house. *'Why all the furtiveness?'* Eventually arriving at his home, just around the corner from the McAllisters, he found Marcus checking under the flower tubs for a spare key.

"We moved that, too many break-ins around here, don't want to help them out! Where's your key?"

"Ah, yes, I left my jacket…"

Anthony waited for the end of the sentence.

"…somewhere…"

With a frown he unlocked the front door and collected some dishes to take over to Donnie's house. Before he could leave, Donnie arrived on the doorstep. "Hello Anthony! Marcus left his jacket, I hope he was alright for his exam as it's got all his pens and calculators in it!"

Marcus appeared at his father's shoulder. "Thanks Donnie!"

From over Anthony's shoulder, he grabbed the jacket and flew upstairs. Anthony scratched his head and shrugged his shoulders at Donnie.

During the ensuing evening the families and students could relax. Marianna made small talk to a few of Marcus' friends. "How nice to have an early finish even if you did have exams!"

"Oh yeah but it's been a good year for that, we had every other Friday afternoon off school."

The sixth formers laughed. Noticing confusion cloud his wife's face, Anthony thought of the timetables that were pinned on the fridge for each McKenzie child. Marcus' schedule definitely had 'revision' marked for Friday afternoons.

"Was that not for revision?" Anthony asked.

"Yeah but you didn't have to stay in school, in fact they wanted to get rid of us as they needed the library space for detentions. That place is a mess!"

He was sure Marianna was wondering how those twenty afternoons had been spent as no mention of time off the school site had been given. Anthony observed Marcus and Noëmi together. As Marcus described the exam experiences Noëmi finished his sentences. They fetched things for the other without being asked. When they thought no one could see they whispered things to each other. As the evening came to an end, Marcus stayed back to help 'tidy up' in spite of his horror of household chores. Anthony walked home with his wife and mused,

"Maybe with the exams done, Marcus now has the opportunity to relax and find a girlfriend?"

"His timetable has always been full, so I'm sure he'll just carry on as he is." Marianna replied.

CHAPTER 49 - BLESSINGS

7 October 2020, Newcastle Royal Victoria Infirmary (RVI).
Marcus
Dr Marcus McKenzie was a man unburdened. Finally, he was now on the three year ACCS (Acute Care Common Stem) with a view to becoming a Major Trauma consultant just like Alex James. He loved his job and cared sensitively for his patients. Today he was in paediatric A&E and was honing his knowledge of Doc McStuffins for the youngsters. He checked his next case and went to the bay.

"No way! It's Doc McKenzie!"

Marcus was stunned. Before him stood the security guard from the Radisson and his partner who was cuddling their sixteen month old.

"Hey! Oliver, right? You got knocked off your bike, literally a year ago! You returned my wife's phone to me! How's things?"

"Yeah, good but Rudi's not well, fever we can't get it down, could it be meningitis?"

Calling his team together, Marcus got to work and Rudi was put on a drip and a number of monitors were connected to record his oxygen sats, blood pressure and heart rate.

"We'll admit him immediately and arrange for you to stay at his bedside."

Within a couple of days Rudi had made a full recovery and was discharged. His grateful parents thanked Marcus.

"How are you managing with the twins?" Oliver asked as he shook Marcus' hand vigorously.

"It's crazy, they find different ways to try to kill themselves every day!" As he joked, a cold feeling came over him. *'Focus on the good outcome.'*

"How is it with baby number three on the way?"

Marcus was stunned; his face was enquiring.

"Your wife, she's often at our hotel, The Radisson in Durham. I imagine she must be close to giving birth by now?"

"Sorry?"

"Your wife, she's expecting any minute!"

"No, we only have the twins! She's definitely not pregnant, I think I'd notice!"

"I'm confused…" Oliver was lost.

Marcus took his phone and showed his latest lock screen photo, "This is my wife!"

As his hand flew across his mouth Oliver let out a cry of something between shock and relief.

"Oh my God! It isn't her! You have no idea how triggered I've been. It's some other woman who's always at the hotel with that blonde bloke. I thought, oh thank God!" Oliver was bent double.

"Okay let me explain what happened."

For Marcus it felt good to relieve himself of all they had been through. Oliver listened and kept shaking his head,

"Marcus I'm so sorry, all this time! Please apologise to your wife! Look, we're often in Paddy Freeman's Park on a Sunday morning with Rudi. I know it's awkward in your professional capacity but if you're ever there look out for us. We'd love to chat and compare parenting notes! Thank you so much for all you've done for Rudi! You've saved our lives! Nothing's more precious than our children eh?"

Nodding Marcus could only agree. Whilst he had shared the photo mix up he was not quite able to talk about the abduction of two of the three people for whom he would instantly die. Therapy was definitely enabling him to cope with the nightmares that often woke him at 3am. Packing the trolley away as Rudi and his family left, Marcus smiled to himself, *I'd actually love another baby…'*

However, the encounter made Marcus uneasy. He realised that a dignified ignoring of Alura's viral video would not do. Staying late at work one day, he prepared his own little montage explaining the pictures and thus proving that the 'wife of the RVI poster boy' was never involved with Digby. Noëmi's nemesis, Alura, had not gotten away with it. Distribution of the clip was facilitated by the TV news crew when they visited RVI to interview the divine Dr McKenzie a second time. This time Alex had encouraged the cameras into his department with gusto.

"What's your message to the public in Newcastle!" The smiling presenter asked once again.

"Stay home and stay safe! Hold your loved ones close! Actually, can I just tell my wife, Noëmi, how much I love and adore her! I'm useless without her." Marcus was making hearts melt.

* * *

The cases against the Honeyfields had been prepared and were not contested. Alura remained in a secure unit and Digby languished in a low security prison. Further investigations into their financial affairs were begun as an adjunct to the existing charges. Guy ensured all details of the charges were made public and he included slander and defamation of character against Alura Honeyfield with regard to Noëmi McKenzie.

Bri Francis did not return to St Wolbodo's that September as she was now a single parent to her new baby daughter who had just been born. A picture of the serene infant was sent to Noëmi.

'Here she is! Béatrice Honey Francis! I'm more than in love! She'll be known as Bea! She's a real blessing!'

Marcus smiled at the picture,

"Do you think it's subliminal, Bea, bee...honey...? Ah she's gorgeous."

Noëmi laughed, "And Bri and Bea Francis!"

The momentary chink of joy in the darkness buoyed everyone. The details had been traumatising. Having re-submitted his medical evidence concerning the death of Isabelle Williams, Alex James was revisited by the angst that had haunted him five years previously. With Guy, he was able to meet Isabelle's parents to bring some so called 'closure'. As Hades had torn Persephone from her mother, so too had Isabelle been ripped from her family. Unlike the daughter of Zeus, Isabelle would not be reborn. Her parents' grief was worsened by the violence of her death at the hands of someone she trusted. Their world darkened once more. A second death was upon them. They mourned.

7 October, 2020. St Oswald's Church, Durham.

Attila

Attila Varga, vicar at St Oswald's, Durham, was a popular man during lockdown. Whilst worship had been suspended, anguish sadly flourished. Those who sought found comfort and blessing. Sometimes people just wanted to sit with him quietly. One lunchtime he was polishing the communion brass in the church lobby. The dusty, brown room was piled high with anything from the church that may harbour infection. A grandfather clock chimed two and he sighed. Placing the cup and plate down, he heaved his tired body out of the faded burgundy velvet chair and smoothed out his robe. Noticing a small stain on the cuff, he licked his fingers to clean it off. He then strolled to a bench in the graveyard. *I really need to find some volunteers to help me with this area, it's always so overgrown. I need one of those modern mowers or a tractor. I'll put a notice in the parish magazine.* In the distance he noticed two young women walking towards him. He called out to them.

"Louisa James?"

One of the girls waved. They approached and sat on the two office chairs he had laboriously carried out earlier that day.

"Father, thank you for seeing us!"

"Ah I'm a Church of England vicar, so call me reverend or simply Attila if you prefer, my dears."

"Thank you, Attila." Louisa made her choice.

"It's interesting how many people have come to me during lockdown with points of faith. Time gives us space to reflect. See a world beyond our own. Look into our hearts!" He caught sight of the wonky gravestones and wondered why death was such a fearful mystery. *Too much focus on the inevitable and not enough on the glory of faith in God!*

Nodding, the two girls held each other's hands.

"We wanted you to pray for us, Attila. We've had a bad experience." Louisa's voice shook. He noticed her eyes were sad.

"My dears, God loves us all. Never fear! God gave his only son, Jesus, so that we may live, He has a place in his church for us all. Life throws us choices and chances but God's promise remains steadfast. God loves you. God will never desert you."

Octavia explained the supernatural experience they had witnessed. Louisa's face was whiter than his Sunday robes. Standing up, Attila beckoned at them to walk around the graveyard with him. As he moved, he spoke with care.

"In the same way God exists, so does evil. Never underestimate how powerful those forces may be. Best never to tamper with the realms of the demons whatever you may think of God; a pact with the devil will only bring death and separation. Thank you for coming for prayer and for opening your hearts. God can give you comfort when you face desolation. God will console you in times of sadness."

Together they prayed and peace came upon the pair.

"Do we need to request an exorcism at the house?" Octavia asked wide eyed.

"My dear, if you wish for a vicar to bless your student house then that can easily be done. Do not worry. Prayer will always bring God's peace into your life."

The girls were a little overcome and with grateful thanks, they walked slowly away.

Attila remembered how he was at their young age. He too had been in love but it was forbidden. Memories flooded his mind. Pushing himself up he caught his breath and steadied himself. Wiping a tear, he felt comfort that he had known what it was to love and consoled himself with the knowledge that he had been loved as much in return. Yet not a day went by when he did not regret the separation.

Attila watched the girls leave across the overgrown path that led to the broken gate. He recalled the angry email from a young couple who lived opposite St Oswald's about the unkempt appearance of his church. *'I must find help soon!'*

CHAPTER 50 - THE PROMISE

23 December 2020, Jesmond, Newcastle.

Noëmi

Just before Christmas Yumi was visiting Noëmi for lunch, with baby Matsu. The Watanabe-Castle baby was a real smiler who slept easily and was as good natured as his mother and father. The two women discussed Christmas plans, as Noëmi sorted baby clothes to lend to Yumi. She held up a small jumper decorated with yellow dinosaurs.

"We're going to Guy's parents, it's a military operation! So much stuff to take. Everyone's excited. I was reluctant to go at first in case his ex-girlfriend Laura was in the village, but it seems she has met someone and is getting engaged!"

"That's fast work! In July she was still trying to mess with Guy's head with her fake cancer story!"

Bruno and Emmanuelle ran about the lounge pushing matching toddle trucks.

"Apparently it's someone she works with. She moved firms and didn't go to America in the end, partly because of lockdown but also because her father's so ill now."

"What about her pretend illness? Did her company find out?"

"Criminal malingering! It's a dismissible offence. She was lucky, they bought her story that she'd simply got better and just like that she changed jobs!"

"Unbelievable!"

"I don't care, as long as she's nowhere near us! Tbh, I think she'd be too ashamed to show her face. What she did is unforgivable." Yumi stacked up the baby items, preparing to leave.

With Christmas bubbles and imminent mixing limitations coming into force, Noëmi's father had been keen to visit. As Donnie arrived, with a rose bush in his arms he seemed energised. Offloading the plant to his daughter, Donnie went to the toddlers and stroked their heads. They screamed excitedly when they saw their grandfather. He knelt to hug them. He smiled as he saw baby Matsu.

"Hello Yumi! What a handsome chap! Back in the room where he was born, hey! And you seem to be coping admirably! N was still wailing on the sofa when the twins were Matsu's age!"

In contrast to Noëmi who clumsily battled through life, Yumi was back to her effortless elegance, even when dealing with a four month old.

"Dad I'd been unconscious for three weeks, I had an injured leg and I was breastfeeding two babies at once! Some days I couldn't even get dressed!"

"You got yourself together for my hen do! Not a whiff of motherhood that night! Priorities eh Noëmi?"

She rolled her eyes at Yumi who turned her attention to Donnie.

"Donnie, how are you doing? You know whenever I see Sarai, it's like she's a changed woman! Life must really be suiting her

413

now!" Yumi gave Noëmi a smug grin.

Whilst her father did not seem to notice, Noëmi gave Yumi a withering look. Yumi scooped up Matsu and added.

"Your hair looks good by the way Donnie!" She gave Noëmi a wink.

"Yumi, get out of here!" Noëmi called to her already out of the door friend.

With a giggle, Yumi was gone. The screeches and babbles of toddlers filled the room again.

"How are you my dear?" Donnie asked his daughter.

"Yeah okay, but…"

He was not listening. She stopped talking. Noticing, he filled the silence.

"Nice colour for the walls, can you give me the details of the paint, I need to…"

"Dad you're not here to talk about room colours now are you!"

He moved to the sofa and she took his hands.

"N, I feel terrible, so guilty."

He hesitated for a moment and then continued with some determination.

"This is hard to say…Sarai and I plan to get engaged, quietly, at Christmas and we're intending to marry, when the time is right for us. In the meantime, Sarai has moved in properly with me, Lucia has your old room. I'm so sorry! I feel awful…" he wiped his eyes and fidgeted some more.

"What are we like Dad! Don't feel bad, it's perfect for you both to have found love again." She squeezed his hand.

"We're so very happy, that's the worst part...although we can't quite believe it. We understand each other. Yesterday Sarai was very upset as she missed Luca so much with the four year anniversary of the crash. Sometimes I want to be alone with my thoughts about Manon, as I did on Monday...fourteen years...it feels like yesterday."

For a moment he was lost. Then he shook himself and carried on with determination,

"None of that's not a problem for us, we both have those days. It's separate from our feelings for each other and it's not some weird polygamy, it's just space for our hearts. We know Manon and Luca are gone, but we don't want to forget them in any way. Never! But we need to allow ourselves to love again, always knowing it's second love for us both. Only one thing leaves us questioning and confused," he wrung his hands together.

"What's that Dad?"

"We went to see Attila the vicar at St Oswald's...we didn't understand how it'll work in Heaven. Everyone's always saying we'll meet again in Heaven. It's been our comfort and what we've both been living for."

"Oh Dad," she realised how hard everything was for them. She put her arms around his waist and he hugged her.

"We've been waiting to be with Manon and Luca in Heaven. We would never betray them. But where would that leave Sarai and me? Our love? Attila helped, he said there's no 'mine' after we die, in Heaven we're all just angels, we'll see each other but it'll be a different kind of love. All love will be perfect in Heaven and our perspectives will be different. Plus God wants us to be happy in this life too. And yet the guilt is still there, Noëmi."

She moved her chair closer to his and felt his warmth.

"Dad, please, no more guilt and shame." She kissed his cheek. Wet, salty, too often he had cried.

Her father nervously filled the silence.

"Here N, this Santoro rose is for your garden. I've been working on cuttings so that the rose can live on and be shared with all of us. That way it's a reminder of mum. When the time's right I'll get some of that white lilac for you too!" Donnie continued to chat away. "Anyway, I've offered to help Attila tidy up that church graveyard. A man of his age can't do it by himself!"

"Dad, thank you. Stop for a moment. Come with me outside and read this!"

From her mustard handbag, she took a letter and then opened the patio doors. Father and daughter walked out with the toddlers at their sides. Tight next to one another they sat on the familiar wooden bench, between the Japanese Acer and the cherry tree. Both were flaming auburn.

Dad

Oh my what a journey together! I'm already crying as I write this!

You and Mum have always shown me how to be and especially how to be true to my promises.

The day Mum left us you took me to see her to say goodbye at the hospital. You told me to be strong and I was determined. As I went in, she sat up, smiled broadly and threw her arms out to welcome my hug. She was better! My prayers had been answered! I ran to her. The warmth of her, the smell of her, how she would giggle. I told her everything would be fine now! She gave a sigh and said that she still had to go, that it was time for her to leave. I didn't understand, I got scared, I searched her face for answers. I now realise the massive effort she made that one last time... for me, to save me from pain. She did not want me to suffer. Holding me she told me her life would be different but her love would still be with us. She told me she loved me and that I was everything to her. I couldn't hold back the tears. I couldn't save her. Taking me by the shoulders she gazed deep into my eyes and asked me to do one thing, 'Look after Dad,' and I promised that I always would.

In spite of the very dark times we have been through since she left us, her love shines on in us. It is a perfect love where you both care more about the other than yourself. Every day I saw this in you both. I learnt from you. I kept the promise.

In all honesty Dad if death had taken me from Marcus that summer, I would only want him to be happy. I'd want him to enjoy his life without guilt or shame. That is because my love for him is more important than my love for myself. This is how Mum feels about you. Now you have to let her win!

Dad, if you can find a path to love again please take it. The love you and Mum have is still there, it burns brighter than ever, I see it every day. It lives on in me! You both showed me what true love is! When we look into eternity, love is the only thing that can fill it. Be kind to yourself and do not deny yourself; chances for happiness do not come often.

Thank you for being everything to me,

I love you Dad.

Noëmi

Father and daughter held each other tightly as they sat beneath the burning red leaves, both protected by true love in the fresh winter breeze.

The end (to be continued...)

ABOUT THE AUTHOR

K McCity worked as a high / secondary school teacher for sixteen years. She is now training for a role in the NHS.

Living in London in the UK with a busy work and family life, she finds escape in writing stories.

K McCity believes in true love, the power of those who support us and the importance of those little people who are so often ignored...

* * *